BEAUTY

BEAUTY
A NOVEL

BRIAN D'AMATO

Delacorte Press

Published by
Delacorte Press
Bantam Doubleday Dell Publishing Group, Inc.
666 Fifth Avenue
New York, New York 10103

Library of Congress Cataloging in Publication Data

D'Amato, Brian.
    Beauty / by Brian D'Amato.
       p.   cm.
    ISBN 0-385-30676-8 (hc)
    I. Title.
PS3554.A4675B4   1992
813'.54—dc20   92-3843
                                        CIP

Manufactured in the United States of America

Published simultaneously in Canada

Book design by Robin Arzt with Brian D'Amato

October 1992

10 9 8 7 6 5 4 3 2 1

BVG

This is dedicated to Barbara D'Amato, who taught me everything about writing and the world.

Beauty is momentary in the mind—
The fitful tracing of a portal;
But in the flesh it is immortal
    —Wallace Stevens,
       "Peter Quince at the Clavier"

Everyone imitated my fuller mouth, darker eyebrows. But I wouldn't copy anybody. If I can't be me, I don't want to be anybody. I was born that way.

                                   —Joan Crawford

PART ONE

THE LCHEMIST

1

An egg floated in the void. It rotated on its vertical axis as the blackness behind it gradated toward a dark ultramarine purple. It moved closer, in microscopic increments. Its surface was absolutely pure, smoother than any real egg and scaleless in its non-space. Rose-colored light fell on it from a source apparently somewhere between the egg and the implied observer, and the light pooled one-third of the way down the surface in a spot that suggested its texture was, perhaps, slightly more glossy than that of a real egg.

Then an irregularity seemed to appear in the lower center of the oval. At first it was so slight, it might have been imaginary: a faint depression, with perhaps a slight bunching-out above and below. The depression and swellings grew, becoming more distinct with agonizing slowness. It was an order of motion that animals or machines never approach, the slowness of plants, or of crystals forming in solutions. Above the irregularity, two more slight indentations, identical round concavities in the pristine surface, manifested themselves with the same intense deliberation. They were symmetrically aligned along the vertical axis. As they worked their way into the surface of the egg, the light highlighted over and under them and shadows began to form, first soft like airbrush marks, then soft only on top and hard-edged on their lower sides.

Suddenly the egg passed over the threshold of abstraction, the invisible barrier that separates a geometric form from the most basic figurative paradigm.

It was a face.

The eyes and mouth became more distinct. The outlines of cheekbones and the hollows under them began to alter the silhouette of the egg itself. A nose began to protrude ever so slightly, and tiny indentations under it developed into near-nostrils. Buds sprouted that would eventually be ears. A peach color began to spread beneath the surface like an Icelandic dawn. Now the eyes had a hairless eyebrow ridge and closed lids not quite separated from the flesh beneath them. The lips were still fused, but they were lips, complete with hollows at the corners and the depression beneath the nose. The wings of the nostrils extruded slightly. The forehead broadened. It was a face, but not a human face. It was a face from some idealized realm beyond death and life, ageless and silent and beautiful. It was still embryonic, and more like mathematics than flesh. But it was becoming an entity.

I typed out HALT F9 on the keyboard. There was no perceptible change, but somehow you could tell the growth had stopped. And I'd stopped it before it had left the land of the undead for the land of the (at least in appearance) living.

I punched in a few coordinates and moved the mouse-cursor over the face, up to the command line at the top of the screen. I clicked it on WIRE FRAME, and instantly a small screen appeared on the lower left of the image, blocking out part of the face but showing it again, schematically, with triangular facets etched in orange lines against dark blue. I moved the cursor down to the region of the eyes and began to program.

After eighteen minutes, I clicked off the wire-frame screen and typed RESUME IMAGE GENERATE on the command line. The egg disintegrated itself, then reappeared a few seconds later, slightly closer. Very, very slowly, the eyelids began to rise. A mirrorlike surface appeared under them, a strange, cold, wet-looking lavender substance. Then the circle of the iris came into view, emerald green against the lavender, with magenta and golden facets shifting under the green like the spicules in Mexican fire opals. And then, as the lids passed the halfway point, the pupils should have come into view. But there were no pupils. The eyes were fully open and the face looked straight at me with the blind, soulless, malevolent blank stare of a demon.

I looked back for what seemed like a long time. I heard a scratching sound at my left wrist and recoiled from the desk, hitting my head against the wall. A coil of paper was extruding itself from my fax machine. I peeled it off and read it:

> HAVE YOU TURNED YOUR RINGER OFF?
> DON'T FORGET, PENNY PENN APPOINTMENT 2:00
> I'LL BE THERE IN 45 MINS. DAVID.

I allowed myself to look back at the screen for a few minutes. I rotated the head through 360 degrees, thinking about the profile and the three-quarter views. The Face was becoming a thing of awesome beauty, I thought, unless I was just flattering myself. I didn't think I was, though. I wondered whether I'd ever really get the chance to implement it. I typed SAVE and shut down the computer and got up. My back cracked a bit. I'd been sitting down for quite a while.

Somewhere in the microscopic binary code of sixty-four megabytes of memory, the demon slept with open eyes. The ghost in my machine.

"Laugh lines. I cried when I got laugh lines. That sounds so stupid, too. What a *stupid* name for a terrible, terrible thing. I just can't deal with it. I also have three horizontal lines in my forehead, and there's one more starting up near my hairline. And I'm getting crow's-feet. *That's* an ugly name. What a stupid name for eye wrinkles. And there's four really, really really big huge acne scars. One's right here, right to the left of my nose, a quarter inch away. And there's one right above the center of my upper lip, on the—on the septum. It's called a septum, right? And the other two—they're right here, on this cheek—you should know that these two have had some collagen shots already. The pores on my nose and to the sides of my nose are too big. They're really unattractive. But my facialists say there's not much they can do about them besides keep steaming them and then putting on the astringent. Well . . . besides the *big* problem, there's a whole bunch of little things . . . but anyway the biggest problem with me, as you can see, is eye bags. Eye bags. They upset me a lot. I was kind of overweight for a while. Maybe I got them from that. I drank a lot of milk shakes in college. You went to that school, too, didn't you?"

Like many of the people I know who went to Yale, Penny Penn said "that school" instead of "Yale" when she was talking to other Yalies. "Yale" is hard to say because it's so pretentious and monosyllabic. It's like saying "fuck."

"I was in your class," I said. "You used to hang out with Hilary Pearl and Andrew Moskowitz."

"Sure. That's great! Do you see them at all?"

"Hilary just bought a theater on Essex Street a few blocks from here. And Andrew's working for Richard Foreman, you know, the sort of avant-garde director—"

"Sure, yes," she said. "Well, I should give them a call sometime. I suppose—maybe I haven't been a really good friend to them. But the thing is, with films, you know, you just get bound up in a really specific kind of social thing, you know, it's really stupid. . . . I really liked being at school, thinking about real thinking stuff. . . . I mean, imagine getting to study with Jacques Derrida, he really is one of the most brilliant people of the century, I think. . . . Is the camera still running?"

"Yes."

"Listen, can we erase that last part, so we don't have the thing about Hilary and Andrew?"

"*Nobody*'s going to see these tapes. They're just for legal protection. But I'm sorry, if they have traces of erasing, they'll be worthless. You know that. We discussed this."

She looked at me suspiciously for a split second. She had a cold streak in her, and it *surfaced* at me. I hadn't seen Penny Penn off-screen since school, where it seemed she didn't remember me from, and I was a little unprepared for the hard-nosed-businesswoman act she was pulling on me. But people who see me in these situations are always tense. They're in a vulnerable position. I should remember how empowered I am at these times. It was a switch since she was the school movie star girl, slinking around with her boyfriend Theodoro, whom I couldn't stand, and her old bodyguard with the walkie-talkie, and I was just the earnest art student.

Actually, I second-thought, not as much of a switch as I'd like. She was still incredibly famous, and I was just a medium-hot New York artist, not any fame at all, really. Only insiders know who artists are, unless you're Andy Warhol. Well, maybe I was on my way to the Warhol level with my new direction. He "did celebrities," too. He didn't have to keep it a secret, though.

"Well, okay, then let's be professional," she said. I had to watch it. I was in something of a position of power, but she could still probably have me crucified if I screwed up.

"Eye bags," she went on. "Dr. Weil said I wasn't a good subject for a tuck because of my delicate skin. He said my eyes would look tight and the scars could show. And tucks just don't last. I mean, I *know* Cher and she really looks strange up close. And Joan Rivers looks *really* strange. Anyway, they use a kind of greenish foundation there for filming, and that pretty much gets rid of them, but I'm no good in person or even on TV sometimes with these things. And Virginia suggested I come and see you."

I had done terrific work on Virginia Feiden.

"Well," I said—I felt like a doctor—"all this seems really minor to me. You look great. And your career hasn't really been based on conventional beauty anyway. I think people respect you as an actress partly because you look different and halfway real. And a lot of this is stuff you could handle, with dermabrasions and ordinary plastic surgery."

"The hell with looking real. The hell with plastic surgery. It's not just little imperfections. I'm not talking about looking in a mirror, I'm talking about watching myself in the dailies and I just don't have what I used to have. I look puffy. My face used to have a really specific memorable quality about it, and it's just lost it. I was bigger when I was fifteen than I am now, and it's entirely because of the face thing. I mean, it's actually harder if you've been like, a child star, everyone in the industry's afraid that no one wants to watch you grow up. Seriously, I can't do ingenue roles anymore as it is. And there's plenty of time to be some old grande dame of the screen anyway. And my career is always on the edge anyway *because* I look real. It's really, really difficult. Okay? It takes constant work. And anyway, I'm just not thrilled about getting old. All right?"

She really wanted it badly. For the same reason everybody else did. She was simply afraid of getting old. She was twenty-nine, like I was, and she looked older than I did.

"All right, I know," I said. "Women just age much faster than men, and their faces age much faster than the rest of them, and it's not fair."

"You're damn straight it's not."

I snickered inside. A bond had been established. She knew I

understood her problems, and she was going to trust me. This was my biggest commission so far. I was excited.

"All right. Let's take some pictures, I'll do a set of drawings, and we'll start in a week. You can look at the drawings on, uh, maybe Wednesday the thirteenth, and we can start next Monday at two. Okay?"

She did the number with her electric date book and said it would be okay.

"Now . . . you know to be prepared for a twelve-hour session, if necessary. And a few days of resting around, not touching anything, and then maybe another session. So I suggest you get a hotel room, anonymously. Somewhere everybody minds his own business, like the Mark. Not an apartment you could be traced to. Try not to schedule any business except phone calls for all of next week, just in case. And I'll want the waiver forms signed then, and we'll make another videotape."

"Can I have a copy of the waiver thing to show my brother?"

Her brother was her manager.

"I can't do that. It's just bad policy. And really, the less your manager or anyone hears, the better it is for everybody. I know that sounds really corny, but that's the way it is." Take it or leave it, I thought.

She said okay.

■

We went through the photo session. I tried to do it the way Timothy would do it. She was a professional, and we were only interested in the head, but it was still a little embarrassing. Photography is a very intimate thing. Nothing remotely like what was going to follow, though.

At about ten, I figured not enough was enough. I switched off the lights and the video camera—I'd run through two cassettes just filming the shoot—and stacked my giant pile of film holders on the kitchen counter. I still photograph with an old Speed Graphic four-by-five, and so I have to switch film holders like a madman. It's a dinosaur of a camera, but it knows what I need and does it. Penny was sort of draping on her coat—a comfy-looking duffel coat—and she got an envelope out of her big floppy bag and handed it to me with a certain amount of reluctance. I walked her downstairs and let her out the door onto Rivington Street. She said, "Bye, Jamie," stepped over some Lower East Side garbage, and let herself into the back door of an ordinary Mercedes. It whisked her away. An unassuming woman of the people. I couldn't resist tearing open the envelope and looking at the check. "Penny Penn, Box 131, Encino, CA. To: James Angelo. Three hundred and fifty thousand and no/100s————dollars."

3

I'd shot about sixty four-by-fives. I walked over to U.S. Color on Bleecker and Lafayette and dropped off the boxes, marked NORMAL/RUSH. I walked home, cleaned up the photo-mess, answered some calls, and walked back—walking's a big part of the downtown lifestyle—and spread the just developed four-by-five transparencies out on one of the light boxes there.

I picked out the ten best shots and laid them out on one side, put the others back in one of the boxes, taped the box shut, and marked it FLUSH. The little place was crowded, even at eleven-thirty at night. Mainly magazine people and one or two grade-B models and fashion and product photographers and their delivery persons who had to get their shots of Naomi Campbell in Agnès B. or Bart Simpson Tofu Bran Cereal or whatever back in time for a morning meeting. Sometimes it's impossible to get anything done in these photo places. I'm trying to cut something neatly, to do a quick paste-up or something, and these models come in with their books and pick up topless shots of themselves and wave them around, just in case the art directors from *Vogue* walk in. It's really distracting. I didn't recognize anyone, except for a cute Japanese-looking model/girl with a strange haircut—some club kid from the neighborhood—so I was a little careless.

"Hey, is that Penny Penn?"

Some goon was leaning over my light box.

"I wish," I said instantly. "She's just a look-alike."

He didn't believe me.

"No, seriously, I'm a professional. . . . I've worked with Paulina and shot a lot for *Elle* and *Interview*—what's the project with Penny? It's an endorsement, right?"

Jesus, I should be more careful, I thought. But I was too excited to wait. I just smiled nicely, scooped up my transparencies, and went over to the counter. At least the place is run by Pakistanis who, I thought hopefully, might not recognize her. Sri Devi, yes, but not Penny Penn.

"Yes, please?" said the Counter Kid, who knew me.

Just to show off to the girl and frustrate the goon's curiosity—he was still hanging around—I hit the kid with a little Urdu. *"Mu je paanch* sixteen-by-twenty Cibachromes *chai hyee,* of each. *Samje?"*

"Haa," said the kid. He wrote out my name and account number on the blue slip. I checked it and nodded. "Four o'clock tomorrow?"

"Accha, shukriyaa," I said, overdoing it.

I left. Maybe I should have skipped the Urdu thing, but I just didn't want the goon to know I was ordering over a thousand dollars' worth of Cibachromes. Why would anyone need ten identical blow-ups of each of ten shots?

■

Penny was human-looking in real life, but in two dimensions she was stunning. Even though I'd photographed her to accentuate her flaws, even using fluorescent light a few times—something all actresses fear like death itself—she still came out looking great, a little pockmarked and baggy but still sexy and just *herself,* with that weird, wistful, incredibly famous strange look in her eyes that millions and millions of people were absolutely gaga for. I should get into photography, I thought. I could be a Robert Mapplethorpe for the nineties, especially now that he's dead.

Still, I was more excited about my own medium. It's less of a *pure* medium, but it's very cutting edge. Science is very hot in art right now. I put one of each chrome aside in an envelope and closed it, suppressing an urge to mark it BEFORE.

I wasn't going to use the computer on this job. I wasn't quite comfortable with it yet. I wanted to do this one the painstaking, old-fashioned way. I spread the remaining shots out on a clean sheet of white homosote on the floor of the studio, dug my gas mask out of its three layers of plastic bags, and put it on. I switched on all the air vents, sprayed invisible adhesive over the photos, and rolled a big roll of prepared acetate over them. I pushed the air bubbles out from under the acetate and sliced the sheets apart with a razor knife. Then I spray-mounted the double sheets to thick sheets of foam-core, cut *those* apart, and stacked them on the drafting board. I rolled over my painting cart—which was stocked with small jars of Golden Brand Acrylics—sat down, and spooned some titanium white, ivory black, burnt sienna, and gel medium onto a Chinette paper plate. I mushed the paint around a bit with a nylon brush and started playing around, rather freely, on the first photograph, a left-side profile. This was like a dry run for next Monday. This was what Penny Penn was going to look like.

There was a mole on the side of her forehead, above her eye. I whisked it away with a flick of the brush. I feathered a little tone into her cheek and added some cadmium red light into the mix. I'm so good, you couldn't see where the photograph ended and the painting began. That's what's so great about Cibachromes, too—they have a nice even painterly surface with no dots, almost like an Ingres painting. After whisking away a few more imperfections on the cheek, I went right to work on the eye bag, lateral view.

This required a bit more skill because the bulge had to be cut into a bit and the nose had to be redrawn slightly behind it. But it wasn't hard. I put the shot aside in less than an hour, and she already looked a hundred times better and ten years younger.

But what if we allowed just a little more poetic license? I picked up an identical view, whisked out a few bumps and bags like before, and just tucked in her very slight double chin a bit. She hadn't mentioned the chin thing, but it wasn't fabulous. It was something an ordinary plastic surgeon could deal with, but with Mark's help I could probably handle it, too. I should get more into structural: The Architecture of the Face, I thought. What I'd mainly been concerned with up to now was surface. Surface and Gloss. Still, those *are* the things that really matter.

You can do a lot with contouring. What if she had just a little more of a depression under her cheekbones, maybe to make them just a little bit higher—not enough to turn her into Katharine Hepburn, not enough to diffuse her essential Penny-Penn-ness, but just a bit, to bring her into the "sophisticated" class . . . not that she wasn't already . . . but just a hint of those waspy aristocratic wing-tips . . . and she looked *really* different. But not bad. And not like someone else. Audiences around the world would be captivated by a new Penny Penn, a mature yet *perfect* Penny Penn, a Penny Penn mellowed by suffering and compassion, yet more alluring than ever. . . .

I figured the fumes from the spray glue had dissipated, so I took off my mask and wrapped it up to protect the filters. I picked up a full-frontal shot. Now *here* I could do *much* better. On frontal, eye bags were the least of her problems. We'd lengthen the eyes a bit, for one thing, and clean up a few problems under the lower lip. Tuck in the cheeks, definitely. It wouldn't be too bad to recover the whole nose, either, and launch those pores she hated once and for all. But I wasn't sure where to stop. Should I recover the whole face? Some of the things I wanted to do were things you could approximate with makeup and lighting. And most of her skin was in pretty good condition. It would be a shame to take too much of it off. And she was young. We still weren't completely sure how long the work would hold up. You shouldn't go crazy over this job, I told myself. Don't get perfectionistic. The most important thing in art is the ability to compromise and make excuses. Still, it would be a coup to redesign a real icon. And she'd be *really* perfect, not just a freakish combination of nature, makeup, lighting, and good camera angles. She'd be an *Über*-wench. An elf. An icon. I went to sleep thinking, she's such an icon, icon, icon . . .

4

On Monday, October 18, Penny was due to arrive at two P.M. My assistant, David Lowenstein, showed up at nine and woke me up. Besides Mark, he was the only person allowed around when I worked. He started setting up the studio, rolling the couch—an electronically adjustable kind of psychiatrist's couch—up onto a big rotating model stand. It came up to a good working height; her head would be at my shoulder level. There was a huge plastic dropcloth, with a cotton dropcloth over that, covering the whole model stand and most of the floor of the studio. I'm a little paranoid about other people's blood, especially in the age of AIDS, so I was extra cautious about splattering it around. He put a clean lavender slipcover over the couch—I want everything to look as little like Frankenstein's laboratory as possible—while I made cappuccino in my favorite little machine. The doorbell rang, and it was Mark Saltzman, my liaison to the world of medicine. He was a little shorter than me, handsome in a sort of dark, curly-haired, Jewish-scientist way. He was wearing his regulation navy sweater and black chinos, which he had at least twenty sets of. He was carrying two big boxes.

"Did you get absolutely *everything*?" I asked.

"Sure, definitely. I got two hundred extra pads, and about five square feet of AS."

AS was Artificial Skin.

"Can I have some coffee, too?" he asked.

I steamed milk and asked him to please set up and sterilize the tools. He grumbled a bit, but he did it.

"Listen," I said, "did you get any tetracycline?"

"You didn't ask for any."

"Well, it does say on her questionnaire that she's allergic to penicillin. Do you think you could, uh, prescribe David some over the phone to the Avenue A pharmacy, and he'll pick it up this afternoon?"

He wasn't thrilled about it, but he couldn't think of a reason to say no. We'd been friends since school, but now I made a lot of money for him, and anyway, he'd turned me on to this whole process in the first place, and now he had more to lose than I did. After all, he was a doctor and I was just a psychotic artist. Speaking of which . . .

"David, could you move those paintings away from that wall? No, stack them so the good ones show."

"Why, you want her to buy one?"

"I just don't want to look like a full-time mad scientist."

"You want to look like a part-time crummy artist?"

I have a really big ego, so I just have to ignore David sometimes.

We unpacked the boxes. Disinfectant. Surgical gloves. Coagulant. Anticoagulant. Sterilized sponges and towels. Disposable skin knives. Liquid Suture, a surgical glue, by Parke-Davis. And in a little green plastic double-walled cold case, with a wisp of dry-ice smoke curling around the edges of the lid, those twenty difficult-to-get packages of Bickerton-Clarke/Experimental Burn Treatment Labs Product #AS 46A. Artificial Skin. The second A meant it was white, undyed. I'd do the dyeing myself.

I checked our rack of dyes and the little blue jars full of our own product, PCS 10. It was damp enough, without any dry patches. But we'd whip it up later anyway. It looked like thick salmon-colored cream. Sometimes we called it Beauty Foam.

■

Penny turned up early, like most people I work on do. I told her to send her car away. She'd cab to the hotel. She looked cold and edgy. She was wearing a Don't Notice Me sweatshirt and jeans and Arche loafers. She was obviously very nervous. Still, before I offered her anything, I took her into the studio and sat her down in the "video chair." I sent David out for the tetracycline—Mark was being unobtrusive in the bedroom area, a mile away at the other end of the loft—and I switched on the camera.

"This is one P.M., October eighteenth, 1993," I said. "This tape is private and will be stored in a safe-deposit box until the year 2075, when the Chase Manhattan Bank or their representatives will destroy it without viewing the contents. Any attempt on the part of unauthorized persons to view or duplicate this tape will result in immediate legal action."

I paused dramatically. I hoped I sounded official enough.

"This tape is only to be used as evidence to protect me, Jamie Angelo, in a court of law should that need arise." Pause. "I'm speaking with Penny Penn, the actress. Penny, you made this appointment yourself, isn't that right?"

"Yes," she said.

"And while you were here, I didn't give you anything to eat or drink, or any drugs of any kind, and I didn't try any sort of coercion or psychological tricks on you?"

"No."

"And right now, you're in perfectly good health and a normal frame of mind, and you're not being treated for any psychological problems?"

"No."

"Could you talk for a few minutes about what you did today, beginning with waking up?"

She was a little surprised at this, but I guess she realized it was to prove she was mentally fit. She went into a lot of detail about moving into the Royalton under a false name and shopping at Charivari. I wished she'd picked a less upscale hotel.

"Okay," I said. "Now, you realize that I am not a licensed doctor and that what you have asked for is an unorthodox and unnecessary treatment that may not be successful, and that could cause problems in later life?"

"Yes."

"And you realize that you will look different, and you may not like the way you look, and you will feel different, and you may not like the way you feel?"

"Yes."

"You realize that the treated portions of your face will be quite numb. You realize you may have itches you won't be able to scratch, and that parts of you will never feel water when you go swimming or take a shower, or feel the wind on your skin. And that persons you are intimate with might notice the difference in warmth between your face and the rest of your body."

"Yes."

We went through some more legal stuff about maintenance of her face through the years. Finally, I came to the important part.

"And at this time you waive any claims you might pursue against me, now or in the future?"

She answered yes, more hesitantly. She'd probably told her lawyer some edited version of what was going on, and he'd thrown a fit. But she was the buyer. I handed her the short waiver form. She read it a couple of times and signed it. I checked the video monitor to make sure she was signing it on camera. It was only one short paragraph.

"Very well, now I'm also going to ask you to sign the retouched photographs you approve. And then we'll start the procedure."

I turned the tape off, ejected and labeled it, and switched it for a new one. I set up the camera and tripod with a good view of the "model stand." I'd turn it on when we started.

"Would you like any Valium, alcohol, or marijuana?" I asked.

■

I only use local anesthetics. There's a tiny, multipronged novocaine needle that they make just for skin surgery. I also spray some ethanol or dilute viscous Xylocaine on minor spots. Anyway, I wasn't going to take off much flesh. She'd agreed to the paintings of her with the double chin and eye bags removed, with the pores covered, and with the accentuated cheekbone. But she hadn't agreed to the most radical study, the one I really was most proud of. I couldn't blame her, though. It didn't look like her, and there was a lot of recognition value tied up in her look as it was. Her look worked for her, so why fix it more than aesthetically necessary?

While I waited for her to get more relaxed, I drew some guidelines on her face with a blue marker and swabbed over them with brown disinfectant. Just to get started, I novocained a mole on the side of her forehead, a quarter inch from her eyebrow. I tested the spot with a needle to make sure it was anesthetized, buzzed the spot with the surgical sander—it looks like a dentist's drill with a tiny sphere on the end—and hit the tiny bloody red patch with a cotton pad soaked in coagulant. It stopped bleeding and scabbed over almost immediately. I brushed on a little Liquid Suture, snipped out a tiny dot of AS, and patted it down. It was whitish, but the dark scab underneath showed through. It bulged a little bit because of the coagulation.

I got out the anticoagulant. This was Mark's Trick: I soaked a layer of cotton pad in the stuff, held it on the patch, and let it seep down through the semiporous layer of AS. The bulge underneath dissolved and disappeared. I'd get out my dyes and match the skin tone later. But from a structural point of view, the patch was already invisible.

I looked at Penny for a minute. It was strange and exciting to be this close to her icon-face. She seemed to be relaxing a bit. She'd had fifteen milligrams of Valium, and it might be kicking in already. It's always a little hard for me to do the next part. But I rinsed the tiny head of the sander off in a plastic cup filled with alcohol, pressed the button, and brought it in on her right laugh line.

•

I hated looking at her covered with scabs. It was three-thirty P.M. She was lying still, so I took a little break and got myself a Natural Raspberry Soda out of the fridge. This was a dangerous stage. What if the building caught on fire right now, or if I slipped and cut my hand off with the soda bottle? She'd be in pretty bad shape. Mark was out, and David was reading *Flash Art* in the Couch Area. And David probably couldn't even get her back to her original looks without me around. Some calls had come in on my machine while the ringer was off, but I didn't want to break my mood by listening to them. I finished the soda and put on a fresh pair of surgical gloves. I picked up an anticoagulant pad in my left glove and a smear of prepared PCS 10 in my right. Generally, as soon as the scabs dissolve, I pat the PCS on loosely. As it begins to harden, I carve away what I don't want with tiny clay tools. I'd fill in the laugh lines first. I called to David and asked him to switch off the Enigma record and put on my favorite disk, the Cocteau Twins *Treasure* album.

■

PCS 10 is really an amazing thing. Mark came up with it with his partner, Karl Vanders, in his research lab at Columbia as something to use in both internal and reconstructive surgery, but it turned out much better for cosmetic surgery. It's not licensed, which is one reason we have to work in secret. Karl wanted to go through the long process of getting it approved, but they didn't have the political clout and it would have had to go through years of testing anyway. It stands for Plasti/Collagen Silver and it's basically microscopically thin silver capillaries—which conduct both heat and air very well—suspended in a base of collagen, with a small percentage of purified protein polyethylene resin added. The resin holds the silver to the collagen and makes the whole substance easy to work with. Collagen, as you may know, is a protein, not some kind of plastic. It's one of the biggest components of skin. You might have seen collagen in a sculpture by Liz Larner, a young Neo-Minimalist sculptor from California, in the 1989 Whitney Biennial. It was a laboratory beaker filled with collagen that had been tinged with soluble fluorescent dye. There were a couple of gold nuggets suspended inside. It was a beautiful little object. Maybe she was trying to say something about the amount of money people put into cosmetic surgery.

Anyway, plastic surgeons have been using collagen refined out of cowhide for over a decade, mainly to fill out minor depressions left by scarring or to tidy up wrinkles. It's usually injected just a little bit under the skin, and it's generally more reliable than silicone, which it's replacing. Silicone really is a type of plastic, and of course they still use it for large fillers like the ill-famed breast implants, but besides maybe giving you immune-system problems, it moves around, it feels cold—Edie Sedgwick, for instance, supposedly used to have to put heating pads on her breasts pretty often—and it's just not easy to control. It's what they use because they don't have PCS 10. Anyway, collagen doesn't have all the problems of silicone, and the body seems to accept it very well, but you can't sculpt it. It just sets into a kind of a hard gel, which doesn't always hold its shape. It kind of dissipates after a year or two. PCS 10, by comparison, is as flexible and, in its way, as permanent a medium as any I've ever worked with. When I use it I feel as excited as I did when I was an undergraduate, when I was a reactionary Romantic Realist and thought that I was getting so good with oil paint that pretty soon I'd be better than Poussin at his peak. PCS hardens slowly, so it can be sculpted easily, and it can take any color. The only color we put directly in it is a heat-sensitive red dye that turns a deeper red when the surrounding skin or the flesh underneath gets flushed and warm. So except for sun tans, which have to be masked by makeup, changes in the color of the real skin are matched by chemical changes in the artificial product. The only other ingredients are some soluble anticoagulants, which keep the blood from clotting underneath the implants and which dissipate in a few days, and a tiny amount of a kind of surgical epoxy. When I'm going to work with the PCS, I whip it up in a tiny laboratory mixer—it can be whipped to different consistencies, depending on the texture of the flesh it has to imitate—and with a capillary measuring tube I drop in between two and ten parts per thousand of the hardener compound for the surgical epoxy. This helps control the hardness, too, and it makes sure that everything bonds to the raw flesh. It wouldn't do to have sections peeling off.

The final set can be extremely supple, sensitive enough to take the facial expression from the underlying muscles as well as real flesh would. The capillaries in the PCS allow the flesh underneath to breathe as much as they would with real skin. But, of course, I do have to take off all the skin underneath where I use the PCS. Otherwise, the skin would go on excreting sweat and pigment, growing hair, and generally gumming up the works.

As I mentioned before, I bind a thin layer of the Bickerton-Clarke Artificial Skin, or AS 46A, over everything. It's probably not necessary, but I think it's a little more durable than the PCS—it was designed to save burn victims who don't have enough skin left to graft—and it blends the whole artificial area in with the natural skin. It's a semi-transparent white color and extremely thin. When I drop it over the PCS—translucent foam, with the darker scarlet of raw flesh pulsing underneath—it feels like dropping a sheet of gold leaf onto an antique frame covered with sticky red bole.

■

I looked over at the "before" photos pinned to the wall to remind me what her pores had been like. She didn't want them, but she'd have to have some or she'd look fake. Pores are difficult. No-body really knows how to do them the way I do. Hospitals use the Artificial Skin on burn victims who've only lost their skin, and it holds up very well for a long time, but it always looks artificial because it's too smooth. I have a little dentist's tool attached to the handle of a soldering iron, and I can make slight indentations in the surface of the Artificial Skin with that, and they hold their shape when they cool down. Occasionally I have to add artificial hairs as well. But that's a real bitch. You have to patch in each individual hair with a scalpel and then trim it. Luckily I've found that, in general, people don't notice the absence of hair.

All that's left to do after the pores is wait for everything to set—about a half hour—and then do the color.

So I did some nice pores on the nose, on the neck, on the place where the laugh lines used to be—and except for the color differ-ence, the transition between the remaining portions of her real skin and the Artificial Skin was completely invisible. Regular plastic sur-geons just can't do the things I do. They don't have a sense of detail. And they don't have the poetry. Actually, poetry is detail, I thought. I was pretty proud of myself.

It was six-thirty. Outside, through the big windows at the west end of the loft, the abandoned buildings were becoming magenta and ultramarine. I started to wonder whether maybe I should have sanded over and reskinned her entire face. Some of her remaining pores were still a bit obvious. Her closeup shots might still have to be in soft focus. I should have just given her the smooth skin she de-served. Well, even Michelangelo had to make some concessions. He had to use funny-shaped marble blocks that nobody else wanted for the *David* and the *Pietà*. And he stopped smoothing everything out so much after a while, too. He wanted a coarser look. Still, I'm per-sonally very into smooth.

Penny was squirming a bit. I could tell the novocaine and the Xylocaine and the Valium were beginning to wear off. I held a cold alcohol jet on her face for a while.

"I'm sorry it's beginning to get painful. We can keep the pain away until you go to sleep tonight. Your face will feel a little tight for a while, and you'll itch for a few days. But your nerves will adapt to the artificial tissue and you'll be comfortable."

She looked as if she could use more reassurance. "This is an absolutely state-of-the-art thing. Your flesh will bond to the PCS 10. It won't affect any of the processes going on underneath. It breathes, it transfers heat, it expands and contracts with your body temperature —and this isn't like a transplant, which your body might reject. The synthetic parts will stay in exactly the same place and match the rest of your skin for a long time."

"How long is a long time?" she asked. She was a little groggy and sounded scared. It's kind of sexy when women—especially really public ones—start revealing their vulnerability.

"We talked about this. I'll give you the folder about maintenance, and enough of the special cleanser to last for many years, and some refinishing fluid that you should apply every couple of months—you know, like it says in the little folder. And if you start to look patchy in a few years, or if the AS gets abraded, or if something happens to your natural skin that keeps it from matching the AS, come back and we'll do some repairs. This isn't like plastic surgery, you know, where you can only operate"—oops, I thought, I tried never to use the word *operate*—"once or twice. . . . I can go on working on top of the Artificial Skin over and over—"

"Oh, that's great," she said. "By the time I'm sixty, I'll be coming in every day."

"As I said in the contract video, I won't charge you for anything after the first process—unless you want something really outrageous —and if I get hit by a truck or something, you know it's not a *totally* secret procedure. All the tapes are in two different safe-deposit boxes, and my assistant knows about it all and he'll carry on the process, and eventually this may be an accepted medical procedure anyway, and in fact I bet if you even got examined by a good plastic surgeon, he'd be able to figure out what was going on, and figure out something to do about it. . . . In fact, be careful around doctors, okay?"

"I can't believe I'm doing this."

She was beginning to slide into the post-op depression phase, and I wasn't even finished.

"Try to relax a little. Okay? Penny? Think how good Virginia looks."

Right after I'd done my treatment on her, Virginia Feiden had come out in a pretty big movie and was getting a lot of press. I thought mentioning her to Penny would get her jealous. Penny was getting a little dubious. I hate that when they've already totally committed. I couldn't let her look in the mirror because I hadn't done the color yet and she looked patchy. Anyway, giving her a mirror would make me feel like a hair stylist. I'd bandage her up like I always did, even though they don't really need it, and give her a grand unveiling in a few days. It sets them up for the change and helps them forget what they really looked like. It's odd, but even when people know they look much better than they did, they still feel nostalgia for their former look. They should think of that first.

"How about another Valium?" I asked. She shook her head. "It's the best drug ever," I said. "Do you think they named it after *Valley of the Dolls?*"

She just squirmed.

"What I'm doing is going to look good a lot longer than your natural skin would anyway," I said. "Face ages fast, you know."

5

I love what I do. It's almost better than painting. And I love applying the dyes best of all. I got out some brushes: a bunch of brand-new filbert-head Kosmos nylons from Pearl Paint, which are cheap but have a kind of gentle springiness nothing else has, and some of my old favorite Winsor & Newton Series 7 sables in each size from 000 to six. I got out my little rack of dyes in dropper bottles. Some of the dye comes from Bickerton-Clarke for use on the AS. But Mark and I worked out some other dyes that seem to be permanent even in direct sunlight. We've mixed up a sort of cobalt violet-looking shade and a terrific bloody red, which as I mentioned is also the only heat-sensitive dye we need to use on the surface. And we have a translucent titanium white so that I can do some nearly opaque layers if I need to. The B-C colors are all different skin shades, and some of them are nice, but it's as though Bloxx Colours only made fifty-seven varieties of "flesh tone." Really, I don't know how anybody gets a decent match when they just use the B-C products. But I suppose since doctors only use the AS on massive burn cases, their patients think they're just lucky they don't look like blackened redfish.

There's a big difference between pigments and dyes. Pigments, which make up most of the colors you generally use for oil painting, are tiny particles of metal or rock that have to be suspended in some medium. Dyes, for example food coloring or oil colors like phtalo blue, are completely soluble chemicals and don't have any particular body to them. Not having body makes them much harder to work with, since they just stain into anything they touch without leaving you much time to push them around. We've added a little bit of a glycerin colloid to our dyes, to make them more maneuverable. But basically it's like working with watercolor that you can only put down once. Actually, it's exactly like working with egg tempera. Am I going into too much technical detail?

"We're done with the sculptural phase," I started explaining to Penny. "I'm just going to do some color for a couple of hours and then you can go home. Okay? You want to move around a bit?" She squirmed, but she was relaxing a bit better. The combination of Valium and the Cocteau Twins was doing the trick. She looked beautiful and helpless laid out almost horizontally in the reclining chair, with a gray sheet draped over her like the stone shroud on a dead saint. The patches on her skin were like the veins in Sienese yellow marble. For a moment she looked French. Medieval French, like the Virgin from Enguerrand Quarton's *Coronation,* the one with the strange slitted eyes.

Egg tempera. If you're not an art history major, you might not know it's what they painted small paintings with in the Middle Ages and the quattrocento, until Jan van Eyck's group invented oil painting. Before that, if it wasn't fresco, it was egg tempera. It's just finely ground pigments, like watercolor pigments, mixed with water and egg yolk, which is still the world's best glue. Maybe we'd be better off if TV hadn't been invented, and maybe the Renaissance would have been better off if oil paint hadn't been invented. Oil paint has a glossy, aquatic richness, it's like looking into pools, and I love it, but tempera has a dustier, milkier beauty. It's unforgiving—you can't move it around. But it's incredibly precise. You can do detail like you could barely even do with engraving. And so the early Renaissance had a softer but incredibly specific look to it, so that I still feel closer to those more distant pastoral times than I do to the cinquecento, which is richer, but murkier, or to the glossed-out Mannerist kitsch that followed that. The quattrocento was delicate and fleeting, but tremendously intimate and still utterly present. I can look at a panel by Sassetta or Giovanni di Paulo and know exactly what they were thinking, and see the traces of their actions and their decisions as clearly as if they'd happened yesterday. It was action painting before Action Painting.

When I was in high school, I was crazy for egg tempera. I really thought I'd bring its kind of purity back to the world. I knew about contemporary art, but I was insanely reactionary even though, paradoxically, I also loved Robert Rauschenberg. I spent hours teaching myself techniques no one else could teach me, all from observation in museums. Ultimately, it all had less to do with my painting statement than it turned out to have with my sideline. In fact, I think it made me the only person who could handle dyes the way I do. Basically—and it's hard to describe in words—the trick is building a flowing tone without being able to mush the colors around. You can only do it by cross-hatching with a tiny brush. Of course, I have some airbrushes, too. But airbrushing's just not the same. I use it if I want to do a decent job quickly, or for some kinds of glazing and shading, like darkening the Artificial Skin under eyebrows that have been partially removed. But with the small sable brushes, you just have to make the cross-hatching so tiny and smooth that it's invisible, the way the really great ones did it. And I have my own pantheon of really great ones, the ones who were able to create these incredibly flowing variations in tone that look so cloudy and smooth, you'd never imagine there was a sort of stern, hard weave of individual marks that was creating the illusion. The difference between flesh in an oil painting and flesh in a tempera painting is like the difference between a modeled clay sculpture and a carved sculpture: the clay sculpture is just smoothed out to get a flowing surface, kind of all-over and vague, but in a carving every quarter inch has been laboriously articulated, and the smoothness is arrived at by the sum of thousands of individual decisions, which make it a more earned smoothness, more felt and alive and pulsing. And there are only a handful of artists I can think of who can get that feeling of a carving in a painting. Michelangelo, my half-namesake, is one of the best, of course, but he's also too tough, too heavy and structural for me to base much of my work on. Botticelli is one of them, but you can see his individual marks. The texture in the skin of a Botticelli painting is like a closeup of the skin in a portrait by one of the really good guys. Albrecht Dürer is much better, and he's an incredible miniaturist when he wants to be, but there's something sharp and unforgiving about his skin. It has character, but not a lot of pulse. Giovanni Bellini is absolutely fabulous, but even though his skin is totally radiant and perfect, it doesn't quite have the sensual life of the two best people. Leonardo da Vinci is the second-best skin painter. Of course, he kind of inaugurated the smoky-oil-paint-sfumato era that I was complaining about, but even as an egg tempera gradation technician, almost no one could touch him. You can really see it best in the portrait of Ginevra di Benci in the National Gallery in Washington, and you can see it in reproductions of the *Mona Lisa*. There's nothing more delicate looking, but the skin is also completely articulated in every point of its surface. There's only one painter, a much more minor painter, who's better: Mabuse. His real name was Jan Gossaert. He was obsessed with smooth skin. You've never seen gradations like the ones he did. In a way, he was very primitive, because he let his love of the perfect gradation get in the way of all his other considerations. His people don't have any bones. Their color is strange—blue-black or greenish, with brilliant scarlets and magentas showing through. Their eyes are bulgey and stare at you. But that skin is just smoother than Teflon. It looks like, if you touched it, it would be frictionless and you couldn't feel a thing. There's something creepy, death-obsessed, and bad-taste about Mabuse. A fascination with perfection and smoothness goes along with a fascination with death. He was a lot like me.

■

I finished the dyeing. I could have done a little more with the color, and I might do more in another session, but I knew she was a smashing success anyway. Although we'd been working for more than eight hours straight, I didn't feel tired, just exhilarated. I felt I was getting so good, I should stop pacing myself and do something more drastic and radical. Maybe she looked a little flushed, but I could always tone her down a bit later. I'd used a slightly freer technique on her than usual, and it had paid off. Just the way Rubens would have orange as a first layer, and then paint grays over it, our heat-sensitive red sort of glows up through the translucent layers of skin and dyes. The whole technique imitates living tissue perfectly. But I like to think it looks just a little bit better. It has radiance.

■

It was 10:48. I told Penny she could move around a bit, without touching her face, of course, and she said she wanted to get up and use the bathroom. David had taken down the mirror in there, of course. But I decided to make sure everything was dry and wrap her up first anyway. I just used a couple of layers of soft cheesecloth, with some loops of surgical tape around the back of her neck and at her ears, and some ordinary pink porous Johnson & Johnson tape over the face to hold the whole thing together. I taped pretty close to her eyes and probably cut down her peripheral vision quite a bit. I let some of the new skin show around her lips, because she had to have lip mobility. She didn't really need much wrapping up, because the stuff I use is pretty stable, but I didn't want her pulling at her face until it was totally set. She went in the bathroom, and David and I cleaned up. He called Scull, the car service we use, and they said they'd be here in ten minutes. They're right around the corner on Clinton Street. I turned off the video camera and labeled all six cassettes with PENNY PENN and the date, and put them in an antistatic, lead-foil-lined briefcase to take up to the bank. She came out of the bathroom and put her bag back together and got into her duffel coat. She put on sunglasses and looked like a pink version of Claude Rains in *The Invisible Man*. I gave her a big hat—I have a bunch of cheap wide-brimmed blue felt hats for these occasions—and she turned up the collar of her coat, and it looked as though she and David could pretty well pass through a dark hotel lobby without attracting too much attention.

"I look like Claude Rains in *The Invisible Man*," she said.

"You're sure they don't know who you are at the Royalton?" I asked her.

"Yes, yes, it's okay, let's go," she said.

"You're going to live off room service for a couple of days?"

"I've done it before."

She wasn't used to looking horrible and weird, and so she was a little cranky. We waited nervously for a few minutes. The car person rang the bell, and David walked her downstairs. I said, "I'll call tomorrow," and typed in my appointment file, "Call P.P. 1:00. 555-1030 ext. 455, ask for Polly Crane."

It was one A.M. I was supposed to meet some friends at a new club called NUM at two. For some reason, I kept thinking about that Japanese girl in the photo store.

6

I washed and astringent-and-moisturized my face. I was careful not to scrub it. Just pat dry. Don't stretch the skin. I ran a little product through my hair—I was very proud of my sort of bluish-red hair—changed into a Peterbilt Trucks T-shirt and my green Isaac Mizrahi jacket, rechecked the hair, went out with David, and said good-bye to him when I found a cab on Houston. I gave an address in TriBeCa from a message card. It was foggy and dramatic, and the damp shine on the Belgian block streets seemed creepy, like the foggy old London of *Dr. Jekyll and Mr. Hyde*.

Was this it? I wondered. Was this all the beauty and glamour that I'd wanted access to years ago? What was I doing, still chasing this phantom anyway? The eighties were over. Andy was dead. McDonald's was into recyclable packaging. Artificiality and surface were out. They were only skin deep. We were into the Sincere Decade. Beauty didn't matter so much as Genuineness did. Naomi Wolf and her band of radical feminists had sent beauty packing. It was a myth, a scam to oppress women, an outmoded, sexist notion.

The fuck it is, I thought. Just turn on MTV.

From where I was, it seemed that the recession of the Sincere Decade had only made the people on top even more ruthless. They'd traded in their Alaïas for Levi's and Birkenstocks, but under them they were meaner than ever.

There was a big crowd of people dressed in black outside a steel doorway. Echoing my thoughts: It looked almost as pressurized as the club scene of the late eighties. I got out of the cab and just shuffled around aimlessly until Calvin Greenaway and Andrew Solomon found me. I was too keyed up to just bag the day and go to bed, but I was tired, and I wasn't thrilled when I found out we weren't just going out to lounge around on banquettes. I guess I'd agreed to watch an evening of performance art. I was already performance-arted out for that week. Or maybe, I thought, for my entire lifetime, and for the ten billion millennia of the next ten incarnations of Brahma. It's kind of a New York complaint. Things supposedly happen quickly in this city, but there's still a tendency to not drag people offstage fast enough. And performance artists usually go on some. That's what I like about paintings, you can just look at them for a second and get the whole thing. I mean, I make them as rich as possible, but it's nice to just get in and get out. That's the most up-to-date thing about painting—it's great for today's lite attention spans.

"Why don't you have that nice girl person along with you?" Calvin and Andrew greeted me.

I didn't want to talk about any girl persons. "Do we need girl persons?" I asked innocently.

"You're the major hetero thing," they responded, almost in unison.

I have such funny friends. Sometimes I do feel hopelessly retro being so much the hetero. They made the doorpersons find our names on the list, and we squeezed through the crowd, through the door, and past a whole bunch of little performance-art-related acts that were set up in booths around what looked like the huge ruined lobby of an ancient burlesque theater. It also looked like a church bazaar in a barn in Pierre, South Dakota. It's unbelievable, the way the art moves in the second the cold storage moves out. Someone was doing a gross-out painting act with food and condiments in one booth; in another, a woman was making up another woman in a dentist's chair, doing some shtick about executive makeovers. My dubiosity level was rising, but pretty soon they got me to a shaky table and we just sat there waiting for the acts to start. It's crazy, a two A.M. curtain for what they call "an evening of performance art." *Evening,* for their information, really means the time between about four in the afternoon and sundown. But maybe I'm the only person who still knows that.

Ariane from Click, who's one of my favorite models, was at the next table with some guy. She was dressed like a boy in knickerbockers and a Gigli vest. She has a kind of long, exotic, can't-place-it face that looks vaguely Oriental. It's a kind of look I'd like to manufacture myself sometime. She's older than you'd think now, but she still has perfect skin without technological augmentation. I was thinking about how great she'd looked in the *Times* fashion section a few months before, tall and willowy and Avedon-ish in a green satin Chanel gown. She'd had a bit part in *The King of New York* with Christopher Walken a couple of years ago. But her big role had been in a movie called *Year of the Dragon.* Her acting in it isn't too good. She just needed a little more method. I bet all you'd hear on the set all day was, "Quick, call the Lee Strasberg Institute, Ariane needs some method."

"This should be kind of okay," Andrew said, looking at the single sheet of Xeroxed program. "Alexia's written a whole bunch of new stuff they're going to try out."

"I think Jamie thinks they should have already tried it out on someone else before he got here," Calvin said.

"Are there any wait—uh, flight attendants around?" I asked. I wasn't very funny. "I'd like to get a Gourmet Natural Black Cherry Soda or a Dalmane or something before—"

On cue, the lights went down. There was a barrage of WWIII–sounding sound effects.

"FROM THE SUN AND FUN CAPITAL OF THE WORLD, MANAGUA, NICARAGUA, THE CUCARACHA THEATER BRINGS YOU THE BUT SERIOUSLY FOLKS IN *SWINGING DOWN TO LA PENCA!*"

The voice on the amp was pretty deafening. I hoped the evening wasn't going to be too socially conscious. At first, they did a couple of media skits, but pretty soon they just started sending out individual acts. Ethel Mendelberger, a drag performer, did a terrific, well-written monologue-characterization of Lucrezia Borgia, surprisingly historically accurate. I was beginning to feel tolerant of the whole thing. There was one Indian girl who did some great impressions and parodies. She even did an aria, *"Mi Chiamano Mimì,"* in the style of Stevie Nicks, and it was very funny. She was kind of attractive in an offbeat way. Her manner was a bit like Sandra Bernhard's, but shyer and less aggressive.

"Who's that?" I asked, whispering directly into Andrew's ear over the noise of some Kipper-Kids-esque food-fight skit.

"It's Jaishree Manglani, she's another sort of poet-comedian thing."

"She's good, huh? Ear for dialect, and all that sort of thing? Did she write that herself?"

"Shhh."

Sure, I'll be quiet, I thought. You couldn't hear a scud missile in this place.

■

Everyone was kind of milling around after the show, so I got the writer, Alexia, whom we knew, to introduce me to the Jaishree person. "I thought your act was really terrific," I said. How many times this month had I said that? But I meant it. *Aap se mihlke buddie couchie hui,*" I added. It meant "I am very pleased to meet you." It was actually kind of a casual phrase, but I tried to use my best accent.

"Thanks," Jaishree said. "Where did you learn Urdu?"

"In Benares," I said, "I lived there for a few months when I was a kid. But I really don't know much Urdu, I know more Hindi. Are you from India?"

"Bombay," she said. "It's pretty pretentious to run around yakking Hindi. You're sure you didn't just memorize a few phrases out of *How to Pick Up Ethnic Women?*"

"Uh, well, yeah," I said, "actually I helped edit that book." She half-smiled.

I wanted to keep in touch with her for some reason, but I could feel my friends edging toward the exit, and Jaishree was drifting off, edging toward the bar, so I thought of something fast.

"Listen," I said, "a friend of mine who's a photographer is shooting some ads for Italian *Vogue* with New York performance artists, and I think you'd be really great for it. You know, you just have to be able to wear a big floppy Missoni sweater. And maybe a *bindi* and *duputa* for atmosphere."

"Are you a photographer?" she asked.

"No, I'm like an artist," I answered.

"Do you have a gallery?"

"Yeah, it's Karen Goode, on West Broadway."

"Oh, unh-huhn."

"Do you follow the, uh, gallery scene?"

"No, not really. What kind of work do you do?"

"Nobody does. Well, my art varies a lot, I don't really have a single style, but it's generally about beauty technology of some kind."

"What's beauty technology?"

"Well, cosmetics, hair care, industrial materials designed to imitate or, um, surpass nature—that sort of thing." I wasn't lying. Most of my straight art really did deal with things like that. Anyway, I'd just given her one of my better stock lines about my stuff.

"Oh, really? That sounds kind of interesting."

Since she was getting interested, I felt I could pull back and make contact later. "Look, I think my friends are leaving. Do you have a card?" I asked.

She fished out a card. I said "Bye," and wandered toward Calvin's last recorded position. He was out in the street by this time.

"Hey, we're all going to Undersheen," he said. It was an after-hours club. "Are you coming along or what? It'll be barrels."

"I'm a dinosaur, I'm just too old for this kind of schedule," I said.

"You're only as old as you look."

"Well, I look like Vincent Price."

"Ew, gag me out with two spoons," Calvin said.

"Look, I've been creating deathless masterpieces since one this afternoon," I said. "All you guys do is sit around all day selling Jasper Johnses for millions of dollars and ordering bruschettas from Dean & DeLuca."

"You're breaking my heart," Calvin said.

I'd had enough of the brittle dialogue. I said good night and walked upstream, away from the other cab-seekers, and got a taxi home. When I got in, there were three new messages blinking out on my machine, but I just didn't have the guts to flick it on. I took two whole Valia, brushed my teeth, and started looking forward to ten hours of nonbeing.

■

The phone rang the next morning at six-thirty. Either my best friend or my worst enemy, I thought.

Shit. It was Ute, an ex-girlfriend. Pronounced *Yootie*. She was crying again.

"Didn't you get my messages?" she asked hysterically.

I picked up. "Hunh?"

"I just can't stand thinking of you going out with that bitch," she said.

She meant Katrina.

"Just because she's pretty and stupid and nineteen years old. How could you do this to me? I was in love with you, and she doesn't love you, she's just some little floozy idiot from Queens who's using you, and you're—just so shallow and a jerk, I can't believe it."

"Well, if I'm such a jerk, I don't deserve you, anyway, you're a very loving person, and you should find someone really nice who cares about you more than I can, not that I don't care about you, I mean, but really, I'm a complete clod and you deserve the best, you know?"

"Damn it, I was in love with you, and think what you *did* to me!"

What had I done to her? I was pretty groggy.

"You dumped me for that slut, and then you didn't tell me right away, and you still slept with me, and I feel dirty and disgusting!"

This was not a well girl. I'd already spent hours on the phone with her earlier in the month, trying to calm her down, but it looked as though she'd regressed.

"Look, Ute, I think you're not a well girl. I really feel like you should get some psychiatric help, okay?" I said. "I'm serious. You're really brilliant, and you've got a lot going for you, and this just isn't healthful behavior. Okay?"

"Yeah, I'm brilliant, I'll never get anywhere, no matter how brilliant I am, because I'm *ugly*!"

"Don't be ridiculous, you're not ugly, I think you're really, really attractive. You know I do. You know how much you turn me on, you know, I still think of you all the time."

"You're *lying*! You just dumped me the minute you found someone prettier. And that bitch Katrina's going to do better than me in everything because she's gorgeous and everybody notices her on the street and nobody notices me."

This kind of stuff really breaks my heart. "Look," I said, "I'm going to start taping this conversation, okay? If you jump off the roof and leave a note saying I drove you to it, I want to have some evidence about your state of mind. Okay?"

I switched on the MEMO button on the answering machine.

"Do whatever you want," she said.

"I want to discuss your behavior a bit with my shrink, okay?"

"I don't need a shrink and I'm not crazy!"

"I'm sorry, and I know this sounds a little bit like verdict first, but I tend to think that the more people assert they're not crazy, the crazier they are."

"That's just stupid."

"Listen, Katrina's not going to do better than you in everything, that's ridiculous, you've got a whole lot going for you and you just shouldn't worry, okay? And I'm not good enough for you."

"Don't tell me what's good enough for me."

"We're going over and over the same things."

"I just can't stand thinking of you with that bitch."

"Listen, for what it's worth, and I don't think we should see each other again, but, uh, I think the Katrina and Jamie thing is pretty much over, so you don't have to think about it anymore. You and she ought to get together and form a support group."

"That's a mean thing to say." Pause. "Well, can I see you today?"

"Let's just chill out, okay?"

"I'm just not pretty, and that's why you went out with Katrina."

"That's total nonsense."

"No, it's not, I'm ugly."

"You're so crazy to say that, you have a very distinctive look, it's a very ethnic look, but it's amazing and great."

"I don't want that distinctive look, I want that white look. You're just a racist, too, you like waspy girls."

Ute was kind of tan-skinned.

"Katrina's Jewish, you know, she's not exactly a wasp," I said.

"It doesn't matter, she's white, and that's what beauty is, looking white."

"Look, I just can't take this *tsouris und drang* right now. Why don't you let me take a shower and I'll call you back?"

She hung up.

■

I showered, got some nut mix out of the fridge, tidied the loft a bit, and called Penny at one o'clock.

"Are you having any problems?" I asked.

"I feel numb, and I'm really itchy in a few places, and I don't dare scratch."

"Well, where the tape is, on the back and sides of your head, you can rub yourself gently, and maybe if you'd rather I could come over to your hotel tomorrow morning and take the bandages off."

"That would be just so great. How about nine?"

I gritted my teeth and said okay. If I'd said it had to be later, she would have known I was just lazy. I was thinking about that singer, Jaishree, for some reason. She had something sexy about her. I dug my wallet and stuff out of my clothing from the night before and found Jaishree's card. It was on some sort of holographic lenticular laser-printed purple and green paper that charged like ocean waves when you looked at it from different angles. I'll have to get some like this for myself, I thought. JAMIE ANGELO, AMERICAN PSYCHO ARTIST. The card said, JAISHREE MANGLANI, YOUNG PERFORMANCE ARTIST. (212) 555-1113. I still had the cordless in my hand, and so I just dialed it.

"We are Jaishree and Alex, the great and terrible, not necessarily in that order," the message machine said. *"Who are you and what do you want?* Beep."

"It's Jamie Angelo, I met you last night, I'm at 914-5858," I said, and hung up. I knew if she didn't call back, I d feel worthless for a while, but I didn't want to push. I'd decided that in general, with answering machines, the less the better.

■

Calvin came over at one-thirty, a half hour late. He looked okay for someone who'd been cruising the Spike or whatever other gay club all night, though. Calvin's the better of my two "society" brokers. He's an art dealer, a real social climber, and lately he's gotten to be a bit of a pain in the neck, always backbiting, and hardly anyone I know will deal with him, but he still works for me. He says funny things, though, and he knows about stuff. He's thirty-one, tall and kind of good-looking in a dark Byronic/Spanish kind of way. Except for his basic personality, he's terrific. He's known informally as Calvin "I'll Do Anything to Meet Fancy Fags" Greenaway.

"I've got a good one for you," he said, "and you've heard of her. It's Laureen McNiel. You know, the one who was married to David McNiel."

"Yeah, that real-estate guy who bought all that art in the eighties."

"Exactly, the one Robert convinced that he should buy all those Jeff Koonses and Peter Halleys."

"He also told him to buy Rick Prol and Holt Quentel."

"Is that so? Well, that brings me to the financial end. She also has some things you might be interested in."

He was digging in his bag and brought out a black eight-by-ten envelope and flipped it over to me. Trying to be cute, I thought. Look at this clown with his theatrical manners and his air of secrecy, acting like he was Sydney Greenstreet in *The Maltese Falcon*. I didn't say anything, though. I pulled out the photo.

"Take a look. We'll save on laundering bills."

It looked like it was nearly three feet high. The condition was amazing: It was apparently complete, and there was quite a bit of paint, black, cinnabar, and Mayan blue, still on the surface. The hideous hook-nosed face of God L—one of the Nine Lords of Xibalbá, the Maya underworld—had huge, blank, staring turquoise eyes and a protruding tongue. His head was encased in a fantastic headdress of three stacked birds, with the cruller-knot over his forehead and the tiny Jester God perched above it. There were wide ear-flange arrangements around the face, and the whole head and headdress emerged from a second headdress in the shape of the jaws of the Cauac Monster, the earth-demon, resting on what looked like a turtle but might have been a stylized crocodile.

I was taken aback for a minute but realized it was best to keep cool. "Just offhand I'd say this was from the Usumacinta region, maybe Dos Pilas or Piedras Negras, an incense burner from the Late Classic Period, about 700 A.D.," I said.

"She mentioned something along those lines."

"But she didn't mention a definite provenance? It's a looted piece."

"I don't know," he said, "she doesn't even have it. Some dealer in Merida owes it to her."

"Who?"

"His name's Antonio Portilla."

"I know him, he's a sleaze," I said. "This is sounding shadier and shadier. How do we get it up here?"

"Send a courier."

"I can guarantee you that Tony'll substitute a fake."

"So go down and take a look at it yourself, I don't know. Don't do it if it doesn't sound like a good deal."

"No, don't get me wrong," I said. "It's a museum-quality piece, and I don't have any idea what it's worth today. It might actually not be as much as our asking price. But it could be a lot, and besides, this must be a documented item, I could never sell it later without a record of sale, and then where would I have gotten the money, and where would she say she'd spent it?"

"You'll have to say you traded a painting for it."

"I don't know."

"I know you like such things, Jamie," Calvin said.

"What's your end, a larger commission for saving them money?"

"Laureen's a little cash-poor at the moment," he said. "I may ask for an Yves Klein drawing or something myself, in lieu of currency."

"I don't know," I said. "I'll have to shop this photo around a little."

"Well, let's not think too long about it," he snipped. "By the way, Laureen's already had a lift and a nose job and chin implant."

"So what, everyone's getting a chin implant lately," I said. "All these women end up looking like Margaret Hamilton."

"Trop mal pour elles." Calvin shrugged. "Fat injections for lips are so big now, too. It's a permanent pout all the way from Gracie Square to the River House."

"So pouty's de rigueur right now. It goes in and out."

I helped him back into his coat and walked him out.

"Chowder," he said.

"Au reservoir."

I *would* shop the piece around. But I was kind of hooked. There was something about the expression on God L's face that I had to have. Something knowing.

■

I didn't bother calling Ute back. I had to go to my psychiatrist at three o'clock that day. I cabbed uptown, and the East River was all white, and there were pink helicopters flying low over it. We passed UN Plaza, and I got a glimpse of a Salle painting through the Edelmans' window on the eighth floor. They were some of the biggest collectors in the world. I'd been to parties there a few times. We zipped under the ominous overhang of the Fifty-ninth Street bridge.

The point of psychiatry is largely just ritual, getting all the way up to Park and Seventy-third, walking into that dark office with the picture of Freud and the tribal art and the lighted-up sea urchins, and doing the news of the week. When I'd started with this guy four years ago, he'd seemed cool and therapy had seemed like a good move, but lately we'd been going around in Möbius strips. He said I wasn't forthcoming enough to do "serious work," as he called it. I wished I could tell him about Penny, but it wouldn't be a good idea.

"I'm pretty cut up about Katrina," I began instead.

"You never really told me much about her," Dr. Brook said.

"She was just *La Reine de la Nuit,*" I said. "I was crazy about her. I know it only lasted nine and a half weeks, but she was just so hot. And she was really smart about stuff that counts. Like she was *really* on the ball about Counter-Reformation poetry. You know, like Scève and du Bellay. All my favorite things. She even knew all about *The Countesse of Pembrokes Arcadia.*"

"What's that?"

"Oh, it's a romance by Sir Philip Sidney, you know, with a lot of poems in it, 'Ye Goat-Herd Gods that Love the Grassy Mountains,' and all that kind of thing, I guess maybe you had to be a lit major at Yale to really get into that stuff, but it's really great, and she was so into it, and she had such a great figure."

"Sometimes I wonder whether you really know what all your priorities are with women."

"No, I don't, that's right, I don't know what my priorities are with women. You're absolutely right."

"We haven't yet figured out why you seem to only go after very ethnic women."

"I don't just go for ethnic women, what's ethnic mean, anyway, I mean they're all very different—"

"Maybe you just haven't found the right girl yet. Do you think you can accept that?"

"No, I can't accept that. I have to have every girl be absolutely perfect."

"Well, every girl isn't perfect. You can't just set up this bargain with the world that if it doesn't do what you want, you'll be upset all the time."

"Maybe I'll make the perfect girl."

"What do you mean?"

"I mean, maybe I'll find the perfect girl."

He didn't answer.

"Oh, by the way," I said. "Ute's been calling me constantly, and, uh, I'm a little worried about her. I taped a phone call of hers. You want to hear it?"

"Sure," he said.

I took out my little portable tape recorder. It takes the same size cassettes as my answering machine. I played the conversation.

"That's not a well girl," he said. "Did she have any kind of religious upbringing?"

"Yeah, as a matter of fact, that's true, she's a Catholic, she went to a Catholic school until she went to college."

"Maybe she feels she's given you a lot by sleeping with you and that you owe her undying devotion in return. You know, sex is a very big thing for Catholics, and they tend to feel very guilty about it."

"Yeah, I suppose, maybe that's it."

"She should get some help."

"I'll tell her you said so."

We were silent for a minute.

"How's the BuSpar doing?" he asked.

"I don't know, I still got one or two little anxiety attacks this week." Frankly, after two months of popping the stuff, I hadn't noticed any difference at all.

"What's a little anxiety attack?" he asked.

"Well, I guess I kind of demolished one of my computer monitors, the portrait monitor that wasn't working."

"How did you do that?"

"I guess I kind of put one of my paperweights through it."

"One of the Lalique paperweights?"

"Not one of the really scarce ones."

"I'm worried about you," Dr. Brook said. He gave me one of his strange bug-eye looks. "You have some very violent aspects to your personality. Are you sure there isn't something you're not telling me?"

"No, no, you get the whole scoop." I decided I'd stop seeing this old jerk and buy some Thierry Mugler jackets with the money I saved. That would probably be just as psychically generative. I'd get my downers some other way. The problem with psychiatrists is that they've been to medical school. How could anyone who's spent all that time in medical school have any insight into a person like me?

"Do you take the BuSpar three times a day like I directed?"

"Yeah, once in a while I may screw up, I don't know."

"It's a systemic thing, you can't just pop it like you did with the Valium."

"Maybe we should dump a couple of cartons in my building's water supply."

"Hmmm," he said humorlessly, giving me the Herr Doktor look. "Well, let's give it another week and see if anything really stressful happens. If it doesn't help, we'll start you on Konzak."

"Oh, no chance of anything stressful," I said.

The King was dying, and the Queen and the Knave were already dividing his empire.

The Valley of the Kunsthandlers, as I thought of SoHo, really was a valley, with low iron buildings on low ground between the crystal mountains Uptown and Downtown. This twelve-block area still dictated what was what in the Vis Biz, and the rest of the world just had to deal with it. When I got out of the cab (five o'clock traffic getting thick) on Broadway and Houston Street, or Zero Street, as I thought of it, I was amazed for the millionth time that you really could see all the way down Broadway as it curled up away from you, all the way past the King Ludwig fantasy of the Woolworth Building to the entrance of Trinity Church, and turning back, all the way uptown past Grace Church, where Broadway veers west, to the top of the Chrysler Building and even the ugly one-angled roof of the Citicorp Center, which I always wished would blow up. But as I walked down into the Valley, I became caught up as always in the subliminal dub rhythm of the art world, a hungry shark dance of money and image and behavioral-sink psychodrama. Everyone came here. Lower Broadway really is the Forty-second Street of the nineties, I thought, trying to make up new lyrics to the Dubin and Warren song:

> *Let's walk faster, there's Brooke Astor,*
> *Filthy rich but sweet,*

Vulgar Gir-ls, from the Boroughs,
Who are indiscreet,
They're side by side, they're glorified—
Where the underworld can cheat the elite,
Faster, Slower,
Fake-er, Faux-er,
Lower Broa———dwaay street . . .

The King of the Valley was Nino Fortreza, the Don, the Lion in the Castle, the dealer who invented Pop Art and focused the eyes of the world on SoHo in the sixties and seventies. The Queen was Karen Goode, who was also my dealer, who started out working with Nino and then took over the Conceptual Painting business in the eighties with Neo-Expressionism and the best of the East Village painters. But she'd slowed down a bit lately. The Knave was Jerry Davidian, the Big Noise from L.A., the Resale Raider, the Lebanese Connection, the Turkish Mafia, the Prince of Darkness. He was moving in on Nino's territory, courting all of Fortreza's artists and buying up their old work, or getting pieces consigned for long periods at long distances and selling them over the telephone, like a Wall Street trader or a movie producer. He had the new clients, film people like Steve Martin and Dawn Steele and Sylvester Stallone. To some extent Nino, who was always the foxy old Neapolitan, knew enough to keep his friends close but his enemies closer. And so he was being really friendly to Jerry, going along with Jerry's deals, getting pieces of them for himself, staying alive and thwarting Jerry's dreams of global domination. But the Don was getting old and forgetful. Sometimes he'd sell a major piece and then not remember which one it was, where he had it stored, or anything. It was only a matter of time until the Prince had the market to himself.

But I was mainly concerned with Karen. I had to drop by her gallery at five-thirty. "Report" might be more like it. Mistress Karen ran the place like an armed camp. She'd weathered some attacks lately, the Art Crash of '91, Jerry's various schemes to drive her out of business—but it looked like she was leveling off again and was going to pull through. It's still one of the only ten or so actually profitable galleries in New York—the rest are basically vanity businesses—and it's a gallery that a lot of people were jealous of me for showing at, but I still wasn't a household word just because I had a show there every fourteen months. It was just a very good gallery. But the public simply doesn't know artists. I was brooding about this as I turned onto West Broadway.

The scene wasn't like the old days anymore anyway, when I'd first come to the city, in the heart of the Boom. The East Village. I missed the limousines filled with European collectors cruising past the garbage on Avenue A at one A.M. to the all-night parties in the back rooms of Gracie Mansion's Gallery, the quick money and fame and excitement, kids right off the street getting fifteen thousand a pop, Keith Haring, Jean-Michel Basquiat, and Andy, all currently dead, and now Kenny Scharf was getting old and crusty, David Wojnarowicz was sick, Debbie Harry was hardly ever around, and Madonna was off doing her own superstar routine worlds away. New York kind of swallows history up. It's too much of the moment. You find yourself somewhere that you know was tremendously significant, and you can hardly believe it's the same place, it seems so new and soulless, even if it looks unchanged.

I pushed in the heavy glass door. There are two glass doors, but only one of them moves, and it moves in the least obvious direction. The gallery was very carefully set up to intimidate visitors as much as possible. I pushed hard on the left door. Of course, I knew by now which door worked. Anybody who didn't know would first try pulling the right door, and then pushing the right door, and then pulling the left door, and then when he finally got the left door pushed in, it was really awkward for him to usher his family or whatever in with his right hand and hold the heavy door open with his left. And usually there'd be a whole bunch of people trying to get out and inch around that door in the other direction, so it was even more tense. And then you ran right up against a white false wall, with the name of the artist on it in specially designed austere-looking press-type letters ten inches high, and you had to maneuver around that. Then when you got around the wall you came face-to-face with the Front Desk Boy. Except he would never look you in the face if he didn't know who you were, or if he did look at you by mistake, he'd give you a look like, "What are *you* doing in here? The Poster Originals Gallery is down the street. This gallery is for movers and shakers and Doris Saatchi, not for some dentist from Tenafly." He smiled at me, of course, because I was persona grata. There was a picture card for the current show sitting on the counter surrounding his nonobjective desk. I knew better than to try to pick it up, because they were always taped down. That way if people tried to pick them up, they'd get even more flustered.

So I smiled at Jonathan the Front Desk Person and struck off into the darkness of the main gallery. They were having a Sigmar Planck show, and there were just three of his tiny paintings in the huge space, spotlighted in a really dramatic way. I have to hand it to Karen, she knows how to display art. Even a dead fish with maggots on it would look beautiful and expensive if she hung it. I didn't bother looking at the paintings. As I walked toward the back rooms, my shoes squeaked like dying mice. Karen has a perfectly sanded bleached-cherry floor and she has it waxed nearly every day, partly to make it look good but mainly so that your shoes will squeak on it and you'll feel small and intimidated. I turned the corner into the second room. There was a blank wall, a gigantic Planck, and another blank wall. The basic message was that Planck was such an incredible perfectionist genius that he only did about one painting a year, and anyway since each one was about as expensive as an Apache assault helicopter, they didn't need to show more than four. And if you were neophyte enough to actually ask the Front Desk Person what the prices of the pieces were, he'd say, "I'm sorry, but this show was reserved before it opened." But of course, if you were intimidated enough by the whole presentation to insist that you wanted to buy something, anything, because otherwise you'd feel second-rate and mortified for the rest of your life, you'd get ushered into the back, and yes, it might turn out that there was *one* little Planck left in the rack because the show was too crowded, and you *might* be able to acquire it before the Kunstverein in Munich snapped it up, and before you knew it you'd be writing a check for more than your daughter's full four-year Princeton tuition for a little brown rectangle with a smaller black rectangle on it off-center, and wondering whether that purchase alone would make you socially acceptable.

I moved the brown-velvet rope aside and stepped up one level into the first of the back rooms. Some people in the gallery watched me replace the rope, and I felt kind of bad shutting them out. They looked as if they were trying not to feel rejected.

The back room was designed so that our hypothetical dentist from Tenafly, not daring to lift the rope, would get a teasing glimpse through the entranceway of the insiders' glamorous world: a Diego Giacometti table surrounded by comfy-looking Knoll International chairs, a de Kooning painting, and a long desk with an absolutely gorgeous pair of secretaries, one male, one female, one blond, the other blonde. The male one always wore a Wehrmacht brown shirt under his Armani blazer and the general joke was that Karen had called up her boyfriend, who's a dealer in Salzburg, and said, "Honey, when you send over the Plancks, could you throw in a real *Übermensch*-looking boy to help me intimidate my largely Jewish clientèle?" The girl, it was rumored, was just some Zoli model who'd barely learned to pretend to type and repeat a few key phrases like "This show was sold out before it opened." I knew all this wasn't true, of course—they were both just Columbia kids—but it was part of the mystique.

"Hi, how are you?" I asked.

"Fine," Conrad said, "we showed some of your work to Barbara Cohn this morning."

"Oh, that's great." I wanted to ask if she had been interested, but that was Karen's territory and she was funny about the help.

"Karen's with a client, but she can be with you in a moment," Cheryl said. "You can go into the outer office if you like."

"Thanks," I said. God, I thought, can you believe the way Karen gets these people to act? I'd been with the gallery for four years, and they still talked to me as though I were a not-so-steady client. Still, the way she abuses them, it's amazing they can speak at all. I walked behind the desk and around into a conference room with a round dark fruitwood table and dim lighting. They watched me nervously. Anyone who works for Karen has got to be a complete masochist. Conrad quit for a while after she screamed at him and tore up a slide in front of him and threw it in his face because he got the label upside down—it was on a Robert Ryman monochrome painting that looked the same either way up—but then he came back because he said he needed more discipline in his life.

I sat down on a Le Corbusier chair—surprisingly comfortable, actually—and waited for Karen. Nobody would even think of bothering her while she was making a pitch. I toyed with my Toshiba

Electric Filofax and flipped through a catalogue for a Nayland Blake show at Michael Werner's in Köln. It was all kinds of torture-instrument-looking gadgets. Nayland's such a kidder, I thought.

After a while Karen manifested herself in the First Back Room, leading some couple I'd seen before out of the gallery. I knew she'd already seen me come in on the security cameras. She spoke with Conrad for a minute and then swaggered in to see me. For a little person, she can really swagger. She was wearing a short Armani skirt with a kind of tattered hemline and a green Armani blazer. The gallery must have an account with Armani, I thought. Actually, it's kind of beat; as far as I'm concerned, the thing these days is not to get too caught up in the Armani thing and to leave yourself open.

"How are you, it's good to see you." She smiled. The smile of a crocodile in couture.

"I'm good," I said. "I'm getting a lot of fabrication done—"

"I have some good news and some bad news," she said. "The good news is that we'd like you to do a show at Peter's in Berlin in April. The bad news is that we want to put your next solo here off until next March. I know that seems like a long time, but we need to make room in September for the show of Rumanian photography."

You didn't exactly argue with Karen Goode. "That'll make it almost two years between shows for me here," I said.

"I know, it'll help build up excitement for the next one. And also, your sign's under the influence of Venus during September, it's a bad time for Libras. It's a very, very bad time for you. Venus is a *bad* planet for you. I can't emphasize that strongly enough. You should just try to stay out of trouble that month."

I clammed up. I'd learned when to. One of the first things she'd done when I'd signed with the gallery was have her astrologer do my chart. You can't argue with the stars.

"Also," she said, "there's an important show at the New Museum coming up that we might be able to get you in. So you won't be without things to do. And we're showing your set of drawings, and it looks like we'll place some of them."

"What about the frames on the drawings? I'd really like to use my signature frames," I said. We'd been having this argument for years. I was almost thirty, damn it. Too old to have this kind of argument with a dealer.

"Believe me, I know what I'm doing, the rosewood frames work much better for what you're trying to achieve," she said. "Listen, I have a six-o'clock. Get a plan of Peter's gallery from Conrad, and I'll see you at the dinner for Planck on Sunday. At Chanterelle."

I guess you just took orders from Karen no matter who you were, even if you were Roy Fucking Lichtenstein. But if that was a meeting, I didn't need to come in for it. She could just fax me my instructions, in code if necessary, and I'd never have to look at her again.

■

I'd been home for about an hour, fooling around with some paintings, when I heard Jaishree leaving a message on the speaker-phone. Fabulous. I was pretty psyched that she called back. I made it to the phone just as she was about to hang up.

"How are you?" I asked.

"I'm tremendously sick," she said. "I've taken five Advils in the last four hours."

"That's the one that's little, yellow, different, and better, like you, right?"

"No, Advil's the one that's advanced medicine for pain."

"That's good, you're so advanced."

"I'm tired of the painkiller wars. I really just need to sleep, I need to get some more Valium—or go back on a good sleeping pill."

"Halcion's really the best sleeping pill, you wake up so refreshed. You don't want to get up all leaden and awful, you want to leap out of bed shouting 'Happy, happy morningtide,' " I said. "It's too bad it gives you brain damage."

"Well, I don't know, I think Valium's fine for that, too."

"But Valium's more addictive," I said.

"I don't think I'm addicted to it."

"I used to really swear by Xanax."

"But Xanax is just a tranquilizer, isn't it?"

"Yeah, it really gets you through the rough spots. It's the only true peace I've ever experienced."

"Oh," she said.

"But I don't really need a tranquilizer. I need something specific for my thinking. I'm off the BuSpar, it really wasn't working for me."

"Well, BuSpar doesn't bring you up at all, it just kind of levels you out."

"It wasn't leveling me out. I'm supposed to go on Konzak."

"Oh, well, that's just the new cool one, it's the drug everybody's talking about right now. It makes it so you don't enjoy sex at all, but nobody cares because they feel so great."

"Well, it's not just because it's trendy, it's supposed to be really specific, you know, an anti-obsessive."

"I don't know if that's really possible. But yeah, I just met you, but I'm sure you could stand to be a little less obsessive," Jaishree said.

"No kidding. I wish I didn't have to take anything, but you know, maybe I wouldn't if I lived in California and surfed to work every day, but in New York, it isn't—"

"It's true, you just can't live in this city without chemical help."

I suggested we get a dinner at Shazeen, a Pakistani fast-food place on Lexington and Twenty-fifth. Surprisingly, she said okay. Maybe it was just the Tuesday-night blues thing, but I guess I also have tremendous charm. At least she admitted she was free. She was honest. "It may be a little too fancy for you, though," I said. "Next time we'll go somewhere less pretentious."

"I saw a mouse the last time I was there," she said.

"When was that?"

"Night before last."

"Well, good, it's probably especially clean today. They'll be on the lookout. I'm glad we're going someplace safe and homey. I'm sick of trying new things."

It was true. A few days before, someone had taken me to a Scandinavian place called Agavit. They served mainly what they called Bleak Fish. In fact, everything on the menu was called Bleak. It was like Dickens meets Bergman. Everything was raw, but it didn't have that fresh Japanese quality raw fish is supposed to have. It tasted raw and rotten both. All I wanted right now was a reassuring *samosa*. Hindu soul food.

8

I'd already sat down and ordered a chicken kebab when Jaishree walked in. She was really pretty, kind of an Indian Julia Roberts, maybe not model-level but fine for the stage, I thought, what with all the "believable-looking" actresses doing so well out there. Her face was just a little bit on the weather-beaten side, though. And her nose and teeth weren't quite right. I guess she was about twenty-eight. She was wearing boots and a floppy grandfather coat and green jeans and a shirt that said CHICAGO POLICE HOMICIDE DIVISION—OUR DAY BEGINS WHEN YOUES ENDS. It had a picture of death, with a scythe and an hourglass, holding out a police badge.

"Hi," I said, getting up—genetic manners, you know. "Is that a real T-shirt?"

"I hope so."

She sat down and started looking through the little "specials" card.

"I mean, does it come from the police department?"

"Yes."

"I wouldn't have thought that cops would have it in them. To be that funny, I mean."

"No, I have a friend who's a cop, he's very funny."

"Do you ever wear, like, any Indian things, like a *salwar kameez*?"

"No, not much, unless I'm doing a nationalist thing of some sort, it gets too much attention. You seem to know a lot about India."

"I was there when I was a little kid. I grew up in Hong Kong, and we went through all the time, because my dad was a foreign correspondent."

"Where did you go?"

"The first place I remember is Calcutta."

"It made a big impression on you?"

"Yeah, it was pretty horrible, when we first got there, you know how they're so cruel to animals in India, I thought the streets were covered with blood. All the dirt streets were running red stuff down the center. Of course, it wasn't really blood, it was juice and shells from, you know, uh, what you call betel leaves."

"Paan."

"Right."

She had the greatest low voice.

"So do you not wear the Indian stuff because Indian society is so sexist?" I asked.

"Yes, I suppose that is a factor in it, sure," she said. There was a sort of quaint British touch to the way she phrased things that was kind of cute. "I was quite appalled at sexism in India after I came here and learned what my rights were. I was fifteen years old then. But, you know, I'd already seen some pretty horrible stuff."

"Like suttee, and all that?"

"Well, not actually suttee, at funerals, but bride burning and things of the sort."

"Bride burning?"

"Yes."

"Like before the husband dies?"

"Yes."

"Did you know anyone this happened to?"

"Well, maybe, it's kind of a secret, I guess—"

"Someone in your family?"

"Well actually, apparently, my grandmother on my mother's side says my mother's uncle did set his wife on fire."

"That's just shockingly barbaric."

"Well, the rest of my family would never speak to him again, of course."

"But this goes on all the time?"

"Yes, it's pretty bad, but there's still a lot of bride burning in India. The police almost always just call it a cooking accident. But I think my uncle did go to jail for some years."

"What do you mean," I asked, "a 'cooking accident'?"

"Well, in India, it's not like it is here, all the women cook all day long, and they stand over a kerosene stove in these saris which trail down and which are usually very flammable—polyester is very popular in India—and they really do burn themselves to death pretty often cooking."

"But why is there so much bride burning?"

"Well, usually it's just for the dowry. You know, a bride in India has to have a big dowry, because women there are just complete liabilities, and so they get killed for that, but also usually it's the *sass,* the mother-in-law, that just doesn't like them because they're not sufficiently respectful."

"Can I just say that I've never been so shocked in my whole life?"

"I'd like a lamb *kurma* and one *naan* and a *keema paratha,"* she said to the waiter.

We got along pretty well. I'm always excited to make a new friend. Of course, I'm just so smooth lately, it's easy. But we were clicking. In general, I hate it when people you've only known for a little while start telling you their life stories, but there really was a kind of super rapport developing between me and Jaishree. Indian women are generally very reserved. Of course, she was a performer.

I sound like a jerk saying it, but I have a good rapport with most women. In my milieu, I feel hopelessly old-fashioned being heterosexual at all, but I really am, pretty much anyway, because I just like women so much. Women have such a sleek modern design compared to men. Men always look so rococo and knobby. And most of the time they're into some stupid macho thing. But I don't think it's macho bullshit with me to like women, I really think it's a kind of identification. I'm not into team sports, I'm much more into outfits and ballet. But maybe lots of men say that.

"How is that *keema*?" I asked.

"It's good. It's not goat like at home, though. Do you want to try some?"

"I have a little problem about sharing food. But thanks."

"What problem is that?"

"I'm just a little paranoid about it, that's all. It's just a little mild hypochondriasis."

We started talking about racism in India and how Indians were so into looking Western. She said when she was a little girl in Bombay, she'd had a recurring fantasy where her face gets totally destroyed in a car wreck, and it has to be reconstructed, and she comes out looking like the Cinderella in a nineteenth-century British illustrated book she had.

"You mean, you thought you should look white," I said.

"Yes."

"What a personal thing to tell me. I hardly know you," I said.

That shut her up, but I hadn't really wanted to shut her up, so I thought of something else to say. "It's funny you should mention that reconstructive surgery fantasy, you know, I'm kind of interested in that stuff myself."

"Oh?"

"Well, you'd just have to see some of my stuff to know what I mean. Want to do a studio visit?"

"What time do you feel it is?"

"I don't have a watch, but I feel it's about eight-thirty."

They'd given us trays, so we picked them up and dumped them out, college style, and put them in the "dirty tray" pile, which looked exactly like the "clean tray" pile. Indians are a little dirty, frankly, as a rule. They're not clean like Japanese or Koreans.

"Well, okay," Jaishree said. "I'd like to see your work, but we'd better go back by my house so I can pick up my messages."

Actresses are crazy for messages.

"Why don't you just call up and get them?"

"Oh, the retrieval function on my answering machine isn't happening. I've been trying to find a place to get it fixed."

"What do you mean, fixed? Just throw it out and get another one." We nodded to the counter lady and walked out.

"Well, it's been pretty good until now."

"I mean, what do you think this is, the industrial age, the nineteenth century or something? Nobody fixes anything anymore, it's all solid state. It's cheaper to toss it."

"You're right. I don't know what I was thinking."

We walked down Second Avenue. It was getting eveningy-looking, kind of dusty-rose light all over, and there were a lot of peddlers with all kinds of stuff dug out of closets and trash cans.

"So tell me more about the car-wreck fantasy," I said.

"Well, it's funny, I'd had that dream or daydream or whatever for a long time, but just a year ago I had a second cousin whose face was totally crushed by a bus in India, and they flew her here for surgery, and you know what's really weird? She has an identical twin sister, and so they brought her here, too, and used her as a model."

"Wow, that's really lucky and strange. So did they graft out of her?"

"What do you mean?"

"Well, the genetic material would be the same. They could use skin out of the sister, and it wouldn't get rejected."

"Really?"

"Yeah. You know, in the future when someone's born, they're going to grow a clone of that person and lobotomize it and keep it on ice to use for transplants."

"I hope I'm dead before they start doing that."

I didn't know what to say, so I asked about the grafts again.

"No, I don't think they took grafts out of Softy," she said. "What's with your big thing for medicine? Aren't you supposed to be an artist?"

"Oh, yeah, it's wrong to have more than one field."

"Yes."

That was kind of a strange exchange, I thought. Maybe she'd felt she'd given too much away with the car-crash thing. But she was supposed to be a performance artist, and they make a living out of giving things away.

We walked down to her apartment, on Tenth Street. It was a fourth-floor walkup, and the stairs were a little squalorous and the apartment had that pathetic messy quality that girl performance-artists' apartments usually have, but it also had an authentic seventies-revival hipness about it and a lot of nice Indian stuff. There were clothes all over, maybe evidence of a roommate. The main thing that caught my eye first was a fish tank done up like an opera house inside, made out of some sort of plastic doll-house puppet theater. It was all lit up with turquoise and magenta light. She said it was based on the passage in Proust about the Opera being like a fish tank, and she started telling me how all the different fish were characters in *À la Recherche*.

"This red one's the Duchesse de Guermantes, and of course, the big fat ugly catfish back there—"

"That's Charlus."

"Right. And then the formal-looking one, the black and white one with the long neck, that's Swann, of course, and that white one is Robert de Saint-Loup, and then the little guppy is Marcel."

"What about the Verdurins, are they in there?"

"No way, I wouldn't want them in my tank."

"Which one's Albertine?"

"Well," she said, twinkling, "I *did* have one named Albertine, but, you know, she just sort of, like, disappeared."

I should have known she was waiting for me to ask that.

"Have you thought about getting any non-fish, like turtles?" I asked.

"I thought about getting some crayfish," she said, "but, you know, I kind of figured they'd massacre some of my fish."

"I know what you mean. They look cranky."

"They just don't look like they're going to wait around for the next infusion of tubifex worms. They look like they've got sashimi on their mind."

"Absolutely," I agreed.

"You know, I started doing the fish thing when I'd just come out of a long, bad relationship," she said. "And I needed something living around the house, but I didn't want anything that would make a whole lot of emotional demands on me, so I thought fish, because they're supposedly pretty self-absorbed. But then I was afraid that they wouldn't like me, and that they'd die, so I got a whole bunch of really little ones that I thought probably didn't have a lot of emotional needs, and if one of them died once in a while, it wouldn't make a difference. So I had a lot of anonymous fish—it was kind of a Warholly-looking thing, about reproduction and identity—and it was great for a while. But then it began to bother me that they didn't have any real identities, and I couldn't have a favorite. So I got one really bright red fish and put it in with all the others. And it *looked* great, but after a while I realized that that red fish was just my surrogate, lording it over all the other fish, it was just a sick replication of my skewed view of the world. The fish were just feeding my neuroses. So I started to feel like, if I was going to have an emotionally satisfying fish tank, I was just going to have to alter my perception of the world. So I started thinking about more narrative things and characters and stuff, and I started adding more different distinctive fish, like each one had something important to offer. But then I realized that Proust was so important to me, what I was really doing was replicating the characters in Proust in my own view of the world. So that was when I bought the larger tank and added the plastic opera house, and now it's a pretty good representation of the novel."

"That's great," I said. "It's a tough novel to do in fish, really, too. I mean, if you were doing *The Old Man and the Sea,* it would be a lot easier."

"I was thinking of doing one based on *Lolita,* actually," she said. "With just two fish, a big ugly brown one and a little beautiful pink one."

"How about a red Quilty one?"

"His car's red, he's not red."

"Are you a big *Lolita* fan?" I asked.

"Sure."

"Me, too." I was surprised she mentioned it. *Lolita*'s one of my favorite novels because, even though it's narrated in the first person, you actually know much more than the narrator. He seems like a pleasant guy, but he's actually a weird pervert and a psychotic killer. So it kind of plays with your expectations. You can't believe everything you read. Maybe the narrator is lying to you about something under a mask of total honesty.

She got her messages off her machine—they went on for at least ten minutes and some of them sounded as if she had some decent agency pushing for her—while I sort of kicked around looking at her books. There was a copy of Edmund Spenser's poetry with a yellow sticker on it that said USED. That sticker was always a giveaway.

"You went to Yale," I said.

"What tipped you off?" she yelled out from under the telephone.

"Stickers from the Co-Op Bookstore."

"Maybe you know some of my friends from the Drama School."

"What year were you?"

"'88," she said.

"Forget it, I'm a dinosaur. Did you study with Austin Pendleton?"

"Yeah."

"I know the syndrome."

For some reason, she also had a few books on pre-Columbian history. I wondered what she'd think when she saw my pre-Columbian library. I have over two hundred. Almost everything major ever published on the subject, in fact. She had a fair amount of South American stuff that I didn't have, though. I'm only interested in Mexico. There was a copy of Mary Miller's *The Blood of Kings* lying open.

She got a different coat, kind of a "fun fur" thing in lavender, and we went out and walked downtown toward my house. It's a loft, of course, but I call it the house. *Loft* is so short and pretentious, it's like saying "Yale."

"Have you been to the Yucatán?" I asked her.

"No, but I like reading about the Maya," she said. "There's something sexy about human sacrifice."

"You should go. It'll change your life."

"Let's cab it," I said when we got to Sixth Street.

"That's so extravagant, I never take cabs."

"I never used to, either. But one day my foot stepped off the curb, my hand shot up, and I've never looked back."

It was dark when we got to the thoroughly unpretentious, graffiti-covered exterior of my building and walked up the three flights of stairs to the green door. The freight elevator was fun but a big hassle to use. The door onto the stairs had an odd painting of a cockleshell with an eye in it. It's pretty unassuming from the outside. When I opened it, though, I could tell she was impressed because she acted blasé.

The loft was nearly four thousand square feet, so it was pretty impressive even when it was messy. It was a long, railroad-style space with the kitchen and studio area on your left as you enter and the living area on your right. Each area was lit by a wall of high windows at the narrow end. The door opened directly into the living-room area, which had three purple velvet imitation-Ruhlman couches arranged around a huge five-foot-square coffee table with rounded corners that was actually a sign from a Dunkin' Donuts shop. I'd stripped off the lettering, of course, and it was just a hard white plastic surface. When you switched on the fluorescent lights inside, it lit up the whole room from underneath and cast great shadows, but it was off right now. I mainly turned it on to look at transparencies and overlays or for hors d'oeuvre parties, when I'd put translucent table-cloths of different colors over it. There were built-in bookshelves on the left, some filled with books—mainly on the movies and on pre-Columbian archaeology, although there was also a bunch of major expensive art books and exhibition catalogues and a shelf full of heavy art theory books in a prominent position—and some filled with trinkets, religious statues from Little Havana in Miami, lava lamps in different colors, and geometrical crystal models. To the left of the living-room area was a desk area with all the computer stuff on it—the Macintosh Quadra, the scanner, the HP5 laser printer, a couple of loose disk drives, a modem, a color monitor and an amber portrait monitor, a television and VCR hookup to that, and the Toshiba laptop word processor, separate from the Mac, which made four TV screens in all on the desk alone, so it looked kind of official. Calvin says that it's General Schwarzkopf's World Headquarters for Third-World Domination. There was a four-line business phone and two answering machines, a radio phone and a headset phone, a good half-tone Toshiba fax machine, and a huge Canon 500 color laser copier (rented) curled up next to the desk like a big dog, with a Scitex hookup to the Mac trailing out of it like a leash. Despite all the gadgetry, though, the place still looked shabby and chaotic, with bills and cash-machine receipts and exhibition announcements strewn all over it. To the right of the office area was the boudoir area, partly around the corner from the living-room area so you couldn't really see it, even though there were no separate rooms. I had a great walk-in closet and a big bed and orchids and cacti and more books and stuff. The kitchen, on the immediate left as we walked in, had all sorts of funky built-in glass cabinets and a huge tile bar-counter hang-out area with a couple of different sinks in it, salvaged by the original restorers from when the place was a plumbing warehouse. All the walls in the kitchen were covered with pinned-up photographs and posters and take-out menus and cards for theater and performance events and all my old exhibition announcements and photographs of me by Timothy Greenfield-Sanders and little Indian trinkets and Hindu calendars and Devali cards with pictures of Lakshmi and

Naryan and the baby Krishna. And then there was a kind of long, narrow passage past the kitchen, off to the left, into the studio.

"Is that a real pre-Columbian thing?" she asked.

"Yeah," I said. It was a Zapotec glyphic pot.

"I'm impressed."

"Then it's all worth it."

She looked around some more and finally said, "What a great space." I wish I had a recording of all the people who've come in over the last few years saying "What a great space."

"Thanks, I bought it myself."

"Are you an heir?"

"Not really."

"So you sell a lot of your art?"

"Yeah, kind of. I mean, it's not always sold with as much attention in the press as I'd like, but it gets sold."

"Uh-huh."

"Would you like a cappuccino? If you'll pardon the cliché."

"Sure. Thanks. You know, I expected your loft to be pure white without anything in it."

"No, that's beat, it's 1988."

My loft had a really rich-looking rough wood floor that was at least seventy years old. There were scars and burns and cracks all over the timbers, but they'd been sealed under about ten coats of polyurethane so they were easy to clean. The walls and ceilings in the living room and kitchen/hang-out area were all different colors, magenta, rich yellow, emerald green, and black. They'd been painted by David Wojnarowicz, the proto–East Village artist, when he'd lived there for a couple of months in 1982. That made it kind of a landmark; it should have been in a glass case in the Smithsonian with a sign, "East Village Loft, Early 1980s." But the old brick walls in the studio were covered with pure Benjamin Moore Decorator White, which is what they use in most art galleries. The studio was lit by six tall, narrow windows that reflected in the dark floor. They faced east, and you saw the roofs of abandoned, burned-out Lower East Side tenements with eroded stacks of brick sticking up in various places, like Dresden after the firebombing, or Brady's photographs of the ruins of Richmond. The tenements had glassless windows that opened onto gaping gutted interiors, and there was florid, rococo ornamentation and lion-heads and rosettes in terra cotta around the windows that were cracked and falling off. The buildings were owned by the city and would never be repaired. There were ginkgo trees growing up through the old courtyards At night, some of the windows would be lit with orange light from the squatters' campfires. There were a couple of ugly orange brick high-rise low-income housing projects from the fifties rising beyond the abandoned buildings, and beyond that there was a glimpse of a trapezoidal section of the blue East River. A few turquoise copper-covered domes from old synagogues poked up here and there, and a couple of them that were still operational rang their bells at dawn and dusk and various odd hours having to do with Orthodox Judaism. There were mourning doves and pigeons hanging out in all the nooks and crannies of the old buildings. Huge flocks of carrier pigeons, raised in coops on the rooftops by old Italian families, wheeled by every once in a while in flickering silver clouds, *L'aube exaltée ainsi qu'un peuple de colombes.* Roosters crowed in the mornings. Someone in the neighborhood raised them for sacrifices in Santeria rituals.

I gave her coffee.

"So let me see some art," she said.

"I'll take some of the veils off."

Most of my stuff is usually covered. I went over into the studio section and took some of the gray cloths off the big pieces with as little grandiosity as possible.

She seemed pretty interested. I cleared out and started bustling with the cappuccino machine the way I usually do during studio visits. I realized there was a tray of surgical supplies lying out, but I thought she probably wouldn't notice them.

She was kind of absorbed in one of my early paintings. It was a huge seven-panel piece that was usually stored. It was called *Nights in the Garden of Allah,* and it was based on the style of Kayaffid miniatures. Each panel was already in one of my "signature frames," a wide, round-cornered rectangular frame in gold or silver leaf with dark striations running around through it, a bit like the grooves in a Whistler frame. It relates the paintings to television—which suggests narrativity—and to late modernist architecture, of course, but I also just think that a round-cornered rectangle is one of the least compositionally obtrusive shapes. It's stable and classical like a rectangle, but it doesn't have the problem of sharp corners distracting you from the smooth surface of my paintings. I have a carpenter-whiz friend in Williamsburg who turns these frames out for me on a moment's notice, and he's one of the foundations of my existence.

The seven nights in the story were inspired by miniatures in which the Prince Baram-Gur sleeps with a different bride, in a different pavilion, each night. The first night, he visits the Princess of Egypt in the red pavilion; on the second the Princess of Greece in the white pavilion; on the third the Princess of Turkey in the sandalwood pavilion; on the fourth the Princess of Ethiopia in the blue pavilion; on the fifth the Princess of Sind in the rose pavilion; on the sixth the Princess of Iran in the turquoise pavilion; and on the seventh, the Princess of India in the black pavilion.

"Is all this stuff you?" she called in. "It doesn't look like one person's work."

"My work doesn't fall into an easily definable style. It's more based on certain ideas," I said. It's a stock line.

The other two pieces I'd uncovered were quite different.

There was one directly based on my beauty research. It was four panels, identically framed. There was the closest thing I could come up with to an "ideal" female face, and then the closest thing I could do to an ideal male face. Each was done in my combination Cibachrome/painting technique. Next to each was a framed mirror. There was an obvious invitation to comparison. It was kind of a cruel piece. I was a little upset that I'd uncovered it. I'm a lookist. It's true. That's the Lesbian-Awareness word for what I am.

There was also one other photo piece, a gigantic four-by-eight-foot print of a grid collage I had made out of three thousand and thirty portrait shots from New York prep school yearbooks, different schools, all between '62 and '65, when everybody had the same hair. All the people were white males. There were some variations that kind of clustered through the piece, like the fatter ones were centered toward the lower left-hand corner, and the really handsome ones were in the center, but basically, they all looked exactly the same, even though they were all different people, and you got tired very fast of looking for variations among them. When I made it, I felt it really dealt a blow to the idea of individuality. Supposedly, people who work in snapshot-developing factories have a tendency toward extreme depression, because after looking at thousands and thousands of very similar snapshots, they get the feeling that everyone is a version of someone else and they lose the sense of their own individuality. Maybe I like really gorgeous people because at least there are very few of them.

9

We had coffee and talked about the work. She was pretty smart about art. "Why so much gold leaf?" she asked.

"It's pure," I said. I didn't want to go into how much I loved the stuff. But sometimes I wished I could just cover *everything* with gold or silver foil. Then the whole world would always be bright and shiny, and I wouldn't have to worry about anything. I'd just electroplate the whole world. For a while, during the late nineteenth century they used to electroplate dead people, particularly dead children. Sometimes they'd dress the gold-plated dead babies up and put them in ornate jars filled with clear formaldehyde and put them on display in parlors. And sometimes they'd just have the hands or feet, with rings on them, in really little jars. I had two of the big ones and three of the little hands in my collection, in storage. I had kept them in my apartment for a while, but everyone seemed to think they were just too creepy. It does seem kind of strange now, I guess, but it makes more sense than displaying some wrinkly old mummy, the way a lot of people used to do. It was a drag I couldn't keep them around the house. It was like the tarantula thing. I was just about to get this tarantula from the Crystal Aquarium Pet Store, and then Katrina said she'd never visit me again ever if I had one. I'd started explaining that Dali and Breton and all the Surrealists used to have pet praying mantises because they liked the way they ate their mates and everything, and so I should be able to have my own mascot insect or whatever, but she just wouldn't hear of it. People are so touchy and unreasonable.

"I should cruise," she said. It was getting late. "Hey, what about that Italian *Vogue* thing?" she asked at the last minute as I fished out her coat.

"I guess Timothy's still dickering with them about it, but I mentioned you. I'll keep bugging him about it."

She looked suspicious, but she'd had an interesting day anyway, I guess.

■

The next day I went over to the Royalton, Penny's hotel, to take the bandages off her. As she'd said, she was listed as Polly Crane. Her suite was pretty messy, and she was pretty nervous when I walked in. She was obviously just dying to get them off, so I cut them away with a little pair of B-D clippers—it was something she could actually have done herself—and took her over to a light away from a mirror to see if she looked okay. She grabbed at a compact mirror, but I held on to it for a second before I let her use it. She looked fabulous. I'd really outdone myself. I didn't think any re-dyeing would be necessary. I let go of the mirror and told her she could touch her face, gently.

"How does it feel?" I asked.

"I'm not sure—okay, I guess," she said. She'd looked in the compact and was trying to maneuver past me toward the bathroom mirror. I let her get by and watched her reaction. She didn't give anything away, but I was pretty sure she was amazed. I thought I should leave to give her some time to get acquainted with herself.

"Would you like me to stick around, or would you just like to call me later and come by when you feel like it?"

"You can leave, sure," she said. She was just standing there looking at herself in one of those wall-size mirrors they have there.

"It'll be okay outdoors," I said, "but you shouldn't go out in direct sunlight for a while." She'd been cooped up in that room for quite a while, but I guess she was used to living in a location trailer. I was going to remind her to wear sunglasses and a hat when she went out, even at night, until she checked out, but then I decided she knew enough to do that and I just left. It was an emotional moment for her.

■

Later, I called up that playwright, Alexia, to tell her I liked her showcase, and she said she'd heard I'd had Jaishree over.

"Yeah, she's really interesting," I said.

"Do you like her?"

"Well, she was really nice to me, you know, and then sometimes I got the feeling she was putting me down, and I don't know why. I mean, I've always felt I was a pretty innocuous person."

"Jaishree has a real judgmental streak. You shouldn't take it personally."

"Okay, but why does she have a streak like that at all?"

"No comment. She's brilliant, though. The only time I ever really doubted Jaishree's intelligence was when she said she liked that Tama Janowitz book."

"Wow, that's pretty bad."

"She'd be mortified if we confronted her with it now, though."

"She must have just been new in New York."

"She was."

My mother caught me on call waiting, and I told Alexia I had to take it. Mom is what is known as a strong woman. She calls about once a week. She started in on the disease issue.

"Are you being careful about AIDS? You know about New York."

"I'm so careful, I'm even worried about getting it from food," I said. "There aren't any little anti-AIDS purification tablets you can carry around and drop into your food, are there?"

"No. Just avoid going out on dates."

"I don't want to have to avoid going out on dates."

"Suppose you were in the army."

"Suppose I were paraplegic."

"Suppose you were."

"Well, that's the main reason for not being paraplegic—being able to go out on dates."

"Well, listen, girls might have AIDS."

"I know. I hate them for that."

It went on like this for a little while, but I managed to placate her. She's actually a pretty big influence on me.

■

I didn't speak to Jaishree that day. Then the next day, Thursday, I called her and asked her if she felt like seeing the Peter Halley show at the Whitney in the afternoon.

"I'm free from four o'clock to five," she said.

I was really beginning to like Jaishree. I don't know about whether I was falling in love with her. The L-word's a major word. But she was really something. She had an absolutely beautiful alto voice over the phone, with a lot of range and depth. The songs she'd done during her performance were the best versions of those songs I'd ever heard.

She had beautiful hands. They were long and dark and expressive, with hardly any lines on them. The palms were substantially lighter than the backs. She was thin and slim-hipped for an Indian, but still extremely curvy and round-limbed. It was a perfect figure, but with something exotic about it. She was about five feet eight inches tall, and there was a lightness and delicacy in the way she moved. Often I'm attracted to people on the basis of how they move, despite my concern about how they look. If they move in a kind of graceful and relaxed way, it's especially sexy. Jaishree had all this grace, but she also had a kind of vitality that Western women never have. Western women are repressed wet blankets compared to Indians and Middle Easterners. Spanish women have a certain amount of life in them. But it s still not up to the Indian level. Jaishree had a smoldering intensity about her that was purely authentic Indian.

And she had brains, and talent, and tremendous ambition. And despite her sweet aspects and her sense of humor—she really camped up her femininity—she had ruthlessness, too. An essential for a career in entertainment. And she had extreme self-respect. She had a core of steel.

And she was beautiful. Not devastating, maybe, but really distinctive-looking and sexy. Maybe not so much like an Indian Julia Roberts, but more like Rekha, the Indian film star.

We met at the Whitney, original uptown version. For a while, the Whitney was opening branches all over, the Whitney Downtown, the Whitney Midtown, the Whitney Stamford Connecticut, the Whitney Dallas, they even wanted to do a Whitney Houston, but that name was copyrighted already. After the Halley show—which was amazing, all those carcinogenic Day-Glo colors—we went into a group show called "The Desire of the Institution." It had some Mapplethorpe photos in it around in the back, two of Ken Moody and one of Brooke Shields, and we sat down in front of them on the "comfy couch" they have back there. It's the only inviting thing in the building.

"Mapplethorpe was pretty into perfection, wasn't he?" I said. It sounded stupid.

"That depends on what you think is perfection," Jaishree said.

"I don't know, sometimes I think everyone has pretty much the same idea of perfection. People are all pretty much the same."

"Yes. They want to be, anyway. I still want to look like Cinderella."

That was a weird thing for her to say. Was she kidding?

"Do you really want to look like Cinderella?"

"Well, no. I don't want to be white."

"Maybe the dark Cinderella? Like the Black Madonna? You know, La Vierge Sous-Terre?"

"Sure."

I was just kidding, of course.

10

She canceled her five-o'clock, and we had a long dinner and went around looking for desserts, and finally she came over and we slept together. It happened so quickly, I thought she must be a pretty promiscuous person. Later that turned out not to be the case. I checked it out.

If only, if only, if only I had had any idea how things would turn out . . . and even though the nightmare part of my life didn't really begin for a while, I wonder whether it germinated right then, whether there were seeds in my mind that night that would eventually grow into hideous mutant disgusto-critters with googly eyes and razor teeth.

At the time, though, I was thrilled with how pure I felt with her. There weren't any weird psychological issues involved in my feelings for her, as there had been with most of my other romantic interests lately. It was a little early to start talking about feelings, but that was what was happening: I was already starting to fall for her. Her thoughts about me, however, were more of a mystery.

She was really something in bed. More or less insatiable, with an amazing body. I was very into the whole sex thing with her. She said, "Multiple orgasms—didn't that used to be a thing in the seventies?"

It turned out she had very beautiful, expensive French under-wear, lacy black front-clasping bras with pearls in the center, and skimpy briefs. Later I realized she had what amounted to an underwear fixation. She'd be out of money and spend everything she had left on underwear. It was one of my favorite things about her.

She left really early the next morning. Before I knew what was happening, she was kissing me good-bye, and I just had to lock the door after her and lie down again. It was a little abrupt but kind of nice, too—maybe she was letting me know that she had a life of her own and wasn't going to waste my time. Or hers.

■

I got up anyway and got coffee into my system because at eleven that morning—Friday—I had to do another interview to prepare for a procedure. It was on that lady Laureen McNiel—a rich society matron, to pigeonhole her in her proper clichéd slot—and her face looked as if it had really taken a beating even though she had already had two lifts. But she was only sixty-one years old, and her body, from what I could tell, was quite good. It's not fair that faces age faster. She showed me some pictures of her when she was young, and it was quite touching. She'd been a beauty queen. But just psychologically speaking, should she really look the way she did when she was younger, or should she look somewhat different? Maybe the latter, I thought. Because otherwise there'd be all sorts of baggage about time and illusion and reality going along with the change, whereas if she looked completely different, she'd just zip off to Bermuda and have a good time. I guess she had had enough of her husband and didn't want much to do with his friends. But had she thought about how she'd relate to *her* friends? I wasn't sure how to phrase the question.

"Would you like people to be able to recognize you, or would you like to try something more radical?" I finally asked. Never ask a yes-or-no question—always give them a choice.

"Won't they just think I look a lot younger?" she asked.

"Wellll . . ." I said, "in the early days of plastic surgery, they really couldn't make people look much different or very much younger, you know. They tried concealing identities that way, and it usually didn't work. But we're using very advanced techniques here, and within reason we can design any facial type." I wouldn't have said something like that a few months before, but lately I was feeling creative.

"Uh, I'll have to think about it," she said. "But basically I guess I just want to look the way I used to."

"Well, perhaps you could leave the photographs for us to study, and we can meet one more time to discuss it and look at the studies before the procedure." I learned to talk that way when I worked at the Jerry Davidian Gallery.

"Well, I guess that would be fine . . ." she trailed off. I was a little depressed after I let her out. When I got back upstairs, the phone was ringing and it was David with good news. He'd been relayed a couple of leads from my two other "shadow sources"—one's a dermatologist and the other's a photographer and occasional modeling agent—on girls who might be willing to have me change their faces for them. I wanted to see whether I could design some supermodels. It would be a great deal for them—they'd be getting for free what movie stars pay hundreds of thousands of dollars for, and they wouldn't have to owe me anything until they started really raking in the bucks. I sat around trying to think of what the contracts should say, wondering whether I should take some lawyer friend like Jay into my confidence. It's difficult trying to figure everything out yourself.

■

Jaishree called, but I had to say I'd call her later because Mark had been bugging me to come up and visit him in his lab and check out some new computer-imaging system he'd gotten hold of. It was way, way upstate at 151st Street. It was only two o'clock, the farthest time away from New York's five-hour rush hour, when I left, but it was still crowded all over. It's always an emotional experience for me to take the subway. It's like sitting through *The Sorrow and the Pity.* I just can't stand the stench and the noise and the wretched refuse of our teeming shores, but lately I'd been blowing a lot of money on cabs and feeling really bad about myself, so to be virtuous I took the train. But it was a bad move. Getting on the F in my neighborhood is kind of scary, and then I had to change at West Fourth, and there were all sorts of those people in clown suits coming through asking for money, and then getting off at 155th is *really* scary, even in the middle of the day. and by the time I got into the worn old lobby—at least it was an old building—I was a quivering wreck.

God, I hate the underclass. I'm sorry to say it, but it's true. They're just so lumpy and bad-looking. Once in a while you find a hidden treasure among them, but not often. There was this guy next to me on the subway whose face was just a patchwork quilt of cut-rate post-accident surgery. He had a really strange misshapen ear and discolorations over half his face, and his nose had been really squashed down and then sewed back onto his cheeks. He had no lips at all—I spent some time puzzling out the slapdash re-creation of his mouth parts—and he was ninety-two percent bald with scraggly tufts. I wanted to stare, but I felt really bad about it, and I think he knew I was looking at him. I'm just Miss Lonelyhearts. I felt like going up to him and saying "I can make you look like Jason Priestley, here's my card," but he didn't look like he could afford it.

On the other hand, there had been a Vietnamese family on the subway with a beautiful twelve- or thirteen-year-old daughter. She had a bright green ski parka and black tights that had HOW ARE YOU? written on them in Day-Glo colors. She had such a perfect face, she was amazingly sexy, although I don't generally consider myself a nympholept. Her little brother had a perfect face, too, and I caught myself imagining kissing it. I have to admit, some little boys are extremely sexy.

11

It had been strange living with Mark in college when I was an art major and he was pre-med. I'd stagger home at three in the morning, sometimes with a girl or something, and he'd be wading through pages full of chemical tables. And Karl Vanders, who lived in a different residential college, was Mark's other nemesis at that time because everything was so easy for Karl. He'd gotten the best graces any pre-med at Yale had ever gotten, as far as anyone could remember. Karl was a prepped-out Horace Mann kid from the East Nineties who'd cruised through Yale in three years and Columbia med school in four and was practically a Ph.D. in microbiology already. But Karl also had kept in touch with some of his artsier friends like me and Mark, and now we were all working together. They had their own lab, three rooms, as some part of their research deal with Columbia. The outer room was for computers and files and had shiny white walls with charts and graphs taped all over them.

Karl was in the lab, too. He was a tall blond collegiate-looking guy in a sweater and big thick glasses, more of a doctory nerd type than Mark, but actually pretty good-looking. Kind of a James Spader knock-off. He wore a white lab coat. "I hear you did the procedure on a major star the other day," he said.

"Yeah, I guess, pretty major," I said, not knowing whether he knew it was Penny Penn. I was a little disturbed that Mark had told Karl anything.

"Is it true she's an MD?" Mark asked.

"What's that?" I asked.

"You know, a muff diver."

"Oh, sure, I suppose so."

"Listen, Jamie," Mark said, "Karl and I get every batch together for each procedure, so I think we should tell him more about what we're doing with it, because it's only fair."

"Well, that's fine," I lied, "but I guess I thought Karl had said he didn't want to be associated with it." Karl was standing at the other end of the room, but he definitely heard that. I wondered if it had come out all right. Karl had a twenty-percent share of the profits from any procedure I did—that had been our arrangement from the very beginning, with Mark getting forty percent—but Karl was really paranoid, he made me give him cash and just hid it in gold or something. He never laundered it or bought anything, and he never came by the studio.

"No, no way, thanks," Karl said. "It's really interesting what you're doing and all, and the money's great, but I only want to deal with the technical end. I like to see how it works out, but I don't want to have anything to do with your business. It's just too risky for my career." He looked at Mark. "I'm just not the type for living dangerously."

"I hope we're not living that dangerously," Mark said.

"I don't think we are," I said.

Mark got some doughnuts out of a refrigerator. "Karl's the original disinterested researcher," he said. "He's not into lifestyle."

"What do you mean?" Karl asked.

"Well, Jamie's got a loft the size of the Plaza ballroom and movie stars and beautiful women running in and out every day and pictures of himself in *Vanity Fair,* and we're living in graduate student housing at Columbia and eating crummy doughnuts. I swear, Karl's apartment is about as big as that centrifuge."

"Look, it just goes with the territory. It's not as glamorous as it sounds," I said. I didn't like the way the conversation was going.

"I know that, but Karl doesn't know that. He's totally not keyed into the art scene. It all seems very grand and strange to him."

Had Karl and Mark had a fight before I showed up? Why was Mark talking like this? Karl looked a little pained.

"It's fine," Karl said. "I don't think I have the artistic poetical gift necessary to take part in your cosmetic work."

"You certainly don't," Mark said. "You're just a numbers nerd, right?"

"Look," I said, trying to change the subject, "if you guys think you could actually get the stuff approved by the FDA, maybe you should start the process. I mean, it could do a lot of good, and it's worth the effort—it doesn't have to be just us who get to use it. We'll keep making money even if other people learn to do it."

"No," Karl said. "It's just too far out, they'd never go for it. You know, those FDA people are like the John Birch Society, they just hate innovations. Forest or B-D or Pfizer could get something like this through the system eventually, but not a couple of kids. Maybe after I'm a really respected doctor, I'll start applying for a patent, but for the time being . . ." He trailed off.

"How do you know someone else isn't working on the idea?"

"Well, I haven't heard of it, and if they are they're having the same problems, no matter what country they're in. And maybe we should at least apply for a patent soon." I noticed he said "we" this time, when he'd said "I" before. "But it wouldn't make sense until I get out of internship and get my own really serious research lab."

"Well, I guess you're right," I said. "I'm not sure it's the kind of thing that could ever really go public, anyway."

"Because it's so weird," Mark said.

"It's just too disturbing for people. I mean, people can deal with knowing that you've had a lift, or whatever, but if they find out that your whole face isn't really alive at all, it's just plastic, they're liable to get grossed out. I get grossed out by it myself sometimes." They looked at me. "I mean, when I see the people I've done, sometimes it just flashes into my head that they aren't really alive, and I get all weirded out by it."

"I don't know," Mark said. "Eventually, people accept anything."

"Maybe," I said.

"Listen," Mark said, punching away at one of the keyboards, "I have to show you this software." He put a three-and-a-half into the disk drive. I sat down at this kind of counter they have with microscopes and pushed aside a bunch of covered petri dishes full of gross stuff. "You can do anything with this, as long as you have a scanner," Mark said. "You can scan and digitalize your photograph and then play around with the proportions until you're satisfied, and then you can store, and it'll type out a list of the quantitative changes. And you can combine different photographs. Apparently some doctors out in California even used this software to combine different models' faces into, like, an ideal beauty."

"I know," I said. "I just saw the article in *Vogue.*"

"What article?"

I pulled the magazine out of my bag. Karl Vanders seemed kind of interested, but he was trying not to show it. We all sort of bent over it. The first thing you noticed was this black-and-white photograph of a woman that was actually a digitalized composite of four models.

"I don't know—if that's the ideal face, she's awfully young-looking," Karl said.

"Yeah, she looks just like Karen Alexander, too," Mark said.

"Well, Karen Alexander was the first one they used. Look."

Karl was already looking at the other page, the one with the four models on it. They'd mixed together full-face shots of Karen Alexander—the very young-looking, light-skinned black model—Laura Lindberg, Cordula, and Karen Young. You could tell what the problem was right away: Laura Lindberg and Karen Young looked exactly like each other, and quite a bit like Karen Alexander, so the two of them combined couldn't override the basic Karen-Alexander-ness of the composite. Cordula looked a little different, of course, more waspy, but one-fourth her didn't do much, and she looked terrible in the shot they'd used anyway. I couldn't imagine why they'd put her in at all. They should have tried mixing in Paulina and Iman, or something, but I guess they were limited to Ford models. What's also strange is that Karen Alexander was always one of my all-time favorite models, but after looking at this article, I'd kind of lost interest in her.

The article was called "Future Beauty" by Shirley Lord. It started off talking about a program like the one Mark had stolen and then it started quoting Derrick Antell, who was a plastic surgeon Mark knew at Columbia. " 'Computers can't predict soft-tissue changes,' " he said. " 'Bone changes, yes, soft tissue, no. If I move the chin forward one centimeter, we know, within reason, you will get one centimeter difference. When it comes to the nose, if someone makes an adjustment on the computer to show a patient how her "new nose" is going to look, it can't and doesn't account for how the skin is going to drape in that area. The end result is a disappointment.' "

"All this stuff they're actually doing is incredibly outdated," Mark said. "But the program's terrific. It'll really help you with the design end."

"Don't worry—I'm going to try out the program," I said. "But look, even this Smith guy uses hand drawing sometimes."

"That's because they're using outdated procedures," Mark said. He read out loud:

" ' "The blueprints of humans produced by electronic surgical imaging don't realistically portray what changes are and are not possible," says Smith. "Whereas when I do overlays with drawing paper on a patient's photograph, using this armory of ideal micromeasurements as a guide, I am able to determine with a better degree of possibility if the patient is deficient in the malar [cheekbone] area—or has too much bulk in the jaw." ' "

"Or looks like a baboon with acromegaly," Karl interjected.

" ' "Perhaps," ' " Mark went on, " ' "the slant of the eyebrows is off, or the size of the nose. It's often such a subtle little thing." '

" 'To the suggestion that their ongoing pursuit of perfection for their patients is creating unrealistic expectations, Antell and Smith have only contempt: "On the contrary," says Smith, "now more and more women of every age want to improve their appearance by making what may be only the slightest change, and more and more plastic surgeons are working with them to discover what can be done to change them from average to exceptional. You could say it's cosmetic surgery coming of age." ' "

He skimmed the rest:

" 'Although undoubtedly there are many sophisticated new tools and techniques available that produce fast visual improvements, it is neurotic to become obsessive about one's appearance, just as it is a sign of neurosis to neglect it. There is a great deal we can do, but too much cosmetic surgery can look terrible. . . . silicone injections . . . microdroplets at very well-spaced intervals of time . . . tattooing . . . for reshaping lips, eyebrows, or areolae surrounding the nipples . . . a special sterilized "gun" is used that can dispatch a mixture of inorganic pigments to achieve an exact skin-tone match (a similar gun is used on the West Coast at beauty clinics like About Faces, Sausalito, California) . . . tattoos real gold into the skin, "because it can stimulate the manufacture of natural pigment." . . . invest hundreds of thousands of dollars in computers . . . Estée Lauder's Personal Profile Printout and Skin Analyzer Machine . . . Retin-A has become the first anti-aging prescription drug . . . chemically treated fabrics with an SPF of 60; a personal sun vane . . . vending machines at the beach that spray you with the right SPF at the touch of a button, towelettes soaked in sunscreen . . . at least one hundred new skin-care lotions are scheduled for introduction next year alone—' "

"God, this is all so incredibly primitive," Karl said. "And it's not neurotic to worry about one's appearance if one is the Elephant Man."

"Chill out, Karl," Mark said. "I thought you weren't interested in this stuff."

"Sorry," Karl said. "I think I'll go play with my slugs." He walked out. I was about to ask Mark whether they'd had a fight but then decided Karl might hear.

"We *have* to get more into computer imaging at least, just as a first step," Mark repeated. "It's silly to keep using these old techniques like drawing and casting in wax and everything. It should all be digitalized. Everything's digitalized now—it's just silly to hang on to the old stuff."

"I guess so," I said.

"You know, in fifty years everyone's just going to be in his or her little sensory deprivation tank, linked up to the cyberspace Virtual Reality system. The idea of actually *making* anything is totally beat. That's not where technology is interesting right now. It's all software. Total digitalization. We're on the edge of the wedge."

He was right, really. A lot of the time I felt I was in the middle of a historical and cultural clash as big as Kalahari bushmen meeting astronauts. I knew all these artistic techniques, or hardly even techniques—metaphors, almost—and they'd been handed down for centuries, and now all this new technology was doing in a second what it would have taken years of labor to do before, synthesizing and rotat-

ing things in three dimensions, colorizing, moving you through invented landscapes, amazing stuff. And it was even more complicated
because there was still something about each of the old techniques
that the machine couldn't capture, some delicacy of line in a chalk
drawing that just wouldn't translate into digital bites on television, or
something about the existence of a real object that seemed like a real
experience when you interacted with it, whereas with the colder
images flashed on a screen, you always felt like just a spectator somehow, you didn't really feel in the presence of something.

But presence can be a strange thing, too—like at rock concerts,
for instance. All these people get really excited to be near some rock
star they've seen on TV. But it's no more real than it is on television,
it's all planned out beforehand and the musicians know exactly how
the audience is going to react. It's just a congregational experience for
the kids—it's the closest thing to a religious experience they have.

Paintings and sculpture can be like that, too, if they're not convincing. They're not really for enjoyment—they're just for people to
pretend to understand and be in the presence of and feel superior to
other people because of it. They aren't really fun, like movies can be.
But I want my procedure to bridge that gap, between movies and
painting, and between art and science. I think of myself as a contemporary Leonardo da Vinci: Beauty and Medicine. He'd be really into
what I do, I'm sure of it. All he could do in the way of serious surgery
was dissect.

I guess I feel like my procedure is just scientific enough in its
materials, but not so scientific as to be cold and dead. I think my faces
need a trace of the hand in them, they need that human care to go
into them or else they really would be robot-masks. The trace of my
hand takes the place of life for these faces. My work is a unification of
art and technology. It's a unification of painting and sculpture. It's a
unification of the living and the dead. It's both figurative and abstract,
completely imitative and entirely original.

And maybe I just wanted to use the old techniques I knew so
well a few more times. I wanted to do one really great project where
all that knowledge would come out. Maybe it's just a really deep
thing I have against digitalization, against the infinite Cartesian grid. If
everything's just reduced to a binary code, nothing means anything

anymore. There's no ambiguity left; things are either on or off. Of course, Baudrillard says that's already happened.

I took the software, though. I said I wanted to give David a call and went in the back room, where they have big humming tanks full of snails or salamanders or something. David was still at home, and I gave him some instructions. He grumbled a lot. I went back in, and Mark and Karl were kidding around with some petri dish full of pink crud.

"Take a look at this stuff," Mark said. "It's for bone marrow injections. You know how when you scrape yourself on something, if your bone gets scraped, it's a real problem and you need all sorts of transplants . . ."

The boy genius thing was beginning to thrash my buzz. "Listen, I should get going," I said.

■

I got back home at eight. I wanted to stay in and paint all night, but then it turned out I'd said I'd go to a premiere for some arty film and a party afterward. I decided not to invite Jaishree because, you know, why smother her with affection at the beginning? But I called the florist and ordered five African purple lilies to get to her the next morning.

At four that day Jaishree called and thanked me for the flowers. She really seemed thrilled. We made a date to meet later. I had to go over to Calvin's house to pick up some ultra-top-secret, for-your-eyes-only paperwork.

It was getting afternoony-looking, and I walked to the West Village. People seemed happy to be in New York and alive.

I'd shown the shot of the incensario to my pre-Columbian dealer friend, Spenser "I've Never Bounced a Piece in My Life" Beckman, and he'd said it was worth quite a bit.

"I think we should go for that piece, plus fifty thousand for my overhead," I said as soon as I sat down in Calvin's overtasteful apartment.

"Great," he said. "If it looks good go down and check it out. You love Mexico anyway."

"Yeah, I guess. . . ."

"Coax some luscious beauty into going with you."

"Hmm," I said. I started playing with a pair of handcuffs that was lying on the couch. Calvin always has great S&M toys.

"I'll see what Laureen has to say," he said.

Suddenly I realized something was wrong.

Uh-oh, I thought.

"Calvin," I said, "could you give me the key to these handcuffs? It looks like I closed one around one of my wrists. By mistake."

"Are you sure it was by mistake?" he called out from the kitchen.

"No, I have a subconscious desire to be beaten and gang-banged at the Spike tonight," I said.

He lumbered back in with a couple of drinks, giggling. "Good, I'll arrange it," he said.

"Look, just hand me the keys to these cuffs, okay?"

"I'm afraid that's impossible."

"Okay, enough bullshit," I said.

"No bullshit. The whole idea behind having cuffs is a kind of domination and control thing. I threw away the keys a few nights ago in order to make the threat of the cuffs more menacing."

"I don't believe you."

"Don't." He laughed and handed me my drink. Natural Cherry Soda with a splash of Absolut.

"Listen, I don't like to sound panicky, but just give me the keys, all right?"

"I wish I could, old boy. At least you didn't lock the other end around a chair or anything. We're just going to have to go down to the Stud Shoppe on Christopher Street and see whether any keys they have fit these cuffs."

Great, I thought. I could see the whole thing: Some clony-looking old bald guy with a moustache and a motorcycle jacket getting out key after key, laughing at me: "Hot night last night, huh?"

"I'm not looking forward to this," I said. I couldn't believe it. Here I was with Jeffrey Dahmer and I'd shackled myself.

"Fromage," he said, meaning *dommage.* Then he began laughing hysterically and tossed me the key.

■

I met Jaishree at Caffe Vivaldi on Jones Street. She already had a big pot of tea going.

"Hey," I said.

"Hey."

I kissed her, trying to act smooth. It's especially strange meeting somebody the first time after you've slept with them. I always try to think of Cary Grant in these situations. I repeat to myself, I'm Cary Grant, I'm Cary Grant, I'm Cary Grant.

"What are you up to?" I asked.

"I just had a callback for a Pizza Hut commercial."

"Oh."

"It was really demeaning, we had to eat cold pizza and pretend that we'd just gotten here from India and we'd never had pizza before and really loved it."

"You really work hard, don't you—"

"The only parts around for Asian actresses are prostitutes like in *Miss Saigon* or exotica on chain-food commercials."

"That's a harsh toke," I said.

"Excuse me? *Harsh toke?* Are you from southern California or something?"

"No, I guess I'd just like to be."

"Great ambition." She was teasing me but she was still obviously in a good mood. I decided to go for broke.

"So guess what, I have to go to Mexico," I said.

"When?"

"Kind of soon. Want to come along?" She didn't say anything. "I'd be thrilled. I mean I realize I hardly know you and everything but you said you were into it—"

"Yeah. Well, it's a thought."

"It'll be megally fun. I just have to pick up one thing in Merida and then we could look at some old cities. . . ."

"What're you picking up, cocaine?"

"Could I get you something?" the waitperson asked. I hadn't seen him there.

"Could I have a hot chocolate and a decaf cappuccino and an Orangina?" I asked. "And a big Pellegrino." He looked at me a little funnily before he went away. It seems like most people drink only one beverage at a time.

"When do you need to go?" she asked.

"Anytime. We could adapt to your schedule."

"Maybe I could get away for four days next week. It sounds expensive, though."

I didn't bat an eye. Joe Cool. "It'll be nothing," I said, "I have a great travel agent. He's psychic, he's probably already got the tickets."

"I'll agonize over it for a day or two."

"Groovy." I tried the hot chocolate. "Yum,' I said. "Breakfast of Aztecs."

12

Jaishree and I were watching the sun go down from the top of Nohoch Mul, at Cobá, the highest pyramid in the Yucatán. I figured that by now the caretakers at the entrance of the Zona Archaeologica had probably all gone back to their huts and wouldn't spot us even if we were out in the open. Jaishree sat on the top step at my left. I just stood on the limestone slab at the apex of the steep stairway, a stairway made more for rolling sacrifices down than for climbing up, feeling the power of the position. In 600 A.D. this had been one of the greatest cities in the world. Swallows and bats flickered above and below us. The twin lakes in the distance looked like gold leaf. A kilometer and a half away, the Cobá group, with the only other excavated pyramid at the site, rose out of the green-and-yellow moss of jungle. There were at least fourteen other tall, tree-covered hills clustered around that gave this section of flat Yucatán Peninsula a mountainous appearance; but they were all originally artificial. Once they were hard-edged and brilliantly painted. I'd spent a lot of time studying what little work had been done on the city and didn't have much trouble imagining what it must have been like: in my mental picture the jungle had vanished, and outside of the vast multicolored rectangle that was the center of the city there were tilled fields, colored by different crops, more like farms in the North American heartland than what we think of as Mexican. Within the city there were only a few trees—huge, ancient,

sacred trees, strangely manicured. Every surface of the vast multilayered complex was stuccoed and smoothed and clean. The floors
of the plazas were smooth and color-coded to the temples, with
walking routes marked out for different ceremonial processions. The
corners of the structures were razor-sharp. The temples were striated
with red and turquoise and white and blue and black, and they shone
in the light of the setting sun like structures of geometricized flames,
internally lit, the huge roof combs over the crowning temples seem-
ing to defy gravity, carrying immense quantities of hieroglyphic information high above the plains, like the headdresses of the kings, visu-
ally weighty and rich but physically insubstantial and fragile.

*The priest took a handsome and heavily drugged fifteen-year-old
captive gently by the hair and made two incisions on either side of his
head, just below the ears. The sound of the screaming muffled behind
the wad of cotton became louder and choppier. Blood spurted out of
small arteries in the twin pressure points. The priest grabbed the
captive's lower jaw and, without much effort since the ligaments had
been cut, twisted it off the head. The fatty skin of the cheeks ripped
across easily. The priest threw the jaw off the platform into the crowd,
leaving an arcing trail of blood droplets in the air. A tall man in the
crowd caught it expertly and waved it around as a souvenir while
other young men playfully tried to grab it. The tongue attached to the
jaw flapped and quivered automatically, evoking a great deal of
laughter. Meanwhile the cotton wad had fallen out of the captive's
mouth, and the screams, inchoate vowel sounds ranging from high
shrieks to low gutturals, emanated furiously from the bloody opening.
The guards had released the prisoner's ankle bonds, leaving his
hands tied together, and they drew back from him to the far ends of
the platform to observe the dance. Unlike captives from Tikal, who
had been trained to endure torture to death without a whimper or
movement, this captive, from a rather backward coastal town,
quivered and shook and danced about like a skinned frog, finally
falling over and writhing about on the stage floor, occasionally spurt-
ing blood into the air like a fountain, and kept thrashing for several
minutes until the loss of blood finally began to weaken him. Eventually, he lay in one spot, curled in a fetal position, twitching spasmodi-
cally. The twitches became fewer and farther between and the crowd
began to get restless again. The bacab, or priest, nodded to the atten-*

dants. Since this captive was dedicated to Kan-Xul, the corn god, and since corn doesn't grow without being peeled first, the prisoner's final torture was being skinned alive. Two attendants held the boy while the priest sliced him carefully down the back. Then the skin was carefully peeled off, the pain reviving the captive. Finally the red skinless corpse was rolled down the steps, and the skin was carefully washed in clear water. The rip in the jaw was repaired. Inside the temple chamber the naked priest was helped into the skin: it was adjusted so the eyeholes fitted over his own eyes and the lips surrounded his own mouth, and he was loosely sewn into it. Finally he emerged to the roar of the crowd and began the last dance to Kan-Xul. He was an old man, but the new skin made him look very young.

The sun was down and Jaishree and I decided we'd better head back, or we might not find our way out of the Zona Archaeologica, which was large and mainly unmarked. We didn't have a flashlight, and it would be hours before the moon came up. And there were these huge pigs grubbing around in the forest, and Jaishree said she'd always been a little apprehensive about pigs. We walked down the steep steps sideways—the best method for pyramids—and got onto the path that followed the old *sacbe,* the ceremonial causeway, back to the Las Pinturas group and Cenoch Mul. The trees on either side looked pale and wan. Darkness was rising out of the scrub. We didn't say anything to each other, not wanting to break the mood. I half expected to meet a ceremonial procession of Maya ghosts, with the cacique in a palanquin carried by four slaves, leading a row of bound captives marching in step with the flutes and clay drums.

I wondered what would have happened if the Mesoamericans had been left alone. If for some reason the Spanish had never invaded, or if the Aztecs had held them off militarily and they had never come back, what would Mexico be like today? Would they have begun using wheels? When would they have begun constructing machines, and what would the machines have been used for? Would they have eventually created a technological culture, with cars and photography and printing and television? And would all of these things have remained in the service of despotic human-sacrifice religions, the warrior ethic, and the amorality of the trickster gods? Would the priesthoods have become rapacious religious empires and warred with one another over artificially produced miracles and the distribution of victims? And, eventually, what if they had come into contact with European culture at a much later date, and fought off the Spanish, and built empires across the sea, and absorbed and influenced European ideas, and been a force in the bloody twentieth century? Would they have allied with the Axis? They probably would have loved Hitler. He had the same expansionist drive and disregard of human life. Would they have invaded North America? Would human flesh have been packaged and sold in supermarkets? Would the lords of Tenochtitlán, acting on the authority of Huitzillapochtli, have nuked the entire rest of the world and probably themselves the instant they got hold of an atomic weapon? Or would they have been isolationist in the face of alien civilizations that had nothing to do with their beliefs? Would there be a descendant of Moctezuma in a seat at the United Nations, signing treaties in a quetzal-feather cape?

It was getting seriously dark. The humid air was cooling and releasing dew. It was filled with jungley scents from weird spores and animals and distant campfires. The birds were making the tremendous noise they make in the tropics, baroque cries and whispers. We came around a bend and there was a big group of big pigs up ahead of us. "Coming around the bend in our red convertible, a pig was seen," I thought. But we didn't have a convertible. There were three female pigs, and one big, big hairy black male pig. I wondered whether they'd been detusked and whether they were still dangerous anyway. We picked some large sticks out of the scrub, trying to be unobtrusive about it.

"Just act natural," Jaishree said. "They can sense fear."

We strolled up to them. Speak naturally and carry a big tree, I thought. We tried to look nonchalant in a way a pig could understand. Black Male Pig grunted at us suspiciously and let us go by. He apparently felt he was supposed to have the run of the place at night.

"That was a big pig," Jaishree said.

"Yep. Big pig."

"Real big."

"Yup."

"The Maya didn't have pigs," Jaishree said.

"They hardly had any domestic animals at all," I said. "They were so different. Even though they invented cocaine and chocolate and coffee and rubber and tobacco and corn and whiskey." (Pause to throw sticks away.) "But we'll never know quite what the Maya were thinking," I said. "We'll never have the same outlook. They're unreachable. Things didn't look the same to them as they do to us. They didn't have our ideas of good and evil. Maybe they didn't have an idea of good and evil at all, only happy fortune and misfortune."

"Gosh, gee whiz, you're blowing my mind," Jaishree said.

We finally got past the Cobá group and hopped the fence at the entrance to the ruins—nobody even looked at us, the caretakers were all sitting around little fires outside their thatched huts a few hundred yards away—and we walked down the dirt road to this thatched-hut restaurant, El Boccadito, to get food. We'd had enough hotel food. There were zillions of stars. A huge bullfrog glopped along in front of us toward the rushes at the edge of the lake.

I explained to Jaishree about the pre-Columbian universe. I love lecturing. The world stretched around us, the turquoise bowl of the land and the blue bowl of the sky, with the nine layers of Xibalbá, the underworld, underneath and the thirteen heavens over us. Venus was up in the West, the most important planet for the Maya, a sign for war. By Venus and the Big Dipper, which pointed to the hidden North Star, we could orient ourselves to the four colors of the quarters of the world. The North was white, the East was red, the South was yellow, and the West was black. North of the civilized world of Mesoamerica was an ever-widening expanse of flat desert, populated by tiny bands of barbarian nomads. The Sun avoided the North. The North lands were a complete blank—a flat, white void. It was Mictlanteculti, the land of the bones of the dead. The East, where the sun was born every day, was the land of life, and birth, and blood. The South, to which the sun was drawn, was a hot, feverish, and golden place. The West, where the sun died every day, was the dark entrance to Xibalbá, the underworld, ruled by God L and the other skeletal death-gods, the Nine Lords of the Night.

We sat outside in the tiny restaurant getting served *tipico* food, lime soup, guacamole, manchamanteles and enchiladas, by a little boy in a bow tie. It was strange being with her where it seemed a million miles away. There'd always been something a little strained about our interaction, but down here we'd just moved naturally into sync with each other. We talked more like old friends.

"Did you feel there were any ghosts on the pyramid?" Jaishree asked.

"Did you?"

"I don't know. It doesn't seem like the kings could just leave the city they built alone."

"I think you'd have to take a lot of drugs and sit up all night in that chamber at the top of the pyramid, if you really wanted to contact them," I said.

"Maybe we should go back in and try it."

"And deal with those pigs? Anyway, we don't have the right drugs right now. Let's save it for our next trip."

"I felt like we were just passing through," she said.

"Yeah. The kings were sleeping down in the royal tombs, waiting."

"Waiting for what?"

"The end of the world."

Across the dirt street, about three hundred feet away, there was a thatched-hut church with a bunch of Maya saying the Rosario. Jaishree had had a Catholic education in India, and I was never sure whether she was really a Catholic or not. She wasn't sure either, I guess. She walked over there after dinner and walked in, into this bunch of peasants. I didn't want to go in because I was weirded out and I had this leather bag that cost more than these people made in a year, so I sat on the dirt outside with these little kids who were messing around and chattering in Yucatec—they looked at me pretty strangely and then decided I was harmless—and watched the service. A woman in one of those spotless white *huipils,* a blouse/dress with beautiful embroidery around the throat, was leading the chanting. There were big wood crosses stashed up in the rafters of the hut, and there were lacy decorations hanging from the beams. They weren't really lace, they were just folded paper with patterns cut out with scissors.

Jaishree seemed to be making friends with the teenage girls. After what seemed like hundreds of antiphonal chants, the service ended and they closed the place up. We gave them a fifty-thousand-peso donation, which is hardly anything, but at first they said it was way over the limit for donations. Finally they took it and said they'd say all kinds of Hail Marys and masses for us. We walked back to the hotel surrounded by Indians. What do they think, living in thatched huts in the shadow of the ruins of one of the greatest cities in the world, a city their ancestors had built out of nothing?

■

It's hard not to fall in love with someone in a Mexican hotel. It's just kind of a romantic place, with the big crumbling rooms around the big central courtyard and hardly anybody there and nothing to do but sit around the pool getting smashed on piña coladas and flipping through books of Maya codices from the library and shooting an occasional game of pool. It's amazing, these big hotels without even telephones or anything out in the middle of nowhere, surrounded by hundreds of miles of thatched huts. Jaishree and I got to know each other pretty well. She was pretty smart for someone so pretty: most smart girls are sharp-featured and drawn, with jittery, nervous movements and vague hair. But she had a lot of grace. I was crazy about her.

We were the only two people awake in the place, sitting in chaise longues and watching the moon rise. I told her I loved Mexico so much partly because of all the bright colors there. "I guess my childhood was kind of austere," I said.

"In what way?"

"There were always places I couldn't go when I was a kid." I didn't think I'd had a bad childhood. Actually, my parents were very low-pressure and tolerant. But I would say it was a rather austere childhood. And there was a deep sense of nowhere-ness to the Massachusetts suburb where we lived after we got back and settled down from all the Asian travel my dad did when he was a foreign correspondent. It was suburbia without even the *jouissance* of California suburbia; it was no-nonsense New England house-after-house with a whole lot of Volvos. The most glamorous thing around was Cape Cod, and even running into the Kennedy grandchildren on the beach in the summer wasn't the thrill of a lifetime. We lived in Brewster, Massachusetts, from when I was eight to when I got out of high school. I remember every speck of our unremarkable shingle-style house in excruciating detail. There was a mysterious bump in the floor of my room, where they used to ring for the maid, and an old skull-like wooden Indian head on a shelf in my room, that always gave me nightmares. I'd just lie around for hours, playing scale-change games with tiny figurines of Spiderman and Wonder Woman and wondering when something was going to happen. I constructed intricate and misinformed scientific experiments out of household materials: thread made out of eggs and yeast, or a rocket that took off when the vinegar in its nose-cone seeped into the wad of Kleenex and baking soda in its base. I drew vast fantasy realms with water-soluble Magic Markers. I wasn't much interested in playing with other kids. In the summers we were out at our farm in Great Barrington and I never spoke to any of the locals. I stayed up late and was too bored to sleep. So at a very early age I got the distinct feeling that the glamorous part of my life was over. I always felt everything was too late. In grade school I thought I was ruined if I made a single faux pas with the rigid social structure. I was withdrawn and constantly concerned with my physical appearance, how I was presenting myself and what my clothes and hair were like. When I was in high school, if I got a single B in any class, I always thought that was the end, I'd never get into any good college and I'd never meet any interesting people. And I lived in a fantasy world that distanced me from the rest of my age group. I always thought of myself as much older than they were. My self-image was a foggy cross between a Romantic poet and painter and James Bond. Once in seventh grade a classmate did an interesting improvisational piece and I made the mistake of saying to another friend, "You know, sometimes kids can be very creative."

And my fantasy world was *about* difference. It was founded on nutcases like Edgar Allan Poe and Oscar Wilde and Coleridge and Nabokov, writers who created great beauty and glamour, and on reproductions of art by Piero della Francesca and Botticelli and Canova, who created physical perfection that could make you cry, and movies on television like *Anna Christie* and *Casablanca* and *Goldfinger* and *The Thief of Baghdad,* movies with cool guys and ethereal heroines in impossible settings. And then later I became obsessed with specific actresses, especially the big stars with the distinctive brands of beauty, Elizabeth Taylor, Marilyn Monroe, Louise Brooks, Anna Magnani, and Catherine Deneuve. There was always this idea of the essence of the beautiful, the glamorous, the connected, the magic sexual power that opens all doors. I couldn't wait to move to Hollywood. Sometimes I'd dial random 213 area-code numbers for the sheer thrill of reaching L.A. When I started developing girlfriends, I was tremendously picky about them. Despite the importunate demands of male adolescent sexuality, which need to be fulfilled instantly if not sooner, and the fact that I was an intelligent kid, I ignored all girls who were not absolutely gorgeous. I would go out only with the class ice princesses, when I could get them, no matter how stupid and dull they were. The most beautiful of all, Amy, was the hardest to get. I finally got to her by appealing to her vanity: I had her pose for me in sculpture class, for nearly four months, while I did a bust of her that was completely idealized, smoothed to a licked-candy surface, with incredibly detailed hair cascading in fanciful spirals around her truncated shoulders.

My parents kind of encouraged the art thing, but they also didn't know anything about it and weren't truly interested. I learned early on that they had their own agenda, which included being left alone by their only child as much as possible. My father would generally sit at his desk typing and shuffling papers for hours with some football game on the TV, and my mother would knit or something, and there was a big sense of eternal gloom.

I finally did get into every school I applied to, partly because I included a big glossy photo of that sculpture and a few other pieces in each application. But even at Yale that beauty, that connected glamour, kept eluding me. It was like a black swallowtail butterfly that I trailed over rocks and beaches and through forests but could never catch. And in my second year there, even though I had no intention of being anything but an art major, I took my first pre-Columbian course, with Mary Miller, and also my first pre-med course. I wonder what I was thinking.

13

We swam (of course without clothing) in the pool and had amazing sex and went to sleep. We were going to drive—actually, get driven—to Uxmal the next day. Jaishree fell into her usual fitful sleep. It was pathetic watching her toss and turn. She was such a wreck. I couldn't sleep much next to my little bundle of nerves, so I stayed up reading and thinking about the Maya. They used to deform their babies at birth. They'd put their head in a kind of vise to make the forehead slope back, and they hung a ball over the babies' eyes to make them cross-eyed, which they felt looked especially sexy. Then they'd get to the tattoos. I've never been much into tats myself, but I kind of like the idea of them. They're so permanent.

■

Sixto drove us by way of Tixcacalcupul, a sleepy colonial town. There's a gigantic church built in 1603 and a few dusty buildings and a market square and a lot of thatched huts. Nothing's happened there since the Conquest. We drove to Mérida, which is in a way one of my favorite cities. It's a sort of sprawling but still somehow small primitive dusty noncity with a bunch of big colonial buildings in the center. They make great buzzed-up tropical fruit drinks there, so we stayed there for hours and got to Uxmal in the evening, as the site was closing, and checked in in time for me to sneak into the Zona

Archaeologica through a spot I know in the fence. The sun was getting to the horizon. I walked into the Nunnery Quadrangle from the back, out past the huge round-cornered Pyramid of the Magician, and up to the high platform with the Governor's Palace. Uxmal was such an integrated whole, a multilayered, multileveled diagram of the Maya cosmos. Every tile on the intricate walls had a specific numerological and calendrical significance. The palace glowed with pink inner light, radiating the heat from the day out of its massive core back into the suddenly chilly blue air. Three big gray-green lizards, one of them easily four feet long, crawled around on its facade, each one climbing a different route upward. They must sleep up there, I thought. There were thousands of swallows and bats flying into and out of the palace in the magenta twilight. A bigger, darker shape darted out of the central door, the door larger than all the others, and flew toward me. I gasped and jumped back a bit, and it whirled to the right and perched on one of the Chac masks above the farthest-north door. It was an owl. Venus was becoming visible above the palace. I walked inside into the central chamber, filled with the shrieking of bats. When this was an active temple, this room must have been the seat of supreme power. It was black and the air was thick. Then I thought I might get bitten by a bat and get rabies so I walked out again. No one was around. It was just me and the Lords of Xiu.

Mesoamerica is the closest thing we have to an alien civilization. Their view of the world was alien: in Mesoamerica, lightning originated in the ground and traveled up toward the sky; the snake, for us associated with the earth, was for them a symbol of the sky, associated with the Milky Way. With us, pillars grow upward; for them, the snake-shaped pillar descended from the sky toward the ground. So in many ways the Mesoamerican world is our world turned upside down. For them, symbols corresponding to "evil" for us, the snake and the bat and the skull and the tiger, are positive, or at least centrally powerful in a cosmos that is by our standards essentially amoral.

That's why they're so fascinating; the Mesoamericans had been isolated from the entire rest of the world since their ancestors crossed the Bering Strait ten thousand years before their civilizations even began. They are the only civilizations that we can say this about; the rest of the world, even the aborigines of New Zealand, all interacted with each other to some extent. And the Mesoamericans reached a very "high" level of civilization independently, higher in most of the terms we use to describe civilization than that of any other far-flung region like Madagascar or whatever. So it's both fascinating in its alien aspects—the trickster model of the gods, the color associations, the sense of time, the imagery—but also somehow disturbing in its similarities. Because the similarities—buildings, writing, court life, so many things—arising despite millennia of isolation, suggest that mankind is essentially limited in his creativity. So the homologies between Mesoamerican culture and our own are immensely sad. People are the same all over. We'll never come up with anything truly new under the sun.

The next morning, Jaishree took an Air Caribé plane back from Mérida. She had to see some of her extended kinship group in Miami. I had one last errand.

I got to Tony's shop at noon. It was on Calle 57 and it was tiny and squalorous. The God L piece was in the back, with tissue paper over it. He pulled the paper off and it was just staggering.

I checked out a couple of things Spenser had told me to look for. The blue pigment didn't react to any of the little liquids-in-jars he'd given me. It was genuine. Tony tried to hit me up for all kinds of money, but after I screamed and yelled and said I'd call the State Department, he let the incensario go for a thousand-dollar finder's fee. He wasn't entitled to it, but you always have to pay a little graft in Mexico or you get beat up. We bubble-wrapped the piece into a big suitcase and I checked it through at the airport. They never X-ray anything down there, I could have walked off with the Sun Stone of Tizoc. When I got back to New York and got the thing home and it was in one piece, it all felt like a drugged-out dream.

■

Mark and David and I finally did the procedure on the society woman, Laureen McNiel. It was two days after we got back and I was finally getting a little sick—I guess I wasn't so invulnerable to tropical food as I thought—but massive doses of Pepto-Bismol and Imodium were helping a bit. Because Laureen was old and puffy I'd decided to take a fair amount of the flesh off, so I had Mark help me with the surgical side. She was under intravenous Valium, which Mark had supervised. He'd brought this whole big kit along and set it up. I'd wanted to use laughing gas, but he said the Valium was safer.

It was an odd feeling, we'd make an incision with a skin knife around the fold of flesh we wanted to remove, and then we'd just peel it off, separating the loose flesh from what was underneath with a flat-tipped scalpel. It was like peeling the skin off a chicken breast. I wondered whether we were taking off so many facial muscles that her face wouldn't be expressive, but Mark said we weren't. At least we left most of the orbital muscles around the eyes, just snipping off the eye bags a bit, and we left the zygomatic muscles that allow you to smile. We did a general lift, too, which is something an ordinary plastic surgeon would do, but not so radically as we did it. We took at least an inch off the top of her forehead and pulled up the skin around it. It was weird, throwing the bits of flesh we'd peeled off into the "infectious waste" basket. They plopped down into the plastic bag with a kind of disgusting *thwop*. We'd also rented a liposuction machine, but it was dangerous to use, aside from being absolutely disgusting. People have died from liposuction. I only turned it on a couple of times. Mark handled the suction and blood pressure and finally said she didn't need any saline solution. We used surgical glue instead of sutures in most places, but it still took forever. It took five hours just to get her to the stage where I could sand down the top layer of the remaining skin and seal the whole thing with PCS.

I did Laureen's hands, too. I'd only done hands once before, even though they're actually the most common thing for conventional plastic surgeons to do. It was tricky making the transition from the back of the hand to the palm and fingertips, which I had to leave untouched. But I think it blended in pretty well.

"Do you think she's been under too long?" I asked.

"I think she can go another hour on the intravenous, and then we should bring her up. But she'll get a lot of pain."

"Well, can we give her painkillers before she's off the Valium?"

"No, I don't think that's a good idea. She might end up like Karen Ann Quinlan."

The last thing I needed was a comatose body to dispose of. Maybe we were getting into more than we could handle. I felt like we were just a couple of kids playing around with expensive, dangerous gadgets we didn't fully understand.

While we were bandaging, I asked Mark whether he was on the outs with Karl.

"What do you mean?" Mark asked.

"Well, you seemed to be teasing him a bit the last time I was up at your lab."

"Oh, he doesn't mind, he's used to getting kidded. He's just a total nerd," Mark said.

"You're sure he doesn't want a bigger cut of our business?"

"I don't know—you heard what he said. He's not into making money. Just don't worry about it."

"How much of the process did you invent and how much did he invent?"

"I did most of it, okay? It came out of our research together, but I brought it into the real world, you know? I rounded up the burn victims and combined it with the Artificial Skin and everything. Don't bug me about it."

I hate having to deal with touchy people. They're such little kids, it drives me crazy. "Let's order an artichoke-heart pizza," I said.

It was after midnight when we got Laureen shipped off and David and Mark had cleaned up and left. I just sat around for a while, chain-eating banana/strawberry Frozfruits and staring at the ceiling. What was the essence of physical beauty? I wondered. Were there rules that went so deep they were genetic? Was it something about balance, or symmetry? Did it have to do with *completeness,* because there was some primal fear of being maimed?

Or maybe the essence of beauty had less to do with something you could somehow measure than with mystery and ethereality. Maybe symmetry, too, helped to make real beauties kind of ungraspable, because there's a tension between all the different forms that makes it hard to put your finger on any one thing. And of course I was thinking about female beauty at this point, and ethereality is a big issue in female beauty. I knew a lot of philosophers had talked about this, but the one I remembered right away was Georges Bataille, who was kind of a champion of surrealism and a pioneer deconstructionist. A lot of my art-critic friends were really crazy about him. I pulled his major book, *Erotism,* out of my shelf. I hadn't cracked it since college, but I found the part about ethereality pretty fast:

The erotic value of feminine forms seems to me to be bound up with the absence of the natural heaviness that suggests the physical use of the limbs and the necessity for the framework of bone: The more ethereal the shapes and the less clearly they depend on animal reality or on a human physiological reality, the better they respond to the fairly widespread image of the desirable woman.

What about all the periods where they liked fat women? I thought. Were they ethereal like clouds and balloons?

I think what I have said is indubitably true. But the opposite, only secondarily obvious, also holds. The image of the desirable woman as first imagined would be insipid and unprovocative if it did not at the same time also promise or reveal a mysterious animal aspect, more momentously suggestive. The beauty of the desirable woman suggests her private parts, the hairy ones, to be precise, the animal ones. Instinct has made sure that we shall desire these parts.

Yeah, sure, I thought. All very true, I suppose. It's going to be a little tough to get both aspects into one face, though. It reminded me of what somebody else, I forget who, had said about why women use lipstick to make their lips redder—because, supposedly, it reminds you of their vaginal lips. I suppose that's true, too, but on the other hand, then you'd also expect moustaches and beards on women to be sexy.

I went into the studio and looked at the row of studies I'd done for Laureen. I compared them with the composite thing out of *Vogue*. My faces didn't have the insipidity of the *Vogue* picture, but they had some of the same problems—lack of character, lack of vigor. Of course, the final version would be animated by a living being. But I needed something more to work toward. I had to experiment a bit, create a supermodel or two out of nothing.

I did a whole bunch of acrylic sketches out of my head. Nothing seemed absolutely sure-fire. I'd done some gorgeous faces, but they were *still* all a little bland, a little too much like the girls in *Mirabella*. And when I tried to make one less bland, and exaggerate certain features, and play around with proportion, then they didn't look universal enough. I tried different ethnicities and different personalities as unifying factors to aspire toward, and it helped a bit. But after a while, I felt that the elements of what would be read as a beautiful face were extremely simple and abstract. It was like cartooning. Cartoonists can suggest a beautiful girl with just a few strokes. It's partly the viewer's knowledge of the conventions of representation that allows him to fill in the gaps, as Gombrich says in *Art and Illusion*. But it was strange to feel that there was an essence of beauty out there somewhere, something very simple and perfect and platonic, and yet not be able to get to it. I wondered whether maybe it was silly to try to design the perfect face; maybe it couldn't exist any more than the perfect painting.

■

I was supposed to go eat dinner with Lucy and Robert, a couple of friends from graduate school, and some of their friends, but I just couldn't bear it. I called the Viet Huong, the Vietnamese place where we were supposed to go, and left a message that I would be too sick to make it. I wondered whether they'd get the message. Probably not, but I was too tired to call again when they should have gotten there. I felt beautied out. I sleep in shifts, not particularly at night, so I knew I could reenergize. I had time for a twenty-minute nap, and then I'd catch this performance of Jaishree's uptown.

It was a shock, after a couple of hours inside, dealing with the most ethereal facial beauty, to go outside on the street and see all these lumpy-faced people, and go down into the subway and see even more lumpy-faced people, like gnomes and trolls and goblins and Maya death gods with horrible misshapen potato faces and mouths oozing crud and spiky beard stubble and all sorts of horrible warts and cysts and sties and pustules, and one old black guy's lower lip had been entirely eaten away by cancer or yaws or something. And I tried to smile and be polite to some blotchy old woman I bumped into on the train, and she smiled at me, and I had a terrible thought: What if she thought I was sexy? It was just the most revolting thought I'd ever had. I suppose when I get old, I'll think young girls are sexy and they'll be disgusted. But of course, I won't let myself get old. Either I'll finally break my rule and operate on myself, or I'll get someone else to do it, or I'll just shoot myself when I get to a certain level of grossness.

But then I started thinking about my art while I was perversely fascinated and horror-stricken by all these grotesques. I decided my art was really completely abstract, not figurative, because, really, these creatures weren't all that different from the radiant vision that I was creating; I was actually just working with the same basic elements in a very confined idiom, within very narrow parameters. And I still didn't know exactly what I was looking for at that place where sex and aesthetics meet. I was working with a refined system of harmonies, balances, textures, and colors, in a more restrained matrix than minimalist abstraction. I was more precise than Jan van Eyck and Myron Stout and Robert Ryman put together. My work was really profoundly reactionary. Like all truly avant-garde art.

What was it about eyes, nose, and mouth that was so important? Eyes, nose, and mouth are some sort of basic metaphor for the structure of the universe. They're repeated all over everything, like houses with a door and a window on each side and a peak over the door, and cars with headlights and a projecting grill with teeth-looking ridges in it, and airplanes, and furniture. There's something so basic about body imagery that we don't even notice it anymore, but it's everywhere, in almost everything.

When I emerged from Xibalbá, the underworld, and walked uptown on Madison, I realized I was falling into this behavior pattern where I check everybody out. I guess a lot of people do it. If I see someone who looks interesting on the other side of the street, I cross over. In a way it's pretty terrible, the way your face brands you as interesting or not interesting. As you walk through New York, everyone's just checking you out, and if you can't cut the mustard facially, you're nothing. I began to really realize, for the first time, what a limit beauty is. It's difficult for a man, especially a "straight" man, to imagine what a factor beauty is for women. Female beauty is just so codified, there just aren't many acceptable variations on it, even with the tremendous rise in acceptance of more ethnic beauties of various types, and so most women just aren't very attractive in a conventional sense. Whereas, supposedly, most men feel pretty good about the way they look. I think most of them look horrible, too, actually. But still, it's nothing like the gulf that separates pretty women from the others. And the others are crushed from the outset, it's a life without recourse, they're trapped in this shell that won't let them get where they want, that keeps them from meeting the people that they want to meet and just being whatever glamorous way they'd want to be, and when they walk down the street they're constantly made aware that no one's interested in them, no one looks at them, and they're just nonpersons, or at least nonsexuals.

And even beautiful women become nonsexuals so much faster than men. They can really only count on about ten good years, from fifteen to twenty-five, and then the lines start to set in, and there's nothing they can do about it. They're trapped in such a narrow time frame, they're already approaching the outer limit of their desirability before they've really had a chance to try it out. They're just day-lilies that only last ten hours. And I was becoming so aware of this, aware of how there was just nothing more tragic, and in a way it made me feel really good about my art, because I was giving people the most valuable thing in the whole world, and not just because a middle-of-the-line Zoli model grosses $300,000 a year, but because no matter how great a person you are, people just don't want to deal with you unless you're gorgeous. It's like death: it's a built-in cruelty that's just part of the system, it's a horrible flaw at the heart of society, it's like everyone is born with a terminal illness. It's in the numbers, like in some of my paintings: You can't live much past one hundred, you're not attractive past fifty if you're a man and thirty if you're a woman, and that's just all the play there is in the system. Just fifty-seven varieties. Only fifty-two cards in the deck.

Time's a weird thing anyway. With all the recording media available today, and all the instant communications and the climate control and everything that's distanced us from natural cycles, all the things that preserve everything perfectly, film and videotape, three-dimensional photography, frozen foods and microwaves and everything, and all the reproduction and replication technology that gives you an exact duplicate of anything, time as a limiting element seems really out of place. My work's kind of a hedge against it, but only an imperfect one. Of course, I planned to extend my practice to include the entire body someday, but even that wouldn't do everything, because those internal organs still go pretty fast. Even though it would cut down on my business somewhat, I'd still really welcome it if someone would isolate the aging process. Aging's tremendously unfair. Life's a bitch and then you die, as Voltaire said.

I saw some girl from behind, with a nice outfit and nice hair, and a nice-looking jaw curve, and I sort of sped up and ran around her to get a look at her, and it turned out she was a weathered, baggy, puffy half-gorgon, just a sharpened caricature of what she must have been just a few years before, and it was such a feeling of disappointment. And she had to feel that disappointment every morning. Maybe the militant feminists and lesbians who shave their heads and refuse to wear any makeup are absolutely right, I thought. You can't make any concessions to received standards of beauty, the whole notion is debilitating, demeaning to women, it's given every woman in the Western world a complex the size of the Graf Zeppelin, it's the biggest psychological disaster since Catholicism, and I'm in a horrible, parasitic, male chauvinist business. But I love it anyway.

I wondered whether I could really get hold of a couple of ugly girls to turn into supermodels in the next couple of weeks. I passed two girls with good bodies but cruddy faces and wondered whether they might be good candidates. It was very overcast and dark. I felt like a vampire, wandering the streets, looking for people whom I could capture and transform into the Undead and grant the gift of eternal youth.

I passed Missoni and noticed some really beautiful mannequins in the window. They were pure white and sort of marbly-looking, just right for all the lilac sweaters they were wearing, but when I looked closer, I could tell that their faces were a little too stylized to be of much use. They had a lot of life, but even so there was a Deco-ish sharpness to their features. Still, I thought, mannequin technology has been producing great-looking models, many of them very realistic, for a long time, and it's all anonymous, which means it doesn't have all the baggage about originality that known artists have to cope with. I made a mental note to get my friend Tobi Ramadan, who runs an architectural antiques place on Lafayette Street, to investigate the mannequin industry. If there was some big warehouse somewhere with a whole range of heads in it, I might just find that some drone had saved me the trouble of designing from scratch.

■

Jaishree's performance was fabulous. She and three other women did a reworking of Gênet's *The Maids* as a sort of TV game show, and it was hilarious, but it was a Saturday and it wasn't a full house and it wasn't a big house. Afterward I told her I figured people just don't go out anymore.

Her name was Rose, and she really wanted to be an actress, and she was very ordinary-looking. She was from Iowa City and must have had a certain amount of spunk to have come to New York in the first place. She was terribly down-and-out. I don't have a lot of access to the underclass world, but I got her name through one of my "shadow sources," a somewhat sleazy photographer who had a studio in the basement of my building. In this area there's probably one in every building. He had long, stringy hair and wore overalls without any shirt and was a complete ugly slob and wasn't even any photographer anybody knew about anymore, but he had all these beautiful young girls running in and out at all hours. They must all have been fresh off the bus. What an ugly racket. I guess he'd been kind of famous in the seventies. He doesn't know what the Process really is and only knows me as a neighbor involved with it, not its principal architect. He rounded her up for me after he heard she had been let out of the hospital after two months of observation after a suicide attempt. Rose and I were sitting in Aggie's diner on Houston Street.

"Would you like some coffee? At least?" I asked.

"Okay." She wasn't very talkative. I wondered how I could be absolutely sure she wasn't a spy of some kind. David said she checked out, but she still could have been hired—by some other plastic surgeon, by law enforcement working for the FDA, by some curious client, a million possibilities. I looked around trying not to seem nervous. I'd met her on the corner of Broadway and Houston, and no one knew we were coming here, and no one new had come in. I was wearing fake glasses and a hat that covered my hair. I still wished I had insisted that David do the interview. He'd been getting kind of recalcitrant lately.

"Do you know what this is about?" I asked.

"Scasi said you were a plastic surgeon."

"That's right. Did he tell you how we're not supposed to work for free?"

"What?"

"Sometimes we want to use new procedures and we wouldn't charge for them, but the American Medical Association won't let us do anything without charging for it."

"Why not?"

"Medicine's a racket. All doctors want to charge a fortune, and they don't want to be undercut."

"They're such a bunch of parasites."

I guess that meant she could relate. I wondered how smart she was. It's often best to treat them as though they were smart. The waitperson brought her coffee and another chocolate egg cream for me.

"What did Scasi tell you?"

"He said you could turn me into a top model and that you've done movie stars."

"Why should you believe him?"

"I don't know."

"Why do you want to try this?"

She didn't say anything. Of course, she wanted it because she was desperate. She was either a hooker already or just on the edge. I didn't want to ask about that.

"Are you sure this is safe, and like, going to work and all?" she finally asked.

"We won't be using any techniques that aren't already in frequent use," I lied. "But the AMA doesn't like the idea of *completely* changing someone's face. It's too flashy an idea. It would threaten their power base."

"Why do you have to change it completely?"

I hesitated a second. "Well, you can look a bit like yourself, but if you really want to be a top model, we'll have to give you a fresh look that people really want. You know, the difference between Naomi Campbell and a million other women is very, very slim. You have to be absolutely exceptional. But I'll show you the drawings and models and be sure we have your approval. Normally, this procedure would cost about half a million dollars." I wanted her to feel she was asking me for something and she would be getting the bargain. Which was true.

"I guess you only do big stars," she said.

"No, I'd work on you, I guess, if you're really not happy with the way you look."

"Of course I'm not happy with the way I look. It's not easy for me to walk by magazine stands, you know?"

"I know, it's a problem."

"I feel so ugly, I can't look at people in the face. It's really embarrassing, I've never had a blemish like this. I used to have absolute baby skin. It's just horrible—every morning I wake up looking worse. I feel like I have to keep people at a ten-foot radius. I took a photograph of the me the way I used to look along to the skin doctor."

I felt kind of bad, but I wasn't going to get her off the subject just because I was feeling softhearted.

"Are you sure you want to go through with this?" I asked.

"Okay."

She said okay too quickly. It was really worrisome.

"No, I don't want to do it if you're even the least bit unsure."

"No, I really need to do it."

There was definitely real desperation in her eyes. Unless she was a really great actress. She had that pathetic dignity and low self-respect and little airs that unsuccessful actresses always have. I should still be careful, though.

"Would ten o'clock on Friday, December tenth, be convenient?" I asked.

"Okay."

"You'll have to stay in a hotel for a few days. We'll tell you where and put you up."

"Okay."

"Someone with a blue hat will meet you at the corner of Broadway and Houston at ten o'clock in the morning.'

"Okay."

She must be used to a lot of sleazy deals and secret meetings.
Was she a hooker after all? How could we make sure she wasn't being
followed? It was crazy, but working with unknowns was actually a
million times more dangerous than working with celebrities. Somebody would have to check out this woman more carefully before she
got anywhere near my house. I hoped it would be worth it. Maybe I
was crazy to try this. I should stick to celebrity makeovers.

Still, we had found her, not the other way around. If she'd been
planted, it had been done very cleverly.

"Oh, by the way," I asked, "Scasi must have mentioned that
you'd have a contract with his office for exclusive representation,
right?"

"Yeah. Yes."

And then it would be up to us to go over his books. That would
be hell, too. Maybe we should just try to get a flat fee out of him. This
whole thing was madness.

But it was for my art.

"You must be about a size six, right?" I asked.

■

On Wednesday we took the bandages off Laureen. I still had to
do most of the dyeing, because we'd worked so long on her face, I
hadn't had time to finish it before. But we kept her away from mirrors
until I was finished, and she was really thrilled. I'd made her look a
little like her former self, but more like Jean Shrimpton, the model
from the sixties. It was a miraculous job, probably the first true total-
alteration surgery that had ever been performed, and I felt very god-
like, but at the same time it just didn't seem like enough to me. I
needed to do something *amazing*.

■

So the Jaishree and Jamie experience had quickly developed into
a relationship. A *relationship*. God, it's enough to make you want to
become a nun. This whole serial monogamy business is so repeti-
tious. But I guess there's nothing else for it.

And Jaishree's career went okay for the next couple of months. She was in a good period. She got a fair amount of press over Thanksgiving. Mel Gussow in the *Times* called her a stunning new talent, the *Voice* people loved her acts, and a lot of doors opened up for her. But she didn't quite seem to be hitting it, either. She didn't get into the *Alive from Off-Center* thing at Lincoln Center. She made a couple of tapes for some HBO things, but they screened them at bad times and didn't get much response, or at least they said they didn't. Her agent kept sending her to all kinds of auditions for TV commercials, and she only got a couple of spots. She'd be eating tacos for Taco Bell for a split second, and that tape and the money she'd earned was all she'd have to show for three days of work and three weeks of auditions. She got depressed. I got depressed. I told her she should just bag the commercials and keep building up support for her cabaret act. If Sandra Bernhard could get so major, I couldn't imagine why Jaishree wasn't swinging it. But Sandra was just kind of in the right place at the right time.

"Your stuff is just a little too obscure and intellectual," I said. "Talk down to people a bit. Nobody ever went broke underestimating the taste of the American public. Flo Ziegfeld or somebody said that."

"Listen, I do what I do, I don't want to talk about it, okay?"

She also began to develop some acne. It wasn't really bad, but it didn't seem to respond to the Retin-A. I can peel all over the place with just a little bit of Retin-A, but she just wouldn't peel. And it became kind of an issue in our relationship because she didn't like it when I mentioned it all the time, but I just couldn't leave it alone. The spots on her face were like melanomas that would kill our relationship dead.

I was getting a little concerned about my own skin imperfections, too. Especially the hints of eye bags and crinkles around my eyes. I began to really lather on the Retin-A and the Lancôme anti-aging creams during this period. It was time for another dermabrasion and maybe some collagen shots. I just couldn't take the idea of roughness, of skin stretching, becoming brittle, losing its elasticity, falling and drooping and developing jowls and bags and lines. It was too disgusting. I was going to be like a shriveled old green pepper, I thought, and I just shuddered and shivered when I thought about myself slipping into that realm of age. I deserved to be forever young. Or die pretty, like Jim Morrison and Arthur Rimbaud and Raphael and all the truly cool individuals.

I began to have trouble with the *idea* of skin secretions. I'd squeeze these little bumps on my face and neck—or I'd get Jaishree to squeeze the ones on the back of my neck—and this white crud would wriggle out, like white worms. And I'd just start shivering sometimes even thinking about the fact that I was probably carrying around a whole layer of unsqueezed-out white crud. Maybe I'd at least get another dermabrasion and chemical peel, I thought. Sand it all down and start over.

Suddenly I realized Jaishree and I had been going out or staying home or whatever for nearly two months. Time sure flies in a condensed narrative. But it flies in real life, too.

In December, Jaishree had to go to L.A. for six weeks to make a film. It was an okay part in a big film, *Song of the Dolphin* with Kevin Costner. I said it was just great, but she didn't seem too excited about it.

"I'm not exactly the ingenue," she said. "I play his 'bookish and rather unpleasant sister-in-law.' I have ten lines, and they still want me there for a whole half of the schedule."

"So make it shine," I said.

"It's not very well-written."

"A good actor can't lose. Even if the script's bad, you'll stand out."

"I don't know."

"Look, I don't know if I can stand all this negativity. Most girls would be thrilled to be in a movie with Kevin Costner. He's the Orson Welles of the nineties, after all."

"Yeah, right."

We had a little talk about whether we would be faithful to each other while she was away. It's difficult to have those kind of talks in our postmodern era without cracking up. I said that since we'd already used the L-word, we might as well at least try to do an Ain't Misbehavin' thing, unless we met somebody we really, really liked better.

"Why can't you just come along?" she asked.

"I'll come out for a few days, but I do have a life, you know.

Unglamorous as it is. I can't just follow you all over the planet." I had a couple of high-paying "procedures" to do that month.

"I hate L.A.," Jaishree said.

"Just learn to drive and you'll love it," I said. "There's always a place to park out there. I can't understand why you don't want to learn to drive."

"I'm better at convincing men to drive me around."

"I guess that's a more important skill."

I didn't think I liked the way I pictured her convincing them. She was such a mega-flirt. I guess it's nothing to be that way when you're a performer. By comparison, artists are stodgy, dowdy, and puritanical.

At a certain point, around early December, just before her L.A. trip, Jaishree was staying over a lot and there were all these calls regarding the Rose project, and Jaishree was asking what they were all about and finding little surgical tools and things, and it was just getting ridiculous that I hadn't told her about my "dark side." Anyway, I really wanted to confide in her about my cosmetic-surgery sculpture thing. One evening, when she found a whole set of scalpels, she asked me whether I was some kind of closet American Psycho.

"No, but I have another thing I do," I said.

"What's that?"

"Well, I'm an unlicensed cosmetic surgeon."

Actually, I wasn't a cosmetic surgeon. I was an Artist. Someday Rizzoli would put out a book of my faces, and Penny Penn would be on the cover.

"You're kidding."

"No, I wouldn't kid about that." I sat down at the kitchen counter and began to play with my cappuccino machine. "I have to ask you not to tell anybody at all about it, in fact. I mean, people know, but just reliable people. I could get in really big trouble."

She was silent. I wondered whether she was beginning to think I was a creepy weirdo.

"It's a little creepy and weird," I said. "But it s also really exciting.

I make designer people. I do plastic surgery procedures that are too advanced to make their way into regular practice. Someday everyone will be doing them, but for the time being, I'm the only one."

I sort of pushed the black leather portfolio toward her across the counter. She didn't look interested.

"Maybe it's not that interesting," I said. I was getting moths in my stomach. Would she just go freaky on me and leave me and blow my cover and ruin everything? "Look, just don't mention it, okay? I trust you."

"No, it sounds really interesting," she said. She was smiling suspiciously. "Do you have any examples?"

"They're in the book. But seriously, it is a little creepy, and if it's going to freak you out, maybe you shouldn't look."

That got her to look. She pulled out the leather loose-leaf binder with the Cibachromes. The first couple were actually the grossest, since they were disfigured burn victims that Mark and I collaborated on when he was interning in pathology. That was six years ago. The "before" shots were disturbing, but I was proud that the "after" shots looked pretty normal. I wasn't allowing myself much artistic freedom in those days; I just handled the PCS better than Mark could. It was nice, because I could tell Jaishree thought I had done a good thing.

"So ordinary surgery couldn't have gotten these people back together?"

"No, not really. There wasn't enough good skin left to graft. The first two were caught in an explosion in a chemical plant, and even some of the unburned skin fell off because of corrosives."

"So you studied medicine, too?"

"No, not really. No."

"So how do you know all this stuff?"

"Well, I work with a surgeon, and I read a lot—"

"Aren't you afraid you'll mess up and kill somebody?"

"I'd be more afraid of a real doctor in a real hospital. They kill people all the time. And it's all basically surface work, you know. Nothing really structural. I don't even have to go in through the nose or the mouth the way regular plastic surgeons do. We use a special compound, and it's all done from outside."

She was looking at the third project I did, an actor named Paul

Garrison. He had really bad acne scars, and then he had had a dermabrasion that didn't work out. There were some big holes in his face. In the second group of pictures, I had filled them in and also done a little rethinking on the nose and brow line. We had also sent him to Dr. Kopf for an ear pullback. His head shot at the end looked a million times better. He was on some soap opera now.

"This guy looks a little familiar," Jaishree said. "Do *you* know who they all are, or did he black out his own name?"

"Sure I know who they are. We just covered all the names on the published stuff. But there are some people at the end you'll definitely recognize."

She flipped through toward the end. "It seems like it's almost all women."

"Yeah, well, that's not really fair, I guess, but I guess I just have more aesthetic sympathy for women. I'm really tuned in to the way women look. I guess it's just because I'm really into my hetero thing, I don't know why."

"So you mean you consider this part of your art?"

"Well, it's got a lot in common with my art. It's like Mapplethorpe, you know—it's a sublimation of sex."

"Why is it so great to be a sublimation of sex? Why do you have to sublimate it at all?"

"I don't know, all art is just sublimation of sex. But I feel like, for once, I'm an artist who's actually creating real sex objects, so it's not exactly sublimation anymore, it's doing something about it. Isn't that great? But one thing I do worry about, in terms of the art thing, is maybe it's not critical enough, it's not exactly 'smart art,' no matter how much thought I put into it."

"It's a little like commercial art."

"Yeah, it is. But actually, I guess I prefer commercial art to fine art a lot of the time. So much more thought goes into it than people put into fine art. I mean, just think about those 'Smooth Character' ads. They're the most clever, manipulative things in the world. Whoever thought of that campaign is a genius."

She had gotten to Penny Penn.

"Jesus Christ, that's Penny Penn," she said. "I don't *believe* you!"

"I'm working on very heavy people now, it's true." That sounded a little mercenary, so I added, "I guess I should do more burn victims and everything, but it's actually much more difficult than the society stuff, because they don't search you out, you have to search them out. And they're much more likely to tell somebody about you than a public person is. They might talk too much even out of gratitude."

"Why don't you publish your process so, you know, you can benefit the world and all that?"

"It isn't just my process. And my partner is working on doing that. But the medical community might just shoot it down. They don't want innovations. It's just politics."

"I don't *believe* you!"

I couldn't tell what she meant by that. I started steaming some more milk, because I didn't know what to say.

"So how did you get in touch with Penny Penn?"

"Oh, I did a minor star who I knew in high school, and she's a friend of hers. But I also went to school with Penny." I made a "dropping" gesture with my hand to indicate namedropping. "Thud."

"Are you the only person who does this?"

"I don't know, you'd think somewhere someone would have to be on to something similar, maybe in Japan or someplace. But I certainly haven't seen any evidence of it in any entertainment figures or anything."

"What about Michael Jackson?"

"Oh, definitely not, no. He's great, a lot of work went into him, but he's definitely all conventional surgery, you can tell. There was a period where he had really bad acne, but the chemical peels brought a real girlish quality back to his skin, you know, but then they left it a little tight. He's down to his last couple of layers of skin, he can't have any more dermabrasions. It looks like he's had implants, too. I wouldn't be surprised if the stuff ended up shifting, actually. But he's certainly about as far as you can go with conventional surgery. And they have done amazing things with him. I'm such a fan of his. And the racial and sexual ambiguity—they're both part of his divinity."

We looked through all the other projects. I'd done twenty-six. She was getting more and more fascinated. Finally she said she thought the whole thing was terrific and kissed me. But there was a certain distance there.

■

The day of Project Rose finally arrived. Ultimately, we'd gotten a room for her at the Sheraton Centre Hotel, which used to be the old Americana. "My Combray," as Calvin calls it, since he spent so much time there when he was a kid. David booked another room at the Gramercy Park, picked Rose up on the street, took her in a cab, switched her from one cab to another going the opposite direction in the middle of heavy traffic—the classic antitail maneuver—took her to the Gramercy, made her change completely from her clothes into a robe and then into something kind of nice, actually, a loose pants suit I had him get at Agnès B., and then he went through her whole suitcase with two different kinds of bug detectors and went over her body with metal detectors and put her in another car and blindfolded her and brought her to my house. If she really let us start cutting her, at least that would mean that if she were working for someone, she didn't know it. It all seemed like a runaround, but you can't be too careful.

Everything was spread out and ready. She let him lead her in, she was totally pliant, and we got started at 3:26 P.M. I went over the drawings and CGIs—computer-generated images—of what I was planning to do with her and she seemed happy, a little weirded out that she wasn't going to look much like herself, but we reassured her with visions of Elite Management contracts. We went over all the secrecy and legal procedures, and she seemed to understand. The operation itself lasted until past midnight and went well. I stuck very closely to the plans, and we even tried matching the measurements of her face to gridded overlays on the drawings and computer monitor. It worked to some extent, but I had to keep making adjustments by eye. Next time, I thought, maybe I'd make a full-scale model and cast it. Especially if I wanted to do something really, truly artistic. I'd let myself go very far with this one, farther than I'd ever gone or would ever go with a commissioned piece, but in a way I felt I hadn't done enough prep work. Rose might turn out to be a major model, but she was still a fundamentally conventionally beautiful major model. Not an artistic triumph, just a technical one.

We wrapped her at one A.M. and bandaged over her eyes as well.

Mark and David drove her to the hotel together. I had to clean up all the crud. As usual, it went into the trash compactor with a lot of turpentine and old paint rags and paint tubes. Nobody would think it was blood.

I went over and stayed at Jaishree's. She asked a lot of questions about the operation and was kind of fascinated. She'd had a little trouble at first adjusting to her knowledge of my secret profession. Of course, it was a weird-out by most standards, but it also bothered her because it reflected on her own insecurities. There was a part of her that thought it was really neat and another part that was extremely dubious. She had a dual nature anyway. She'd been such a smart student, but she really wanted to sing and perform and all those things. It was important to her to be glamorous, but then she also had this real smart streak, the streak that had been the great English student, that said it wanted to go to graduate school someday and become some major literary theorist or something and change the world. And she had terrible trouble reconciling these things. Many of my generation at Yale and wherever had the same problem: We all wanted to be really smart, but we were fascinated with Cher, with Madonna, with Elizabeth Taylor, and we never knew where our campy side left off and our serious side began. She asked me again why I really did it.

"Well, frankly, I'm kind of crazy, I guess. I have a *really* big Pygmalion complex."

I hoped that would forestall any comments from her to that effect.

"Have you talked to your shrink about this?"

"Well, he's a doctor, you know. I don't think he'd really be into it. It's true, there isn't always too much for us to talk about."

"Why do you want to do this, anyway? Just money?"

"Sure."

"No, really."

"It's really just for money. No, that's ridiculous. It's artistic, it's brilliant. I feel like my stuff's kind of the dawn of a new age, you know, if that doesn't sound too ditzy. Anyway, who looks at static art anymore? Nobody in the big outside world has even heard of Ross Bleckner or David Salle, let alone Jamie Angelo. It's all just recording media that people ever see. So I realized that the only way to keep doing static art was to do static art that people would record. And the only thing they'll consistently record is a star's face. You know, Andy Warhol became kind of troubled in mid-career because his films weren't getting him taken seriously in Hollywood and he had to do portraits of whoever the Hollywood star machine decided was major. So he tried to find "superstars," like Edie and Ultra Violet and International Velvet and Nico, and promote them from the ground up, but none of them ever got as big as he had hoped. So he started *Interview* magazine to try to get in on the ground floor of the celebrity mill, you know, to get a little more control over the whole process. I think that toward the end, he might have been happier if he were just a big movie producer. He realized that was where the force of the culture was going. You know, though, 'Andy Warhol' sounds a lot like 'Woody Allen.' Sometimes I think they're the same person. Anyway, my thing's more different, more affirming, in some ways."

"Sure." There was a pause. "What do you mean, the new age?"

"Well, you know, I'm in the beauty industry, and there's a lot of people out there who think that whole thing is really demeaning to women. And it is. I mean, obviously, the way really beautiful women get treated is totally unfair to other women. Men too, good-looking men get treated better. But it's really glaring with women."

I wondered if she was taking this personally. But I figured she was tough enough to handle it.

"So, sure, it's a problem," she said. Meaning what was I going to do about it.

"Well . . ." I knew if I launched into it, I'd go on for a while.

"Well, what?"

"There's a tyranny of aesthetics going on," I said. I turned on the TV and turned the volume all the way down. There was an Obsession ad on, with beautiful models, just as though I'd planned it. "It's more of a cosmic problem than just making the lot of most women very hard. This culture is dying aesthetically in every other area, but there's one level on which it's obsessed with beauty more than any other culture has been." I felt as if I were giving a lecture. "Facial beauty is kind of a controlling metaphor for everything our society wants. Of course, it has a lot to do with sex, but that's just the tip of the iceberg. It's also about youth, and power, and transcendence, at least a kind of transcendence from ordinary human emotions. That's why models act dumb, not because they are dumb, although a lot of the time they are, because they've never had to think, but anyway they act dumb because they know they aren't supposed to act human in any way. That's why Andy Warhol started off acting dumb. He picked it up from models. He was obsessed with glamour, and he decided that was the way glamour was supposed to act. Today beauty's about anti-humanness, it's abstract, it's about trademark and fame. That's one reason ethnic is so big—we need something distinctive enough to be signaturized but still absolutely perfect in some way. So instead of truly unusual-looking people, we're starting to pick on different ethnic groups to give new fuel to the glamour machine. Maybe our culture is so aesthetically bankrupt right now because we've sublimated so much of our desire for beauty by filling the world with reproductions of beautiful faces. If you've got the faces right there, who needs great architecture, or trees and flowers, or anything? Maybe all the great architecture and flowers and everything were just sublimations created by people who didn't have access to many beautiful faces, or at least they couldn't possess them sexually, and needed to create a substitute that they could live in and own."

"Listen, I've got to be on the plane at seven tomorrow," Jaishree said.

■

I had some uneventful days. I made art and enjoyed early spring from a safe distance, through my closed window. After two weeks out in L.A., Jaishree called and I heard her voice on the machine saying it looked like there were big problems with the film and she couldn't get any straight answers and she didn't know whether to stay or go and getting other work out there was a nightmare and all the cabaret contacts she had out there were tremendously flaky and she hated Plasticland and really didn't know what to do and was more or less at the end of her rope. I'd been working on paintings and I had to tear myself out of my gas mask and turn off my airbrush compressor and run out of the studio. I punched on the speakerphone and then switched her to the headset phone and started trying to calm her down while I played with an Etch-A-Sketch.

"I'm old and shabby and sick," she said. Her voice sounded scruffy over the line.

"No you're not, you're absolutely beautiful."

"Really?"

I always loved the way she said "Really?" when you said something she liked to hear. She was almost a parody of femininity. Her glamour was at stake, and she really wanted to be glamorous more than anything.

"Really," I said, "really, really, really."

17

Rose got her contract with Elite after just a few tests. She'd turned out amazing. So beautiful she was almost ugly, as Calvin used to say. She was booked for most of the New York and Milan fall line shows within three weeks. She called one of my call-forwarding safety numbers every once in a while to tell me how grateful she was.

Jaishree came back. L.A. hadn't agreed with her. I picked her up at Kennedy at ten o'clock at night. I wouldn't say she'd lost her looks, but she was kind of haggard, with folds around the eyes I didn't remember and a sort of pulled feeling to the mouth. There were also tiny networks of hairline wrinkles running through her nose and forehead that I didn't remember. I said she looked great.

"I played tennis in the sun a lot," she said. "It aged my face three years."

"Didn't you wear sunscreen?" I was in shock.

"I didn't at first, and then I got all dry feeling, so I did," she said. "But you know, I'm dark skinned, it seemed natural to me."

"But really, baby, you're in the display professions, it's important, you should always wear sunscreen."

"Look, I don't want my career to depend on my looks. That'd be a stupid career. Anyway, my face is bouncing back. It may not really be three years."

"I just got such a shock when you said that."

We were silent for a while. How could she damage herself like that for no reason? Was she out of her mind? It was like trying to hurt our relationship or something. How could she do this to me?

"Will you always wear sunscreen from now on?" I asked.

"I don't want to talk about it, you're getting psychotic," she said.

She stayed over at my house more and more for the next few weeks. I kept two humidifiers going so her skin wouldn't dry out. She wasn't getting much work. I liked having her around, but it was occasionally hard to work because I had to keep up with her alternating fits of fierce optimism and utter despondency. We found we were almost exactly alike in our personalities—self-centered, manic depressive, flaky and flirty, aggressive, hyperactive, given to outbursts of foolish enthusiasm interspersed with long periods of self-loathing. She let me wait on her a lot. It was okay, I kind of enjoyed it. And her parents had basically been in charge of their group in India, so she'd gotten used to being waited on at an early age. I suppose I got the notion that maybe I should fix her face up a little bit sometime during this period, in mid-March, sometime when she was complaining, in her pathetic, plaintive way that was always half playful but partly serious, that she felt shopped out and less than attractive. It sounds sexist, but it was that sort of pathetic quality that really got to me. She was pathetically feminine. She never mentioned the surgery idea herself, but she seemed to mention her looks an awful lot, so much that I wondered if she was hinting at it. She had this way of looking in her compact mirror—I'd bought her a couple of cute Deco compacts out of an auction early in our history because I noticed she took out her compact so often—and putting on lipstick in restaurants and other public places, and she did it with such deliberation and intensity, and such a nineteen-twenties level of coquettishness, that it made you wonder whether she was really such a feminist as she made out in her act. Her act, incidentally, began to focus more than ever on the unfairness of aging and sexist expectations on women and on unreasonable expectations created by the beauty and fitness industries, and occasionally drifted into tirades against pornography and other supposed forms of exploitation, tirades I didn't agree with and which we had hours of fights about. She'd scream and throw things and say I was a sexist pig and generally make me wish I lived somewhere where all the neighbors weren't in the art world and didn't gossip.

Toward the end of March we both felt our relationship was getting to the stage where there would soon be too much damage to continue, and she walked out for a while. We talked on the telephone endlessly anyway. Even after she said she was trying out another boyfriend. I told her to wear a body condom or have herself dipped in latex in case we ever got back together. She said there wasn't any chance of our getting back together, but then she was back, not officially of course, in about another week. I said I wanted to send her out for testing before we slept together again, and she eventually agreed on the condition that I get tested, too, and I said that I already had been four times and that I put on surgical gloves before I even looked at *Hustler* magazine, but she insisted and we both got tested, and we were both okay, always a terrifying and purgative experience in New York in the nineties; I recommend it to everyone. That brought us back together a bit, and she explained, over numerous Vietnamese dinners, that she didn't really like other men as much as she liked me, but that she had trouble staying with one person for very long because she simply had an experimental relationship with the opposite sex.

And it was true that a lot of men seemed to find her irresistible. She wore mainly skimpy low-cut black outfits by Norma Kamali and Michael Kors during this period, and there was something about the way she behaved that was just obviously intentionally provocative, so that absolute strangers three times her age would strike up conversations with her at every opportunity. Usually she didn't mean anything by it, but she had a way of leading men on that would drive them to distraction. We joked about how she had the soul of a gay man: flirtatious, experimental, a self-conscious parody of femininity rather than the real thing, whatever that is. The flirtatiousness carried over into her act, and it had gotten her as far as she had gotten; it didn't quite move her onto the next rung, though, where the big-money acting jobs were. Around this time her career took a bit of a downturn. She got sick a lot, with various systemic things that were never terribly serious but didn't seem to go away, and she had to take all kinds of strong antibiotics and pain-killers and downers and hang around inside for weeks at a time, watching television and canceling gigs. She decided not to go on the road this season, then couldn't get much backing for a new venture in New York. And she didn't want to

keep playing little places like La Mama and the Knitting Factory because that way lies marginalization. So she listlessly only showed up
at the auditions her agent sent her to and hardly ever got anything. I
asked once or twice whether she thought I was a bad influence on
her, and she said no, I was great, she was just going through a sick
period. By April, she had gotten better most of the time but still wasn't
the self-promotional powerhouse she had been. She withdrew from
her friends and read a lot and didn't return phone calls. I made a
couple of short art-related trips to Austria and Germany myself during
this period, so I wasn't really keeping track of her situation, and when
I got back she was sick again.

"I can't stand this for you," I said.

"I'm not thrilled myself. I'm supposed to have a lobotomy next
week."

"What?"

"Actually, it's some kind of nasal surgery. For my sinus thing. But
I just said, great, while you're at it, take that messy brain out, too."

"Maybe you should confine your black humor to the stage and
not spring it unannounced on those who care for you."

"Yeah, yeah," she said in her high, "pathetic" voice.

"Will they go in through the nose or the mouth for the nasal
surgery?" I asked.

"I don't know."

"Are they going to make an external incision?"

"I don't know."

"Jaishree, you have to ask these things. You can't just let doctors
do whatever they want with you, they're dangerous people, they can
kill you. Is it a general anesthetic or local?"

"I'm sorry, I just didn't ask."

Whenever we were out with friends that week, she kept insisting
she was going to have a lobotomy. Calvin thought she was hilarious.
He called me the next day.

"Is this General Schwarzkopf and the Committee for Neocolo-
nialism?" he asked.

"Give me a break." It was all I could think of to say.

"I'll tell you, meeting your mistresses is like taking a walk
through the Michael Rockefeller Wing."

"Thank you."

"How's Lakmé?"

"Who?"

"You know, Lolita Bhagavad-Gita."

"She's fine. What did you think of Jaishree? To use her real name."

"She's a real girly girl. Very feminine."

"I guess that's good."

"It's great, just enjoy her. Have sex with her. But remember, be safe. I'm just Doctor Ruth these days. Be safe.'

"I'll remember," I said.

"Have you ever just pulled up a woman's skirt and fucked her like in the movies?"

"Uh, well, kind of, ah—"

"Hetero life is *so* primeval," he said.

■

The nasal surgery went fairly well. They did go in through the nose and the mouth, and they only needed a local anesthetic with intravenous Valium. They said they'd cleared up a couple of obstructions and that would be it. I stayed with her the whole time, partly because I cared about her and partly because I'm fascinated by real surgery and try to observe it whenever I can. I made a big fuss about getting to be in the operating room with her, and she went along, and finally they said okay.

While I was sitting in the waiting room of this clinic up on Sixty-first Street for what seemed like two whole days, I thought some more about the possibility of doing the procedure on her. On the one hand, I was already beginning to imagine what I would make her look like, and it was an exciting idea to pull out all the stops for her, to do the face I'd always wanted to do for someone who really had the talent to make it work and who I really cared about and everything. But I was sure it would also do weird things to our relationship. She'd be dependent on me in a strange way. She'd go through all the dislocation that comes with the change, and I'd be her only guide. She'd feel that I didn't really like her the way she was. She'd accuse me of spending all this time with her just to set her up for an experiment. And I really did like her the way she was, although I was beginning to recoil violently from her various imperfections and wasn't feeling too sexually attracted toward her lately. And just feeling sorry for her would be the wrong reason to do anything. But did I just feel sorry for her? Not really, I thought. I really just wanted to help.

And it would be a tremendous high. I'd do something for her that would just set the world on fire. And how many people get a second chance? She'd kick with the face I'd give her. She kicked now, except she just didn't have that edge that extreme beauty gives you.

And I wondered, how would I feel about her if I completely changed her face? Could I love my own creation, or could you only really love something that was somehow The Other? Or would I be able to create a face that really *was* her, that would somehow express her personality in a more perfect way?

■

Finally, one Sunday we were just sitting around my house in the afternoon, enjoying the warmth of pretending to be a married couple by reading the *Times* and eating lox and bialys and sun-dried things from Dean & DeLuca, and she said, "My crystal's flashing."

"What do you mean?"

"You know, *Logan's Run*. My crystal's flashing, and it's time for a change."

She was always making references to *Logan's Run*. It was emerging as a really seminal film, in her estimation. For those deprivation cases who haven't seen it, it involves a future society where everything's just perfect until you're thirty, and then this crystal you have on the palm of your hand starts flashing, and you have to give yourself up to jump into this big disintegrator machine.

"You mean you're going to escape from the Zayles Fort Worth Mall with Michael York?" I asked.

"No, I think I'm going to go to graduate school next year."

I was kind of stunned. "What about the performance career and everything?" I asked. "You're just getting off the ground."

"Jamie, I really love doing it, but it's just not happening. It's not going to go anywhere because it's just too rare a thing for it to go anywhere. I'm practically thirty, I'm too old to really hit it, you know that."

"Well, you know, you want to write and direct plays and every-thing."

"Oh, maybe, I don't know, I don't really want to talk about it."

"Anyway, you're not getting older at all."

"People are either twenty-five, forty, or a hundred. And I feel I'm nearing forty."

"But really, Jaishree, sweetheart, your career's important."

"It's important for you, maybe. It makes you feel good to tell everybody that I'm a performer, it's just a male ego-trip thing for you."

"Oh, that's ridiculous. I'm happy with whatever you do."

"Sure."

"Look, if I'm doing something that's really bothering you, I think you ought to tell me about it."

"You're not doing anything, I just think you don't really care about my mind. Much."

"Jeez, that's such a cliché, there are plenty of dumb girls around who I could go out with if I wanted to."

"So go out with them then."

"I'm not sure I can take this particular mood."

We were silent for a while.

"Look, do you really want to be Mr. Chips?" I asked. "You'll be cooped up in Stirling Library with Agatha Frump and Rotunda the Librarian, and you'll be wondering why you're not the toast of New York."

"I'm not the toast of New York now."

"You just need a pushier agent. Something will break next sea-son, and you'll be on top, and you'll wonder what all this was about. The grass is always greener. All those lit-crit twits would give any-thing to be glamorous actresses."

"I don't feel glamorous anymore. And I want to do something more with my mind."

"So write and direct some plays or something."

"It's not the same. And I'm tremendously disaffected with the entertainment industry. It just isn't based on quality or talent. I don't want to deal with it anymore at my age."

"What if you were twelve years younger?"

"What do you mean?"

"Nothing."

"You want to do one of your face jobs on me?"

"I didn't say that."

"You don't like the way I look?"

"I'm crazy about the way you look. *You* don't like the way you look."

"What ever gave you that impression?"

"Nothing. Look, if you want to look ten or fifteen years younger, you're lucky that we can do that. Otherwise, let's not discuss it."

"Let's not discuss it. I find it insulting."

"Fine, I think I'm going to go see that Julia Roberts movie, want to come along?"

"No. And why don't you see it twice while you're at it?"

"I'm sorry if I offended you," I said as I found all my stuff and walked out.

■

I couldn't take the lit-crit grad school thing because I just knew the whole syndrome too well, and as much as I loved literature, it was fundamentally a drag. I knew the whole routine, Ute'd gotten her Ph.D. while I was with her, and it was megally beat. Becoming an academic, the little petty department squabbles, the scrounging around for thesis topics that were obscure enough, the teaching positions at obscure midwestern liberal arts colleges, the faculty dinners, the university press publications, the department politics, the closing-in-on-oneself—I'd just been that road before and couldn't deal with it. I mean, I knew the whole syndrome of being a performer too, but at least it was theoretically more adventurous. It wasn't really much more glamorous, not really, because nothing's glamorous from the inside, but at least you didn't always know exactly what was going to happen next. In academics, even if Jaishree became the next Harold Bloom, she was still essentially going to have every aspect of her life mapped out for her. It was just the kiss of death for our relationship.

Over the next few days, though, I got the feeling that she was thinking about it a little bit—from things she said and asked about little details of the "procedure," from catching her looking through my Before and After books, a hundred different things. It was finally getting truly springlike and even in the heart of Megalopolis there was a faint whiff of new buds and flowers and green growing things and it seemed like a time of new beginnings. She didn't mention graduate school again, but she also didn't make many moves to get her career going. I was distracted by some art business for a while and just let her simmer. I still wasn't sure myself. Then we were in a bookstore and I bought some magazines with Rose on the cover, and we looked at them when we got home, and Jaishree said it was kind of great what I'd done. So out of the blue I said, "Okay, let's just do it."

"Do it?"

"Let's change your face. I'm tired of this whole thing. We can do it, and I know it sounds stupid, but I almost think we're destined to do it."

"I don't know, Jamie," she said—she hardly ever called me Jamie —"of course I've thought some more about it, but I don't know, there's a lot about this stuff we don't know yet. How do you know it won't be like a silicone breast implant?"

"Well, it's inert," I said. "It's not going to react with anything. The protein-polyethylene foam in the PCS is just like another kind of flesh or something, it just sits there, it doesn't migrate. The proteins in the real tissue bond to proteins in the polymer chains. People have been walking around with this stuff in them for six years, so far. And there's no sign of any problem. Mark did a biopsy on our second patient a few months ago and everything was fine."

"Hmmm."

"Maybe I could just turn you into a supermodel. Better than Rose."

"Yeah, right."

"I'm serious. I'm not sure you realize what an advanced process I'm using here. I could rebuild you from the ground up. You know how creative I am. Come on, Wendy, come with me to never-never land, where you'll never ever grow up. . . ."

She said I was crazy, of course. I told her to give the idea a little time to sink in.

"I don't think so, no," she said. "Definitely not."

◾

I worked on a new series of paintings that week. They were more heavily pre-Columbian-based. Jaishree went to the health club a lot, where she went when she really wanted to think. She lifted weights. Another macho gay male affectation. She could bench-press as much as I could. She was definitely ruminating. Her wheels were turning.

A few days later—it was a Friday, and she'd stayed over—she was going out the door and said, "I'm thinking about it."

"About the face thing?"

"Yes."

"You know, I like you the way you are. It should just be what you want."

"Well, I don't know, but it's just an interesting thing to think about."

And she left.

◾

That day I was supposed to meet her at an opening at the Metropolitan Museum at seven. I hadn't known it would be a big deal, but there was a huge crowd outside the museum begging to get in. It was almost like Nell's in the late eighties. These days, they probably just wanted to get free crackers. I was supposed to meet Jaishree at the main entrance, but I didn't see her. I thought she'd be late and went down the steps to the little side entrance to see whether we could get in there if she did show up. It was open, and she was standing next to it.

"Hi. I guess you know about the side entrance," I said.

"Yes."

"You know a lot."

The opening was for a show of new stuff, in which I wasn't included, in the new wing of the Met. The new wing had been designed by Kevin Roche and dubbed "the Roche Motel" by Robert Pincus-Witten. It was a pretty boring building and a pretty boring show, partly because I wasn't in it. No, actually it would have been boring anyway. The real action was on the other side of the museum, around the Temple of Dendur. I bet the ancient Egyptians threw some pretty expensive parties in that temple themselves, but we were definitely giving them a run for their money. You'd think there was no recession, that everyone wasn't moving to Park Slope and keeping whole grains in jars. We ate complicated food and said hello to people, but the band, which was set up right in front of the temple, was really massacring a sort of Kurt Weill medley, so we decided to bag out for a bit. Some guy with silver hair who looked familiar was hanging around the crudités, looking at us.

"Do you recognize that, uh, guy?" I asked.

"No, is he important?"

"I don't know, he looks like somebody who knows somebody, not somebody who is somebody."

"In this city, if you know somebody, you practically are somebody."

Apparently they'd kept the rest of the collection open, too, in case any of us somebodies wanted to wander around. Jaishree and I went out of the Egyptian wing, past the sarcophagi, into the lobby, up the main staircase, past the Tiepolos and through the Rembrandt room into the room with the early Vermeer, the one with the sleeping girl with the widow's peak. It was nice to see the stuff without having to push people aside. It was like being there on a Monday, when you get to go if you're a friend of someone who curates there.

"I'm feeling strange about this surgery thing," Jaishree said, right away. "I think you're just going to do something that won't have anything to do with me at all."

"Well, we're going to collaborate on the design," I said.

"That's not it, it's just the idea of getting designed. It's not natural, it isn't going to be me."

"You mean it's not going to express you, you know, express your personality?"

"No, it won't."

"Well—does the way you look now express your personality? You know, in China, they give kids what they call, um, a 'milk name.' A milk name is what the kid has until he's old enough to choose his own name. And people should be allowed to choose their own names, don't you think?"

She didn't answer, but she sat down on the bench in the middle of the room. There were a couple of old ladies there, too, but I just made the commitment to ignore them, sat down, and went on talking.

"You know, for all I know, the new design's going to express your personality much more. I mean, you were born with your name and your face, and maybe they've *influenced* you, but they don't really *express* you. You've just grown into them. And come on, think of it as an adventure, it's a new thing, you're the first person who'll ever have this experience. Isn't that exciting?"

"All we ever do is talk on benches in museums." She paused for a minute.

"Well . . ."

"And how will I work it out with Paul and my other agents and the unions and everything?"

"You'll work it out."

"Maybe it's just sick. You're sort of sick, you know. And I like my face, for your information. It's not perfect by your stupid male standards, but it's really nice and I got it from my mother and father and they love me."

She was getting a little loud and a little heavy. The old ladies were looking around. I hoped she'd look at them and decide she'd do anything to avoid looking like that.

"Listen, I'm not asking you to do anything. And it's true, I think you have a great natural face. And there are enough people bugging me to do the procedure on them as it is, so we can forget about it anytime."

That stopped her. We got up and went into the next room, the one with the really classic Vermeers, and sat down on the bench in front of *Girl with a Pitcher*.

"How do you think Penny Penn feels about having a plastic face?" she asked.

"I think she feels fine. She's always taken fame with a grain of salt anyway. And she's thinking about her career, making people happy and stuff."

"Maybe she just makes people jealous."

"I don't know, everyone's just so thrilled to go to her movies after a hard day at work."

"How does she feel about not being real?"

"It doesn't matter whether she's real or not. Nothing's real anymore, it's all just a simulacrum."

"Who says that, 'simulacrum,' Baudrillard?"

"Yes. I guess you're an intellectual, too."

"Oh, give me a break. You're such a jerk." She paused. "Well, what does that *mean*, I mean, certainly, there are a lot of fake things around these days—"

"No, it's not just that there are a lot of plastic things around, it's more that we don't have a concept of the real anymore, everything just aspires to some ideal version of something that doesn't actually exist. And those ideal versions are in the realm of the hyperreal, and everything else is just a simulacrum of them.'

"So it's kind of Platonic essences and stuff."

"No, it's much darker, it's that there's no possibility of a real action anymore. It's that self-consciousness has come to such a state that nothing means anything. Everything's a lie, even if it's the truth."

She seemed kind of skeptical, which, God knows, I could understand, but I went on anyway.

"Baudrillard gives the example of how, when some terrorist sets off a bomb, for instance, even if a Leftist group says it did it, you don't know whether the Left really did it, or the Right did it to stir up the public against the Left, or whether the Centrists might have done it in order to discredit all extremists, both the Right and the Left. And it doesn't really matter who did it, because it serves the needs of all of those groups. . . . And everything's like that, you can't say or make anything that's true anymore, everything's just a caricature of itself."

"Ahh-huh . . ."

"So in a way, Penny's just as real with her plastic face as anybody with a real face, because our whole concept of faces is based on simulating an unreal ideal in the first place, and she simulates it better."

"As far as I'm concerned, Baudrillard's one of those people who gives bullshit a bad name."

We were silent for a while. It's corny, but we were both pretty enthralled by the Vermeers. He's a cliché, he's everybody's favorite, but he still really packs a wallop, especially if you just sit in front of one of his paintings and give it time to wash over you.

"For all I know," I said, "your real personality will be a lot more visible to the world if it comes to it through the medium of ideal beauty."

"That sounds great, but what's ideal beauty?"

"Every age has its own different ideal of beauty. And the people who get listened to are the ones who partake of that ideal, and there's nothing you can do about it, you can't single-handedly change the ideal, it's just bound up in the ethos of the era, but if you want your work to get noticed, you'll have to conform to that ideal a bit. There's no objective standard."

"Well, what's the ideal of our time that you're going to turn me into?"

"Well, that's actually a tough question. I've been thinking about it a lot lately. And I guess the ideal of any given time is usually expressed by a couple of models or actresses. In the thirties, I think Garbo was pretty much it, for instance. But what's strange is, the ideal of the time is also kind of invisible. There was a really successful forger named Van Meegeren, who sold a whole bunch of fake Vermeers he'd done to the Nazis, and anyway, he did an early Vermeer *Christ in the House of Mary and Martha,* and he gave Christ a face almost exactly like Garbo's, but nobody noticed it at the time because Garbo was the ideal. She was both the epitome and the ground-zero of beauty. Everything else was measured by her. And that's something I want to get at."

Jaishree said, "Uh-huh."

19

Two more weeks went by. Jaishree went back to L.A. for a couple of days to work out some new representation because her contract with her old agent, who wasn't pushy enough anyway, had run out and she needed better representation. I got the feeling over the phone it wasn't going so well. Then the morning after her third day there, she called and said okay, start getting some sketches together. She must have seen too many fifteen-year-olds around the studio. I felt a real thrill inside. This could really be the beginning of something big. I called David and gave him some urgent requests, and then I had to go out to meet with some curators and dealers about a catalogue project. Then I stopped at New York Central Artist's Supplies and bought a whole bunch of prepared panels. I was too excited to prime surfaces myself. I staggered into Paradise Loft, saw the message light flashing, and indulged in not playing the messages. I moved some paintings around to make a blank place, hung four of the panels up on some masonry nails that were already in the wall, and dragged over the painting cart. I wanted to start before I even looked at a single source. I wondered what essence of beauty had filtered down to me through all the people I'd seen and remembered.

■

The next morning a messenger turned up with a package from David. He'd spent a few days with a camera and tiny tripod at the New York Public Library Photo Archives, and he'd shot seventeen rolls and had them rush-printed at U.S. Color. There was a bill attached for $1,856.32. It's only money, I thought. I dumped them out, and he really had gotten some good head shots, all either full-face or profile, just as I'd specified. Of course, the sizes were different and the lighting was often very different, but I thought the program could probably allow for that. I also noticed, though, that what looked like a full-face shot was often subtly tilted up or down, and so a lot of shots had to be disqualified.

I wanted to do real serious research on the essence of beauty. I already had an interesting file on beauty aberrations—cosmetic adjustments that other cultures (it's only other cultures that seem strange) have used to make people beautiful: bound feet, Ubangi lips, Mayan cross-eyes and receding-forehead-boards, the giraffe women of the Congo, the Long Ears of Easter Island—it all proved that *difference,* and not classicism, is the hidden standard of beauty: things that stand out get remembered. And it has to be different from other groups, but standardized within the given group. But somehow I thought that file wouldn't do for this project. So to supplement David's work I cut the heads out of the full-face shots of the good models from about twenty back issues each of *Vogue, Glamour, Elle,* and the Italian and British *Vogue,* Paris *Vogue* and *Zoom* and *Harpers and Queen* and *Interview* and some modeling agency books. I'd also picked up a few hard-to-get years'-worth of *Stardust,* an Indian film magazine that I got from a place on Twenty-seventh Street, near Shazeen. Lexington in the Twenties is the real Little India. East Sixth Street is mainly for tourists.

There weren't many full-front shots in the *Stardust*s, but I got a few precious ones—two of Sri Devi and one of Rekha, the two most famous Indian actresses, three of Dimple Kapadia, a sort of upstart starlet but really pretty, and one of Smeeta Patil and six of Najma. I also had a few other head shots of Najma and three of Shabana Azmi, another Indian film star, and a few really old Indian glamour shots of actresses I didn't recognize, that David had found. In two of the Azmi shots she looked old, but in the last she looked really alluring. All of these plus the shots of Yasmeen Ghauri from the big magazines ought to give me enough Indian Look to work with, I thought. I resized the images on the Canon 500 laser copier and spread the Western models out first, on huge sheets of foam-core, roughly grouped into genres of facial style and coloration, kind of like my "prep school individuality" piece. When I finally looked at it all—standing on a ladder looking down at a floor filled with faces—I was pretty disappointed. There were some standouts, but none of them really blew me away. Or maybe they all blew me away. Maybe most of the people were just a little too standard, a little too blandly perfect, to be really sexy in a memorable way. Or maybe seeing them all together leveled them out.

Sexy was not the same as beautiful. A lot of the sexy ones weren't beautiful, and a lot of the beautiful ones weren't sexy. Whatever I did would have to be both.

Another thing I noticed, when I looked at a lot of different photos of the same person, was that a face might have three or four different essential aspects, depending on angle and expression and age and other more subtle factors. These aspects were often very different from each other, but there were only those few basic "looks" for each face. And you can see this in Al Hirschfeld's work, for instance. He's got two or three distinct ways to caricature any given celebrity. Fundamental character can be conveyed with only a few lines. It's like the soul of a face. But each face has more than one soul. And the faces with the most souls are the most beautiful.

I'd also taped about sixteen hours or so of MTV the other day, and I fast-forwarded-and-paused through it to the shots with beautiful girls in them. I began to experience beautiful-girl overload for the first time in my life. There were just so many of them, and they were all so great, and some of them were even distinctive. I took some stills off the television with the Scitex and added them to my list. I began to feel like the idea of designing the perfect face was stupid, that I might as well just choose one of the really outstanding faces and go with that. Use an appropriational strategy.

I printed out the "paused" frames from the TV on the 500, through the Scitex hookup, but they came out kind of grainy. I also went back through the magazines and set aside the photos of the models that looked somehow distinctive enough for the trademark face I wanted. I had several pictures of most of them, including a lot out of the model books that Kimura, a friend who's a model at the Dodge Agency, had gotten from Dodge and most of their rival agencies. Too many were in color. Color's so confusing. It wasn't the first time I'd wished you could just switch your eyes to black and white.

I boiled the "distinctive" stack down to about a hundred girls. In a way, any one of them could have been or could become a major star. It's mainly luck, and a bit of talent, and whether that particular face just happens to strike a nerve with the public. You can never tell what the public's going to do. Look how they've gone wild over the sort of Ivy League women, Jodie and Glenn Close and Meryl Streep, and none of them are really glamorous-looking. It just happened that the public went preppy crazy, and they liked actresses that fit that image. In fact, it was almost as though they didn't want beautiful actresses because they wanted people to think that they liked certain actresses because of their acting ability and not because they were beautiful. It's a total Masterpiece Theatre sensibility. The middle class wants you to think they read the best books and see the best movies, and they end up being totally masochistic because those books and movies that they think are good aren't artistic and aren't even entertaining. And anyway, the whole idea of acting is a big fallacy in our society. I don't think acting in films is really about acting, it's not about being convincing. It's about celebrity, it's just about being famous and *pretending* to be convincing. And if you're famous, you can't be convincing. If people wanted their movies to be believable, they'd cast them with unknowns.

It was the same kind of thing in the art world: the least pleasurable stuff is assumed to be the smartest. Thank God it wasn't like that in the fashion world. But still, maybe you could just never tell what would fly. Maybe it was silly to try.

Finally I got the nerve up to try Mark's software. The composite-imaging thing actually has a long history that Mark didn't know about. There's a computer artist named Nancy Burson who's done composite portraits by superimposing, for instance, frontal shots of Nixon, Stalin, Mao, Reagan, and Gorbachev to arrive at the portrait of the archetypical dictator. Some of her things are pretty neat. And there was a piece in *Vanity Fair* in the thirties where they did the same thing with the ten top male and female stars of the time. I dug up the article out of an anthology I had, and the composite woman was quite beautiful—a little hazy because of all the superimpositions but still a clearly new thing—but she wasn't exactly *memorable*. She did look very thirties—more round and doelike than the composites those surgeons in California had come up with. But I thought that maybe if I were careful to stick to similar genres of people, I could arrive at some good superimpositions that would give me the proportions I wanted.

I booted up the disk—it said PRIVATE PROPERTY NOT TO BE DUPLICATED OR CIRCULATED UNDER PENALTY OF LAW—and punched HELP. A schematized face came out on the screen, in green lines, and then it said LOAD FROM SCANNER. The first thing was to figure out how to get all the full-face shots the exact same size. It turned out you could just feed them into the scanner, and it would automatically plug them into this standard-size matrix, which was pretty handy. Then you had to line up the eyes and mouth and central axis of the face on this little diagram with two dots, a vertical line, and a little line crossing that. There were also ten "mapping points": It said MAP POINT ONE: MOVE ARROW TO CORNER OF EYE AS SHOWN ON ICON. PRESS ENTER. The "icon" was a little schematized head in the corner of the screen with an arrow pointing to the left corner of its left eye, and you had to use your mouse to line up another arrow with the left corner of the left eye of the scanned photograph. It wasn't too difficult, although you had to compromise a bit in terms of whether the eyes or the mouth would correspond exactly to the diagram. I wondered whether Chuck Close, the painter, had this gadget. It could do his work for him in a second.

HELP said, ENTER # TO MIX.

I thought I'd do a really composite one, so I typed in 20. I hadn't punched in the names of all the models, but I decided to start with some I recognized, and I led off with Karen Alexander, the way those doctors in *Vogue* had. Then I called up the picture of Paulina Poriskova and superimposed it on Karen Alexander. Paulina's head was a bit bigger, and I didn't know how to work all the real intricacies of the program, so I scaled it down manually with the mouse. I got it to what I thought was the same size and typed in MIX-PREVIEW. The disk drive thought for a minute, and then this great transracial image came up on the screen. The program was great, because instead of just superimposing translucent pictures on top of one another, the way you would with real photographs, it arrived at a digital mean among all the characteristics of the two faces. You could see the faces change, kind of like the melding faces in the Michael Jackson *Black and White* video: a vertical wipe went across the screen and scanned the alterations onto the existing face. It wiped across once, very slowly, and left a strange, incomplete cross, but then the wipe went over it again, much faster, and left a very slick-looking composite. Some of the time it looked funny or lumpy because of differences in lighting, and I had to switch into the manual-override mode and alter some stuff by hand—or with the mouse, actually. But I arrived at a pretty great face. I wondered whether it would interface with the colorization program that was already on the hard drive. There are so many things to deal with in computers. I went back into the image files—it actually took almost a minute or so for each face to come up on the screen—and I mixed in Whitney Houston and Shari Belafonte. I was going to mix in Cindy Crawford, but then her eyes started bugging me, so I used Christie Turlington's. Christie Turlington's eyes are just so much better than Cindy Crawford's. Cindy Crawford's eyes look human, like mine. They're little and flat and they have wrinkles around them. But Christie's eyes are absolutely *ethereal*. I mixed in a shot of my friend Kimura, even though she wasn't really the type I was after. The composite woman was still a little white-looking, so I punched in Najma, the Indian singer. She didn't affect it much, so I mixed her in a few more times, and the image got better and more exotic. I mixed in Dimple Kapadia twice, and she helped a little. She was more Western looking, but Indian women definitely have a certain sensual quality about the way they look that's very hard to describe. I only had one space left, so I called up Karen Alexander again and punched her in. She didn't affect it much.

I printed out a hard copy. Somehow you believe in things more when they're in hard copy, even if they're duller than a TV screen. My Mechanical Bride was a great face, but there wasn't anything unbelievable about it; it might belong to any young perfect model with a trace of Indian ancestry. It wasn't necessarily going to set the world on fire. In a way, Ariane alone was almost better than my composite. Well, it's nothing I can't handle, I thought. I was still pretty excited about the gadget. I typed RESET and started on another composite. This time I called up Najma first and added two Arianes to her. It was much better. I mixed in Paulina again, but it was a mistake, and I had to add another couple of Najmas and Arianes to get rid of her influence. The face was good, very feminine-looking. Maybe too feminine. Just for the hell of it, I found a head-on photo of myself and mixed that in, too. It was an interesting effect, you just saw a hint of my personality in the mix, so subtle you'd probably miss it. But I was arriving at some sort of *Über*-person, a synthesis of many, kind of an Oversoul.

The four composite prints I finally got out of the scanner and pinned up on the homosote wall came out beautiful, but a little bland. Oddly enough, although I'd separated them from one another by the facial types I was aiming for, and I'd tried to make them all different, the composites looked fairly similar to each other. Without the particularity of an individual, the abstract elements of a face—eyes, nose, mouth, chin, and hairline—tend to become mechanical elements without an apparent animating force. I began to feel that maybe an appropriative strategy was not going to work for this particular project. I was going to have to be more creative. I hate being creative when I can steal something, but I'll do it if I have to. I also began to feel that instead of working from the perfect beauties, the empty-headed techno-mannequins from the land of the slicks, maybe I should look to the real icons. The babes of the screen. And the babes of the canvas. We needed something that looked much more primal, more basic, more vital, not like some fifteen-year-old twit from Helsinki in a Kenzo shirt.

Maybe it was a total waste of time trying to design a definitive face. Maybe there was no such a thing. Maybe, I thought, the problem was that I was thinking "definitive." Maybe I should think "evocative." Maybe I should let myself be *really* creative, do something really strange, and just give it a try. Run it up the flagpole and see whether anybody salutes it. And I was definitely looking for inspiration in the wrong places. There'd always be a million nearly perfect-looking models around, and some of them would rise to the top just by the luck of the draw. But maybe I should think sexy, think of a face that Jaishree could use to sex her way to the top, the way Marilyn did. Something unique, something stylistically right for the mid-nineties. But timeless, too.

At least I had something to work toward. I wasn't just sitting around the loft wondering what new-looking *tchachke* I could manu-facture. Jamie had *purpose*.

I looked through my movie books and magazines and loose files marking pages for a stack of photos of the sexiest women of all. Going backward in time.

Different faces had obsessed me at different times. For a while a year or two ago, I'd been seeing the face of Linda Evangelista every-where, and it would sneak up on me out of the back of my mind when I wasn't expecting it, an abstract sort of mental caricature of the essence of her look, that sort of elfin sharpness, that kind of fifties-indigestible mean-looking downward strike of her eyebrows. Like a beautiful little demon crouching in the corners of my vision. But now I hardly ever thought about her.

Madonna. Catherine Deneuve. Marilyn Monroe, of course, but was she really beautiful or just sexy? Anita Ekberg was more classi-cally beautiful, but she somehow didn't have the soul that Marilyn had. Elizabeth Taylor, too, wasn't so much perfectly beautiful as somehow sexy in a womanly way, even when she was fifteen in *National Velvet*. The young Veronica Lake was incredible, but Lauren Bacall was somehow sexier, more knowing. There's something about looking *knowing* that's very sexy. Maybe it's the "I've got a secret" trick that actors use. There was mystery there, too. The old stars were so much more amazing than the new ones. The real love goddesses of the screen were gone, or at least relegated to soap operas. People can't take amazing beauty in a major star anymore. At least not in a female star. People are just too wise and self-conscious to believe in it. Most big stars today are just interesting-looking, at best. But Jaishree would bring the love goddess back. She had enough obvious talent to convince anyone. And the chain reaction of fame would start, and everyone would believe that she was just a freak of nature.

I was thinking of picking out twenty or so of the best faces of all time and just shooting them into the scanner with the video camera—even though that would make them more grainy than cutting them out and feeding them in directly—but when I got up to turn on the camera, I realized how tired I was. I was too tired to sleep, so I took a BuSpar and a half a Valium and pulled out my notebook and a copy of Theodor Adorno's *Aesthetic Theory* out of the shelf and sprawled on the couch. It was another thing I hadn't looked at since John

Hollander turned me on to it at Yale, but something had reminded me of it. I flipped through it. Sure enough, there were a couple pretty apropos things. I copied them down, they were so good. Maybe they'd been dormant in the back of my mind for a long time:

> The dreadful powers understood as the compulsion that ema-
> nates from form are lodged in the midst of beauty itself. The
> concept of blinding glare (*das Blendende*) articulates this ex-
> perience. The irresistibility of the beautiful, originating in the
> sphere of sexuality and passing into art through sublimation,
> rests on the purity of beauty, its distance from materiality and
> effect. . . . The affinity of all art with death is most noticeable
> in the idea of pure form imposed on art by the living manifold,
> which is thus snuffed out. . . . Art's ultimate function, then, is
> to grieve for the sacrifice it makes, which is the self-sacrifice of
> art in a state of helplessness.

He didn't know what it was really like, of course, the way I did. But in his austere German way, he did get a lot of the main issues across. I flipped around the chapter on beauty:

> Contrary to what Hegel thought, the beautiful in nature is close
> to the truth, except that at the moment of greatest proximity it
> beclouds itself anew.

Yes, hard to pin down, that's for sure. He didn't know the half of it, though.

> The drift is that art aims at realizing the articulation of the non-
> human by human means. Pure expression in art works, freed
> of all interfering factors including the so-called stuff of nature,
> converges with nature.

Well, that was what I was trying to do, all right, converge with nature, but it wasn't like I could get a formula for how to do it out of any of this stuff. I sort of staggered into bed. It was getting blue outside, with purple clouds. Beclouds Itself Anew, I thought.

20

The next morning, Jaishree came back from California and I took a plaster cast of her face. If I was going to rebuild her as drastically as I wanted, I was going to have to have a perfect idea of what I was working with. I wouldn't be able to change the position of her eyes, nostrils, or mouth. Everything else I could play around with, and I could even get Mark to help me remove some flesh surgically if I wanted to dig in anywhere, like hollow her cheeks out a bit, for instance. Just looking at her, I didn't think too much flesh was going to have to come off. She had kind of a small face that would leave me some room for a lot of creativity. And her big, kind of googly eyes were going to come in handy, I thought. They wouldn't be googly when I got through with them. I'd fill in around them, and especially under them, and make them heavy-lidded and mysterious. They'd be huge and beautiful and doelike. "Whoso list to hunt, I know where is an hind,' as Sir Thomas Wyatt said. I think.

The couch was covered with a white cotton dropcloth. The floor under the couch had blue plastic all over it. There was a table with five half-full buckets of water, a box of surgical gloves, and a big bucket of pure white powder.

"Is that plaster?" she asked.

"You sound a little alarmed, dear. People pay George Segal to cover them in plaster."

George Segal was an artist who did plaster casts of people.

"Fine," she said. "I love being covered with plaster."

I could have made a synthetic moulage cast or something, but I wanted to do the cast the old-fashioned way, even though it took longer to use plaster than it did to use some of the new waxy plastic compound things. This was dental plaster, the kind they use for taking casts of teeth, and the level of detail it picked up was amazing. And it didn't warp or sag or shrink at all, it gave you a perfect reproduction. I didn't want to deal with a wobbly sheet of plastic, I wanted the exact position of her features. I had her lie down on the couch and gave her a Valium and put her hair in a bathing cap and started constructing a shim line out of thin pieces of plastic down the center of her face. She squirmed a bit when I put on the putty-glue.

"Don't worry, it's just putty, it comes right off," I said.

"I'm a very ticklish person," she said.

A shim line is what keeps the two halves of a plaster cast apart. You have to do it at the highest point, at what they call the axis of bilateral symmetry, because plaster's not flexible and can't travel around a bump. So when you're doing life masks you always have to put the shim line right down the middle. Finally the line of blue plastic shims ran down her neck, over her lips and right along the middle of her nose, all the way over her hair to the occipital bone at the back of her skull. It looked like some surrealist costume, drawing an enlarged version of her profile in the air.

"Please don't try to talk at this stage, or I'll have to redo the mouth," I said. "Just grunt if you have trouble breathing through your nose."

She grunted, but I didn't think she was serious. I started mixing plaster. Mixing plaster is a feeling like nothing else. You have to have done it to know what it feels like. And you just have to work with plaster awhile, and get to understand its rhythm, to be able to do it. Basically, plaster has about a fifteen-to-twenty-minute life cycle. It doesn't dry, it hardens, getting pretty warm as the chemical reactions take place, so it goes through all these stages, from milk to mayonnaise to rock, and you just have to match what you're doing to the proper stage. For the first coat on something you want to reproduce exactly, like a face for instance, you do a spatter coat.

I sprinkled the plaster powder around on top of one of the

buckets of water with my dry hand and mixed it with my left. You kind of strew it in order to get it all through the water, with no lumps. You can tell when the mixture has absorbed as much of the powder as it can take, because the powder stops sinking into the water and just floats on top. As soon as this happened, I gave the milky-textured stuff a last swirl, pulled the glove off my dry hand, and said, "Okay, I'm going to put a straw in your nose, all right? Don't say anything."

I got my other glove off and picked up the straw. It had some soft earplug wax around the end. I put that into her left nostril, mushed the wax around to make a seal, and bent up the accordion-pleated straw so it jutted out at a good angle. I didn't have time to put on another glove, so I just dipped my right hand into the bucket of plaster and started to spatter it onto her face by flicking my fingers. It made pure white clear-edged little circles on her dark skin, like bleach spots on a sheet of leather. She winced a bit.

"Please don't wince," I said. "Relax your eyes."

Finally, her head was totally covered in plaster. She looked really strange, and you would have thought she was dead, except you could see her chest rise and fall. I knew she was uncomfortable from the heat of the setting plaster, but it's best to wait until it's actually cooling down to take it off, even though it seems hard. So I cleaned up and let her sit for a while. She probably thought I'd forgotten about her, but she couldn't say anything. After a few minutes I told her it was almost over and I inserted some thin chisels into the shim line. I wiggled them around and finally the halves started to separate. I pulled on the left side—it was difficult because of the suction—but finally it came off into my hands with a sucking sound. It was odd, seeing her with half a face and the other half covered by a white shell. When I finally got the other half off, she was pretty mad.

"Sorry. That was the most unpleasant part of the entire procedure," I said.

She just glared at me to indicate she didn't believe me. I brushed the two halves of the mold very carefully with sealer while she went to wash her face and comb the bits of plaster out of the edges of her hair. I was already mixing more plaster to make positives out of the new mold. It's great to be an artist, you always have something to do with your hands.

■

Bernini said that marble sculpture has to accentuate and caricature because if you just coated someone's face with whiteface, you'd barely be able to recognize her. It was true. The white plaster positives of Jaishree's head, when I finally dug them out of the negative plaster mold, didn't look anything like her. And even worse, the whiteness accentuated all her skin irregularities and pores and acne and crud, so she really looked hideous. It was just as well she'd gotten bored watching me and left. I mounted the masks on four Styrofoam wig stands that I'd gotten in her size and smoothed some plaster over the backs, so they looked like real heads. It was eerie, a row of four white goblins with closed eyes. But they had all the information I needed; the eyes, lips and nostrils were in the right place. I turned a blow dryer on the first one for a while until it was totally dry. There was a horrible mess all over the studio, but I started getting out my plasticene clay and pressing it onto the cast anyway. I worked until midnight. I only took a couple of phone calls. I remembered that Virginia Feiden was on Letterman that night, and she was one of my best jobs, and I hadn't seen her for at least a year, so I turned it on. It took him a while to get through Penn and Teller, but after the third commercial break she came on, very grand, in a strapless turquoise Kamali-looking dress with side slit, and the audience was really hooting and everything, and she looked great. She sat down, and they switched to a closeup.

"So I understand your movie's coming out on Friday?" Dave said.

"Yes, it's called *Demon Spawn VI,* and it's a kind of comedy-horror takeoff on movies like *The Exorcist* and *Aliens* and like that."

Somehow, she seemed a little stiff. She wasn't using her face in quite so mobile a way as she used to, I thought.

"So do you get eaten by monsters and all that sort of thing?" Dave asked.

She laughed, and a new closer camera angle came on. She was wearing a *lot* of makeup. I wondered why she didn't just trust the color of the face I'd done for her? I'd better get a look at her and make sure everything's all right, I thought. It was kind of a stiff laugh she was doing. I turned it off. Letterman's getting so self-indulgent lately, it's hard to watch him.

21

The next day, I got another package from David. It was a batch of color laser Xeroxes of beautiful women from painting and sculpture through the ages and in all cultures. It was an unbelievable set. It would have made a great art book. I went through and picked out the best ones, laying them out in patterns on the studio floor. They weren't for mixing on the computer, they were just for inspiration. I already had the positives of the heads I'd mixed pinned to the walls. There was also a row of views of the demon-head, the alien-looking 3-D being I'd generated on my industrial design/animation program. It was haunting and beautiful, but somehow too frightening. Too much the Queen of the Vampires.

I padded around between the rows of faces. Madame X. The Mona Lisa. The Madonna of the Misericordia by Piero della Francesca. Six Raphael Madonnas. Three Leonardo Madonnas. Venus by Bronzino. Venus by Scopas—I should copy the eyes from that one a bit, I thought. Two Madonnas by Pontormo, also with great eyes. Very round eyes, with something imploring about them. Eurydice by Poussin. A Madonna by Poussin. Vermeer's Dutch girls. Whistler's model in a kimono. Rossetti's Lilith, the dead Elizabeth Siddal, the heavy-featured pre-Raphaelite vampire. Nefertiti. Empress Li-Lan. Princess Senouie of the Upper Kingdom of Egypt. Prajapati from Kajuraho. The Queen of Ethiopia.

I put the stack next to the "movie goddess" stack. It had most of the obvious ones. Madonna. Elizabeth Taylor. Marilyn Monroe. Joan Crawford, Marlene Dietrich, and Bette Davis, who were all in the same category, as far as I was concerned—distinctive and perfect for black and white but kind of harsh and indigestible. Ingrid Bergman. Penny Penn and Virginia Feiden, of course. Ann-Margret, the young Vanessa Redgrave, and Brigitte Bardot. Lauren Bacall and Veronica Lake. Veronica Lake was really one of the best, but she was too harsh-looking for Jaishree. She knew something, though, with that mysterious hair. Mystery is very important. Nita Naldi. Louise Brooks. Gene Tierney. Jodie Foster. Virginia Madsen. Rita Hayworth. Anita Ekberg. Alice Faye and Marion Davies. Lauren Hutton. Grace Kelly, especially. Most were the type you admired, and some, like Marilyn, were the kind you instantly, instinctively fell in love with. Of course, that was the kind I needed to understand.

I spread them all out next to the "models" exhibit. My beautiful old floor was completely covered, and there was no room to walk. I took off my karate slippers and padded around in socks on top of the photographs, thinking. It was a beautiful day outside, but I was soaking it up through the light in the room anyway. And I was in the presence of so much beauty, maybe more at one time than anybody had put together before. It had the feeling of new terrain even though it was composed entirely of familiar images. Somehow, the very best pictures of the very sexiest ones, Madonna, Marilyn, Elizabeth Taylor, and Nita Naldi, had something in common with the stack of the most beautiful women from the world of painting, from the days before movies. I started moving certain images from the south end of the loft toward the north end, near the windows. This would be the "top of the stack."

In the "painting" category, the *Mona Lisa* was on top, but other than her and Madame X—who was disqualified in a way because she wasn't actually a beautiful face, just the most elegant thing ever—the best were all Madonnas. And wasn't the *Mona Lisa* really a Madonna, too? They all had the same look in their eyes. And that mysterious smile. A look that maybe Marilyn had the most, out of all the star pictures. It was heavy-lidded, it was dreamlike, it was somehow beatific, it was knowing—it was really the look of the Madonna, the old Madonna. It was maternal.

It went back further than the Madonna. It went through Venus to the primal fertility goddess. The faces on the Hindu temples at Kajuraho had that mysterious smile of ecstasy that Marilyn and Mona had, too. They were all more Venuses than Aphrodites. The Karen Alexanders and Brooke Shieldses and Penelope Trees of the world were Aphrodites. But only the Marilyns drove people mad.

Madonna. Marilyn Monroe. Mona Lisa. It's no accident that the names of the three sexiest women ever begin with M. Of course, M represents breasts. And it stands for MMM-MMMM good. In fact, when Pepsi did its blind taste-test thing against Coke, they put Pepsi in a glass labeled M because it's the most "positive reaction" letter in English, so they say. They put Coke in glasses labeled Q because Q stands for *queasy* and *queer*. Everyone thought Pepsi tasted better because they all just love the letter M. And M also stands for *mystery*. And it stands for *money*. But it's really M for *Mom*. Their mystery is in their motherliness. It's the first thing we love. And there's always something mysterious about your mother. She's always bathed in awe, no matter how you feel about her as a person. It runs very deep. There's something girlish and sexy about Marilyn, but what distinguishes her from the other screen beauties, what makes her *hors de concours,* and what still drives people so crazy about her, so that her fame keeps growing and growing forever, is something maternal about her, something very warm but also dark and mysterious in her smile, La Vierge Sous-Terre beneath the platinum, the catacombs under Chartres Cathedral, and it's no wonder men—and women—go crazy over her because she represents that primal incestuous moment at the heart of being. Men want to be taken care of by her. And Madonna, of course—she's come close to reincarnating her. Madonna's obsessed with Marilyn. But Madonna goes deeper, because she's the new Madonna. "When you call my name, it's like a little prayer." Of course it is, when your name is Madonna. Just being named that did something to her. And now she has that look of the archetypal mother as well. Like a virgin. Which means, like the Virgin. And again, her dark hair slowly revealed itself to us beneath the blond shell. She has such a look of beatitude now, like a real Madonna. And the Mona Lisa: she is dark, of course, right on the surface. But she's darker inside. Pater said she had been dead many times, "like the Vampire, and learned the secrets of the grave." She knows some secret, of course. And she is a Madonna. But it's a secret about us, because she is really our mother, with a mother's knowing smile. And like they say, she looks like Leonardo himself. But not because she is his self-portrait, like they say, but because she is his mother. It's very primal. It goes back to the sea itself, to when our ancestors lived in the womb of the sea. Marilyn—Mona—Madonna—Maria: *mare, la mer,* the sea. Ave Maria, *la Reine de la Mer.*

Maybe Jaishree would have to have a new name beginning with M. And she would have to have that look in her eyes, the timeless mystery look of the universal mother. And she'd have it perfectly. She would be the essence and culmination of ten thousand years of the symbol, beyond the Venus of Willendorf, back to the sea itself. And for the first time, everyone on earth would know the symbol. Because now it was possible. Practically everyone on earth recognized Michael Jackson and Ronald McDonald, so it would take only a little more press than usual for them to recognize her. And she'd bring the world together. Just one universal thing, and maybe it would really be a force for peace. It sounds corny, but I was really rolling on the idea. She'd be a kind of one-girl We Are the World. She Are the World. She'd get into politics, as a kind of guiding hand. Everyone would be so crazy about her, they wouldn't want to fight each other. And her look would last for a long time. She'd take on the radiance of immortality. But she'd be accessible, real people would actually see her, because for once, she'd be as perfect in the flesh as in the images on the screen. She would be the greatest work of art ever, the first true artwork in a living medium. She'd be a Mona Lisa for the twenty-first century. The Mona Lisa isn't so big because it's a great painting, but because it's a great image. It's a great face. I'd do an even better face. My little craft in my little studio would usher in an era of world peace. And what was her name going to be?

She'd just have one name. It had to be a distinctive M-name. I switched on my Toshiba and started typing all the feminine M-names I could think of. I wondered if there was a database of names somewhere that I could search. Mona. Mari. Mara. Marissa. Moira. Marisol. Mandy. Masha. Minnie. Melody. Mindy. Mabel. Maggie. Millie. Molly. May. Maleficent. Malacai. Muriel. Missy. Mar. Maniera. Madeline. Mahasti. Magda. Marina. Manisha. That was a good one, since it was an Indian name. Malloria. Milana. Mireille.

Out of all of them, Madeline, Mahasti, and Manisha didn't look so bad. Mahasti was an Iranian name. It was exotic but a little harsh. Madeline sounded exotic, but in a French sort of way. I did kind of like it because of an allusion: it was the code name for Noor Inyat Khan, an Indian princess who worked undercover for the Allies in Paris in World War II. She was quite a character, she also wrote children's books. It's one of the most romantic stories of the war: She was parachuted into France, captured by the Gestapo, and escaped, and even after all her contacts in the Resistance were captured and she was cut off from any support, she continued to broadcast information out of Paris until she was captured and killed in a concentration camp, a few weeks after D-Day. But I didn't think many other people would know that. Mireille was good, but it was French in a hard-to-pronounce sort of way. Manisha is an Urdu name meaning "heart's desire." It sounds like an exotic older form of Maria. It was good, but too hard for Americans to pronounce. But it had the right nationality if we were going to keep playing up the Indian angle. I started trying to think of other Indian names beginning with M. Then I remembered there was an Urdu form of Manisha. Minaz. *Minaz*. It sounded absolutely perfect. Ancient but techy, too. The Antique Future.

And stressing the India thing would be perfect. She'd represent the Third World, but the older, more sophisticated Third World, and she'd be as ethnic as a white person can be, so people from real racist areas could still deal with her. Like the white-looking black girls who are so big right now, Lisa Bonet and Neneh Cherry and Whitney Houston and Jasmine Guy. Except she'd be bigger. Something different. It's the new hot ethnic group. With Mira Nair's films getting so big, a really big Indian star would be absolutely sure-fire. I'd make her sexier than Marilyn—a Venus, fertility goddess, a timeless incarnation of the essence of Woman for the twenty-first century.

I got out my plasticene clay, thinking about that look in the eyes.

22

Four identical pure white plaster Jaishrees stared at me in a row. They sat on identical sculpture stands in front of a wall covered with drawings, photos, and CGIs. It was midnight.

I know a commercial sculptor who made the original positives for the Cabbage Patch Kids doll heads, and other doll heads and toy action figures like Rambo with the kung-fu grip, and she taught me about working with oil clay, or plasticene. It comes in a lot of different degrees of hardness, and of course the hardest is the most precise and the most difficult to work with. I used a mixture of different hardnesses for different parts of the head. They're all the same cream color. Around the eyes, where I worked very close to the actual plaster cast underlying the plasticene, carving with tiny tools, I used the hardest kind. I used the softer clay on the chin and cheeks, where I could move things around a lot more. Where I felt she could actually use a little less flesh, I chipped away the plaster with an electric chisel, but I didn't have to do that very often. Jaishree had big eyes and a little face, and I figured I'd be able to do whatever I wanted to do above the surface of her actual face without decreasing the relative size of her eyes significantly. I pressed some oil clay onto three of the four casts, and then I worked on one for the rest of the time. I wanted to have a few going simultaneously so I could make different decisions and tries without tearing down things I'd done before. After a while I looked at a clock and realized I'd been working for six hours without stopping. It was a great feeling.

Doing the clay thing made me think about Irvin Kienner, my sculpture teacher at Yale. He was really great. He was a huge Austrian bearlike man with incredibly strong arms and a bad limp. His leg had been hit by shrapnel in World War II. He'd been drafted into the Luftwaffe and was in a training camp that was destroyed by an American daylight bombing run during the last few days of the war. Oddly enough, my other sculpture teacher at the school, David Lutz, had been a bomb-sight operator in one of the B-29s that were on that same bombing run. They didn't meet until they got to Yale in the seventies. Irvin was a real Bauhaus type, terrific at abstract constructions, wonderful at talking about the tensions operating in models of crystals or in the gigantic self-supporting helixes he used to make out of two-by-fours, but he was also great at figurative sculpture. His own figuration was a little austere, a little smooth and muscular and *Übermensch*-looking, and he also did this series of giant vultures that really looked like Nazi eagles, but he wasn't a Nazi, he was the sweetest person in the world. I was the absolute star of the figurative sculpture class for a couple of years. I never sculpted when the model was in the room. I'd just do drawings, a very simple style of contour line drawing, from every conceivable angle, from very far away or from very close up, never in the middle of the room. And then, some night when nobody else was around the studio, I'd come in and bend around one of the biggest armatures to the right position and throw a whole lot of clay on it, and within a half hour I'd have a great rough study of the figure, already way better than most people's, and then I'd just make the outlines correspond to my drawings, which were all over the wall, and by morning I'd have this terrific figure sculpture, huge, with a really "resolved surface," and I'd unveil it at the next class and everybody would rave about it, and that was it. It was a perfect method. It was so much fun. That was around the time I took a few pre-med classes, too, so maybe I had a vague idea of this cosmetic surgery thing even then.

I was happier with my art in college than I've ever been since. I was naïve. I knew about contemporary art, but I was obsessed with figurative painting and sculpture and thought I could give it a meaningful place in the art of today. But when I got to graduate school at the School of Visual Arts in New York, I realized it couldn't have the place I thought. For a while I was hopeful for it because of Clemente and Chia and Fischl, and they were bringing it back to some extent, but then I realized that what they were about and what made them interesting weren't the things that I loved about figurative art; the things I loved about it were the precision of beauty creation, and I just couldn't find a place for it in the stylistic progression of art history. So I expressed my concerns about beauty and time and death in other ways, more abstract ways.

But I always remembered my really retro undergraduate sculpture period as a kind of innocent pastoral era in my life, when I was just *obsessed*. Kind of like the sculptor in the great Balzac story "Sarrasine," when he finds the perfect model, an opera singer, and obsesses over her, and then he kidnaps her and finds out she's really a *castrato*. It was funny, but I associated that story with that period in my life, not because of the sculpture thing but because the story was used in a book we read at Yale for comp lit, the Barthes book *S/Z*. It's kind of a textbook of deconstruction. I thought I might still have it and went into the study area of the loft and found it and got my notebook. It was getting blue with rain outside. I switched on a light and found the part in the story—which is printed as an appendix in the back of the Barthes book—where he sees the singer for the first time:

> At that instant he marveled at the ideal beauty he had hitherto sought in life, seeking in one often unworthy model the roundness of a perfect leg; in another, the curve of a breast; in another, white shoulders; finally taking some girl's neck, some woman's hands, and some child's smooth knees, without having ever encountered under the cold Parisian sky the rich, sweet creations of ancient Greece. . . .
>
> The artist never wearied of admiring the inimitable grace with which the arms were attached to the torso, the marvelous roundness of the neck, the harmonious lines drawn by the eyebrows, the nose, and the perfect oval of the face, the purity of its vivid contours and the effect of the thick, curved lashes which lined her heavy and voluptuous eyelids. This was more than a woman, this was a masterpiece! In this unhoped-for creation could be found a love to enrapture any man, and

beauties worthy of satisfying a critic. With his eyes, Sarrasine devoured Pygmalion's statue, come down from its pedestal.

I skipped to the part where he finds out her horrible secret:

"What a joke!" Sarrasine cried. "Do you think you can deceive an artist's eye? Haven't I spent ten days devouring, scrutinizing, admiring your perfection? Only a woman could have this round, soft arm, these elegant curves. Oh, you want compliments."

She smiled at him sadly, and raising her eyes heavenward, she murmured: "Fatal Beauty!"

Then he finally realizes it's true, she's a eunuch.

Then he gets killed. I went back to the beginning of the book, Barthes's classic deconstruction of the Balzac text, and looked up what he had to say about it:

Beauty (unlike ugliness) cannot really be explained: In each part of the body it stands out, repeats itself, but it does not describe itself. Like a god (and as empty), it can only say: *I am what I am*. The discourse, then, can do no more than assert the perfection of each detail and refer "the remainder" to the code underlying all beauty: Art. . . .

According to Sarrasine, the perfect statue would have been an envelope containing a real woman (supposing she herself were a *masterpiece*), whose essence as reality would have verified, guaranteed the marble skin applied to her (this relation, in the opposite direction, gives us the Pygmalion myth: a real woman is born from the statue).

It's true that only a make-believe woman could really represent all Woman. It's just too much for one girl.

23

I invited Calvin in to see what I had been doing so far. He was one of my very few friends who was in on my whole project. I didn't worry about him much because I knew him from way back and he was into some pretty shady stuff himself with all the weird nightclub and art deals he did. He was also really smart about art. It felt strange doing a studio visit not about my paintings but about something that I was going to create on a ground of living flesh. But I needed to get away from solipsism. Isolation can be good for an artist because it lets you get to new levels of imagination. You need to divorce yourself from the world a bit. But I was also in the business of communication, especially with this face, and it wouldn't do to get it all done and think it was the greatest thing I'd ever seen on the planet and then find out that everyone else considered it rather ordinary. And that can happen. It's called *amour propre*, love of one's own, *Chef-d'Oeuvre Inconnu* syndrome. You can get so bound up in your own issues, formal issues that are internally generated by the sculpture itself, that there's no conduit open between the work and real life. Art has to be an alternative to real life, but it can't be completely closed to it. It's hard to describe.

Calvin came in wearing a big green duffel coat from Banana Republic.

"How are you?" I asked.

"Va bene."

"You look great," I said. I hadn't seen him for weeks. His shoulders were bulging.

"Thanks, I'm going to Radu every day now."

"I can tell." Radu was the gym of the moment.

"I'm really competitive about my looks lately. I can't wait to walk into the next ACT UP meeting."

"It's a competitive scene."

"I know, and I'm really working it, it's the tail end of my youth, and I want to ride it for all I can get out of it. I'm going for major bulk," he said, hanging up his coat and revealing a SILENCE = DEATH T-shirt over a lot of muscle definition.

"It's really all about beef now, isn't it," I asked.

"Yeah, beef, and also abs. A really flat abdomen's harder to get than beef. It's the final frontier. People with a flat stomach just slice through life. You should really work out more. Except I guess women aren't as picky about male bodies as men."

"No, they want sensitivity."

"How tiresome."

I offered him coffee and cookies, but he said he was mainly eating salads and powdered proteins.

"What's your Gravitron level now?" I asked.

"Sixteen."

"Yeah, sure." I'd barely made it to level nine the one time I'd tried the machine, and I'd nearly gotten a hernia doing that.

"Are you *jaloux* of my Gravitron level?" he asked.

"I'm already losing sleep over it."

"So anyway, what are you working on?"

"Well . . . come up to the lab—and see what's on the slab," I said.

We walked into the studio, and I pulled the veil off the best head.

"Is that the final version?" he asked.

"Yep. There's my Last Duchess," I said.

He didn't say anything for a while. Then he said, "It's totally different. And I think it's going to be very powerful."

I was more interested in how he behaved than what he said. From the way it seemed as if he couldn't take his eyes off the head, I thought I was doing all right.

I unveiled the others.

"They're just the most holy things I've ever seen," he said. "Is Jaishree going to be able to handle it?"

"I think so."

"She'll kill with this look."

"You mean that?"

"*Sérieusement,* they're absolutely triumphant. I have no helpful criticism at all."

"That's okay, it's a help anyway."

"I help you by just living."

■

I did some other preparatory things over the weekend. I felt Minaz would have to be associated with clothing in particular colors, especially dark emerald green and a sort of ultramarine-blue-lavender-purple that I had only one swatch of but my designer friend, Bellina, said she'd have copied at her factory. Minaz also had to have a special scent, which would be based mainly on sandalwood to point up the Indian theme, and a kind of haunting exotic-sounding theme music that would follow her around as much as possible. My friend Al who does mixing for Madonna came up with a really good track for me in exchange for some art. It sounded like a cross between Annan Shankar and Enigma. I wanted him to retape it in a loop so it could go on for at least four hours without a repetition.

And Romeo, my hairdresser, and I were working on a special hairstyle. It had to be *à la* the old Bo Derek *"10"* look with the beads, something copyable but really distinctive. So far it was a kind of knotted braid thing with peacock feathers. Starting a fashion trend is very good business.

Monday was a really good day. I didn't go out at all. What got to me more than anything else was my growing realization that I was pushing a limit. There was a certain level of beauty beyond which things just became fuzzy and indefinite. Apart from all the symmetry and smoothness and everything else beauty has to have, it has to annex mystery, there has to be undefinability in it. But working toward that, especially with a single, opaque sculptural material like plasticene, was like reaching for a wall of fog.

One of the main things would be to leave her open for a lot of possible makeup changes, so she would be able to change her look drastically, the way Joan Crawford did and Madonna does. But unlike them, she wouldn't have to grow old.

It's better to suggest than to be specific. You really needed very little to suggest extreme beauty, just a few lines, really. As a child, some of the images of women I fell in love with the most were just line drawings in illustrated fantasy books. And the real girls I fell instantly in love with the most were always the ones who were half-glimpsed, on the other side of the street at twilight or driving past me in cars, and I suppose if I had gotten closer to them, the magic would have vanished. And the most desirable girls you see today are on video, where they're always moving and seen through a watery grid of pixels and completely inaccessible. And to fix this shifting effect in clay was impossible.

But this was going to be one of the strangest faces ever. It really was abstract. All the time I'd put in as an abstract artist was paying off in this figurative project. I was working on such a basic level, with the basic sign of human existence. What was it about eyes, nose, and mouth that was so important? Eyes, nose, and mouth are some sort of basic metaphor for the structure of the universe—or did I say this before?

I felt I was going to be the last artist to relive that experience that Balzac was talking about, the experience of creating ideal facial beauty, in a meaningful way. I was going to be Leo, Mike, and Raph for the last time. I was the first to do what they did, in a twentieth-century way. A twenty-first-century way. Suddenly there was a reason for all the beauty lore I had internalized for so long and had then realized had no place in the art of the present. I'd made it a place.

It was getting late, but I was a regular Sarrasine. By now, I was sleeping mainly in the studio. I couldn't bother to walk the twenty-nine steps to my boudoir area. Anyway, during these last few days, I didn't want to admit to myself that I was going to sleep, I always thought I just wanted to lie down for a little while. I lived on garlic chicken from Empire Szechuan. I wouldn't even order in Microwave Lean Cuisines from the grocery because they required too much preparation.

Night was falling again, and I could tell from the color that it was going to be cold outside. I wasn't going outside, though, I was going to see this thing through. I felt like the cliché of the obsessed artist.

And I hadn't shown the final design to anyone. Calvin was going to be the only studio visit before the design was executed on flesh. I was like the hero in the other Balzac art story, *"Le Chef-d'Oeuvre Inconnu."* He's a famous nineteenth-century painter who works for years on his greatest painting and never shows it to anyone, and when he does show it, it's just a huge meaningless jumble of lines, and everyone's horrified. They didn't have abstraction then, of course. It was all a cliché, I thought for the twentieth time, the obsessed artist. But on the other hand, I was in a kind of happy state that I'd actually found something to obsess about. It was exciting. And I wasn't just making a jumble of crud. I was getting close. The head was taking shape and approaching something very primal. I'm getting there, I thought, as I lay down and looked at the last one of my row of heads. I was getting to that primal mystery thing, and the less the head looked like any real living human that I could think of, and the more it resembled some kind of sphinx, the closer I was getting to it.

Maybe I was getting maudlin and pretentious in my isolation, but I pulled out my Oscar Wilde anthology.

When they asked Phidias what model he'd used for the head of Zeus, he said he used a line from the *Iliad* about Zeus shaking his hyacinthine locks. That's how I felt. I felt I'd gotten to the point where looking at other visual sources wasn't going to help. I had to get inspired on the basis of ineffable things like poetry.

In a dim corner of my room for longer than my fancy thinks
A beautiful and silent Sphinx has watched me through the shifting gloom.
Inviolate and immobile she does not rise, she does not stir,
For silver moons are naught to her and naught to her the suns that reel.

Definitely the effect I was after, I thought. This whole thing was really about time. The Face had to exist outside of time, but still be human. I looked at it again. There was something too perfect about it. It needed a flaw. Something subtle, but a flaw. A sign of mortality.

A mole.

Of course. What would Marilyn or Madonna or Cindy Crawford be without their moles? Nothing, I thought. Or a lot less. It's interesting that moles are called "beauty marks." What was it about them that made them so alluring? Are they like a sign that you can approach the goddess?

I spent a long time composing its position, but I finally decided the black spot would go nearly a centimeter above the left corner of her lip. A hair off to the left. The abstract element would round out her effect. It would make her unique and human and sexy and some-how pathetic. Because a mole is an intimation of death.

24

When you're by yourself in a house and you don't go out, you focus on your books a lot more. It was great. I hadn't read anything but magazines for years. I found the line from Plato, in the *Lysis* dialogue, that was kind of the ancestor of a lot of beauty theory. Socrates says:

> Beauty is certainly a soft, smooth, slippery thing, and therefore of a nature which easily slips in and permeates our souls.

I read a lot of Baudelaire. He had a darker take on the issue. He was good on the cruelty of beauty:

> *Je suis belle, ô mortels! comme un rêve de pierre,*
> *Et mon sein, où chacun s'est meurtri tour à tour,*
> *Est fait pour inspirer au poète un amour*
> *Eternel et muet ainsi que la matière.*
>
> *Car j'ai, pour fasciner ces dociles amants,*
> *Des purs miroirs qui font toutes choses plus belles:*
> *Mes yeux, mes larges yeux aux clartés éternelles!*

> I am beautiful, mortals, as a dream in stone,
> My breasts kill each man in his turn, and they
> Were made to inspire in every poet his own
> Great love, as silent and eternal as clay.

Because, to fascinate my love-slaves, I
Have mirrors which make every object bright:
My eyes, my giant eyes' eternal light!

The eyes thing again. Eyes really were the seat of beauty. Like the Elizabeth Taylor thing. Eyes, large eyes, doelike eyes, eyes are so weird, they don't look like anything else to do with bodies or fleshiness or anything, they're round and abstract, and they come in strange colors, white and black and green. What was so magical about large eyes? Maybe eyes are just magical in general and bigger eyes are more magical. Of course, bigger eyes make you look younger. But they're also the windows of the soul, you know, so when you have big eyes, you're intimate with everyone, because they can see into your soul. I'd been reading too much.

I drew some eye designs in color for a whole day, ordered in pizza at ten in the evening, and went to bed at three. Over the next couple of days, I narrowed the heads I was working on from three to two, and on Friday, I narrowed them down to one. People called me and wanted me to go out, but I said I was sick. I spent about five hours Friday night on the design of the epicanthic folds around the eyes, and then one hour, in a fit of inspiration, in elongating the entire head. I used a slightly cubist approach to the sculpting, so that she wouldn't just be smooth and doll-like but slightly faceted. And it was elements of the facetization that would make her completely unlike any other human. It's hard to describe in words, but I designed the *planes* of her face to be in different places from the planes in other people's faces. I simplified the flow a lot. But it was very subtle because all that structure was veiled behind a layer of smoothness. You'd have to be a figurative sculptor or a plastic surgeon to notice it. Around four, still dressed, I fell asleep.

■

When I looked at what I had done the night before in the morning light, I felt I was really getting somewhere. The face was less human-looking. It reminded me of something, but I didn't know what, and then I remembered Lika. She was a painting student I'd been crazy about during a summer painting program in Skowhegan, Maine, when I was a sophomore. I'd done about fifty portraits of her.

They were all put away somewhere in my parents' barn up in Great Barrington, Massachusetts. But I remembered what it was about her that I could never quite get, and that kept me doing portrait after portrait: there was something too long about her face, the proportions were off somehow, but she was still incredibly beautiful. There was something wistful and strange about her, like the tune "Greensleeves." She was purely gorgeous, but somehow not so cliché-perfect that she'd be left out of the "serious actress" category. It was a distinctively ethnic face with a strange slant to it that fascinated.

I remembered a sunset I'd seen with Lika from the roof of the Art and Architecture Building at Yale. It was all ultramarine blue and magenta, and the faux-Gothic towers glowed like pyramids covered with gold leaf, and Lika wore primarily purple and magenta, but she had emerald green eyes. It was right after the Mount St. Helens eruption, and it was the most spectacular sunset anyone could remember. She looked like Helen of Troy with burning cities behind her.

■

I did a separate head of Lika from memory. It took hours and hours. I wished I had done what Leonardo da Vinci did and come up with numbered codes for all the different types of features and their variations, so I could remember any face from just a set of numbers. But I got close to her. I looked at the other three heads I had done, the first one done from scratch, which was pretty blobby now, and the second two, which were mainly synthesized up from composites done on the computer. After a while I decided what we really needed was to plug the features from the second composite into the proportions of the Lika head.

Since there was always the chance that I would create something that wouldn't photograph the way it looked, I kept snapping shots of the designs in all possible lights and altering the heads more in terms of the photographs than in regard to the way they looked in real life. I was glad that I'd worked a bit in modeling agencies and fashion photographers' studios when I'd first come to New York. People don't realize how unforgiving the beauty industry is. There's very little room for anything less than mind-boggling. Only one in a thousand of the beautiful girls who want to be models can actually be models. And the people at the agencies can tell in about a half a

second whether a girl has a chance or not. Luckily the acceptable
ethnic range of models had expanded a lot in recent years and there
was a little more give in the system, so I felt I could be creative. The
modeling business was becoming more like acting: distinctive offbeat
looks could be promoted to stardom if they seemed to strike a chord.

■

There's a kind of a plane running from the outside corner of the
eye down to the corner of the mouth, and I made that plane almost
flat in my model, with just a hint of curvature to it. It gave the face a
sort of "beauty overload." I think there's a point in a painting or
sculpture, just before it gets too busy, when everything is articulated
together and the accumulated articulations go just over the edge of
comprehension, over the point when the viewer can take them in all
at once, and that's the point of aesthetic critical mass, when the real
beauty happens, when there's a chain reaction of effects that expands
into a symphonic complexity out of a finite number of decisions. And
this plane did it for the final head.

I was elated, like I was on Xtasy. Imagine having the power to
give people a second chance. To give them almost eternal youth. I
could turn straw into gold. Something out of nothing. I could give
beauty, fame, money, power—it was incredible. It was as though I
were Ponce de León and I had discovered the Fountain of Youth. I
was a god. And I was immortal, I was a shape-changer. A werewolf, a
vampire, a skin-switcher. I could be anything I wanted to be, anyone
at all.

25

The face was always present now. When I closed my eyes, it looked back at me nearly as clearly as if I were looking directly at the sculpture or the screen. If you look at anything quite a bit during the course of the day—a painting you're working on, or just bunches of blueberries, if you're in the country and you've been picking blueberries for hours—images of it tend to repeat themselves in front of your eyes when you're tired and about to sleep. But this was a little bit more radical than that.

The effect of the face was inhuman, almost geometric or robotic, with a hint of the computer-generated demon-face, but also somehow warm. A mass of contradictions. And I just had to hope that the warmth factor would be increased to a human level when Jaishree animated the face with her expressions. It would be a cold face for print but warm for film and video. That was the best combination.

■

After two more days, I felt I couldn't take it any farther. I kept covering it and uncovering it, and looking at it in the mirror, and every time I saw it fresh, I gasped.

The final version was long and oval-faced, almost egglike, definitely a little too perfect and a little alien-looking, but otherwise what would be the point of doing the project at all?

The eyes were a combination of Mysterious Asian and Wide

Doelike Hebrew/Indian/Egyptian. But they were more than that, they were too geometric for human eyes. They were almost perfect wide ovals with very heavy round lids. They were something no one had ever seen before. But there was a maternal look in them. It was totally otherworldly, but had an essence of something very affectionate and cozy. I shouldn't really praise my own work so much, but I put a lot into it, it worked out amazingly well, and I think I deserve a little credit.

The next thing was to cast this plasticene version in plaster again. Then I'd work on the coloration. I canceled all my appointments for the next week and mentally scheduled the Minaz Project for exactly a week away. There were a couple of dinners I was going to regret missing, but there was nothing I couldn't reschedule except a visit to Jaishree's parents on Thursday.

I made four plaster casts from the original positive. Over the next few days, I spent quite a bit of time playing around with my paints and the four identical heads, thinking about coloration. Of course, I could just do a standard dark color and change it any way I wanted with makeup later, but I wouldn't trust makeup people once she was out of my hands, and anyway, part of the beauty of my technique is that the subjects don't have to wear much makeup. And they don't look as if they're wearing makeup. In one shot, I can do all the eye shadow, contouring, lip colors, and everything that women have been doing every day for centuries. For the Minaz eyes I did a more subtle variation on Garbo's makeup. When she'd first done it, it was a revolutionary adaptation of a stage-makeup effect: her eyes were widened and extended by dark corners on the lower lids. My version was difficult to do, but it was undetectable and would last forever.

Ideally, she wouldn't wear *any* makeup, not even base. I wanted to get a really distinctive permanent skin coloration. Something with a real glow. But since she was going to be somewhat dark and exotic, it would have to be a sunset glow. I remembered when I was a kid learning to paint, how many times I used to drag my painting box and sheets of Masonite and a huge steel easel down to the beach on Martha's Vineyard after dinner to try to capture that sunset glow. I was obsessed with Poussin at that time because I thought he had done it better than any other painter. And yet nobody seemed to recognize what a colorist he was but me. Even people who liked

Poussin would talk about his composition, but not his color. Or if they did talk about it, they'd just say it was waxy, dark, and artificial. But he was the only painter to come close to the experience of completely saturated dark orange light that I experienced at sunset. Actually, in a couple of paintings Bonnard tried the same thing. But Poussin seemed to have had the exact, identical experience I had. I thought it was just the most beautiful thing in the world—not looking at the sunset, but looking away from it, at the sand and the grassy bank and the dark green trees with the tiny white houses showing through, and the red cedar roofs of the houses, all these colors completely changed to double-nature colors, colors that were themselves but were also shot through with a huge component of saturated golden red, and behind that, on stormy days when the setting sun would slide out from under the rain clouds, the darkest, richest purple-blue anyone had ever imagined.

I tried to approach Minaz's face more as a landscape than as a portrait. Her color should make people think of the magic days from their childhood when everything was bright and new, but also incredibly old and full of dark secrets. Everyone would look at her and think of home, and mother, and mystery. So she'd be dark, rather unusually reddish, and with a sort of golden sheen over her skin. Her outlined lips—Jaishree's Indian lips were naturally outlined, and I kept that idea while changing their shape—would glow out of her like dying coals. Her hair and eyebrows and lashes, of course, would remain pure black, and we might just rinse in an iridescent wash of dark blue, for the rain clouds. I spent all Thursday up at Mark's lab, on the telephone with a cosmetics technician, designing a small round plastic wafer of color for the iris of her eyes, which we'd have to get fabricated and then sandwiched into special contact lenses. It would be a lenticular color, printed by computer in stripes under a layer of clear microscopic triangular ridges, a bit like the kind they use in 3-D postcards. It would flicker from one color to another with the tiniest movement, from a green somewhere between emerald and turquoise to a strange lavender, almost magenta. When the colors in the sample we came up with were visible together, it was like looking into a melting opal. She'd really be the girl with kaleidoscope eyes. Two days later, I got the prototypes back from the optics lab and laminated them into the final painted plaster cast. I didn't want to show it to anybody, but it really did suggest a landscape to me. She was like the side of a smooth cliff, with dark hanging gardens falling over the crest, lit by the light from the burning cities, with twin caves that, defying gravity, tunneled into the precipice, giving you a glimpse of green and lilac pools.

26

That night Jaishree and I went out in my van, which I hardly ever use, to visit her family in Jackson Heights.

"So what have you decided about telling them about the face thing?" I asked.

"I don't know, I have problems with my family, but I don't want to hurt them, I don't want them to think I'm just dead. I mean, it's the same thing with my friends, it's a real problem. I want to go ahead with this, and I have confidence in your work, but I can't lose all my friends."

"I don't know, there's not really any solution."

"Well, we'd better think of a solution," she said, "because otherwise you're not going to be able to do this. I mean, you can get any number of ugly girls without any friends and turn them into dumb supermodels, but I'm a talented person, and I have a support structure already. I don't like the way I'm getting to look, I'm totally sick of it, but we have to come up with a way for me to keep a lot of my friends. I think we should do the car accident story."

"Listen, I'm sorry, but for the hundredth time, if we do the car accident story, eventually people will find out it wasn't true, and they'll know you're faking something. You can't just make up a car accident, even if you do go away to India or somewhere, even if you stay away for a year, someone will figure out it's not true."

She was quiet for a minute. We finally got over the Fifty-ninth Street bridge and turned left onto Northern Boulevard. It was getting dark.

"What's it going to be like not to be able to talk to my friends? No one's going to recognize me. It'll be like dying "

"Well, it'll be an adventure," I said. "But if you're satisfied with the way things are going now, don't do it."

"No, I'm not satisfied with the way things are going now. Of course I don't like seeing idiots without any talent get ahead of me just because they look better. It's crushing, in fact, okay?"

"Okay."

"But I still don't know what to do, it's still going to be very strange. Take a left on Ninety-ninth Avenue."

"Yes, it'll be strange," I said. "You'll be one of the first people ever to have this experience. It'll be kind of like being blind all your life and then getting your sight restored."

"Or the other way around."

"Yeah."

"So what have you got designed for me?

"Something really good. Maybe you should take a look."

"I don't know."

■

Her parents and little brother were really nice to me. The apartment was pretty small, one floor of a row house on some street off of Northern Boulevard. There was a large, probably occasionally violent father, a silent, shy diminutive mother in a sari, and a juvenile-delinquent little brother. The house was Western-style Long Island suburban with clear plastic over the furniture. There were little Krishna and Siva dolls around, and a lenticular 3-D picture of Sai Baba, some nineteenth-century Hindu saint. They were a little suspicious but tremendously hospitable, like all Indians, and they fed me all kinds of *samosas* and *pakoras* and authentic Sindhi home-cooked mega-spicy goat-meat things that I'd never had. The father talked about how rich his family had been before the Partition, in 1948, and how they'd been lucky to get out of Lahore and across the border into India alive. He also told me about how once he had actually witnessed the Rope Trick, how the magician's boy had run up the rope, and the magician had run up after him and chopped him into bloody bits, and then had put all the cut-up body parts into a basket, and the boy had come out whole. The mother, who didn't speak English, kept telling Jaishree to feed me more and saying Jaishree was too thin. She spoke only Sindhi, so I couldn't understand. I tried some Urdu out on the father, though, and he was impressed even though I was messing up. They ate dinner late, and we didn't get back to Jaishree's apartment until after two. She started getting ready to go to bed. She seemed pretty upset, and I wondered if she wanted me to stay over, but I didn't want to. I liked her a lot, of course, but that evening I didn't have any particular sexy feelings toward her.

"It's amazing that you got out of that environment and became a hip downtown creative personality," I said.

"Well, you know, it was because of Jeff." Jeff had been an acting teacher of hers at Queens College when she was an undergraduate, and she started going out with him right after he gave her an A. He was kind of connected and had moved her into some performance-art circles. The next year she'd somehow managed to transfer to Yale.

"He really dicked me over, though," she said. "He was a pathological liar. He was sleeping with two other girls at the time. I freaked out, and I'm still picking up the pieces."

She got into bed. "I'm pretty scared and upset," she said. There was a little bit of a tear in her left eye, and it made her look so young and pathetic, it nearly broke my heart.

"Try not to think of anything but how smooth you're going to look."

"What's so great about smooth? Is that all there is to life, trying to be smooth?"

"Well, I don't know, smooth's kind of a key thing. Smooth is everything. Sorry, I didn't mean to be flip. But yeah—it's sad, but if you're not smooth, you're just not considered attractive, no matter how great you are in every other way, you know. . . ."

"It's really just sexist bullshit, you know," she said.

I had the light on and I was looking through the Former Ivy League Lit Major section of her bookcase. The Harvard Classics. Chaucer to Gray. Collins to Fitzgerald. Edmund Burke.

"Calm down for a minute. Okay? Could I read something to you while you go to sleep? It's not exactly a bedtime story."

She didn't answer.

"It's from *On the Sublime and the Beautiful*. Okay? 'Section Fourteen—Smoothness.'"

She seemed to have stopped crying.

> The next property constantly observable in such objects is *smoothness:* a quality so essential to beauty, that I do not now recollect anything beautiful that is not smooth. In trees and flowers, smooth leaves are beautiful; smooth slopes of earth in gardens; smooth streams in the landscape; smooth coats of birds and beasts in animal beauties; in fine women, smooth skins; and in several sorts of ornamental furniture, smooth and polished surfaces. A very considerable part of the effect of beauty is owing to this quality; indeed the most considerable. For, take any beautiful object, and give it a broken and rugged surface; and however well formed it may be in other respects, it pleases no longer.

She whimpered a bit, but I was kind of proud of myself for finding the right passage nine years after John Hollander read it to us in class. "Isn't that great?" I asked. She wasn't asleep, I think, but she wouldn't answer.

■

When I got home, Jaishree called and said she didn't want to do the procedure and I should find someone else. I didn't say anything, I just said "That's okay" and said good night, because if I begged her to do it, it would just alienate her more, and if I said I thought she was right, she'd know I was using reverse psychology. I'd kind of expected something like this at the last minute. Still, I got pretty depressed. I could do the procedure on somebody else. I could use a version of the design. But I'd designed the Miraz head for her. And for her talent, too. With her talent, she'd just kill with that face. I took one and a half Valia and went to bed, but I was still too tired and depressed to sleep. I lay down on the couch. It was a huge couch covered with a clean rough canvas drop cloth, and it had one of my favorite big pillows on it, and that comforted me a bit. I could hear the telephone ringing and people I didn't want to see leaving messages. I fell in and out of sleep, many times. The sunlight hit the outside of the closed Venetian blinds at noon and then went away, and the glow behind the blinds turned purple, then blue, and then the black and orange of the night and the sodium lights. I must have been lying here for over fourteen hours, I finally thought. But I was in deep depression and didn't want to get up for another fourteen hours at least. I thought maybe I should read something, but then I figured it would just depress me to see that someone else was doing something interesting when I wasn't doing anything at all. The same thing with television and all media in general. Maybe if I could find a historical work written by a boring person about poor unfortunates getting killed, *that* wouldn't depress me. But I didn't think I had anything like that around the house.

27

The next day I had an errand to run, picking up some small versions of my signature frame at my fabricator's girlfriend's apartment, and I was trying to keep my mind off the Jaishree thing, and on the way back I passed New Video on La Guardia Place and wandered in. Something leaped out at me from the "Classics" rack: *The Bride of Frankenstein*. I couldn't face anything, I didn't want to do anything all day, so I thought, I'm only dead once, I'll watch some flicks. I ended up renting *The Bride of Frankenstein, The Bride, Seconds, The Island of Lost Souls, Dark Passage, Johnny Handsome, The Island of Dr. Moreau, The Fly* (the remake), *Darkman, The Phantom of the Opera* (the original), *Death Becomes Her,* and *Batman* I figured I might as well confront my problems in a roundabout way instead of trying to escape. On the way home I bought a half a pound of whitefish salad and some creamed herring and bagels from Russ and Daughters. Jewish soul food. I was pretty depressed. I got home, turned the phone ringer off, and curled up around the screen, in my private escape-from-reality chamber.

I watched *Seconds* first. It was one of the best. It's about someone who gets his face changed and turns into Rock Hudson. I'd seen *Phantom, The Fly,* and *Batman* before, but I wanted to check out the Horrible Face scenes. They were all presented as unmaskings, except that The Fly, Jeff Goldblum, had a pretty yucky face already and Geena Davis just kind of pushed it off to reveal the supposedly even more horrible but actually kind of E.T.-cute fly face underneath. I wondered whether if I showed some of the scenes to Jaishree, she'd change her mind again and decide to go through with it.

Dark Passage was great. The first part's all shot in first-person point of view, of a prisoner escaping from San Quentin, and then he gets his face changed and he's Humphrey Bogart. In a way, it was a better strategy than using two actors, the way they did in *Seconds,* because you were always really aware in *Seconds* that it was two actors. *Johnny Handsome* was kind of the same type of thing, except in the late eighties with Mickey Rourke, and he had a horrible face to start with and then he becomes a criminal after he gets his face done. It didn't make too much sense, though—you'd think he'd just be so happy to get good-looking, he'd never do anything bad. It was already seven o'clock, but I was into a whole day of spacing out, watching VCR. I heated some frozen tortellini, and the only thing I had left to make sauce for it was garlic, oil, and anchovies. A great TV snack. When I got back, the machine had finished rewinding the Mickey Rourke thing, and I wanted even more escape, so I popped in *The Island of Lost Souls.* It was really, really terrific. It could almost replace *Barbarella* as my favorite B film. It's an H. G. Wells story about a mad scientist, Charles Laughton, who makes people-shaped creatures out of the flesh of different animals, and he's got a tiger-man, and a pig-man, and a bear-and-gorilla man. It's a little dated because now we know there are a lot of complications with stuff like that, but it's a great fantasy. Maybe I'd expand my own practice in a similar direction sometime, I thought. How about an art form that would be more closely based on medicine, something that involves anesthesia and pain and bloodletting and weird drugs and hallucinogens and crazy grafts and senseless transplants. . . . Of course, I guess that's kind of what the ancient Maya were into. It's one reason I'm so crazy about them.

I ran out of movies around midnight. I switched to regular cable and watched ads. There was an Egoiste perfume ad with a lot of models screaming out of windows in a hotel, and Rose was one of them. She was by far the most beautiful, and I hadn't put one-tenth as much into her design as I had into Minaz. And it was all a waste. Fuck, damn, shit. I punched my thigh a few times.

I flicked the channel to MTV. *House of Style* was on. It's a special fashion feature they do, with Cindy Crawford as the host. Surprise, they were going to have Naomi Wolf, my old classmate and author of *The Beauty Myth*—the great mega-feminist tract of 1991—scream at Camille Paglia and other luminaries about how images of beauty oppress women. I could hardly wait. I ran and got some Dove Bars for video snacking. By mistake I'd bought some with the crunchy nut sprinkles on the outside. I hate that kind, I only like the smooth ones. Nuts are like eating wood. I found three smoothies and threw out the rest and curled up again in my Media Center.

I fanned out the magazines on the coffee table. All of them from 1993. Great covers. Linda Evangelista, Nikki, Kimura, Julia Roberts, Yasmeen Ghauri, Claudia Schiffer. If beauty was so problematic now, they had a funny way of showing it.

But the Sincere Decade was right about one thing. Garish makeup was out. Whatever I did—if I ever did anything again, if I didn't just give up—would have to be so natural-looking and also so perfect, it would make makeup obsolete. And the other good thing about the nineties was the multiplicity of looks out there. Ethnic, boyish, pouty, stern—the whole catalogue. It wasn't like when you didn't look exactly like Jean Shrimpton you were ugly. And really, that had opened up a lot. It made room for artistic creativity. The Minaz Design was very far out, almost nonhuman, but I knew I could still get away with it. It was weird, almost abstract, but paradoxically it would be closer to the Universal Essence of Beauty than a more average, generalized face could be.

On the TV, Naomi was telling Helen Gurley Brown that she was a traitor to her sex. Naomi had balls, all right And she had some points. It's true that most beauty products don't work and that women are unfairly forced to spend forever making themselves look sexy but not too sexy, and all that stuff. But at the heart of her book, there's a conviction that beauty is totally culturally determined. And I don't know if I can buy that. I think there are biological buttons. Culture has a lot to do with it, of course. But culture has a lot to do with everything. What can you do, get rid of culture? Change it so that it doesn't determine anything? Then it becomes a nonculture.

Anyway, there's more to Beauty. Part of it's culturally deter-mined, and that part anyone can draw and any good model can imitate. But there's also something undefined, something that can never be expressed in words, a demonic/angelic ghost inside, that only a few women ever have.

I guess I'm more interested in working the culture toward its potentialities. I want to make anything possible. Why settle for less just because less is natural? Computers aren't natural. Television isn't natural. Should we give them up? Ultimately technology always becomes a good thing. I want my work to help people. It's just that pioneers are always misunderstood. Or am I sounding too much like the Mad Scientist? Well, Vincent Price always was one of my very favorite actors.

■

I was trying to avoid thinking about it all day, but seeing Naomi's gig made me go into the studio and uncover my final version of Minaz. It really made me sad. I couldn't use it on anybody else; I really cared about Jaishree, and it was specific to her. Lost beauty, I kept thinking. It was four-thirty in the morning. I turned everything off and saw the light blinking on my machine and couldn't resist listening to the messages. The last one was from Jaishree. "I've changed my mind. I'll be over at three tomorrow to start the procedure." Click. There was a tremendous flood of relief through my entire body, as if I'd just thrown up something that was making me sick. I felt light and excited and tired and just staggered into bed.

■

When she came over, everything was absolutely spotless, everything was laid out, there was a perfectly white sheet on the "lounge chair," and there was a golden glow outside, diffusing through the Venetian blinds and layering all the tools with a gauzy-looking rose color that made them look ancient and perfect. I asked whether she wanted to see the final design for the head, and she said no, she'd trust me, she probably wouldn't like anything I'd do because it wouldn't be her, and so I might as well go ahead with whatever I thought was best. That surprised me a bit. She saw the design in reverse, though: I'd left the plastic mold I'd made from the final design lying out on one of the tables, covered with one sheet of clear plastic. You couldn't tell much from it. I was going to check to see that everything was in the right place, that I hadn't made any miscalculations—although I knew I hadn't—and then press the PCS into the mold, sand her face and remove some of the flesh, and finally bring the molded PCS down onto her face like a very delicate mask. Then I'd work on her some more, directly, because I knew there would be a few things I'd want to change.

I'd stocked the fridge with easy-to-eat Indian foods like *dhal* and *kurmas,* and I had all of her favorite tapes in a row in front of the machine. The video camera was running, but David and Mark weren't coming in. I wanted to do this one solo I'd have to do a little structural work myself, taking out a little cartilage. I'd never done it before, but I'd seen Mark do it enough times. I might send her out for work on her teeth later. In the meantime we'd cap them. I had clay ready to take an impression of her teeth at their current state so I could get the caps made even before her bandages came off.

David was supposed to call every two hours to make sure things were going well. I'd be working for a long time, I thought. I hoped David wouldn't fall asleep toward the end. But I knew it would be all right. I had some amphetamines to keep me going if it dragged out, but I'd done twenty-hour operations before without chemical help.

I gave Jaishree ten milligrams of Valium and helped her onto the couch. She said she didn't want any music, but I asked if I could put on some old canons and she said okay. She was wearing a really comfortable-looking yellow Indian pajama-outfit. I arranged some sheets around her so I wouldn't be distracted and pulled her hair back and wrapped it up. She seemed pretty relaxed. I looked around to make sure everything was ready. I changed into the cotton karate outfit I wear to work in and pulled on my surgical gloves. The sun was getting low outside. For inspiration, I'd pinned a blown-up Xeroxed text from my notebook to the wall, next to all the drawings and digitalized mixes and the photographs of the finished model—which I sometimes found easier to work from than the model itself, the way it's easier to do sculpture from drawings—and right above the checklist for the operation, which went all the way from washing the original skin to bandaging the finished product.

I padded down her face with disinfectant and picked up the dentist's drill with the sanding brush. I couldn't believe it. We were going ahead! We were actually going to do it! I was practically jumping up and down, but I managed to focus the energy into my hands. I felt like a Maya priest, standing on top of a red-and-blue-and-black pyramid, at sunset, surrounded by thousands of supplicants, holding an obsidian sacrificial knife over a perfect nude body tied onto the stone altar with gold-plated thongs:

"Lord of Blood, Sun Lord, God of the Smoking Mirror, Maker of the Blue-Green Plate, Maker of the Blue-Green Bowl, I offer you this gift and the best of my skills on this holy day 12 Lord 18 Death in the year 12.19.0.2.0. nineteen years before this sun is destroyed and the new cycle of life begins, in the memory of the ancient Kings, that they are not forgotten in these last days."

PART TWO

THE LAYED GOD

28

The following Friday afternoon, Penny Penn was supposed to come over to make her final payment. I had the receipt all written out for three paintings. I had to give her at least three, or they wouldn't be at all plausible as covers for what she was really buying. She was still paying me much more than the market value of my work. But I'd just have to say, if I ever got audited, that they were old pieces with sentimental value that I hadn't wanted to part with, but she'd wanted them anyway and paid an outrageous price for them. Art's a terrific laundering tool, and a lot of money does get laundered through the art trade, but that's also why I was afraid the IRS might think I was a drug dealer or something. I'd been living pretty large for the last few years—the payments and maintenance on my loft alone were about as much as the gross national product of Bolivia—and so I had to report quite a bit of income, though I didn't report it all. Last year, I'd reported about two-thirds. The other third was stashed away. About a hundred and ten thousand was in cash and Canadian gold coins in a safe-deposit box in Connecticut, just in case I ever got into real trouble. It was wasteful to lose all that interest, but I consoled myself by repeating that it was really the cautious thing to do. The rest was in antiques and old art that I'd bought anonymously. I had no idea at all what it was all worth. I had a pretty good-size storage bin in Williamsburg filled with Lalique paperweights and Ruhlman tables and Beaux-Arts cast-iron garden sculptures and boxes full of Bakelite plastic bracelets from the thirties, and so far I'd done pretty well on them. You take a big hit on antiques right after you buy them, but I'd bought pretty well, and, since the crash of course, the stuff was going up all the time. I also had a couple of safe-deposit boxes for the postage stamps and the rare editions—I had three complete sets of a privately printed deluxe fifteen-volume set of Burton's translation of the *Arabian Nights,* which I had no idea of the value of—and another box in a bonded art-storage warehouse on the West Side where I kept the big-name art I'd been able to collect. But art is much harder to buy anonymously. I had a small Yves Klein *Anthropometry* (a body-print painting), a couple of really early Ross Bleckners, three early Warhol shoes and a small Warhol *Marilyn* in pink and silver, a four-by-six-foot Peter Halley that luckily came apart into two pieces, a complete edition of five photographs of Lisa Lyons by Robert Mapplethorpe, photographs of Orson Welles, Mary Boone, Jerry Davidian, Leo Castelli, and Robert Pincus-Witten (together), and myself, by Timothy Greenfield-Sanders, a Johns lithograph, and pieces by Jeff Koons, Milan Kunc, Matthew Barney, Rona Pondick, Bruce Nauman, Robert Morris, Saul Steinberg, and Andres Serrano. I also had some old stuff and collectibles in another box in the same building, prints by Maxfield Parrish, Frank Frazetta, and Jean Delville, a portrait drawing by Sargent, and a big set of original watercolors by Vargas, my favorite bad artist. And I had my "Beauty" collection at home, racks of vintage original studio portrait prints by Man Ray, Horst, Stieglitz, Roman Freulich, Hans Namuth, Hal Phyfe, Whitey Schafer, and Lazlo Willinger, and glamour shots by Avedon, Screbinski, Newton, Bruce Weber, Mapplethorpe, Greenfield-Sanders, Herb Ritts, Steven Meisel, and Annie Leibovitz. I had a real roster of the distinctive faces of the century, even before I started using faces in Mark's pirated software. Finally, I had a lot of pre-Columbian stuff, some Mayan, Mixtec, Toltec, and Aztec, but mainly Zapotec incensarios, or incense burners, including, now, the incredible Classic Maya one we had gotten from Laureen. They had been hard to buy anonymously, but I'd gotten most of them through friends from dealers in Mexico City. I had at least thirty turquoise lip-plugs and a lot of small figures, Tlaloc, Quetzalcoatl, and Coatlicue, from Tula and Teotihuacán, and I had a carved Mixtec crystal skull with coral eyes, the symbol of Venus in its evil evening manifestation, that was really worth a fortune by now. Basically, I was doing pretty well for someone my age. But since I couldn't insure anything, I had to keep all these collections in a lot of different places as well, in case some of them burned down. It was a little nerve-racking. One of the things on my list to do was figure out some way to sell all this stuff off, claim I'd inherited it or something, and shelter what I got. But I had to figure out some really airtight scheme. I'd probably have to buy goods overseas somehow and then import and sell them. But that's one of those areas where you can really get into trouble. Another thing I'd just started doing to shelter money was getting people to auction off some of my legitimate artworks and then planting people to bid up the value of the paintings. They'd also make sure my gallery shows sold out. They'd buy them with my money, and I'd kick back some of my share to them. Then my prices would go up and my art would become more profitable. It goes on all the time. The trouble was, it was tricky to keep it plausible if my own art career wasn't going well on the critical and media-exposure end, and it was only going so-so. I'd gotten a big piece in *Flash Art* the month before, so I was on a bit of a rising curve. But every artist feels he's not doing as well as he might. So I was juggling a lot of things.

Actually, it would be a help if Penny Penn really did put something of mine into her collection and showed it off. Apparently she already had a pretty big collection of vintage photographs, and she wasn't a dummy about art. So I was kind of anxious about the studio visit. I had six possible paintings for her to choose three from. I was running out of work, and I was supposed to have that show in Germany soon, and I didn't know what I'd show. I'd have to get David and a couple of other people to help me make some photograph-derived pieces really quickly.

The buzzer rang. "It's Penny," the intercom said. I couldn't get much of a view of her on the little TV screen. I'll have to redo the lighting on the security systems, I thought. I buzzed her in and threw out a couple of pieces of trash while I waited for her to get up the stairs.

She looked amazing. She was in a blue shearling jacket and a little pillbox hat, a real neo-Jackie look that contrasted with the "don't notice me" style that she'd affected before. Maybe the transformation had given her a lot of confidence. Superstars need confidence too.

"Let me take a look at your face," I said. I brought her into the light. There were one or two little things that I wouldn't have minded touching up with some dye, but they were small and nobody would notice them but me, and I've found that my subjects tend to like to forget that their face isn't really their face, and I try not to mess around with them unless I have to. Nevertheless, I asked her if she could schedule another visit to New York in a couple of months. "I want to put in a lot of maintenance on this one," I said. "There shouldn't be much. After a couple of years, the PCS itself may begin to develop a few laugh lines and wrinkles and things, but they can be repaired very easily." She didn't answer. "Anyway, we talked about this before."

"Let's take a look at your art," she said.

She seemed to actually like the paintings, and she picked out the best three without too much trouble. She said she was going to hang them in her house on Captiva. I wondered whether that was an honor or whether it meant no one would see them. She said she had to go, gave me the address to ship the paintings to, handed me the envelope with the second check, kissed me, and went back down to her car. The last thing she said was that she'd call me in a couple of days to get me tickets to the New York premiere of her next film. It was opening in L.A. in three days. She certainly hadn't taken much time off from work. I wondered what all her friends and support structure thought had happened to her. Two weeks at a spa would *not* have had this kind of an effect.

"Bye," I yelled after her. She was a busy girl. It was fun getting kissed by her, but obviously she kissed a lot of people, and anyway, I knew from school that she didn't really like boys. She tried to keep that quiet, though. The public still wasn't yet ready for it from a major star.

■

It was six, time to get over to Jaishree's house. She'd been cooped up long enough.

I walked out and double-locked the lower door. It was a really cold, brisk high-pressure day with alternate blazing sun and clouds. I walked toward SoHo, past Ratz's deli, a really dirty place by the way, even though it's famous. It's not even kosher. As usual, I was disgusted by the smell of charred flesh billowing out the vents from the piles of corned beef. I passed Orchard Street and all the stores selling ribbons and buttons and fabrics and bows. There was a big new styleless, soulless apartment building across Houston Street on the right. It had ersatz funky "East Village"-looking details on it—there goes the neighborhood into a whirlpool of self-consciousness, I thought.

I passed the really smelly old man who asks me for money. I used to give him all my loose coins. Now I just can't bear touching these people, and I just mutter "No, sorry," and keep my eyes fixed forward and that seems to be the best way to deal with them.

I was on the shady side, of course, but as I crossed Bowery, I had to step out into the sunlight and I didn't have a hat or even sunblock on, and I could just feel the ultraviolet rays burning into my flesh, destroying the elasticity of my skin and aging me years in seconds. I turned my head away from the sun, but I could still feel it on my cheeks. I hurried toward the shade under the next bank of buildings. Hazards on every side.

■

Her apartment was a mess. Her roommate would still be away for another week. While she'd been sitting around with her bandages on, I'd spent some time with her and talked to her about performance art and about India. Eventually, I began to understand what it meant to have grown up there. She had had a personal maid all through her childhood. Labor means nothing in India, everything's done by hand. Her family had lived in a five-story stone house, with stone floors and multiple balconies, in the Juhu Beach section of Bombay, a huge square building with a yard that they called a compound surrounding it. Until they were fifteen, the girls were not allowed to leave the compound alone. When she was a little girl, she thought that the Child Krishna came to life out of a statue she had in a niche on her wall and played with her. No one taught her to read until she went to Catholic school when she was seven. The nuns didn't exactly try to convert the pagan children, but they did teach them moral parables out of Christianity and she grew up with an odd mix of gods. Her family were followers of that nineteenth-century Hindu saint, Shirdi ke Sai Baba, or Sai Baba of Shirdi. He'd worked miracles like using water instead of oil in a lamp, and he cured his followers from beyond the grave. I'd seen pictures of him at her house, always the face of an old man in a skullcap. Besides the 3-D one I'd liked in their living room, her mother had done a couple herself every year, in colored pencils, and she put them in silver-plated frames and wreathed them in fresh garlands every couple of days. The family was in the clothing business and always had gorgeous silks and embroideries all over the place. They expressed themselves through clothes. But Jaishree had mainly worn Western clothing in India. It was one way her family set themselves apart from the lower classes. One of her traumatic memories was the looting and riots and martial law following Indira Gandhi's assassination. Until she got Shakespeare in school, her main impressions of the West came from Nancy Drew books, *Star Trek* (which ran on the one television channel once a week), and a few fairy-tale books like her *Cinderella*. But once in a while it turned out later on that she had gotten snippets of other things, like the *Canterbury Tales* or Scott's *Lochinvar,* out of short excerpts in her textbooks. She had been largely ignored by the family and said India was monotonous except for the festivals. There was a festival for Ganesh, the elephant-headed god; there was Holi, where you get to throw colored water and powders on people, and Devali, the winter festival of lights. Everybody got little lamps made of mud and put them all over the house, on the railings of the balconies, on the eaves, and on the front steps, and every building in Bombay glittered with hundreds of gold lights. She had thought snow would be icy and hard like the frost in a freezer, and she was amazed when it turned out to be soft. She still ironed her clothing constantly and mended and sewed stuff herself because women in India are practically born with a needle in their hands, even though she was beginning to feel it was degrading. It was interesting to see her iron things. I'd never ironed anything myself in my life. I just bitch at dry cleaners.

She still had the bandages on. I was sure the dye had cured by now. I started unwrapping the bandages, slowly, trying hard not to shake. I was excited enough not to be in a hurry. Finally I got down to the layer of thin nonstick plastic. It was semitransparent, and you could see her face through it a little. I was afraid to take it off, and then I did.

She looked fragile, like a newborn. She looked paler than I thought she would, and strange, but familiar, like a painting you did in school that you've just pulled out of the attic after ten years.

"Get a mirror, please," she said.

I was shocked. It moved! I'd forgotten that it wasn't the plaster model anymore.

"Can you do that again?" I asked.

"What?"

"Speak."

"Of course I can speak."

It was a miracle, like an Egyptian statue coming to life.

"I want a mirror," she said. "I know you brought one." We'd taken all the mirrors out of the house, including the one from the bathroom cabinet, in order to remove the temptation to take the bandages off.

"I don't know if that's a good idea right yet."

"Why, did you screw up?"

"No."

"So give me a mirror."

"I just think you should get used to it gradually."

"Just give me one."

I pulled out an old platinum Deco compact with a dark, cracked mirror that I'd brought for the purpose. She grabbed it and looked in. She kind of froze, and then she moved it all over. Then she dropped it and ran over to the kitchen to look at herself reflected in a black plate. It didn't work, so she started looking for shiny pans. But she couldn't find anything that gave her a good view. She was pulling pans out and throwing them on the floor, making a lot of noise. I just sat there on the bed. Finally she found a *thali*—a steel Indian plate— with a shiny bottom, and she spent a lot of time with that. I didn't say anything. I was afraid of breaking the spell. She was balanced between a sense of loss, of feeling that it wasn't really her anymore, and wonder at how amazing she suddenly looked. And then it wasn't what she expected. She'd expected something more conventional, I guess. More like Claudia Schiffer. This was new.

"Jaishree, I've got something to ask you, and I don't think you're going to like it." She'd calmed down a bit after two hours. It was getting dusky outside.

"Oh?"

"I think you should rename yourself."

"Rename myself what?"

"Minaz."

"Don't be ridiculous."

"No, seriously, I've given it a lot of thought. Let me explain all the considerations, okay?"

"There's absolutely no way I'm ever going to change my name to Minaz. I had a horrible little second cousin named Minaz."

"Look, let's just give it a little time to sink in, okay? You can't go by Jaishree, and I don't think you'll be able to come up with anything better."

"I'll think about it."

"Let's spring you on the public. You want to go to a Whitney opening?"

She was a little dubious, but I got out her favorite sari. A sari, like a Roman toga, is really mainly for formal occasions. Jaishree had been wearing some *salwar kameezes* lately, long bright-colored shirts with embroidery and mirrors over a kind of harem pants in some contrasting color. They were impressive but easy to wear. Saris, on the other hand, take forever to wrap and pin up in all the right places. The one we both liked was black with dark ultramarine and plum-colored Punjabi paisley designs, with a dark burnt-orange geometric border. It looked Beardsleyesque and decadent, like something out of *Les Fleurs du Mal.* We squeezed her into the short black blouse, got her into the sort of slip-skirt that they wear, tucked the top edge into the skirt, and draped and pinned the train over her left shoulder.

She hadn't been out of her apartment since I'd driven her there in the middle of the night, all bandaged up from her operation. She'd been ordering in food, and I'd been taking out the trash for her. She was extremely self-conscious, and it was time to get her out in the real world or she'd explode.

I was beginning to feel I'd surpassed my plaster model. She was my first complete living artwork, and I was incredibly excited.

"For the time being, I'll introduce you as Galatea Trilby," I said.

"You have a great sense of humor," she said. "You just bring out the lightest aspects of the most serious things."

■

The Whitney opening went really well. The face was magic.

Even though there were a lot of professionally gorgeous women there in some pretty amazing outfits—there were a couple of the latest orange-metallic versions of those very sculptural Issey Miyake things with all the pleats, you know, they're run through a giant pleating machine after they're sewn together, so they really have great wild folds all over—even with all of these seriously dressed people around, Jaishree—Minaz, that is—did tremendously well in the sari. She was the only Indian woman there, maybe the only one in the New York art world. And the face—the face actually succeeded beyond my expectations, if that was possible. I could tell that people were looking when they pretended not to be. There was a hush and a whispering that just followed us around like a wind. A lot of people I didn't even know tried to strike up conversations with her, and with me, but generally I glared them down, although she was polite but aloof. I couldn't imagine anything more perfect, cutting a swath with her through the top floor of that horrible Breuer building, with Richard Prince's austere art on the walls, and everyone looking at her, and many of them wondering who I was, and the ones who did know me wondering who she was.

The party afterward was at the Marriott Marquis Hotel, in Times Square. I don't know whose idea it was to throw an art world party there—I guess it was because the tackiness went with the campy media theme of the exhibition—but the hotel was only for tourists so a lot of the people in the entourage we'd attracted hadn't been there before. I'd been there once just to ride the elevators. No one seemed to know in exactly which of the revolving cocktail lounges the party was supposed to be, and after we'd all ridden up and down in those Tylenol-capsule-shaped elevators five times, we were a little jittery and disoriented. And then the hotel was built on a whole bunch of different levels, and you could see one from the other, and artsy people kept calling to us from levels above and below us, telling us that the party was somewhere else, and so when we finally ran into Lisa, who had curated the show, and she helped us find the revolving lounge, we were all already pretty punchy and giggly. Jaishree, or Minaz, seemed to be getting a kick out of it, though, and she was getting a lot of attention. So finally we sort of swept into this revolving lounge and sprawled out on big chairs around tiny tables and started ordering eight-dollar drinks. But it still wasn't all all right, because you'd start talking to someone who was sitting on one of the banquettes, and you'd notice they were kind of drifting away from you, and it turned out that the inside bar part of the restaurant was revolving, too, in the opposite direction from the direction the ring of cocktail tables was moving. Except the people who were sitting there kept saying that they were stationary and we were moving, because they were the same relative to the outside surround, but the people around the tables said that the outside surround was moving, too, relative to the views of Times Square, and so our ring might really be the stationary one, and so they all got into an argument. Some people collared one of the cocktail waitresses and tried to get her to explain what was moving and at what rates, but it was like trying to get a Maori tribesman to explain Friedmann's model of the expanding universe. She finally said it was all moving and left. I asked another one whether we could get any food, and she said all the kitchens were closed.

"How about room service?" I asked.

She said we couldn't get room service here, so I suggested we each chip in twenty dollars and rent a suite and order in room service and watch X-rated HBO until six in the morning, but they were all such a bunch of squares, they weren't into it. Maybe the mirrored ceilings and the disorientation and the slow revolving and the upside-down views of Times Square and the sepulchral piano player were beginning to take their toll, because everyone was getting kind of somnolent. I felt like a tourist in my own city.

When we left the party at four A.M., I knew Jaishree was secretly thrilled. I'd introduced her as Minaz a couple of times, and she had just gone with it. She didn't seem to mind leaving her old identity by the wayside. "It's like being born again," she finally said in the taxi.

We got back to her apartment, and she was so keyed up, she started pulling outfit after outfit out of her closet and throwing them all over the room like the scene in *The Great Gatsby*.

"I just don't have a thing to wear. I mean, I've got dozens of outfits, but I still don't have a thing."

"Look, okay, let's just hit Charivari when it opens and blow a couple of thousand dollars and you'll feel better, okay?"

"I don't know—"

"It's cheaper than therapy, right? And it opens in only six and a half hours! Let's go get breakfast."

"Okay."

■

A bunch of us—you might call it the Art Gang—hung out at the Erectheon Diner until dawn. It's not really a diner, it was an upscale artsy place, and Calvin and Bertrand and some other friends of mine were eating there at a big, big table, and we sat down with them. Sexuality is such power, and she was just totally drunk on it. I could tell that every other woman at the table absolutely hated her for stealing all the femininity. But you couldn't take her too seriously about it, either, if you knew her. She was too meta-level. She knew she was doing an act. And I knew she was hyperreal in more ways than one. She seemed to have learned how to make her new face work. Her expressions were surprisingly mobile. She really got a lot of expressiveness out of the plastic that I didn't think would be possible. I had designed her with a little more of the aloof ice queen in mind, even though I also wanted her to look warm and motherly, but she put a kind of bouncy, girlish twist onto the act that I wasn't expecting. Once in a while she lapsed into her old performance voice, kind of a brash American accent, and I was afraid that some of the other people besides Calvin, who had met her when she was Jaishree, might catch it and get weirded out. But they didn't seem to notice. As soon as everyone else was laughing loudly about something, I sort of whispered to her.

"Remember, try to keep up that Bengali British accent, okay?"

"What are you, my manager?" she asked.

Uh-oh. She's getting a little uppity. Drunk on new-found sexual potency. I've created a monster.

She was eating very well, too. I mean, sometimes eating is a problem for people who've just had my procedure. But she was going through some pretty difficult, messy stuff, like frogs' legs in coconut and lemon grass, as though she'd been doing it all her life. I winced whenever she got any curry on her new face, but I knew it really wouldn't stain. It's just that proprietary streak. I had to get rid of it, I thought. It was going to ruin my enjoyment of this whole operation. Anyway, she really ate very daintily. I can't stand messy eating. It makes me crazy.

People kept coming over and trying to meet her. I kept introducing her as Minaz, and she didn't seem to mind. Finally everyone got up to go, and Calvin got the bill from the seven-foot hostess.

"It's about eighty-five dollars apiece," he said.

"Okay, Jamie's counting," somebody said.

Everybody started handing bills to me. Suddenly there was a huge pile of crumpled twenties and fifties and hundreds in front of me. It was really bumming me out that I'd become the Master of Ceremonies. I started putting the money in hundred-dollar piles.

By the time I'd counted it all, everyone had gotten their coats from the Amazon and were putting them on.

"There's still a seventy-dollar deficit," I said.

"I wish we could figure out who does that and stop inviting them," Calvin said.

It looked as if I was going to have to make up the deficit myself.

■

Minaz and I walked through the park until eleven A.M. and went over to shop on Madison. We weren't tired. We went into place after place, buying stuff like it wasn't going out of style. We went into Charivari and started poking around.

"I need some long black gloves."

"Yeah, Madame X gloves."

"Madame X doesn't have gloves," she reminded me. "You kind of remember her as having gloves, but she doesn't have any."

"I know, but you need the kind of gloves that Madame X *would* have if she *did* have gloves."

"Look," she said, "don't get fixated on the gloves thing, we have to decide on that Monake dress so they can get it ready for Friday."

"It's great," I said. "He's my favorite designer, because he does very night-looking things with very day sort of fabrics, so you can take them anywhere."

"Yeah, I think we should get it, I like it." It was a sort of scarlet corduroy sheath. "It's very texture."

"We're really getting into *Vogue*speak—"

"Yeah, isn't it awful?"

"Listen," I said, "we have to think about business for a minute. We should get you some head shots right away "

"Well, Ben can do it—"

"No, didn't Ben do them when, you know, before, as Jaishree?"

"Yeah, you think we should get somebody else? How about Scott Walters?

"He's way too upscale for head shots. He'll do the Barney's ads of you later. But for now why don't we use Timothy, he gives great head shots and he's really nice."

"Okay."

So the ball was rolling.

30

I dug out my Toshiba and gave
her the information to set up an
appointment with Scott and went
home to sleep. I guess she didn't need to sleep anymore. She
wouldn't need beauty sleep, that was for sure. I just got home and
sleepily, automatically opened my mailbox. When you're new in New
York, you feel as if you hardly get any mail. By the time you're
successful enough to be ready to move out of the city, you get so
much mail, you never want to see another piece of mail even if you
live to be as old as Jimmy Stewart. I was somewhere in the middle of
that continuum, maybe easing into the second phase. My box was full
of crud, and most of it didn't look like goodies or good news. There
was something from Penny Penn's office asking me to call her manager. I'll get around to it, I thought, and went upstairs and just collapsed on the couch. Paradise Loft was a total wreck, a lot of the
dreck from the procedure was still all over everywhere. It wasn't even
safe to leave it lying around, but I just hadn't been able to deal with it.
The final positive and the mold for the Minaz Design was wrapped in
gauze and boxed. I'd destroyed all the sketches and notes and other
positives, but I couldn't bring myself to wreck those two. They'd have
to go to a safe-deposit box. And there was the stack of videotapes.
That should go in a separate box.

I'd been awake so long, my skin was starting to break out. It was
bumming me out a lot, but I didn't even dig out my astringent. I

suppose it's obvious by now that I'm pretty into skin care. In fact, I guess one of the things that kind of steered me onto this track was, I had really bad acne around the time I was a freshman in high school. It wasn't mainly on my face, it was on my chest and my back, and it was quite disgusting, big red sties with little whiteheads in between in clusters and scabs where they had popped.

It was horrible, I felt really self-conscious about it, although not many people saw it—I got out of the ordinary locker-room scene, which I couldn't stand, by switching to ballet in my sophomore year —and my girlfriend at the time didn't seem to mind. But I guess it got me obsessing on skin. I used sun lamps, natural sunlight, benzoyl peroxide, Clearasil, erythromycin solution, Nivea, every single Neutrogena product, and it still only helped a bit. I had some scars for a long time, and I used to break open vitamin E capsules every day and rub them on them. But I still have blackheads and whiteheads sometimes, I guess most people do, and I've never done any of my procedures on myself. You know, a barber can't cut his own hair. But what may seem a little sick is, there's a tremendous feeling of satisfaction out of squeezing blackheads and whiteheads and even full-grown pimples, although it's pretty painful. It's such a satisfying feeling of release. I still remember certain pimples I squeezed years ago, that gave me such immense pleasure. There was one that was a big cluster on my back, and I'd squeezed it for a while without much results, and there was a real feeling of pressure building up inside, and then I just picked at it for a minute and tried squeezing it again, and suddenly this tiny, thin jet of pus just shot out with tremendous force, spraying a big cream-colored spatter all over the bathroom mirror, and I felt such release there, it was like an orgasm. And it turns out a lot of girls really get into this stuff, too. Because, you know, when I'd see a zit on Angelica's face or Ute's chest, for instance—she would get some during her periods, she had pretty oily skin—I'd just squeeze it out, and at first she'd get grossed out. But then she'd see some on me, and she'd squeeze them, and those little strands of dried oil would wriggle out like white worms, and she'd get kind of turned on by the satisfaction of it, too. And so we'd kind of go around, checking each other out, grooming each other like monkeys do. I guess it's a primal urge. We'd show each other the little nuggets of crud we'd dig out of each other, and we'd be really happy to get a big one. I even got hold of one of those instruments they use for facials, a little dentist's-tool type thing with a blunt disk on the end with a hole in it. And that really works amazingly well, you run it over a blackheady area, and all the white worms just automatically goosh up into the groove in the back of the disk. Honestly, people who do facials for a living must be in heaven. Still, I get a different sort of kick out of providing a skin that doesn't have any pores to clog. It's really the purifying urge that's so great about cleaning skin, anyway. And I get so much of that stripping off the yucky real skin and grafting on my terrific substitute. So I guess I've worked out the skin obsession in my life this way. Edmund Burke was really right about smoothness. There's a real urge for it. But it's not just smoothness, it's some kind of purity, or lack of infection, or something. It's primal.

■

When I woke up, it was dark, and Minaz had come over. I'd forgotten that I'd given her the key. She sort of came over to the bed area and snuggled in next to me. I didn't know what to think. I'd never even kissed her new face before.

We kissed. I knew every millimeter of her face. The face. I stroked it, and it felt warm, not as warm as real skin, but warm enough. If I didn't know, it would have fooled even me. It had a slightly different kind of resilience to it. I'd stroked it before, of course, in a more professional way. I wanted to be gentle with it, because it was my work, and it was still possibly a little fragile, but I also got filled with a sexual urge to rub it and hold it and possess it. As I kissed her, I became fascinated by the place where the lips, which had only been reshaped slightly and recoated with the barest minimum layer of AS, faded into the inside of her mouth, which was still all her. Her tongue was her own. It was there before I'd done anything to her, and licking it and playing with it with my tongue seemed doubly intimate because it was like her as a child, before the change. And holding her head so close, possessing her in that way, was something no artist had ever really been able to do before. Of course, writers fall in love with their characters all the time, and I suppose painters and sculptors have, not just Pygmalion, but lots of them—but this was bringing it into real life. And I felt that the role of the artist today was not to create fantasy at all but to shape life the way it has to be shaped. And I was starting at the top, with the human body itself.

She was excited. We started taking each other's clothes off. I unwound the sari off her slowly—it was hard to do while she was lying down, but she sort of twisted around and rolled around on the bed, and the long silk wrapper just went around and around like an unfurling sail. Finally she was in the short silk blouse, almost just a halter top, and a slip skirt. I pulled the slip up over her head and bent over her while she unhooked the frogs on my karate suit. As I got the sari blouse off and unfastened the hooks in her bra front—it was black and lacy—I just got incredibly excited, as though I were back in high school. I'd never been one for big breasts, but they went so well with her perfect Indian figure, she looked like the girls on the temples of Kajuraho, and she was so timeless and brown all over. She was covered with fur, the way Indian women are, a very soft, delicate grain of black patterning her all over. The fur on her back ran in a beautiful V-pattern, like a greyhound. Stroking her was incredibly exciting. Her dark nipples really looked hard and exotic. I sucked on them for what seemed like an hour, trying to get as much of her breasts into my mouth as I could. She was really squirming around, and she said she wanted me inside her, so I managed to dig a condom out from under the mattress, opened the package, with some difficulty, with my teeth, while she giggled at me, of course, and finally got the thing on and got on top of her. She was very tight, and I slipped my lubricated penis in very gently. I like watching a girl's facial expression at this point. She had such an excited, beatific look on her face—*my* face—I wondered, was it her showing through, or was it all me, had I just constructed her for this expression, or for the implication of this expression when others saw her? Because it's the implication of that expression of ecstasy that really turns people on about sexy faces.

We rolled over so that she was on top of me. She was moving over me and getting really excited, and I had both of my hands on her genitals, working one on the front, on her most sensitive part, and feeling around in the back with the other. I suppose I'm making myself out to be a major sex technician, building myself up in a stupid macho way. Well, it's hard when you're a heterosexual, and you really enjoy sex, to avoid sounding that way. But I just really get into it. We got into a good shaking rhythm together.

"Mmmmmmmmmmmuuuuh, mmmmmmmmmmmmuuuuh," she said, making great little noises.

She was getting ready to come. "There, there," I said.

She rested on top of me and shook all over and came, in her own time, kind of the way she might have done it if she were alone. She had a look on the Face that really lit it up large. She had a really sweet voice for moaning. I hadn't quite got to the coming stage, so after a minute of resting I pulled myself out of her gently and took the condom off.

"I want to come on top of you," I said.

She rolled underneath me, and I started rubbing my penis up and down between her breasts. Eye contact is really important in this kind of maneuver, and she was looking up at me, so I was very excited. I wanted to come all over her face—*my* face, my best art work to date. It was really self-indulgent, but I'm a self-indulgent bastard. I needed to see that stuff squirting all over my living sculpture. I drew out the scene for a long time, but finally I did it. I was shaking and making incoherent noises. I smeared and caressed the come around on her face, gently, into the deep shadows over the eyes and around the perfect corners of her lips.

"Is this okay?" I asked.

"I like it."

"I really like it, too."

■

I went to sleep for a little while, I guess, and when I woke up, she was sleeping, too. She looked beautiful, childlike, but a little less puffy and relaxed than most people do when they're asleep. She has a very consistent look, asleep or awake, I thought. And then I realized that she wasn't real, she was just a plastic thing, like a doll head, and I shivered all over, suddenly I was seized by a wave of revulsion, as if I were sleeping with a dead thing, or a giant slug, or just a plastic inflatable sex doll, and I just started shaking and not wanting to touch her or get anywhere near her, even though she was my own work and I loved her. Maybe it was weird because she was my creation, too, she was my daughter, in a way. She woke up.

"How are you, *sunum,*" she asked. *Sunum* means "sweetheart."

I scrunched down in the pillows. "I'm really sleepy," I mumbled. "Is that okay?"

"Oh, yeah, you're so cute," she said, petting me.

I kept thinking of a ceramic mask.

31

The contact sheets of Minaz's head shots came out absolutely fabulous. They'd done a hundred and forty-four shots, one roll in full Bengali regalia, with a hanging gold and diamond *bindi*—that's the dot or jewel worn in the center of the forehead—and big hoop earrings and a shiny contrasty sari that was good for black and white. They'd done two rolls of Western, girlish-looking ones in dark sweaters, and two more rolls in a more casual embroidered Indian outfit, with more Western hair. Almost every shot was perfect. I'd designed her without a single bad angle. Timothy says that most people have about three and a half good angles and they look terrible from every other angle, and that of all the people he's photographed, only Matt Dillon looked equally good from every direction. But he'd add Minaz to the list when he saw this. I couldn't wait to get her to that opening on Wednesday the fourteenth of September—it was a long way away, but not too long to plan ahead for the ticket of the year—and have everybody ask about her.

■

I figured we could get in a shoot with Timothy on a Monday, when he was least busy. I called him up early in the morning—he has kids, and he's an early riser anyway—and he actually answered the phone himself.

"It's Jamie," I said. "It's been some time."

"I've been really sought-after lately. Wait a minute, I'm getting a call."

He kept me on hold for about two minutes. I wandered around the studio picking up pieces of plastic.

"Sorry," he said when he got back on the line.

"Who was that who was so important you had to keep me on hold for an hour?" I asked.

"Julia Roberts,' he said.

"Oh."

"What do you say to someone who's done as much as she has?" he asked. "She wanted me to take her portrait. '

"You just say, you're the greatest, you're the best, I hope that I can pass the test,' I said.

He said he had an hour before he had to go to lunch with Thommas Amman and Julian Schnabel and Ahn Duong. I said I had someone for him to meet.

"You mean Minaz? I've already heard about her through, uh, Calvin. Supposedly she was at the Whitney opening last week, but I didn't see her."

"I guess she made quite a stir, if you've heard about her already."

"Well, I'm anxious to meet her. How about eleven-thirty?"

By the way he said it, I could tell he was considering the possibility of doing a shoot. "That's great," I said.

"Bye."

I called up Minaz and made her promise to meet me at eleven. "Bring a whole lot of ethnic stuff, especially nose rings and things," I said.

"What is it?" she asked.

"Just in case he wants to do a quick shoot. You'll have to get used to these sorts of things," I said.

■

We walked around the corner to Timothy's house. I thought how great it was having him for a neighbor. It was a beautiful day, and I was with a beautiful girl, the most beautiful girl ever, in fact, and I hoped we'd run into somebody I knew on the short walk. We went through the little iron gate and I rang his bell. His family was the only one in the building, but he had a lot of other doorbells to fool burglars into thinking it was a tenement. They had names like Blanche DuBois and Stanley Kowalski on them. I kept telling him that he was assuming a large degree of illiteracy on the part of the underclass, but he felt it wasn't a problem.

Timothy opened the door. He looked exactly like John Malkovich, and I could tell Minaz was struck by him. He was very struck by Minaz. He'd seen a lot of models, even though he didn't shoot as many models as most photographers, and he knew she was something special. He didn't stare at her, though.

"Come in," he said. I introduced Minaz, and he was very polite. "We're doing some tea. I'm on the phone with *03* magazine, in Japan, though. I'll be with you in a second. He led us up the short flight of stairs to the first floor, talking on the radio phone.

"I can't be in Osaka on the twenty-fourth, I have a shoot here. Very important photography. Here, in New York. On the twenty-fourth," he said, very slowly and clearly. "I appreciate the offer, but I will not be able to come until the twenty-eighth, as we planned. *Domo, arigato.*"

I pointed out a picture of mine that Timothy had hanging up in the stairwell. It was a very clean geometric piece from a long time ago, not characteristic of my work now, but Timothy liked it a lot. He generally liked very clean abstraction—maybe, I thought, because that kind of painting was actually closest to the issues he was dealing with in his very classicizing portrait photography—subtle shifts of emphasis and tone, an inch could be too much. My painting was between a Peter Halley and a Tishan Hsu; good company, I thought.

The upstairs had raw wood floors and good Federalist antiques and Persian rugs and a lot of advanced art. There were also some big paintings by Timothy's father-in-law, who was a first-generation Abstract Expressionist. There was a Schnabel and a Clemente and just a lot of great stuff. We walked through to the kitchen, which actually faced out on a little backyard garden, and sat down around his sort of rough country-looking table. I helped us to some Earl Grey and unwrapped the strawberry millefoglio I'd brought.

Timothy was an original East Village pioneer. In 1977 he'd bought the five-story rectory of a church that had been demolished. He'd probably bought it for about $30,000 and now it was worth more than a couple million. He'd done some other real estate in the area, too. A lot of top artists do a whole lot of real estate for one reason or another. Timothy had a beautiful wife and two beautiful daughters who went to Grace Church school, the only truly hip and together downtown grade school, and who got a lot of media exposure for nine-year-olds. He shot mainly portraits of hip people, especially artists, and had managed to straddle both the fine-art world and the commercial world. He'd had shows at both Mary's and Leo's, and he also did immensely successful ads for Barney's and Bergdorf-Goodman and a lot of other things. He brought back the celebrity endorsement ad, in a way. Those big Herb Ritts Gap ads that were all over a couple of years ago weren't as good as his stuff, but they were flashier journalism. They were ridiculous, they'd say "Gap Pocket-T as customized by Jody Watley." Their shirts were so ordinary, they had to be "customized" before anyone cool like Jody Watley would wear them.

He'd done a shoot with Penny Penn the day before, for Armani. Lately, he was just on the phone eighty percent of the time.

Minaz and I started helping ourselves to figs and chèvre. It was getting on toward noon.

"Should we pierce your nose?" I asked. "I can engineer an invisible hole."

"My mom used to bug me to get a nose ring, too."

I knew that her mentioning her mother meant she was thinking about the identity problem.

"So, shall we make up a new identity for you, take you up to Canada, and bring you back in on a working visa under the new name?" I asked. "Don't answer right away."

"Let me think about it."

"It could get to be a problem, the identity thing," I said.

"For the time being, I'm using my own papers and just using Minaz as my stage name."

"Well. Okay."

"And I've decided I'm going to call some of my really good friends and let them in on our little secret. They must be worried about me."

"Well, let's take that slowly, you may not get the reactions you'd like. . . ."

"No, I know most of them are going to be horrified."

We sat quietly for a minute.

Timothy got off the phone. "I actually got a check from *03* today," he said. "They're so honorable, I never expected to actually get paid for a single photo credit like that. It's only four hundred dollars, though."

"That's okay, that's a good dinner," I said. We went down the stairs into the office/studio. It was a big ground-floor room, the size of a whole floor in the rest of the building. The part where he actually photographed was kind of beneath the level of the rest of the room, and it was very clean and spare, with lights, cameras, and backdrops. The office area was businesslike but also filled with art. The big Polaroids of Penny were already up in a place of honor. She was wearing a really nice gray Armani men's suit and looking mature. There were big Polaroids of Jodie Foster and Cindy Crawford and Karen Goode. There was a glass table with copies of all the latest issues of the magazines and catalogues that Timothy had work in. There were *New York Times Magazines*, Comme des Garçons catalogues, *03* magazine—a kind of *New York* magazine for Tokyo—Japanese *Esquire, 7 Days* (defunct), *New York* magazine, *Allure, Mirabella, Elle, Harpers and Queen,* the *London Times* magazine, and a whole bunch of other goodies. He'd evidently been busy since I'd last been over.

"I don't know about Comme des Garçons," Minaz said. "Five hundred dollars for a T-shirt, I don't know. . . ."

"I think they should be even more expensive," I said.

There was another glass-topped table that was lit up and had transparencies that had been taken from positives done on the big Polaroid. They had acetate overlays with grease-pencil notes to the retoucher on them. There was one of Donald Trump wearing a Hickey-Freeman suit, and the note said "eliminate shine," with an arrow pointing to his watch.

Timothy didn't do many standard fashion shots. He did classical half-length portraits, mainly. When he did color he used the giant 22″ × 30″ Polaroid, owned by the Polaroid company, that was in its own special studio in the Puck Building at Houston and Lafayette. That way, each of his color shots was a unique work, like a painting, and not infinitely reproducible like most photographs. Of course, it was also just a great camera. The color was unusually rich and it was completely un-grainy. But for this shoot he was going to do black and white. He had two huge wooden cameras that he used, a 22" × 30" Dierdorff from the thirties, and a Calumet that was more recent. They wheeled around on big antique wooden stands with silent rubber wheels. The Dierdorff also had a video camera and recorder and a black and white monitor attached to the top of it, so that Timothy could instantly see how what he was shooting looked in black and white and so he had a videotaped record of every shoot. He had every shoot he'd ever done in this studio filed away on videotape. A lot of the people he'd shot had since either become tremendously important or died, usually of AIDS. He had shots he'd done of Orson Welles and Mary Boone and Andy Warhol and those kind of people in simple frames along one wall of the studio, and there was a real sense of history in the place. But new history. History moves fast in the art world.

"Are you wearing any makeup?" he asked Minaz.

"No," she said. I wondered whether he would believe her and whether he would notice anything strange about her face. He did look kind of closely at her, but then he seemed to worry that he was making her self-conscious and turned away to mess with the cameras.

"I just got back from Paris, shooting for Tokado," Timothy said. "It was terrific, all we did was get perked around in a stretch."

"That's great," Minaz said.

"And I just did a shoot with Marla Hanson this morning."

"The model/slash/actress?"

"I hope she hasn't heard that expression."

"She's really fun."

It's no wonder the Marla Hanson case hit such a popular nerve. The destruction of beauty is a really key motif. It wasn't just a savage act, it was an assault of male feelings of helplessness and rejection and sexual resentment against an icon of sexuality. It was iconoclastic in the original sense. Bataille would have had a field day with it. Of course, Marla looks great now, although I could do it better. But I'd be exposing myself, of course. So I can't do her.

"Your friend Minaz is fabulous," Timothy said. "I don't usually shoot on spec, but let's just expose a few right now, okay?"

"Do you think they'll come out in something?"

"I don't know, we could probably get it into *Interview. Interview*'s a good start," Timothy said. "Although it's flash-in-the-pan city."

"Look," I said, "it's fine for someone who hasn't even been cast in anything yet. We'll worry about being a flash in the pan later. Right now, we should be lucky enough to be a flash in the pan."

The shoot started very slowly. Timothy had a way of loosening people up that was different from most photographers. Most fashion people have them jump around and lie down and get up and take their clothes off and put them back on and all sorts of stuff to loosen them up. But Timothy wasn't really interested in "getting through the mask"; he kind of *liked* people's masks. He was more interested in getting the quintessential way that people presented themselves to the world. So he asked Minaz to move around a bit, but then he got her to sit down and positioned her head very carefully. The natural light diffusing down through the ceiling-floor bathed her in a sort of Leonardoesque *sfumato*. The dark-gray chalky paper backdrop had a kind of Mannerist look.

He talked a bit while he was changing film holders.

"Most people only look good from one or two angles, except for Matt Dillon. He looks good from anywhere. But I think maybe Minaz is giving him a run for his money."

I knew he was going to say that.

32

I had an important dinner that night with about eight dealers and curators and collectors and another eight artists and artists' escorts. I was really psyched to spring Minaz on them. And we'd invited Alan Hirsch, her best movie connection, and Calvin and Andrew, of course, and Bertrand Villiers. Alan's kind of an agent and producer. He used to be with Triad, but now he's got his own agency. I knew him because he handled a lot of Virginia Feiden's blossoming career. He's kind of a hustler, but he has a lot of energy. Bertrand wrote for a lot of Condé Nast magazines but also owned part of LHOOQ, the club, and he did a lot of real estate stuff, too, so he was getting major. The two of them could do quite a bit for Minaz if they wanted to.

We had to go to an opening first, at the Andrea Burgin Gallery. I wasn't eager to go, but I knew the artist and had to. Minaz was going to meet us later at Café Tzara. The restaurant. So far, we were just me and Andrew and Bertrand and Bertrand's girlfriend, Francine, who was a model. She had a bit of a southern drawl. Southern is the new power accent.

The opening was filled with all the usual suspects. Larry Kinko from the Jerry Davidian Gallery was there, up to his old tricks.

"Did you get the auction results?" he asked me, without even saying hello. There had been a big Contemporary sale at Sotheby's that afternoon.

"No," I said.

"Never mind, I'll get it from somebody else," he said, and walked away.

"Are any of you friends with this artist too?" I asked my little group.

"No, why?" seemed to be the general answer.

"This stuff is harshing my wave," I said. They were only the worst paintings you could possibly imagine. They were all pus-green and crusty and abstract.

"What's wrong with them?" Francine asked.

"They're just too MFA," I said.

"What's that stand for, Museum of Fine Art?"

"Master of Fine Arts. It's a degree." It was the worst thing you could possibly say about an artist. Francine didn't get it.

Andrew was introducing me to a friend of his, a painter who showed at some inferior gallery. I didn't get his name.

"What kind of painting do you do?" I asked.

"They're kind of abstract, kind of organic forms, lots of drips, direct oil painting . . . uh . . . ."

Wow, he really knew how to make his work sound exciting.

"Great," I said, "I'll look forward to seeing your show."

I'd remember to avoid it like a PTA meeting.

We pressed a lot of flesh and left. On the way downstairs Bertrand said, "Alex is sweet, he's attractive, his work is just *so* hopeless."

"Yeah," I agreed, "those icky green touchy-feely surfaces and everything. And he was talking all about them as 'indices of desire,' and shit like that."

"Yeah, those titles are like, they scream: 'Hi, I have a very marginal understanding of Derrida,' you know?"

■

Café Tzara was underdesigned, and it wasn't huge. The food was actually fair-to-good, now that they'd stopped trying to serve Venezuelan food, which they couldn't do convincingly. But there was no way to put your finger on what made it such a hot place. Which was, maybe, why it *was* such a hot place; it was the place to go for people who wanted to look as if they felt they didn't have to prove anything.

Taylor Mead was there, as usual, in his same seat at the bar.

"It's amazing how old he is," I said to Bertrand.

"Yeah, I think they have him bolted to the bar stool with some kind of back support system, you know?"

"So there'll always be at least one nominally famous person in the place."

We gave our coats to another beautiful black seven-foot Amazon Coat Check Girl and sat down at a big table. People would cruise in at their own speed. I hoped Minaz would arrive last and make an even bigger impression.

■

"The only commodities anyone has are beauty, money, power, and fame."

"What about talent?"

"It comes with fame. But beauty is the one that nobody talks about. It's like there's a tacit agreement not to talk about it. And that's what kills these girls."

Robert McEllivey, a Fairly Famous Novelist, was holding forth against Bertrand on the subject of wannabe models.

"It just breaks my heart, the way these girls come in from the Midwest, and they don't know anything, and these old guys send limousines for them and get them to sleep with them and get them hooked on all kinds of drugs, and eventually they just die of an overdose or they get dumped and kill themselves, or somehow, their lives just end up badly. They just come to this city with no direction. Somebody should warn them."

"Well, they can make decisions for themselves, some of them make the right decisions. What are you going to tell them, anyway? Watch out, there are bad people in this city? They can't listen to stuff like that. Anyway, what you're talking about has been going on since ancient Rome."

"I know. But I wasn't around in ancient Rome."

"Well, no," Bertrand admitted.

Our waitress kind of intruded on us and started explaining the specials. She was a major waitress right now because she'd recently been written up in *Interview* as "What's It Like Being a Waitress at the World's Most Glamorous Restaurant?" We listened politely, and she kind of rolled away.

"What's that top thing she's wearing?" Andrew asked.

"It's an Ozbek bathing suit top," I said.

"You're right," Bertrand said. "That's exactly what it is." I love being asked questions I know the answers to.

Peter De Boer, a pretty successful painter who shows at Pace, came in with Calvin and the Japanese dealers we were all supposed to meet.

Kago and Nakasone were in gray business suits, not badly fitting or anything, really nice suits, but still somehow they didn't look as at home in them as Bertrand, for instance, looked in his Armani. They were both wearing kind of nice loud bow ties that I liked. We exchanged a whole lot of formalities, and they sat down.

"Do you mainly wear bow ties in Japan?" Francine asked.

"No, in Japan we wear straight ties mainly," Nakasone said.

"But in New York you get to cut loose a little, right?" she said.

"Yes, we love New York," Nakasone said.

"How's *La Rêve en Pierre?*" Bertrand asked me.

"Who?"

"You know, the Princess of Samarkhand and Ind."

"She'll be here any minute."

"And all those agencies are basically pimp rings anyway," McEl-livey said. "I mean, they take these really stupid girls—not like Francine, however. . . ."

"No, I know, I agree," Francine said, "Modeling's so stupid, you just do this, and this, you know, you feel so dumb." She was striking one silly fashion pose after another.

There was a kind of a hush settling over the restaurant. Everybody looked up. It was Minaz, entering, alone, striding like a gazelle past the tightly packed tables. She was absolutely resplendent. She wore a *salwar kameez* made from the dark lavender-magenta fabrics we'd picked out as her signature color. She had gold sandals and toe rings with bells, and a hanging *bindi* with a sapphire, and a thing on her hand that went over the back with silver chains and attached to a ring on each finger. Her hair was done in the signature braids. She stopped traffic. Everyone just fell silent and gawked. It was like something out of a fairy tale. Her face had a kind of sensual serenity to it, like a bodhisattva. I could tell that everyone in the place, straight women and gay men included, were excited by her. Her face was just a beacon, something completely dazzling and untouchable and be-witching. I almost felt I'd overdone it.

During the stalemate, I pulled a chair over for her. I let the silence settle and then started introducing her around.

Everyone tried to act fairly cool and couldn't manage it. Francine said it was a lovely outfit. And Kago said, "I am pleased to meet you. You are extremely beautiful." He gave a little bow.

She behaved perfectly. I was sure, at that moment, that I'd started something big. This dealer, André, was really staring at her.

Minaz started talking to put people at their ease. She was so vivacious that eventually the mood became less tense. Francine asked what the hand-thing was called and then asked her if she'd ever had a nose ring.

"Jamie keeps pestering me to get a nose ring," Minaz said. "So does my mother. He's exactly like my mother. He even looks a little like her."

"Listen," I said, "you say that one more time, and I'll tear up your green card, wrap you up in your sari, and ship you back to Bhopal."

"Yeah, I'll get married-arranged and I'll be reducing milk for the rest of my life."

"You'll probably get sutteed. In six months you'll be a pile of charcoal briquettes floating in the Ganges."

"It's called the Gunga," she said.

"I pierced my own nose once," Francine said.

"That's difficult, piercing your own nose," Bertrand said.

"Yeah, I bled so much, I fainted. I was kind of a fashion victim. I pierced my ear, too, and I still have a piece of gold stuck in there." She felt around in her earlobe.

"Self-mutilation's just such a big deal these days," Minaz said.

"Yes," I said, "that's one reason I'm so into the Maya."

"Oh, I love that stuff, too," Francine barged in. "The Pyramids of the Sun and Moon and everything."

"That was in Teotihuacán," I said. Pause. "I don't know," I continued, "I'm mainly interested in the Lords of Quiché, you know, the Mayan kings." Everyone at our end of the table was silent, so I went on. "You know, lately, it turns out they really weren't that much more peaceful than the Aztecs. They used to torture their captives for years, sometimes. And they used to mutilate themselves a lot, too. They used to pierce their earlobes and soak the blood into paper and burn the paper, and that was their main offering to the gods. But the blood of their captives was a big offering, too, so they used to keep them around alive for a long time so they could get more blood out of them. They cut their hearts out eventually, too. But that was on special occasions."

I got the feeling people were beginning to think I was weird and creepy.

"Tell me, when the Maya abandoned all their temples and everything, do you think they went to Venus?" Francine asked. "That's what my guru says."

"Uh, I, ah—I don't think so, no," I said.

"Kago-san has a pretty big collection of pre-Columbian art," Calvin whispered to me. "But he can barely tell Olmec from Toltec."

"I got mutilated myself the other day," Peter, the painter, said. "I got tattooed."

Everyone begged him to show it off. After a lot of protestations he took off his Paul Smith jacket and rolled up his white short-sleeved shirt to reveal his left shoulder.

It was a hard-edged solid black oval/lozenge shape, about the size of a small lime, tattooed on horizontally. It was very minimal.

"Paul Auchincloss, you know, that Neo-Minimal painter from Andrea Burgin, designed it," he said. Everyone seemed pretty impressed.

"Can you ever get it removed if you get tired of it?" Francine asked.

"You either have a tattoo or you have a scar," he said.

That's not really true anymore, I thought. But I wasn't saying anything.

Minaz said, "There was this biker guy we knew who used to bike across the country and sleep outside a lot, and people used to hassle him when he was asleep, so he had open eyes tattooed on the outside of his eyelids. He also had "fuck you" tattooed on his inner lower lip so you could read it if he pouted at you."

Everybody laughed a lot at that.

Peter said, "Somebody who was in the tattoo place when I was there had a Jesus face tattooed on the top of his bald head, and when he moved his head muscles, the eyes would open and close."

We got to talking about how people abuse their bodies, too, and got onto the subject of anorexia. I told them about how when I was at Yale, every girls' bathroom just reeked of vomit. Bulimia was a really big thing in the mid-eighties. Now the full-figure girl is back, so it's okay to have flesh, and women don't hate their bodies quite so much. But every one of my friends in those days was just eating jars and jars full of peanut butter and bags of potato chips and then sticking her finger down her throat all day long.

My *crème brûlée* finally came. Then the coffee finally came. We were settling down to post-prandial depression. McEllivey had put away more than a bottle of wine by himself and was giving Kago some kind of drunken tirade about New York Japanese restaurants. Kago was smiling and nodding politely.

"Does Kago-san understand anything he's saying?" I asked Bertrand.

"How could he understand it? *I* can't understand it."

"Does he know that Robert is a really famous writer and everything?"

"Look, the Japanese are just so star-struck, they think everything's fabulous. You don't have to worry."

"You know," I said to Bertrand, "lately I've been feeling like I might move to a lighthouse in Canada and paint really intricate still lifes of grapes for about fifty years. You know with really realistic water droplets running down the sides?"

"Why?"

"I just can't juggle everything I'm supposed to juggle much longer."

"Join the club."

"And I'm disappointed," I added. "When I was in school, I thought the art world would be glamorous."

"Nothing's glamorous on the inside."

"I mean, those housewives in Cleveland who read about the art world think we have a really exciting life, but they don't know how tough it really is."

"Let's *andiamo,*" Calvin said.

Minaz and I talked to Bertrand while we walked up to Houston.

"Seriously, what did you *really* think of Peter's tattoo?" I asked. "I mean, as a work of art?"

"I thought it was one of the most critically acute tattoos I'd seen, definitely," Bertrand said.

"What were those Japanese dealers doing there?" Minaz asked.

"Paying for everything," I said.

Alan came up to walk with us. He'd been talking to Bertrand earlier, but I couldn't hear what they had been saying. Bertrand started talking in a "confidential" tone to Minaz:

"Alan's heard a lot about you, and he saw your picture in *Interview,* and he'd like to send you to an audition with Harold Corman, from HBO, for a start. Did I get that right?"

"Yeah," Alan said. "I also want you to go over to Eileen Dodge and get some color fashion shots for your portfolio. I mean, we don't necessarily want to start you out as a model, but you'll need more than black and whites for the Coast. Even though they're very artistic black and whites."

The Coast. We're on a coast, too, I thought for the hundredth time.

"Except don't tell Eileen about me or the HBO thing, just get in there some other way."

"I know one of her models, she's an old friend, she owes me a favor," I said, getting excited.

"Okay, okay, do it that way," Alan said.

Yay! I thought. I looked at Minaz. She looked blasé.

"So, are you coming to Sound Factory?" Bertrand asked me.

"I guess so," I said. Minaz indicated that was okay. "If you want. I have no ego anymore. No will of my own." It was two-thirty.

Everybody said good night. We got in four separate cabs. I held Minaz's hand. I still had that funny urge to move to a lighthouse in Nova Scotia and paint still lifes.

33

I was a little worried about introducing Minaz to Kimura. Kimura had gone to school with me, and now she was a major brunette at the Dodge Agency, except they'd kept her in Spain and Italy until a couple of weeks ago. She'd just gotten back from some spa in Texas, the Golden Hind or something, where she went to keep her weight down.

Kimura had stayed over at my house one time, when I was still living with Katrina. She'd brought a makeup case the size of a steamer trunk. She had five times more makeup with her for just one night than Katrina owned. She went through seven towels the first night and five more the next morning, not counting the little medicated paper pads she brought with her. She found my Borghese anti-aging eye cream, the one that costs seventy dollars a jar, and used it up, probably on her feet. In the morning she'd lain with her head tilted back with little antipuff pads on her eyes for two and a half hours. Actually, maybe she really needed all that because she had really bad skin, even though she was a top model. The Retin-A only helped a bit. I'd thought I used a lot of Retin-A, but it was nothing like Kimura. She needs Retin-A like Ethiopia needs rice. You could almost tell her skin was bad, if you got her in daylight. But she also took Accutane, and that controlled it. Accutane is for skin beyond hope. It's so bad for you, it even causes birth defects. But if you're really good-looking, why would you want children?

At four, we met Kimura on Fifty-seventh Street and Sixth. It was starting to rain.

"How's your art?" she asked.

"I don't know," I said. "I mean, it's great, but it's not getting as much press as it deserves. The only cool thing to be in art right now is a real activist."

"*I'm* an activist. I led a revolt when I worked at Saul, Rice. We demonstrated against Styrofoam cups."

Saul, Rice, Ruskin, Groton and Keillor was a big entertainment law firm.

"That's great. You're a regular Barry Commoner."

"Yeah, they gave up using them in the water coolers. I mean, it was totally out of self-interest about the way I looked."

"Why, you don't look pretty holding a Styrofoam cup?"

"No, I don't want the plastics to make the ozone layer go away so I'll get skin cancer and look all yucky."

"Oh, yeah."

"I'm pretty crazy about skin cancer," she went on. "I'm wearing SPF 60, and UVA block under that. Always wear total UVA block because ordinary sunblock just screens out one kind of rays, and there's a whole other kind. You have to just accept that the sun is your enemy. The sun is the red meat of the nineties."

"Yeah, and red meat was the sugar of the eighties."

"It's true, that was one of the worst things about the seventies, that sugar had such a bad rap. Sugar was the fat of the seventies."

"I love Styrofoam," Minaz said.

"What do you mean?" I asked.

"It's just really difficult to keep myself from eating Styrofoam," she said. "Like when I'm drinking out of a Styrofoam cup, it's all I can do to keep from swallowing the cup along with whatever I'm drinking. One time when I was three, in Bombay, my aunt gave me a whole bunch of Styrofoam Flintstones Building Blocks, and they left me to play with them, and when they came back the blocks were gone. And I threw up five times and each time it was a different color. I guess if it hadn't been for that, I'd still be eating the stuff."

I didn't quite know how to respond to that. I felt like telling her she wasn't supposed to be a performance artist anymore, she was supposed to be a dumb model.

"So what do you think Eileen Dodge is all about," I asked, "with all those models living in her house and everything, is it just about money or is it some lesbian power thing?"

"I don't know," Kimura said. "It really works for her, though. Sometimes being kind of crazy really pays off."

We walked past that big red nine at 9 West Fifty-seventh Street. The Empire of Signs, I thought. Kimura was looking at Minaz in a funny way, but Minaz wasn't saying much. A woman of mystery. We went in, and the guard at the desk gave Kimura a big smile, but he spent more time looking at Minaz. Kimura pushed 18—the little plaque next to the number just said DODGE—and just before the door closed, two other models got in. They were waspy blondes, dressed in standard model outfits, jeans, T-shirts, and big bright nylon duffel bags. They were pretty stunning, and taller than Minaz, but they still looked pretty jealous when they saw her, even though they were keeping their faces as blank as possible the way most models usually do.

The elevator door opened on a big desk with a girl in glasses behind it. There was gray carpet everywhere—you could tell it got shampooed twice a week. The Land of the Headhunters. Kimura went right to the desk girl, cutting the other two models off, and told her she was supposed to see Eileen right away.

"Well, I guess you can go in, she's anxious to see you. How was Spain?"

"It was really hot and smoky, but fun, I guess. They work for one hour a day, and eat, drink, sleep and have sex for the other twenty-three."

"I could handle that," the girl said.

"Thanks, Cathy," Kimura said as she led us off toward the right. Cathy looked at Minaz sort of curiously. There was a brass sign on the door that said EILEEN DODGE.

I told Minaz to wait outside. I wanted to go in with Kimura first. She was a little nervous. "I've gained some weight over the summer," she said. "I've shot up a dress size." I opened the blond wood door for her, and we went in. Eileen Dodge's office was pretty small, but with a great view of Fifty-seventh Street in the rain and a lot of framed magazine covers that reminded me of the pinned-up covers in U.S. Color Photo Labs. Eileen looked about sixty, but she must have had her face lifted at least three times. She was sitting on the top of her desk trying to peel off one of her see-through galoshes. It was a little strange, because she was barefoot under the galosh, and you could see her toenails were painted with some color a lot like Elizabeth Arden Iridescent Peach.

"Hello, Kimura," she said.

"I know," Kimura said, "I've gained some weight over the summer."

"You can say that again," Eileen said. "Welcome to the Dodge Hippopotamus Agency. I've never seen so many fat, dumpy models in my *life*." Her galosh came off with a tremendous *thwop*. "I think you'd better put on a leotard and step on the scale and let Dianne measure you."

"Okay," Kimura said. "Don't worry, though, I'm on Optifast and I'm going up to Racebrook Springs for the weekend, I'll be okay."

"Good, because the good news is, we're going to send you down to Fort Worth for a Ritts shoot in *Glamour*."

"Oh, that's great," Kimura said, trying to act blasé. It was a break for her.

"Who's this?" Eileen asked.

"Eileen, this is Jamie Angelo, Jamie, Eileen."

"It's nice to meet you," I said.

"What's going on?" Eileen asked.

"Listen," Kimura said, "Jamie's a friend of mine who's come up with a new girl who looks really promising, and Melissa thinks so, too—"

"Well, Melissa can send me the visuals."

I put the copy of *Interview* open to Minaz's full-page photo down on Eileen's desk. "Just take a look at her," I said. I was already opening the door and pulling Minaz inside.

"This is a real imposition," Eileen said. But then she looked at the magazine and at Minaz and quieted down. Minaz just stood there looking blank, not blinking, like we'd practiced. It was a big strain for her not to say something witty. Eileen got up and walked about eighty degrees around her and stood still for about ten seconds. Then she went back to her desk and started unfastening her other galosh.

"Get Melissa to take down her information and schedule a test with Sam for this afternoon," she said.

"Okay, thanks," Kimura said.

"No, no thanks, nice to meet you, Mr. Angelo, and what's your name?"

"Minaz," Jaishree said.

"Eileen," Eileen said, trying to get her other galosh off.

"Bye," Kimura said. We walked out. When we got past the secretary into the hallway, Kimura whispered, "She's really excited if she schedules a test for the same afternoon. She never does that. She's really, really psyched."

"Look, Kimura, I've got to run downtown, do you think you could help schedule this thing and I'll try to get back for the shoot?"

"This is a real imposition," Kimura said, mimicking Eileen. "But okay. You don't have to come back for the shoot, Sam doesn't like anyone else around anyway."

"Is that okay, Minaz?" I asked.

"Sure," she said.

"Will you give me a call?"

"Maybe, sure."

I couldn't tell whether she was mad at me or not. Since the transformation, it was pretty difficult for me to tell what she was thinking at all.

34

So Minaz's life moved into its "model on the way up" phase, a period of endless bookings and shoots and clothing changes and agents and trips to Morocco and Madagascar and Manila and God knows where, and telephones ringing, and car services picking her up and being ready when she got finished to move her to some other place, and everything being taken care of for her because, as everyone knows, models are completely handicapped and irresponsible, mentally and emotionally. They're another species, almost like cats, beautiful, selfish, vicious, and retarded. So people just move them around and take pictures of them and otherwise ignore them. In one week, she was sent to Oran and brought back because the photographer couldn't show up, and then sent again, and then sent to Milan and from there to Madrid and then back to New York. One day I went to shop at Barney's for a welcome-home gift for her, and there was a whole gang of her there, unmoving, five garishly swimsuited, variously wigged Minaz-clones staring down at me with lifeless eyes through the window. Apparently a mannequin company had made a head design based on her; kind of an interesting reverse-switch, I guess, but I lost interest in shopping that day. That same month she did a lot of fall-couture runway work in Milan, and for a week her hair got washed, tinted, hot-rolled, sprayed, and washed again four or five times a day, and she had to put special hair-rejuvenating proteins on it overnight and sleep in a bathing cap. Her nails were done and redone until they broke and she had to use glue-ons. Gianni Versace insisted on a flaming red color that turned out to be automobile enamel and only came off with acetone. Dolce & Gabbana had all their models wear peach and beige nail polish, and then they had it stripped off so that nobody else could use it. She had spirit-gum burns all over her body from an off-season swimsuit show. Some of the suits were so tight and skimpy, ordinary spray-glue wouldn't keep them in place.

As we'd discussed, she always insisted on *removing* her facial makeup herself, but she still had some scares with makeup artists who insisted on applying base directly with their fingers. She told them that she had a low body temperature and to be gentle with her easily bruised skin.

Minaz was a super hit in Milan, but by the time she got back to New York, there were booking problems, and she only got booked for a couple of New York fall lines: the Irving Monake show and the two Ralph Lauren shows. I said it was hard work anyway and she didn't have to do it, but she said it was good business and if Iman and Naomi Campbell could still do runway, then she could, too. She surrendered herself to it even though she felt stupid being a manne-quin, because her career was on a steadily rising curve and it had only been a month and a half, and she wasn't yet pegged entirely as a dumb model. Maybe she'd have to get the kind of buildup Uma Thurman got, getting slipped into films through the back door.

She was always busy, and I hardly ever got to get photographed together with her, but I did ask her to come along on a shoot I had to do in a garage with a bunch of four other presumably trendy New York artists and a couple of Japanese curators for that Japanese maga-zine, *03*. Timothy was going to do it, and then he got somebody else to do it instead. It was at ten o'clock on a Thursday evening in a big drafty garage with a fake Jackson Pollock on the wall behind us, and they wanted us all in leather. The photographer was glad I'd brought her. I'd had some drinks before and it was all just a big blur. The photographer started trying to get us excited.

"Sex, drugs, rock 'n' roll!" he yelled at us, snapping his Nikon frantically. "Insider trading! Pretend it's the eighties again! Whatever you're most into! You're all going out to make millions of dollars! A little more cleavage, that's it, okay, your eyes are carrying this whole shot, flirt with the boys, more downtown, more cynical, okay, now you're all angry, you're mad and upset, you're going to sue your dealer for millions because she sold your paintings to some jerk and pretended she lost them . . . yeah, stick that paintbrush in your boot, like that . . . excellent, that's good styling. I should take you along on shoots with me. Let's get more neck. Okay, now all we see is neck.

"Okay! You're mad, you're cynical. You're downtown existential personalities who don't give a damn about anybody or anything. More *Angst*! More attitude! *Slaves of New York. New York Stories.* Like Nick Nolte in *New York Stories*—you know, really, really intense and angsty. Yeah, Grrr, grrrrr, rough, rfff, rufffff, *rrrrrrrr* . . .

"Okay, now you're happy, you're just kidding around, you're totally cool and jokey, let's move, let's have more physical contact, yeah, yeah, rrrrr, mmmmmmmmmmrrrrrrrrr, *yummmmm,* good, that's fabulous, okay, Minaz, you're carrying the whole shot, you're like 'why am I with these guys,' you're bored, you're disgusted, okay, Muse, more leg, that's right, flirt, sex, flirt with the camera, give it to the camera, play with the camera, yes, that's great, you're happy, you're young, you're signed on with Zoli, *things are looking up*! MMMMMMMMMMMMMMM! Yeahhhhhhhhhh. . . ."

"It's so exploitative," Minaz said. "Exploit me!"

"Does anyone have any powder?" I asked. "My nose is really shiny."

"Here, there's powder on my cheek," Kiri said. Kiri was one of the curators. "Rub your nose on my cheek, and you'll pick up some powder."

"I have to stand on something, I'm short."

"You're short and shiny. Vanity knows no bounds."

"What do you have on underneath that?" the photographer asked Minaz.

"Like, a body suit."

"Can you take off the jeans and just show legs and a shirt?"

"God, this is so exploitative."

"You know they won't let the photos through the Tokyo airport if they're too racy."

"That's only pubic hair. They have special bureaucrats over there to brush over the pubic hair in every issue of *Playboy* by hand," Kiri said.

"It's the ancient art of calligraphy," I said.

"We need to get more cleavage. Okay, there, it's showing up."

"I have *some* cleavage . . ." Minaz said.

"We know you have some, we just have to get it in the shot—"

"I know all these stylists who pretend to be gay, they're like, 'here dear, I'll tape you up,' and they're actually flaming heterosexuals. Especially with, like, *Cosmopolitan*, where they really push the whole front up like this—" The photographer demonstrated the maneuver.

"So where do we see you in print lately?" one of the other artists asked Minaz. The putz.

"I'm in *Elle* this month . . ."

"Great."

"First time in the American edition."

"Where did they have you before that?"

"Milan."

"That's nice."

"Okay, Minaz, don't flirt with the help."

"Hey, Kiri, you look really tough in the leather. That's a long way from a kimono," someone said.

"That's a *Glamour* Don't," someone said.

"Wouldn't that be jive?" someone else said

"Think about how this is the last shot, you're so happy, you're going home, you're going to make millions of dollars, you're all so young and fresh and good-looking, imagine ten billion Japanese teenagers masturbating over this picture, that's it, yeah!"

Kathleen the secretary brought in a big basket of complicated pastries from Balducci's, and we picked at them and said good night and all walked off into the fog.

■

The Monake fall couture show was supposed to start at seven, which meant seven-fifty. Since it was her first big New York runway event, Minaz, Jerry Solomon, Calvin, and I had a late Dean & DeLucca take-out lunch and hung around the house and then walked the nine blocks from my house to Broadway and Spring Street. It was good for her to be with people who knew her and knew about her transformation, she said. It was cool, breezy, early spring weather with menacing clouds cruising by. There were a lot of people standing around outside, and for some reason only Calvin and I were on the list, and Minaz had to convince the Monake Fashion Police to let Andrew in.

The show was in a big, big loft, really the whole floor, of this cast-iron building owned by the dealer I used to work for, Jerry Davidian. He was planning to open another gallery here, eventually, when the time was right. In the meantime he was renting floors out. The top floor was the new offices for Randt Publishing and was already beautifully paneled in Jerry Style. But on three, the clubby-looking mahogany-and-brass elevators opened out onto old raw wood floors spotted with white paint, exposed girders and pipes, white cast-iron Ionic columns, and half-finished drywall. The white canvas-covered runway was very long and ran the length of the space, and there were a few hundred white chairs set up on either side of it, each one (in front) with a large name written directly on the back in black marker: IVANA TRUMP, CHRISTIE BRINKLEY, MERCEDES BASS, JACQUE-LINE SCHNABEL, LADY MISS KIER. Most of the chairs were already occupied. The backstage area was off to the right, screened by drywall, and the platform for the video crews was way down-runway to the left.

Minaz excused herself and went backstage to get gotten ready.

"I'm going to sit in Liza Minnelli's chair if she doesn't show up," Andrew said.

I said I triple-dared him.

"She'll never make it. Many of the chair labels seem extremely optimistic," Calvin said.

Sandra Bernhard sort of breezed in, tall and beautifully ugly in a black-and-white-check Monake business suit, and most of the photographers congealed around her setting off flashes.

"Fresh from another flop," Andrew said. "The program says she wrote a rap for the show."

"Even Milton did some commissioned work," I said.

"Sure, Milton Berle did a ton of commercials," Calvin yelled over. He was getting separated from us by the crowd.

Rose was on the program, too. She'd kept her name, but nobody knew her from before. Scasi had sold his contract with her to Elite, and so now we weren't getting anything from the deal, but Mark,

Karl, and I had still netted nearly a hundred and fifty thousand dollars from the whole thing, which wasn't too bad for an experiment. She'd also been acting in a few things, but she wasn't really very good. It would be interesting to see her compete with my latest design. Of course, I knew which would win.

I was about to sit in a chair that it looked like no one was going to take and then this pushy gray-haired woman from *Details* magazine moved in and said it was hers because it was marked to Annie Flanders and she couldn't come, so this woman had come instead. Okay, bitch, I thought, I can stand, I'm not proud. I don't have a chair. I don't have a life. I'll deal with you later. We all ended up standing behind the last row of chairs. People came in behind us and couldn't see a thing.

A handful of models came through the crowd, getting there pretty late—I guess they were just coming from the Bill Blass show at the Pierre. Nobody paid much attention to them. Christie Brinkley came in, and people paid attention to *her*.

"I . . . don't want clever . . . con-versation. . . ." Calvin started singing.

"What a big compliment that song was," Andrew agreed. "But I like her Just the Way She Are myself."

Everyone rustled around for a while. Spike Lee came in, a walking billboard in a baseball cap and a jacket with the names of all of his films embroidered on it. The photographers mobbed him for a minute and then eased up and got into position. More waiting. The crowd got noisier. Bruce Weber came in. Azzedine Alaïa and Claude Montana, both better designers than Monake in my opinion, managed to get to their seats, and finally the lights went down, loud *Candide*-overture-esque music started up, the runway lights went up, and Linda Evangelista and my friend Kimura strutted out in the first of the fall line: apparently a hybrid of Mexican Peasant and Frank Gehry–like exposed stitching and industrial materials, all in shades of pumpkin and avocado. Under these layers of hell-fabrics they had tight-fitting see-through black chiffon blouses over black lace bras that clearly showed their nipples. I liked that part. But the line was hideous. However, on the runway, on such great models, it couldn't help looking great, too. Just wait till the clients got it home. Ten years ago, all runway models were beautiful, and people weren't looking at the clothes. So they made the models ugly for a couple of years. But now they're getting beautiful again because otherwise people won't look at *anything*.

"I'm not sure about Monake," Andrew said to Ellen, this girl who was next to us. "I mean, the detailing's great, and they're really clever, but to ask seventeen hundred dollars for a cotton skirt, I don't know—"

"I think it should be *more* expensive," Calvin said. "Anyway, half of it's just for the fetish value."

I was upset Minaz hadn't opened the show, but maybe Monake was saving her for something. He was.

She sauntered out alone—everyone else had been paired—in what the program described as a "Shirley Temple Black Rubber Do-It-Yourself Coat with Wild Cherry Collar and Cuffs; Celadon Pebble Silk/Lovat Windowpane Tweed All-in-One-Dress." It was a strange ensemble but a grandiose one, and she carried it off amazingly well. A lot of runway models, including Linda Evangelista, can look ugly up close because their features are so strong—they have to project—but the Minaz face projected despite all the subtlety I'd put in it. She had a short brown wig and different makeup and looked totally different. But perfect. She was only five-foot-eight, and so she was short for a model, just an inch over regulation height, but she walked with that easy swaggering grace that it takes some models years to perfect, and she animated her haughty look with tiny hints of smiles —less broad than the other models' smiles, but warm enough to win the audience over. All the models were being pretty warm this season, actually—apparently the nineties are the Friendly Decade. She flipped the jacket off, exposing *her* nipples through the Celadon Pebble Silk, turned around, and strolled back. The irregular staccato of flashcubes swelled to a steady strobe. She got more applause than anyone had so far, partly because she was a new model to them but also because she had such a distinctive look, the look of a star.

There were five sets, and she came on once each set, which meant a lot of changing, but she didn't look ruffled. Rose was great, too, but there was no contest. The last set, which was titled "Urban Pow-Wow," seemed to involve a pre-Columbian theme.

"What fresh hell is *this*?" Calvin asked.

"These clothes are really harshing my wave," I said.

"They're beyond belief," Ellen said. "Wretched. Not acceptable."

"I'm warming to them," Andrew said.

Sandra's voice came on doing her rent-a-rap over an Indian-sounding drumbeat, something about "shake it, girl," and Beat on the Street and "wear it hot and wear it cool" and "It's all about Monake." Next thing she'd be performing sonnets to Baby Wipes. Rose, Kimura, and some other mannequins walked out in hand-embroidered sheaths. Some old lady in Honduras had probably gone blind making these things. Naomi Campbell came out in a sort of pseudo-Aztec deerhide outfit with leggings and intricate sandals and anachronistic gloves and got a big hand, but Minaz, ending the set, emerged in a fantastic sort of intricate Maya thing with shell bracelets and painted-on tattoos and a huge headdress with turquoise ear flanges and little Jester Gods and cascading green-gold feathers that looked like Quetzal feathers but were really dyed ostrich. It was really kind of great, and she carried it off and was awesome without taking it too seriously, and she just blew everybody away.

The house lights came up. There was constant applause. All the other models trooped out, and Monake sort of flapped out, stocky and jolly in a white turtleneck, and flopped briskly down the runway waving to friends and especially to Spike and Sandra and bouncing his fist to the music—somehow Sandra's rap had segued into a stirring klezmer version of *"Hazenu Shalom Aleichim."* Minaz and the other models surrounded him and clapped. Linda and Naomi kissed each other on the lips, trying to steal the show. After a couple of thousand extra pictures, they all trooped back. Calvin, Andrew, Ellen, and I hung around while everyone clawed their way to the exit.

"She was amazing," everyone said to me.

"I'm writing an article on 'Chic Women of the '90s' for *Mirabella,"* Ellen said. "She should be in it."

"She even made that junk look good," Calvin said, uncharacteristically praising one out of two items in the same sentence.

"Do you see anyone with a cellular phone I can borrow?" I asked. No one had.

"I can't imagine why I don't have one," I said.

Some people from Spumoni Rotweiller, a kind of major art gallery that shows a lot of Italian stuff, came over and started talking to us. I tried to introduce everybody.

"I liked your show," one of them—Arlene, I think—said to me.

"That was nearly a year ago," I said, "I'm amazed you remember."

"No, uh, it was great," she said. She was really pretty, she'd been a model herself before going into the Vis Biz.

"What did you think of the line?" the other one, Kevin, asked us.

"It was death," Calvin said. He had been trying to edge over to talk to Spike Lee, but Spike was already engulfed in a mob of people oozing into the elevator, so he'd given up. He twitched his round head around frantically trying to find someone more important than us to talk to.

"That ostrich stuff, that was just megally skankular," Kevin said.

"What did you think of that new model, Minaz?" I asked.

"The sort of oriental-Indian looking one? She was terrific," he said. "She has a certain ineffable quality."

"I know exactly what you mean," I said.

"Aren't you going out with her?"

"Well . . ." I said.

"Jesus," Kevin said to Calvin, "some new model comes on the scene and the next thing you know he's sleeping with her. That cock."

"Excuse me?" I said.

"Word gets around," Andrew said.

"That Aztec princess dress was the most repulsive garment I'd ever seen in my life," Calvin said. "And most of the leather looked like stuff you could buy at Canal Street Jeans. He's falling apart, as far as I'm concerned."

"Oh, I don't know, I think the Aztecs might have liked it," I mumbled.

"Wait, we want to hear more about Minaz," Kevin said. "She's an actress, too, right? Glen O'Brian had a thing on her in *Interview.*"

"She's incredibly talented," I said. Some more lights turned off. The place was emptying out. Some of the models were already coming out from behind the false walls in their street clothes. Naomi Campbell was signing an autograph. "I'm going to run back there for a second. Hang out, okay?" I said.

I walked backstage. Kimura and Nikki were ostentatiously topless, trying to get into their jeans. Bellina, a woman we knew who works for Monake, was talking to a tech man at a computer disco console and waved to me distractedly. I didn't see Minaz at first, but then she came into view around one of the huge circular racks of already-plastic-wrapped couture. She was in her jeans and T-shirt, talking into a microphone held by that pushy silver-haired lady from *Details*.

"The best thing about modeling is getting a chance to bare your mammary glands to the pervasive Male Gaze," she was saying.

"Do you think modeling is exploitative?" Ms *Details* asked.

"Oh, God, no, how could parading around in underwear in front of ten trillion people be exploitative?"

Some other reporter came in and asked her to come out and do an interview with Naomi and Linda. "Okay, come along," she said to me.

"Can you be that proper little Indian girl?" I asked.

Linda Evangelista and Naomi were sitting on chairs labeled LIZ SMITH and JERRY HALL. One of the reporters pulled over a chair labeled ANNA WINTOUR for Minaz.

"You seem to be the new star of the circuit," one of them said to Minaz. "Where do you come from?"

"Bombay," she said.

"Are you friends with Naomi and Linda?"

"We've just worked together a couple of times, but they've both been very helpful. I'm just a tyro," she said.

"Minaz is great," Naomi said in her English accent. Linda looked upset that she wasn't front and center.

"Now, you, Naomi and Linda and Christy Turlington used to call yourselves the Inseparables, isn't that right?' Ms. *Details* asked.

"That's right, uh, sadly, Christy has pneumonia this week so she couldn't make it, otherwise she'd be here," Linda said. "Otherwise, she'd be here. Nobody wears Irving's clothes like Christy. I think she's just the best person and she's really down to earth, and it's great when the three of us get together. . . ."

"So Minaz, you do other things besides modeling?" one of the male reporters asked.

"Yes, I'm acting in something on HBO but I also have my own act that I hope is more artistically sound, and I'll be doing that at the

Kitchen and then at the Orpheum, on Third Avenue, in November. . . ."

She was obviously doing all right so I went back to our little group. Bellina had come out and was being critical of her own accessories for the show.

"I just think that homeboy jewelry look is passé," she said.

"Shall we go focus on food?" Andrew asked.

"I have to go eat with the office," Bellina said.

"I have to find a phone," I said. "I'm going upstairs to Randt to see whether they'll let me use one." Randt was Jennifer Randt Publishing. They put out *House and Furnishings* and *Art World* and all those kinds of things. I got into the mahogany elevator with a strong feeling that I'd shortly be excluded from Minaz's career. It was just something about the way she acted with me lately. She was a new, independent creature. Like a sculpture doesn't need its creator anymore, once it's in a museum; it belongs to the people who look at it. Maybe eventually I'd be excluded from the rest of her life, too.

35

Alan, the agent, put Minaz in a music video without even asking me. "You can't just do editorial and runway, we have to get you more advertising," he kept saying. "Editorial doesn't pay at all." And he felt that some MTV work would help get her into the really lucrative cosmetics-commercial track. It was a little ironic, the thought of Minaz doing cosmetics commercials.

She was going to be "the girl" in a narrative piece by some hot new band called My Last Duchess. Alan had helped rush the video into production as soon as their song "Disco '82" made it onto the charts. I got a message on my machine: "It's Minaz. The song's up to number four in *Billboard* this week. We're shooting at Mother's Sound Stage at 200 East Fifth Street, Studio B, Chromavision. I'm on from four o'clock to eleven. Stop by." Beep

I'd been planning to go to Philadelphia that day to do some photography at the Museum of Monstrosities. It's all full of two-headed fetuses and no-headed fetuses, autophages, and other creepy stuff in jars. It's really fun. But then I thought I'd want to be around for Minaz's shoot.

Around five o'clock that evening, I put my makeup case in my bag and walked over there. It was up three flights of crummy stairs. But it was a big square sound stage, only they weren't using the sound, of course, and they had a camera crane and a dolly and everything, so someone had spent at least some money. They'd hung a huge gold lamé curtain over the cycloramas, and it gave the place a kind of *Chorus Line* effect. There were about twenty dancers milling around, all obviously non-union, dressed to the height of this year's clubby fashion in black-and-white polka-dot skimpy things with lots of ethnic necklaces and bangles made out of cowrie shells. There was one token white guy dancer. Alan was walking around flirting with some of the talent, so I said hi. He took me into the little office.

"Have you heard the song?" he asked.

"No," I said.

"Oh, great. Well, Minaz should turn up again in about ten minutes. Are you still acting as her personal manager, or what?"

"Well, we can both do some managing, but I don't need to make any money on this right away, or if she thinks I should, I'll work it out with her. I mean, I trust her and you. . . . I mean, basically we'll have to talk. . . ."

"Okay, Minaz and I may have to draw up some papers, though."

"That's fine. Can I go talk to her?"

"She's getting makeup done."

"Actually, that's why she asked me here," I said, "I'm more of her image consultant than her manager . . ."

I trailed off as I headed toward the dressing room. I pushed open the door and got hit by all the usual sweat and hairspray and makeup smells. It was kind of nostalgic. I hadn't been on a film set for a couple of years, and it was exciting. Who cares about paintings? I thought. I looked around at a couple of cute black dancer girls getting their hair spiked up. Suddenly I realized it was Minaz in the far corner. Two people were working on her. She looked totally different. Absolutely stunning, though. But I'd built so much flexibility into the system that a little bit of makeup and hairstyle had changed her completely.

"Hi," she said. She was so impassive lately.

"Hi, can I take a look?" I asked. She said she didn't mind. They'd done a decent makeup job, but somehow they'd lined her eyes so she looked much more Oriental, and she had a kind of tan Pan-Cake on. And they'd overdone the contouring. She looked incredible, but a little harsh. I would have done it much better.

"Do you think I could play around with your makeup a little?" I asked.

"Um . . ." Minaz said, "uh, Israel, this is Jamie. Jamie's kind of my personal image manager."

Israel was a kind of burned-out artist-looking guy with long, dark hair and a cigarette. I could tell he'd be incredibly hurt if I adapted his makeup.

"How do you like my makeup work?" he asked threateningly.

I didn't say anything. It's a Warholish trick. Sometimes it works to just hang out and be silent. Finally Minaz said it. She was the star, anyway, she could say anything she wanted.

"Um, Jamie thinks it's great, but he'd like to adapt one or two things to fit the specific concept of this video."

"Well, I'm supposed to be in charge of makeup."

It was a really tense moment. This time neither of us said anything. Finally Israel walked away in a blue funk.

"Thank God this isn't a union video, or AFTRA would break my legs," I said.

"Listen," Minaz said, "I'm sure you can do better, but I'm not into generating all this friction on the set."

"Sorry. In the future you can insist on doing most of your own makeup. We'll go over it together, we can work out a lot of different possible looks for you."

"Fabulous."

"Did Israel notice anything unusual about your face?"

"No."

"He's blind."

"I was glad he didn't."

"Some people may notice that you don't sweat under the lights."

"I'll just tell them I'm Wonder Woman."

I started sponging off the makeup. I heard Alan's voice outside yelling, "You guys look like you're sleepwalking. I want to see some attitude. More *attitude!*"

"It sounds like the dancers don't have enough attitude," Minaz said.

"Is Alan directing or producing or both?" I asked.

"There's this guy, Ed, around somewhere, he's supposed to be the director."

"Hold still, please. I think I'm achieving that ineffable quality that's going to make you the heartthrob of millions."

I'd taken off most of the base and just used powder, although I didn't really think she needed even that, I'd put so much into her coloration, and her surface wasn't shiny anyway, it was just good and consistently satiny. But I didn't really have much experience preparing people for video work, with really bright, all-over lighting, and so I thought I'd better err on the safe side. I'd kept most of Israel's mascara job, but changed the eye shadow to a lighter shade of green, something fantasy-ish but not as emphatic. I did a little bit of contouring around the cheekbones. I didn't think she needed any more.

"Who decided on the hair?" I asked. It was way spiked up into a kind of super-topknot with beads around it.

"This guy, Kelly. What do you think?"

"Well, it's saying *something*. . . . It's certainly too complicated to change, anyway."

Someone came in and said they were ready for Minaz on the set.

"Thanks, something went wrong, I'll just be a second," she said. She got up.

"Wait, I have to redo the lips," I said. "I can't *stand* glossy lips!" I started getting out my three colors of Japanese matte finish lip powder. "This is the best red color in the world," I said. "They don't even sell it in this country because it's too toxic."

"We're just going to deal with the lips I've got," Minaz said, and got up. She was getting uppity. I should have wiped off Israel's lip job before anything.

She walked out onto the set. I put my makeup away and slunk behind the camera. The dancers were arranged in kind of a *West Side Story* conga line, and Minaz was getting ready to kind of weave through them. It wasn't quite what I would have done with it. It might be fun to direct some videos, I thought. If Robert Longo can do it, I can do it.

"All right, let's go back to the pickup after the bridge," Ed was yelling. "Keith, you know where to start the eight-count?"

"Let's rehearse one more time," Keith said. He was evidently the hip choreographer. He had a sort of Peter Max shirt with peace signs on it and hair with a kind of Islamic-tile pattern cut into it.

They started running through the routine. I started to feel like it was out of my hands at this point, so I wandered off the stage into the hall outside where the food had been. One of the leathery guys from The Last Duchess was poking through the mess. He said there were still some shrimp rolls left, and I found two that were still in their wax paper, so I wasn't afraid to eat them.

36

While they were cutting the video, Dodge scheduled Minaz for a few cosmetics advertising shoots, which meant big bucks. It looked like she was going to start off straddling the modeling and video worlds, which was great, I guess. A session with Scavullo had gone as well as the one with Timothy, not as artistic, but very slick. She even got a *Mirabella* cover scheduled and got into the HBO thing Alan had talked about without even an audition. I guess there wasn't any difference between an actress and a model anymore. You were just the all-around girl or nothing. The HBO project was some political-based docudrama, and they were rushing it into production in time to be topical, so they shot her part in six days and it was ready to air ten days after that. She worked all the time, and we hardly even went to any clubs or parties or anything. I'd kind of been looking forward to going to things with her a lot, because she looked so great, but things were happening too fast. So I worked on my paintings and personal finance programs and cleaned up the Loft in Space. It was getting to be June, and New York was beginning to bum me out. I felt like I was due for a vacation.

■

She looked great on TV, even though I wished it could pick up more of the exquisite detail I'd worked so hard on. Her acting was great, too, even though the script was terrible. It was some fluff about forming a new Eastern European republic. The press for the special was good, but not as many good photos of Minaz as we expected. She had a good writeup in the *Voice,* but the shot of her was crummy, and she got a big thing in *TV Guide,* which is starting to try to publish "serious" articles now, but they didn't quite get her radiance in the shot, which looked like it had been taken straight off the show itself. Still, it was enough. I got a telephone message from Minaz two days after it aired:

"Listen, I got a call from Judy Newman at *People* magazine. They're ninety percent sure they want to do a spread on me, and they know Timothy, and they'll let him do the photography. And Alan's sending me to L.A. to test for a Brian de Palma film. Isn't that great?"

Yeah, great, I thought. All I'd been doing was working on histori-cal-dialectically significant masterpieces that very few people would ever see, and she was jet-setting around like Pia Zadora. I was excited about her career, but I guess I hadn't quite realized that I wasn't going to be getting any recognition for her success. Somehow I'd imagined I could keep something secret and still take the credit for it. Only people would think it was all too creepy.

I said "break a leg" like a really good sport and let her hang up. Maybe I'd done enough. I'd gotten things going, and I didn't have to play manager to Minaz anymore. She was pretty much in Alan Hirsch's hands right now as it was. Maybe I could sit back, see what happened, and get on with some of my art. Until I took credit for the faces—and that was way, way in the future—I should think about my painting more. I had kind of an urge to get back into fantasy. And Karen at the gallery had suddenly said she wanted to do a small back-room show soon, to coincide with that thing at the New Mu-seum. And I had some great new ideas, kind of informed by my work with the faces. It wouldn't be bad later if there was some sort of a tie-in.

■

Minaz flew to L.A. without coming by to tell me. Just a phone call that woke me up at eleven in the morning. I guess she was pretty excited about the whole thing, and I couldn't really blame her. The picture sounded a little silly from what Alan told me, but at least she was on a steadily rising spiral. She said she'd fly back for my opening. Somehow the opening didn't seem that major anymore. With Minaz away and the art season winding down for the summer, and with my shows coming up in September—which was a good time because you're more likely to get reviewed then than at the height of the season—I kind of felt like getting out of town. I was a little depressed that Minaz didn't want to stay with me even though I was beginning to realize that I had really mixed feelings about her. In a way, maybe I really had loved her for herself alone, as they say, including her flaws, and that included her facial flaws. Now that she was perfect, I somehow felt kind of excluded. Like she wasn't mainly for me, she was for the whole world. And there was tension there because she had been so defined by me. She needed to re-create a separate identity for herself.

The only thing that was keeping me in New York was my schedule of procedures. I'd asked David and Mark not to make any new appointments a couple of months before, but there were still a few commitments left. I'd seen off The Laureen, now totally transformed, and she seemed happy, and that was the one I really cared about. The others were just egotistical second-rate actors and actresses. I didn't even feel like extending myself with them. I'd extended myself with the Minaz Project, and look where it had gotten me.

I got out of bed at noon. I took a shower and wiped the steam off one of the magnifying mirrors and looked at myself. I was kind of shocked. I looked old. My laugh lines were really visible. There were incipient eye bags. I was getting puffy and droopy. I almost ran into the studio to get some tools to fix myself up with, but I resisted the impulse. I had kind of a rule never to operate on myself. I'd probably mess up. I'm squeamish at the sight of my own blood. And I wanted to be more sure of the procedure and wait until someone else was trained enough to do it. That day would be pretty far away, though. David didn't really want to learn to do it and Mark didn't have the poetry. One of the things on my To Do list was find a trustworthy apprentice. A sorcerer's apprentice.

In the meantime, I reconciled myself to conventional skin care. I did my morning ritual, from shaving and astringent through sunblock. I came out looking a little better. I decided not to gel the hair. I'd just keep brushing it back with my hand today. I have pretty great hair. It's a funny almost purple color—very odd for an Italian. Everybody mentions it. I've got a lot of it, too. God, can you imagine if I started going bald? We'd really find out what obsessiveness meant.

I sat around for a few hours, looking over the money-manager programs on my computer—the tax one and the secret one—and it looked like I was doing okay. I was afraid the market was peaking on some of my collectibles, but the auction season was over. Really, I could afford three months off. And I had a standing invitation to stay at a big empty house in Key Biscayne, with a studio and everything, over the summer. The owner had some of my paintings and didn't want to rent to strangers. So I'd just give him a couple of paintings at the end of the stay. It's a little odd to do Florida in the summer, because no one's there, but if you make full use of air-conditioning and SPF 50 and hats and sunglasses and never go outside in daylight, there's really no reason not to. And I didn't want to go back up to Connecticut, the way I often do in the summer, because I'd be too tempted to keep driving down to New York, and anyway, my parents were in Massachusetts, and I didn't feel like dealing with anyone. And Europe was out, because setting up a studio was too much hassle. You can get Mussini oil colors at only two stores in Brussels, and that's it. I don't understand how anyone paints anything over there.

I called up David and told him that we'd have to put the remaining appointments off for at least three months, to be on the safe side. I said he could tell them I was sick. He wasn't thrilled about it.

I called my fabulous travel agent in L.A.—he's at a place called Xanadu Travel, they handle mainly top actors, they'll even advise you on your personal problems and write a doctor's note for you if you suddenly decide you don't want to go—and left a note and a key with the trustworthy downstairs neighbors to take care of my plants and fish. They just had to put a slow-dissolve food cake in the tank every two weeks. I threw out everything in the refrigerator and packed a few things. I left all the incriminating stuff that was still in the house in a box marked DAVID. He'd hide it over the weekend.

The last appointment I had was visiting my shrink. I'd been bad for the last few months and had canceled over and over. I cabbed uptown with my two bags so I could go right to the airport as soon as I got sane.

"We're not doing very much serious work lately," he said as I staggered into the eternal murk, fifteen minutes late. I dropped my bag of books and put the leather bag, with the laptop in it, carefully down on the soft part of the couch.

"I've been bad," I said. "I deserve to be punished."

He just frowned. "What's that?" he asked.

"It's a Wash'n Dri," I said. I was cleaning my hands with one of those little lemony-wet paper towels.

"How often do you wash your hands during an average day?" he asked.

"Oh, I don't know, not too many times, uh, let's see, one, two— three or four hundred times a day, I guess. No, that's not true. I'm just kidding. About, oh, six hundred times. Joke. Just a joke."

Dr. Brook was so humorless these days, it was scary. He just looked at me. "They come in packs of twelve," I said. "I guess I use up a pack or two a day. I mean, when it's hot and I can't wear gloves around."

He just sat there silently, implying that there was a great deal wrong with me. Finally he spoke:

"This fear of contamination from outside usually occurs in peo- ple who fear imperfections in themselves," he intoned. "It goes along with the perfectionism and the hypochondriasis and everything else. I really think we should get to the heart of all this. I think there's something you're not telling me. I'm going to ask you again: Are you sure you're not gay?"

"What would being gay have to do with anything?" I asked. I was surprised he'd ask such a dumb question. "All my friends are gay, and they're practically as boring as straight people. What would being gay—"

"Well then, what else is it you're not mentioning?" he asked.

I was kind of stymied. There *were* a couple of things, after all. Dr. Brook wasn't a total idiot.

"I agree that we're not going to get anything done until I can put more time into this," I said. "We're going to have to wait until I get back from Florida."

He handed me his bill with a shrug-off gesture as I left. I walked into the bright sunlight and got into the first cab I saw and got whisked to LaGuardia.

I felt great in spite of all the scorn from my damned therapist. It was fun traveling, fun making spur-of-the-moment decisions. I got on the flight just in time, without a care, to speak of, in the world.

37

I was alternately shooting pool and swimming in the pool in this big empty house. I hadn't done much painting yet because I hadn't totally set up the studio. I had MTV on, and I recognized Minaz's video. I'd seen the director's reel, but it was different seeing it on real TV in another place. Suddenly you realized people all over the world were actually watching this thing. From the buildup the MTV people gave it it sounded like it was doing really well. I should ask dear Alan's office to fax me Minaz's press clips, I thought. He knew I'd "discovered" her—he just didn't know how much—and now I got zero credit.

When I first got to Florida, I'd followed Minaz's career mainly through the women's magazines. Women's magazines are amazing. For one thing, they *can't* just be for women, but a lot of women do read them, so there's a real auto-erotic suppressed lesbian strain going through the entire culture—women's magazines are our entire culture, as far as I'm concerned—that doesn't usually get acknowledged. And they're *entirely* devoted to an unattainable ideal of beauty, certainly unattainable for 99.98 percent of their readers. Just trying to keep up with that ideal really does keep women subjugated, I guess. But what can you do about it? And what's weird is the magazines are also getting more *like* women: soft, and thick, and glossy, and filled with fragrances, and there was even a period where some of them talked to you mechanically, although that seems to have cooled down a bit, thank God. There was an interview with Minaz in *Model* magazine. It was kind of a contrast to the other interviews with models. For instance there was an interview in the magazine with a model named Deirdre:

——How did you first get into modeling?

——I was hanging out at this mall in Ashtabula, Ohio, where I'm from, with a friend who was doing a fashion show there, and the Creature Features hostess, Lucinda, came up and asked me if I'd ever done any modeling.

——And then what happened?

——It turned out she was a scout, and I didn't really want to do it because my friend was crying because she didn't get asked, but then later I thought okay, because I could use the money and it would be fun. And then I did some catalogues and then they sent me to Eileen Dodge.

——And how did you come to live in Paris?

——Eileen just thought I looked really American, I guess.

——And what are your interests other than modeling?

——I'm really, really, really into music. Rock's my favorite.

——What plans do you have for the future?

——I don't know, you can't model forever. I was thinking about learning how to be a sound technician.

■

Minaz's interview started out:

——What got you into modeling?

——*The Countesse of Pembrokes Arcadia.*

——What's that?

——It's only the most important English literary work of the sixteenth century.

——What's it about?

——Beauty. And Nature, and loss. Pastoral stuff, you know.

——So you're quite an intellectual.

——For a model. Of course, Vanna White's intellectual for a model. I like to think of myself as kind of a Theodor Adorno with breasts.

——And what do you most want to achieve in your career?

——I want to give every other woman in America a complex the size of a Greyhound bus.

It went uphill from there. But I was proud of her. Nobody would get it, but maybe they'd like her even more.

■

There was also an ad in *Elle* with Minaz in it that really surprised me: they were using her to sell *glasses* this month, which I wasn't thrilled with. She looked great in them, though, although I hadn't particularly allowed for that eventuality in the design. "A face is like a work of art," the copy ran, "It deserves a great frame." Yep. But it's too bad all those overweight, ugly *Hausfrauen* in Idaho can't buy the face along with the glasses.

She looked so great. She lit up the page. She'd worked out how to use her eyes and her facial muscles to make the face even more expressive than I had planned it to be. It was all really worth it. She had a preternatural face to match her preternatural talent. It was obvious to me at least that she was going to be the biggest thing ever. My calculations had been correct. Oddly enough, there was an ad for Nike exercise-walking shoes on the facing page that said:

LIPOSUCTION
STRAIGHTENING
WAXING
TONING
RHINOPLASTY
SALON TANNING
ELECTROLYSIS
FACE LIFTING
TUMMY TUCKING
IMPLANTS
HYPNOSIS
ZEN
MASSAGE THERAPY
DERMABRASION
CHEMICAL PEEL
LAMINATES
ACUPRESSURE

IRIDOLOGY
HYDROTHERAPY
REGRESSION THERAPY
WHEN YOU'RE TIRED OF IT ALL, JUST DO IT. NIKE.

Ridiculous, I thought. As if just exercising could ever do any of
the things for you that all those processes can do. It's horrible the way
some people try to convince you that you can't buy beauty. Or that
you can buy it in a pair of running shoes.

She was in one Revlon ad with Linda and Rose. "Unforgettable
Lashes," it said. "Oh my God, I've forgotten her lashes!" I thought.
There was also a seminude shot of Minaz in *GQ*. Her bare breasts
gave her a tremendous feeling of vulnerability. There's a tension
between breasts and eyes, I think. It was very sexy to think of her
exposing herself. Glamour photography: the lure of celebrity, exhibi-
tionism, and immorality. Wow.

■

Alan's office finally started sending me all the relevant magazines
and newspapers and even reels of the talk shows she was on. Her
film hadn't even been released yet, and she was already becoming a
household name. It's amazing what a well-oiled publicity machine
can do. They tried to make sure all the articles about her stressed her
mystery aspect. What was most interesting were the reactions different people had to her beauty. I'd succeeded. People were going crazy
about Minaz's strangeness and her mystery. I was glad I'd left a lot of
room for makeup to change her look: she always looked different,
and it worked for her. But she always looked like herself, too. Someone in *Vogue* said she had "that indefinable something that Brigitte
Bardot had, that steamy sensuality and animal verve." On the other
hand, *Elle* said she had "a delicate, ethereal beauty that seems entirely
divorced from the earthly realm, a starlight magic that is elfin, mysti-
cal, remote." And *Harpers and Queen* said she was the "exotic In-
dian/American of the '90s, the apogee of ethnic chic."

Some of the articles were kind of disturbing. People were getting
obsessed with her. One boy from Arizona had hitchhiked all the way
to L.A. to try to meet her, and when he couldn't get onto the lot he
took an overdose of angel dust and died. I'd really struck a chord.

Next thing, someone would probably shoot the president for her. *That* would be something for me to feel proud about.

■

As it turned out, I really did get a lot of painting and art fabrication done. Florida was like being marooned on some hyperreal asteroid, and all I could do was work. I was kind of inspired by the Minaz Project, and I did some stuff that related to some of my thoughts while I had been working on her. She'd called occasionally over the course of the two months she was filming, and we had good chats, but we didn't talk about the "relationship"—a word I've always hated, anyway. Her calls had stopped a couple of weeks later, around the beginning of August, and I wasn't about to call her myself. So what if she was hanging out with Kevin Costner, that Orson Welles of the nineties? At this point, I figured, our relationship was about power. When I was the next Andy Warhol—but I'd be a virile, handsome Warhol, a Warhol for the fin de siècle—then she'd come crying back to me. So I did all these great paintings. They were more traditional, less messing around with photographic processes and weird materials, but I figured I could get away with traditional stuff again at this point because I didn't have as much to prove. I sent Karen a plan of a false wall I wanted put in the back room of the gallery, to block the natural light, and a swatch of the warm gray color I wanted the gallery walls painted. I didn't show the work to anyone. I was kind of paranoid, I guess, because I'd heard recently about a friend of a friend whose graduate-school work had formed the basis for a show by a Major Artist, a show I'd really liked when I saw it. Apparently this painter had showed up at SVA to "guest crit" the students' work, and she had been really taken with this series of studies that this girl, L'Tania, had done. They were done with a technique she'd invented herself, which involved some kind of Lycra Spandex. "This is what makes doing these crit things worthwhile," the Artist had said. A couple of months later, L'Tania walked into the Major Artist's show at Fortreza and saw stuff she'd done that was almost an exact copy of her imagery and technique. But there wasn't anything she could say about it because she didn't want to ruin her relationship with the Major Artist. It happens all the time. So I just worked in the air-conditioned studio alone and only went out after dark.

I hung out drinking sweet coffee and eating *plátanos rellenos* with friends in the small art community in Miami, mainly ex-Cubans who lived in Little Havana and made obsessive art based on religious icons. I had a short fling with a Vietnamese singer who played nightclubs around Miami and St. Petersburg. I loved the Deco district and hung out at the hotels there all the time, soaking up the Ersatz Constructivist architecture and the peach and turquoise—everything in Miami Beach, including the sea and sky, seemed to be peach and turquoise.

I talked to Mark fairly often. He was having problems at the lab. Karl had walked out in a huff over some minor thing and now he was afraid he wasn't going to get another grant this year. I told him I'd do some more procedures in the fall so he shouldn't worry about money. I was a little concerned about whether Karl would try to take our processes with him if he left for good, but Mark said he wasn't really interested. He might get some high-level position at Johns Hopkins. I asked him whether he had alienated Karl by making fun of him. I remembered that scene in the lab when Karl had gotten all huffy. He said they hadn't been getting along, but that it was Karl's fault because Karl had a bad sense of humor.

I called my shrink a lot. Even before I went to Miami, my general irresponsibility had forced our relationship to degenerate into calls instead of visits. "I can't handle it, let's just do phone" was my battle cry with him for a while. He seemed to think I was running away from something. I kept saying that if I got as successful and rich and powerful as I wanted to be, I'd be happy no matter how messed up I was. He didn't think that was a healthful attitude, and we kind of argued back and forth from there.

Timothy came down to shoot the Fine Young Cannibals while they were on tour and we hung out in his cabana at the Eden Roc. The hotel had a great kind of faded splendor, and they'd filmed the beginning of my favorite movie of all time, *Goldfinger,* right there—behind the bar, where they had glass where you could see into the pool. I was pretty thrilled with that. I rented a convertible and zoomed around deserted suburbs at night on the way back to Key Biscayne. I became a connoisseur of shopping malls. I swam in the pool and shot pool on my host's great regulation pool table, and I'd practically forgotten about New York altogether when I realized I barely had two days to arrange shipping for the work I'd done and get back in time for the New Museum thing.

At one point I found a whole lot of old magazines in the trash next door, and I spent days reading them by the pool. Completely by accident, I came upon this horrible article by Romain Gary in an old issue of *Holiday* magazine from the sixties. Calvin says that without *Holiday* magazine, life isn't worth living. It set me thinking. It was so misogynist. He tells this really male chauvinist story. Listen to this pretentious bastard:

> A friend of mine recently underwent a severe ordeal. He is one of the most brilliant European art dealers, and his personal collection of portraits by Italian masters is justly famous. He married a young and beautiful girl and prided himself on his wife's lovely looks, almost as if she were a particularly delightful item in his art collection. Then, one day, somebody—probably an envious competitor—sent him a photograph. The face looked exactly like his wife's—exactly alike, in fact—except for the nose, which was beaklike. My friend glanced at the picture and showed it laughingly to his wife. "What an extraordinary resemblance," he said, "except for that terrible nose." . . .
>
> The young woman appeared embarrassed and said nothing. Then, a few days later, came another print of the same picture. This time there was an anonymous note: "The pride of your collection is a forgery." Once more, my friend showed the picture to his wife, and the poor girl confessed everything. Yes, the picture was hers. Two years before her marriage, on the insistence of her family, she had had her nose altered by a plastic surgeon. There was a silence, while my friend stared at his masterpiece in shock and horror. As he was to put it to me a few days later, after he had moved into my house pending the divorce proceedings: "All my life I have had a craving for authenticity. No one ever succeeded in fooling me—not even the famous Dutchman, Van Meegeren, who had cheated the art experts of Europe with his forgeries of Vermeer. And here, in my own life, in my own heart, I have been mercilessly cheated, deliberately misled. What I revered and cherished as a masterly stroke of nature was but a fake, a fabrication, a forgery. I cannot love her any more. There is nothing in my heart but disgust and shame." It will be interesting to see

whether this interpretation of forgery will be accepted by the French courts. I hope so.

Honestly, I'm not making this up. Can you *believe* some people?

■

Penny Penn's next movie turned out to be her biggest, even bigger than *Trucker,* the one that had made her famous when she was thirteen. The sexier face had done wonders for her. She was a key figure in Hollywood's New Credibility. Suddenly she was taken seriously as an actress, and she'd become a sex symbol, too. The timing couldn't have been better. It was almost certain that she was going to be nominated for an Academy Award. And she'd really paid me the other two-thirds of the contracted amount, too. She was so honest. I was reading about her in the *Times* when I got a call from Max Ringer, who's a director at the New Museum. Surprise, they'd have quite a bit of room for me there in September, and he needed the work in two weeks.

"It's all at the gallery," I lied. "I'll arrange shipment with Karen." I was trying to be cool, but I was pretty thrilled. Finally, a show at a decent institution so I could take my friends there and not have to slink around like a slimy salamander. Suddenly, everything was going well all at once. I had to get the shippers over here in a hurry. As I started packing up my stuff, I noticed I'd really kind of trashed the place. They'd have to have their floor sanded down.

38

I had a week left in Florida. The work was shipped off. After a perfect summer, the sky was beginning to be overcast most of the time, and I wasn't into that muggy tropical-storm feeling the place has. I mainly hung out in the big white bedroom reading magazines and making calls. For some reason, maybe because I was alone, I couldn't stop thinking of Angelica, my major girlfriend in college. She was older than I was. She had been in the Architecture School, and now she was married and living in Germany. She had been quite shy. I was absolutely crazy about her. I kept replaying in my mind all the scenes that led to our breaking up. I had been sorry about it, but I'd known it would happen. I was too young to be committed to her, and the knowledge that I couldn't stay with her forever, the shadow of our eventual breakup, had poisoned the last months of our "relationship." When you get to a certain point of affection, it seems like you have to move past that into the sphere of real commitment or it creates unbearable tension. She couldn't stand the knowledge that I was a fickle young person, that I couldn't control my wanderlust, and I knew I couldn't let it go any farther because I was just too young, she had to get on with her life, all that sort of thing. Women age so much faster than men. It's not fair. She used to make funny expressions and raise her eyebrows, and I would smooth down the skin of her forehead with my hand because she was beginning to develop lines there. Whenever her face started to look a little puffy in the mornings, I'd bring her washcloths in a bowl of ice water and make her soak her face in them. It began to bother her a lot. But I swear, I didn't go into that relationship obsessed with facial beauty, although Angelica was very beautiful. It was more that the signs of her aging were signs of the inevitability of our eventual breakup, and I just got overwhelmed with the sadness of time, the inexorable weight of aging, and I wished I could arrest that flow, not even so much for myself as for the girls. Nobody probably believes this about me, but I really did love each and every one of them.

Under the strain of our impending breakup, Angelica's face had started to break out, rather unexpectedly since she'd had great skin for the first year we were going out. I used to get all sorts of benzoyl peroxide products for her, and I'd convince her to go down to the city on weekends in order to get facials at Georgette Klinger. That's when I started obsessing on facials myself. Now I have a couple every month, unless I'm in some godforsaken place like Florida. I have to hand it to Mariza at Georgette Klinger at 980 Madison, she really does a good facial, forgive the plug. One of the pleasures my clients must really miss is getting facials. But they have other perks, like looking eternally stunning. Mariza used to really kick on the exfoliant, partly just because she knew I loved it. But it doesn't go far enough. I need some kind of mental exfoliant. . . .

The telephone rang.

"It's Minaz."

"Hi, it's nice to hear your sweet voice." She really did have a sweet voice. It was low and very feminine. Suddenly I realized that I'd designed her face largely as a frame for her voice.

"So, are we going to your opening?"

"Uh, yeah, if you can go, it's all set for the fourteenth."

"Okay, that's great. The film's scheduled for a release on the tenth."

I wasn't going to say anything.

"There isn't any New York premiere," she said, reading my mind, "but you should come out to L.A."

"I don't know," I said, "it's the worst possible time because it really conflicts with the art thing. You know, I've got a little show opening at my own gallery two days after the New Museum show." I

had a feeling she didn't really want me to show up. She was probably
sleeping around a lot, but I felt I couldn't begrudge her that.

"You're a major artist these days," she said.

"Yeah, it's like being a major Ping-Pong champion. Nobody
knows who you are."

"I feel really sorry for you."

"You should, everybody knows who you are."

"We're not getting jealous, are we?"

"No, I think it's great. I'm really psyched about the way your
career is going."

"It could be over before it starts," she said.

"Why, is the film going to be bad?"

"No, it's going to be all right. It's not going to be a major classic
like *Terminator 2* or *Barbarella,* but it's going to be all right."

"So what's the problem?"

"I don't know about my acting," she said. "I'm not sure how I
look when I do things anymore. I'm not sure I'm expressing anything,
I may just be wooden. I'm not sure my expressions are really what I
think they are."

"Well, you know, you don't have to be too expressive for
screen."

"No, I know, and everybody likes what's in the can, I just don't
know myself what anything's going to look like. I've been getting the
cameramen to play the video playbacks for me after the first take and
then working from that. I just can't tell what I look like. I feel kind of
outside myself. I don't know who I am anymore."

"I don't know, either," I said. It was true. Since the change, she
seemed like an entirely different person. She really did act differently
—more confident and yet also more insecure, and much more inscru-
table, even taking into account the differences of expression in her
face. But she also really *was* different. Her own outlook and idea of
herself had totally changed.

"Did you hear about that kid from Tucson?" she asked.

"Yeah, that's rough."

"You're a good artist. There are people camped outside the gates
every morning trying to see me. The cops chase them away, and they
come back in the middle of the night. And I get all this psycho mail. I
have two secretaries working on it. But I sign all the pictures myself.

A lot of the mail's really weird. It's from men and women both. And they tell me how great I am, like I'm some sort of religious figure for them. I've gotten over sixty paintings that people have done from photographs of me. Most of them are really bad, but a lot of them are *incredibly* detailed. Like they paint every little hair. And they put me in these kinds of icon-looking aura things, you know, sun-rays."

"Nimbuses," I said.

"That's right. Don't you think that's a little weird?"

"Nimbus patterns go back to ancient Egypt. All religions have used them. The Maya—"

"Seriously, I think I'm having an odd effect on a lot of people."

"Maybe I overdid it," I said.

"A lot of the paintings come from people in prisons," Minaz went on. "It's kind of scary."

"I'm sorry. It's nothing that any rock star doesn't have to deal with every day."

"I don't know."

"Look, you're successful. Let's not lose sight of that basic fact."

"I don't know," she said again. "I'm not sure I enjoy it as much as I would have. I feel so abstract, all my feelings are totally different from what they used to be. That's why I haven't been comfortable around you—it's weird that you're still the same. The whole thing with my family and my friends and the secrecy of it is totally bizarre. I don't know what to say to them. They don't know what to say to me. I don't feel like the same person."

I stretched out on the turquoise canvas couch. There was a slowly rotating ceiling fan overhead. It gave me the feeling I was in some old Bette Davis movie set in Singapore.

"Maybe it's a totally new experience and that will give you a new dimension," I said. "You know, a dimension nobody else has."

"I don't know," she said. "I've gone through the whole thing, and it hasn't exactly been mind-expanding. I thought it would be purgative and cathartic and everything, but it's just been weird."

"I don't know what to say."

"There's nothing," she said. "Look, I'm going to make the best of it."

"You make me feel bad for putting everything I could into this project and everything—"

"I'm not a project. This whole thing was all about you, not about me at all. I'm less than I used to be. I'm just a you thing."

"Listen, Minaz, I think that's something of an oversimplification."

"My friends call me Jaishree."

We were silent for a little while. "Look," I said, "let's talk about this when we both feel better. I'll pick you up at about six-thirty on Friday, before the opening."

"That's another thing about *you*."

"Look, you're the big star. And you're nothing without your talent, whatever I do."

"I don't know." Pause. "I'll see you on Friday." Click.

I just lay there. New times, new innovations, new psychodrama, I thought.

■

It was a rush to be back in civilization, such as it was. We'd decided to hire a car to go to my New Museum opening. I picked Minaz up at the apartment on Fifth where she was staying. It was some producer's place, right under Robert Redford's apartment. When she got in, I got a real rush, like I used to get when I was in college, in a cab with a beautiful girl, zipping down Broadway toward the Ritz. She was wearing a sari, but she seemed souped-up and Tinseltowny, somehow. I was in the back of a terrific stretch and I was on the way to the hottest party in town with the hottest actress in the world, and I'd engineered the whole thing myself. It looked like things were working out, and I felt really, really great. Minaz, on the other hand, seemed a little pensive.

"Sometimes I feel like it's just you, it's not me, and it doesn't matter," she said.

"Look, it's your talent that's going to see you through this acting thing."

"What do you mean, 'acting thing'? It's just a phase?"

"Yes, dear, I have very high hopes for you. First president of the World Federation of Peaceful Governments."

We zoomed past the park, past the Plaza and the Sherry Netherland, and into the shopping stretch of Fifth, which was all lit up, and past the Public Library on Forty-second. Everything was going so well, even the lights were with us. At the Flatiron Building we merged into Broadway. I felt the life of the city pulsing around in me. If someone is reading this in the far future, if this manuscript survives into another age and New York has crumbled into ruins—or, let's say, what's left of it has also crumbled into ruins—and some historian of social mores wants to know what the greatest city of the twentieth century was like, maybe I should explain that Manhattan exerted such a powerful hold over its inhabitants—it seemed like the center of the universe—partly because most of the city was laid out as a vast metaphor for time and the body. The island was oriented north to south, and it had the proportions—one across to eight vertically—that Vitruvius had prescribed for Doric columns as the ideal proportional equivalent of the human body. Central Park, at the heart of the city, represented nature at the heart of man. The rest of the city, the clothing districts and food districts and entertainment sections, represented the civilized parts, and the pornography district was at the crotch-level of the city. The towers of the World Trade Center were the feet sticking up. Of course, with the ethnic areas, the city was a microcosm of the world as well, with its different ethnic districts making a jumbled-up Disneyland of all nations: You could cross over the Italo-Chinese border on Mulberry Street, turn right on Sixth Street, and pass through Little India on your way to the Ukraine.

If you entered the city from the downtown end after you got out of the confused mass of the financial district and TriBeCa and then SoHo, the Valley of the Kunsthandlers, you came to Houston—Zero Street—and began the grid system. The streets running east and west —at least the ones the upper class had to think about—numbered roughly one to one hundred, a significant number, about the maximum number of years of a human life, the number of significant degrees on the Fahrenheit temperature scale the number of pages that make a story a book. The streets represented the ages of man. The twelve wide avenues, running north and south, corresponded to the twelve hours of the day as the sun moves from east to west. And the odd-numbered streets went west, and the odd-numbered avenues went south, so there was a certain numerical draw to the city, and every intersection was pervaded with numerological, iconographic, and cultural significance. And the citizens of the city became inextricably linked to it, emotionally dependent on it, unsettled anywhere else, not just because it was the capital of the twentieth century but because without knowing it they had identified their own bodies with the city and oriented themselves over the vast grid like genii spread out in the sky.

Maybe I should also explain that at the end of the twentieth century, New York was ruled by evil real estate barons and their kept politicians, and the barons built themselves huge guarded marble towers and parked gigantic yachts with helicopters on them along their docks while mobs of raggedy homeless derelicts froze to death on the streets or crowded in the underground train stations. I don't think anyone short of Dante, or at least Dickens, could describe the subway, with its screaming machinery, ghastly stenches, deafening but indecipherable public address speakers, crumbling masonry, giant rats that apparently knew the train schedules, and teeming masses of people crushed together and occasionally pushed over the edge of the platforms to get fried to a crisp on the electrified Third Rail or chopped to pieces by oncoming trains. The street level was only somewhat better, a total chaos of beggars, businesspeople, models, vendors, taxis, and dinotherium-size delivery trucks driven at insane speeds down narrow eighteenth-century streets by immigrants who barely knew their way around the city. But as you rose higher and higher in the mirror-faced artificial mountains, you came to heavenly prospects, gorgeous apartments and offices with ravishing secretaries and clean white bleached-wood floors, until, at the top floors, you were in the sky offices of the Barons' lairs, the ultimate overdesigned power-pads of the time. But it was rarefied up there. It was too isolated from the life of the town, and you felt you really could be anywhere, Tokyo, L.A., Chicago, London, or anywhere. The best way to see the city was to get driven around in it, at street level but protected. You felt as if you were getting the grit through a clean straw. It's probably hard for someone from the future to imagine.

Or maybe the future will be the same.

We got out at the New Museum, and everybody looked at us. It was a definite kick. Max Ringer was standing around outside, welcoming people and helping them get to the doorman through the crowd. He was death-pale and ugly, like a Dick Tracy villain.

"Your work looks great," Max said. "And your friend looks great."

"Thanks, yes, they all do," I said.

He shepherded us inside. I noticed a Jeff Koons photograph
pretty near a glimpse of one of my pieces. I'm in good company, I
thought. "Seriously, I think the skin piece is really good," Max said. I
didn't think he'd had a chance to see it before the opening, since he'd
been out of town, and he certainly couldn't really see it tonight because there were tons of people in front of it, but I didn't want to call
him on it just in order to be a crabby artist. It was a good piece,
anyway. It was the only one that used the material I use in my surgical
line. It was a dyptich, two panels each about two feet tall, framed in
my signature frames. The one on the left had Artificial Skin stretched
inside it, and it had foam underneath the skin so the surface bulged
up slightly. It was an absolutely perfect expanse of skin, painted with
my special Mabuse cross-hatching technique, and flushed slightly
with a few different kinds of rouges. The companion panel was identically framed, but it was a scabby-looking, irregular, jagged field of
clotted, wrinkled crud, in mottled colors. It generally inspired disgust,
but once in a while, in some lights, it looked more beautiful than the
smooth panel.

Even though I should have just been working the crowd, I felt I
had to push around, dragging Minaz by the arm, and see how my
stuff had been hung. There were two other pictures that had to do
with time. Both were huge. And they were pretty well placed, in the
first room. One was just a gigantic long rectangle of perfectly flat
plastic, framed in black lacquer. It was painted a dull, flat, nonreflec-
tive neutral gray, except for a strip of lavender at the extreme left. In
the top left-hand corner, at the top border of the lavender strip, was a
tiny curve of inset opal wafer, which was abruptly sheared off by the
leading edge of the gray expanse. The opal was a good one, twenty-
eight carats, filled with every earthly and unearthly color you could
imagine. But it was very small. The painting, of course, contrasted life
and the immensity of death. Not subtle, but effective, I thought.

The other was a long multiple relief. It had been suggested by
peppers. Green peppers and red peppers, which are really the same
thing. Well, when they start off, when they're just sprouts, they're
really round and bulgey, they just look young and bursting with life.
When they're sort of mature, just turning red, they're really strong on
structure. And then, of course, they start to get old and shriveled, and
all the surfaces that were convex and bulging become concave and

collapse inward. So they're a great visual metaphor for the ages of man. The relief I did had balls of smooth plaster, iridescentized, growing out of a small round ball into a big, mature ball and then shriveling up. They were in rows of ten each, reading left to right and down, seven rows in all. Threescore years and ten. The iridescent colors changed along the way, too, from peach to tan and then to dreary brown and pallid corpse-gray. They were attached with invisible wires to a black velvet background, and there was glass over them, so the whole effect was like a very large old shadow box.

My mentor from graduate school, Robert Pincus-Witten, came in the door in a flurry of scarves and hats and called me over to talk to him while he tried to check his coat.

"Do you hear about the auction results?" he asked. There had been a big sale at Christie's that afternoon.

"No, didn't you?"

"No, I had to teach today, damn it," he said. "Never mind, I'll find out."

"Thanks for asking me how I'm doing."

"Oh, how are you doing? Your work looks great. Why are you wearing sunglasses at night? It must be 1986, you look like Michael Musto."

"I'm just waiting to get my eye bags removed," I said.

"Oh, I'm sorry, yes, that's a good idea. . . . I haven't seen the art you've got here yet but I know it's brilliant—hello, Nino!"

He had to chat with Nino Fortreza, the *éminence grise*. Max came over again.

"Listen," he said, "the dinner's still going to be at Café but we've moved the party from the Puck Building to The Venus Interface," Max said. The Venus Interface was a new club. He gave me a couple of Xeroxes of the address.

"I'm not sure I want to go," Minaz said. Her moods were very changeable lately.

"For the time being, I think it would be good to get used to going to clubs again," I said. "You're doing great, but we still have to get you around, just the way Madonna got around. Okay? We want you on Page Six a few times. I know it's a strain, but we'll make it easy on you."

"I'm really sick of going to clubs."

"Look, you can't just lounge around filming all day, you have to work a little, too. Now, we really ought to be at Café by nine-thirty."

"Jeez, okay, why don't I go home and change into the off-the-shoulder blouse thing with the harem pants—I *hate* this!"

"All over the world, people are dreaming about being beautiful and going to private things at New York nightclubs that get written up in Page Six, and you get to do it and you hate it."

"Yes."

"Listen, I think you ought to wear a *duputa* with that blouse, just to push the Indian thing a bit more, okay? Minaz?"

"Okay, okay, okay."

She was just acting upset. I was teasing her, and I could tell she was really thrilled. She was poised on the brink of major power. And so was I. We were a great crossover team, art and media. Like Arthur Miller and Marilyn Monroe. But for the nineties. And I'd keep doing my "face art." And ultimately, I thought, it wouldn't be a secret anymore, and people would be more interested in my designer people because they were artistic creations. In the future, people will be known partly on the basis of who they are designed by, like clothes and apartments. Maybe then I'll have moved to L.A., have sold the loft and gotten out of this cesspool, and have a really clean, swanky plastic clinic that's like a cross between a waxing salon and an art gallery, with receptionists, and a big office, and all sorts of modern equipment. It would be legal and great, and every single star in Hollywood would be hanging out there, and I'd be the Artiste, it would be like *Shampoo* meets Peter Paul Rubens, a little sleazy and plastic and Hollywood, but after all, that's what this era's about, that's where the monuments we leave behind come from, so that's really the place to be.

We talked to lots of people and I got congratulated and we started to walk out, pushing past hordes of curious people, and my blood just froze. Something was wrong, and I didn't know what. Somebody. Off to the left. I looked around and saw who it was. Some horrible-looking girl with a sharp face. She was across a table full of champagne and Pellegrino bottles, looking around. Then I knew who it was. It was Virginia Feiden. The first major star I'd worked on. She was there with this punk-rock-looking guy from some white rap group that she hangs out with. There was something wrong with her face. It was worse than it had looked on Letterman. It was falling apart. Or not really. It had shrunken somehow. There was something wrong with the process. I was dizzy. Suddenly I realized she had seen me and was coming toward me. Since I was wearing tinted glasses, I could pretend not to see her. I edged behind people, elbowing them out of the way, and dragged Minaz behind me. For some reason I could barely hear anything. The crowd was a faraway roar. I hadn't been so scared since I was a little kid. What about Minaz? What about Penny Penn? We got around the thing, out the door, and up to Houston Street.

"What's wrong?" Minaz asked.

"I just suddenly feel tremendously horribly sick," I said. "I have to go home. Okay? Okay?"

"Jeez, that's crazy. Are you really sick? What's wrong?" she said.

"I'm okay, you don't need to come with me, I just get dizzy spells once in a while lately. I just have to lie down, I'll call your cellular number later."

"Are you sure?" she said. She really looked worried.

It was agonizing. There weren't any taxis. She followed me all the way up Broadway until I found one. I got in.

"I'll be fine, uh—I'd like to see you tomorrow," I said, and slammed the door.

I was slipping into the abyss. Virginia wasn't interested in art. She must have come there to find me. Confront me. What had gone wrong? I felt weak, and I was shaking like I had a fever and there was an earthquake going on, too. Everything was going to crumble. Disaster, Disaster. Doom, Death, Violence, and Despair. I felt all alone in the world, suddenly. I just stared blankly out the window.

Maybe I'd just dreamed the whole thing, I thought. But I hadn't. I knew it was real, and it had really been Virginia.

And, I thought, Minaz has a time bomb ticking under her skin.

PART THREE

THE **R** OAD TO
XIBALBÁ

When I got home I didn't know what to do, so I started eating. I should have felt too grossed out to eat, but sometimes I have the opposite reactions to things from the ones I should have. I was very shaky. It was as if I'd been in an elevator that had dropped unexpectedly and fast, or I'd stepped up to a nonexistent stair, or stepped off a curb without knowing it was there and gone pitching forward into the street. It was those things combined with the awful moment when you realize something you thought was good is actually quite different, when you see that the lovely young girl is actually old and wrinkled, when you suddenly realize someone you're attracted to is horribly fat, when you find that a friend's betrayed you, or when you suddenly get a blob of empty terror in your stomach because for some reason you think you have a terminal disease.

I called Mark. It's generally a bad idea to call people on weekend nights, but this was major. After I left two messages and called again, he finally picked up. I wondered whether I should get out of town for a few days and try to find out some things from there. But when he finally answered, I started to tell him about Virginia. Then suddenly I couldn't go on. I wasn't sure it was a good idea to say anything over the telephone. He started babbling about some new process.

"Actually," Mark was saying, "this whole thing with the plastic is a little beat. I mean, PCS was a good thing when we invented it, but things have gone way past that now. You're a good artist, but you're just not up-to-date. We have to get you into genetic engineering a little. You know, for a long time researchers have been working on developing tissue that can be coded with any individual's genetic material. Then you could sculpt in real living flesh, and the body wouldn't reject it. Skin, too. It could *really* make people young again, and it wouldn't get numb or cold, and it could heal itself, you wouldn't have to repair it. It's something people have been researching for a long time, but I think I've worked out the perfect way to grow it."

"What's that?" I asked.

"What are you eating?" he asked.

"A kiwi blintz."

"I think it's disgusting when people eat over the telephone."

"Not as disgusting as when they eat in person."

"It's all right. Anyway, you know what an ovarian cyst is? Sometimes a woman gets a big cyst in her ovary, that develops out of an egg. But it's not fertilized. Well—they tend to have teeth in them and vestigial eyes. I guess it's a little grody, they're lumpy things with bones and teeth sticking out. They're bad starts at people. In the old days they thought they were real abominations, because they didn't have souls, and they meant you were a witch.

"But anyway, I think we can grow spare tissue that same way. If it's a woman, we can just use the egg, and replicate the conditions of the uterus, like with test-tube babies, and if it's a man, well, it's going to be trickier, but we could probably make the sperm behave like an egg. And I think I know what causes those cysts to develop. And they can get big, supposedly one woman in California had a three-hundred-pound one. So then we'll separate the right kind of cells out of that mass of stuff and put it in some kind of temporary binder, and you'll have real living sculpting material, from the same individual you're working on. It'll be fantastic."

I guess I'm pretty unflappable, because I managed to get down my last blintz. "Is this really a serious possibility in the near future?" I asked. "Maybe we should train people and float shares and everything."

"You bet. I've got some demo experiments set up at the lab."

"What do you mean, demo experiments?"

"Well, they're little living things I've done with animal tissue. Just wait till I show you."

"I have to talk with you about something. I'll come up and meet you tomorrow morning at eight o'clock, okay?"

"Isn't that a little early for you?"

"It's really important," I said.

"Okay, I'll be there. Maybe closer to eight-thirty, okay? Bye."

I hung up. The thing with Virginia had really shaken me up, and I was kind of shivering. I didn't know what I was really thinking about it, so I just kind of went along with a normal routine. I looked over the studio, which I hadn't been in in three months, took another half a Valium, and went to bed. I wondered what Mark had in mind to spring on me tomorrow.

■

"This is the new plant," Mark said. "Kind of Brave New World, don't you think?"

It was. Maybe a little more modern, but basically the well-equipped genetic engineering lab: rows of gleaming tile tables, each with a beige-plastic-encased scanning electron microscope on one side and a computer and monitor on the other; walls lined with closed glass shelves stacked with petri dishes and measuring instruments; four large centrifuge machines on one wall; a refrigerator probably filled with jars of serum for growing tissue. Through a glass door there was a fully stocked operating room, not like the jury-rigged one in my loft, but not like an emergency room, either: no electric defibrilator, no racks of sutures, just an adjustable table and all the racks of little tools you could imagine.

"I haven't done much with humans yet," Mark said. "But you've inspired me to be artistic. Check out the testing cage area with me, okay?"

"What's that?"

"Well, it's just some experiments, mad scientist stuff, you know. But it's pretty humane. I have a really high percentage of survivors."

He led me through an airlock door into a low, dark room, smelly in spite of the constant hum of air vents. The walls were divided into glass-fronted cages, like the ones at the Klein Science Building at Yale, where they do the primate research.

"These are just some things I've been kidding around with. This one might be kind of a good mascot for nightclubs and restaurants. It has a kind of a downtown look."

He switched on a bluish bank of lights inside the cage. The thing was about three feet tall, covered with beautiful black hair or feathers, with long, ostrichlike plumes sprouting from its head. It was walking around, rather delicately, on four human-looking arms with long fingers. It must have been very light, because as we watched, it started climbing hand over hand up a tree branch inside the case. It paused for a minute and blinked at us with big, dark, long-lashed beautiful eyes.

"So it's partly human?"

"Well, part of it was grown by the ovarian cyst method out of human tissue, but it was genetically altered to correspond to the chromosomes of a capuchin monkey. It has a capuchin brain. They have great personalities. That long, beautiful hair it has is howler-monkey hair. It would really make a great, uh, pet for the truly hip, or maybe . . . I bet a lot of heavy-metal type people would buy one." Mark had a sort of evil leer on his face.

"Have you ever seen The Island of Lost Souls?" I asked.

"No. What's the connection? Look, I've got something really gruesome in here. I figure at first our biggest publicity will come from horror films. So I've got this really scary critter."

It was scary. I shivered. It seemed to be in a case with extra-thick glass, and there were bones and feathers scattered all around the chicken-wire bottom. It was a mammal, pinkish, about three feet long, scaled like a pangolin, with little back legs with big claws and comparatively gigantic spiked forearms, like a praying mantis. Its head stuck out on a sort of stalk, and darted and turned about, snapping angrily at the glass. It had bulgey cat's eyes and a huge long mouth, filled with multiple rows of teeth that were much too big for it, like a barracuda's.

"As Andy would have said, that's really great, Mark," I said.

"It's actually pretty gross. But I think we could sell it to John Frankenheimer or whoever that guy is who makes all those really gruesome horror films. You know?"

"I don't know," I said. "It looks like it's in pain."

"Well, it was bred to have a cranky personality."

The last tank had a truly half-human creature. It was about five feet tall, preternaturally thin, with multiple-jointed arms and a row of six breasts like some of Louise Bourgeois's sculptures. It had beautifully coiffed curly red hair all over its head. It was moving around in the tank, dancing incredibly slowly, with its hair undulating in slow motion, too. Suddenly I realized the tank was full of water. The music coming out of it was very muted, but it must have been loud inside the tank itself. I didn't recognize it at first, but then I realized it was the Valse Triste. It turned toward me, and it had Minaz's face. She was mouthing the same phrase over and over, and I tried to read her lips. It was hard to get, but then she stared right at me and mouthed it distinctly: "I hate you. I'm going to kill you. You're already a ghost."

40

In general, I think it's a cheap shot in movies or books when something ridiculous and improbable happens, to weird you out, and then it turns out it was all a dream. It's such a turn-off. But this really had been one of those dreams where I thought I was awake, and for a while afterward, I had real trouble separating what was fantasy from what was reality, especially since my life bears a close resemblance to fantasy. For a minute I thought maybe the whole beauty technology thing had been a dream, too. I'm just a painter, I thought. And I'm a harmless abstract painter, not a twentieth-century Bosch who sculpts out of living material. The whole idea was insane. I never grafted any ridiculous plastic compounds onto anybody, I thought. But it wasn't true, I looked up and saw some of Minaz's head shots pinned to the cork wall, and I remembered Minaz and what Virginia was beginning to look like, and I wondered what was I going to do about it, and I just lay there and sweated. It was gray and bleak outside, with wind, echoing my mood. What time was it? 5:43 A.M., no, 5:44, the digital clock indicated at me out of the gloom. I've got to get an analog clock, I said to myself. I don't mind knowing it's around 5:45, but those threes and fours really offend me. Shit and corruption, it was three hours before I could talk to Mark, and five hours before I could start making any real phone calls. What should I do for the next three hours, reread a few cantos of *The Faerie Queene*? Always worth doing, but I didn't have the heart today. Maybe my life is a little too complicated, I thought. I should try to do something to cut down the stress a little, like sell the loft, move to Hawaii, and lie on a lava beach smoking dope for about ten years. It could be done. Many had tried it, and most were perfectly satisfied. Enough is enough. I'd just about convinced myself when the phone rang. I was so nervous, I grabbed it before the machine had a chance to get it. Stupid.

"Hello?"

"Mr. Angelo?"

"Yes."

"This is Aaron Iskowitz calling from Saul, Rice. I'm sorry to call you so early in the morning, but I've been trying to reach you for several days."

I didn't say anything.

"I'm in Barcelona with Penny Penn, and she has some rather urgent questions to ask you."

"Very well, could I speak with her?" I choked out.

"She's relayed her questions to me. I'm getting a flight from here arriving in New York at three o'clock this afternoon, and I wonder if we could set up a meeting."

"Well, today's very hectic for me, but perhaps you could call when you get in or give me a number where I can reach you?"

"This is extremely urgent, Mr. Angelo. It's regarding some sort of a treatment that I believe Ms. Penn and Ms. Virginia Feiden received from you."

I was thinking clearly enough to shut up at this point. He'd talk again in a minute.

"Mr. Angelo?"

"Yes?"

"Shall we say five o'clock at our offices at 672 Avenue of the Americas?"

"You mean Sixth?"

"Yes."

"Give me your number there, and I'll let you know if I can reschedule my day."

"It's 609-7000."

"All right. I'll call there around noon."

"Very well. Thank you, Mr. Angelo."

"Thanks."

I hung up. Shit, shit, shit, shit, shit, shit, shit, shit, shit, shit, and corruption. Could this be happening? It was weird, something going wrong with Penny at the same time that Virginia began to look wrong. I didn't know what to make of it. But I knew it might be about time to skip town. But then, I couldn't do that, I had everything here, I had a whole major art career that was finally getting going. I'd just have to deny everything, imply somehow that someone else had access to the tapes, and somehow also offer to do repair work on Penny and Virginia if it was possible. My mouth was dry.

But what was the problem? Nothing could have possibly gone wrong. There were people walking around, people on whom I'd used some of those techniques years ago, and I knew they were fine. It was weird, there was some crazy conspiracy going on. Did some doctor get his claws on them and mess them up for no reason? And was something going to happen to Minaz? I was still in love with Minaz, I thought, despite her messing around and my occasional wave of revulsion. But in today's relationships, those things are minor. I couldn't think of anything to do but get through the day more or less as planned, spend the morning getting a few things ready just in case I really did have to skip town, and then meet with Mark like I'd said I would and take the matter up with him. And then I'd try to meet this killer lawyer, Iskowitz—in a public place—if I'd worked out what I was going to say to him. I started looking through my closet. I didn't have a thing to wear. I was down to my last clean suit, a double-breasted pinstripe Versace thing that made me look like a gangster. I'll just have to go with it, I thought.

■

Mark's "demo experiments" turned out to be a lot less spectacular than I had fantasized. They were just little petri dishes of growing tissue from frogs and California slugs. Giant California slugs generally get used for neurological research, because they have big, easily exposed nerves, but Mark was using them for his tissue rejection research just because they were easy-going genetically. The slugs were in a big flat aerated tank, and they were really quite large, like garden slugs but as much as eight inches long, and with ridges on the sides for aquatic locomotion, kind of like nudibranchs, and they were mottled brown and yellow. Of course, the outstanding feature of slugs is the eye-stalks. But really, it's kind of hard to describe something like a slug; basically you had to be there. Mark had a couple of Dr. Moreau-ish ones that he'd cut up and grafted together. One was very short and stubby, one was extra long, like an eel, a composite made of several genetically identical siblings, and one was really somewhat monstrous—it branched into two large heads, both of which had about five eye stalks, and it had much larger and more powerful locomotion ridges than average. But it seemed to have trouble getting around the tank. It was kind of a Quasimodo, powerful but crippled.

"It's a good thing I have the lab to myself for the semester," Mark said. "Otherwise I could get into trouble with the ethics committee about unnecessary cruelty. But *franchement,* I've been working with these critters a long time, and I don't really have much respect for them as individuals. They're pretty brutal, in my opinion. Like they go cannibalistic pretty easily. Not a lot of family feeling between them. It's every slug for himself."

"Mark, this is really fascinating," I said, "and I'm glad to see it, but I've got a whole lot on my mind right now, and we've got to sit down and talk, and then I've just got to get back downtown. I'm sorry. Listen, we've got a real problem. Some of the stuff isn't going right."

"Like what?"

"Let's go outside." I wanted to ask Mark what we could do about the degeneration problem, but suddenly I was afraid someone might overhear us, or the lab might be bugged. And Mark might get scared and disassociate himself from the whole thing if I didn't come at him in the right way. He's a little mercurial and uptight, and I could see him just throwing up his hands and trying to blame the whole thing on me. I had something on him, too, of course, but I just didn't want him running scared when I needed constant expertise. I had to get him outside.

We walked out through the dingy hall with the old blond wood walls and the battleship linoleum on the floor.

"Why are you being so mysterious?" Mark kept asking.

"Did you see Virginia on *Letterman* a couple of months ago?"

"No, I didn't see it—"

"Well, I saw Virginia last night, and I got a really disturbing call from Penny Penn's lawyer this morning. It looks like some of the stuff just isn't holding up. They're starting to look different."

"Shit, well, what is it, are they peeling?"

We got to the big door, pulled it open, and walked out onto 151st Street. It was still drizzling.

"I don't think they're peeling, exactly. It looked more like Virginia was shrinking somehow, but we'd better take a look at them."

"Maybe they're just making it up."

"I've got a meeting with Penny. You'd better not come along. We'll keep you out of her lawyer's sight. But I want to be able to reach you."

"It sounds like you need a lawyer."

"I'm going to tell Jay everything when I get home. But I won't tell Iskowitz anything. Just stay put, all right? I'll tell you whatever I can find out."

He was obviously really worried that I was going to blab about him, but he didn't want to come along and there was nothing he could do to stop me from going. Finally he said, "I'll stay in the lab until I hear from you."

"Okay."

I wanted to keep Mark from skipping town and have him available. I could always throw him to the wolves later.

■

I called Jay's office, but he was in Atlanta and it took two hours to get through to him. I couldn't tell him much over the telephone, and I didn't want to take another lawyer into my confidence. I'd worked with him for a long time. I gave him a few hints of what was going on, and he said that if I knew Penny socially, I might as well meet with Iskowitz and find out what was going on, but I'd better not say *anything*. He'd be back in a week, he said, and we'd go over it. I thought he'd sound more surprised that I was into such weird shit, but I guess he'd seen it all.

The elevator up to Saul, Rice, Ruskin, Groton and Keillor didn't have floor numbers, just the names of firms. Saul, Rice had the whole top three floors. The elevator doors opened onto a vast wall of Sienese yellow marble with the name of the firm carved into it, lit just right so you could read it. What if they got a new partner? They'd probably have to fire a few associates to pay for replacing the slab.

The receptionist was at a desk to the side. She looked up. It was a big abstract desk, set high. I walked up to her with a fair degree of coolness and told her that I was Mr. Angelo for Mr. Iskowitz. She asked me if I could please wait for a moment.

The waiting room had a big brass table and puffy Knoll chairs and newspapers on racks and all the current magazines, including *Artforum,* spread out perfectly on the table in a beautiful fan shape. Some low-paid employee, undoubtedly a woman, must have to come by every twenty minutes and fan out the magazines. I didn't sit down. It felt too dentisty.

Pretty soon another girl manifested herself and asked if she could lead me to Mr. Iskowitz's office.

There was something strange about the main floor of the office. It was a whole open floor and was fairly brightly lit with incandescent track spots, but the space was broken up by huge circular pillars, twice as wide as they were tall. They made the ceiling look lower.

The walls were paneled with vertical ash strips. As the girl led me around one of them, Aaron Iskowitz stepped from behind the column and came up to shake my hand. He was in a beige custom-made sack suit made out of nubbly tweed. His face was kind of old-looking and whiskered and pitted, even though he wasn't that old, and I didn't want to touch him, but I forced myself to shake his hand anyway. He had a really official-seeming, go-to-hell handshake.

"Mr. Angelo? Thank you for coming. Would you come into my office, please?"

We walked past several big birch-slab desks with less beautiful and presumably more efficient secretaries behind them. Pretty soon, we were in the land of predominantly male secretaries, and then we came to Iskowitz's office door. It was unmarked, so he must be important. He ushered me in, and my first impression was of clean, thin Venetian blinds looking out over the orange city, with the Pan Am Building looming like the inevitability of death itself, cutting a swath through the light. He sat down behind his desk, which had only a green-shaded light on it, and I sat down in a Mies chair made by Knoll International, not a Barcelona Chair but a later one. It was a big office, austere except for the huge Kherman rug on the floor. There were built-ins full of law books on either side of the desk, and there were also some art books and philosophy—Dworkin, Nozick, stuff that made you feel you'd neglected your reading. There was one painting on the wall, behind his desk, and when I turned toward him, all I could do was stare at it. It was a huge gold Warhol *Marilyn,* a single one. A good one, a million-dollar painting. She had such menace in her eyes, and such menacing teeth. I remembered what Robert Pincus-Witten had said about the Marilyn paintings, that they were variations on Leonardo's *Medusa,* and Marilyn was the monster that turned men to stone. But not by ugliness, but beauty. The Gorgon was beautiful. It was a flashy painting for a lawyer to have, but I guess not for an entertainment lawyer. They were a different breed.

"Mary, could you ask Ms. Feiden if she would like to come in?"

He was speaking into a hidden intercom. The green light wasn't exactly flattering. It gave him that kind of reptilian sheen. I started picking at a hangnail. It was getting really bloody and disgusting, it was more than just a hangnail now, it was developing into a callused sore. It was absolutely disgusting. I'd have to remember to soak it in water for a couple of hours later. It was really bumming me out.

He turned toward me. "Ms. Feiden and Ms. Penn and I thought we would discuss this matter with you in an informal way first."

The "first" sounded a little menacing to me. He spoke in the careful way all high-priced lawyers do. He thought before every word. He had a glacial calm about him that made me feel like I had a perpetual nervous tic.

I tried to keep from twitching and looked at him. I noticed a couple of ocatillo-cactus-looking plants behind him that I didn't like. They looked all spiky and rough.

Virginia came in, alone. I was sitting in the visitor's chair closest to the windows, away from the door, and I only half-turned toward her. She was kind of wrapped up in a leather coat. She had a Hermès scarf around her head.

Her face was too small. The PCS seemed to have contracted and sunken in. She looked kind of skull-like, but not like an actual skull, more like the statue of the old woman at Reims Cathedral that looks like her face has sunken around her bones. And there were other irregularities. Lumps under the surface that shouldn't have been there. But the outside, the laboriously dyed and sculpted PCS was still there, covered with a heavy layer of base makeup. There were two round surgical bandages on her left cheek, each about an inch in diameter. She was wearing large dark glasses, but you could kind of see her eyes, and for a second they glared out at me with sheer hatred and loathing, and then she looked away and sat down in a chair on the other side of the big desk, looking at Iskowitz.

I sat silently. He started talking.

"Ms. Feiden has given me an account of a surgical procedure you performed on her that has led to a disfiguring and potentially life-threatening condition in the region of her face. May I ask you if it's true that you performed any operations on her?"

"I'm not sure I should say anything in this situation without my lawyer present," I said.

"You realize that of course anything you say in this informal conference is just between us," he said.

"Yes."

"Would you feel more at liberty to speak if we held this meeting in one of the bonded conference rooms?"

Of course, that's what the circular pillars were. Guaranteed soundproofed and unbugged. "I suppose so," I said.

We trooped out of the office again. He brought along a cordless phone. We went up to one of the cylinders and pushed a button. The door slid aside with a dry hiss, revealing a softly lit interior with a circular leather bench surrounding a circular five-foot-diameter table. Very James Bond, I thought. I let them go in first.

It was an oddly intimate setting for a hostile meeting. I couldn't bear to look directly at Virginia.

Iskowitz started explaining a few things to me, without asking the question again. If it turned out to be true that I had caused their conditions, he said, I could very easily be charged both with practicing medicine without a license and with reckless endangerment. And I wouldn't stand much of a chance in the liability suits they could serve me with. I'd lose everything.

And if either of them died, of course, it would be a lot more serious.

Then he called Penny in Barcelona on the cordless speakerphone. She'd had the same symptoms and had been examined by a doctor who had been "appalled." He asked her how she was doing. Her voice came through the speakerphone full of panic and hate:

"It's shrinking. Shrinking. I'm in real pain. And it's getting more painful every day. I'm on pain-killers, but they're not helping."

The implication, I guess, was that she'd sound pretty pathetic at a trial.

Finally it seemed he'd made his whole presentation. He clicked off the phone.

"I can't really say anything at this point," I said, "but what do you want me here for if all this could have been done in writing?"

He hesitated a moment. He looked at Virginia and back at me. Then he said, "I've been told that you made some videotapes of the so-called operations and some interviews with my clients. It would greatly facilitate an agreeable settlement if you were to turn the tapes over to us and sign away any rights to them, legal and otherwise."

No, it wouldn't quite do for those tapes to turn up in court. They might not keep me totally out of trouble, but they'd been pretty carefully worded. Certainly carefully worded enough to greatly embarrass movie stars in the popular press. I still had a card.

"Well, I'll have to think over my response to these allegations," I said. "I'll be in touch." I got up.

Iskowitz pushed a button and the door slid open and he got up, too. We even shook hands. I didn't look at Virginia.

"Thank you for coming," he said.

42

I didn't have any answers for him for the entire following week, no matter how many times he called, and finally, on a Monday morning, a process server came to my door with a summons: *Jane Doe and Alice Roe vs. James Angelo.* Clever bastard, hiding their identities. How much was he trying to nail me for? The bottom of the page said, "Damages in an amount to be determined." More clever. The court date was only three weeks away, which meant they'd pulled strings. The document was cold and scary. I wasn't sure whether to call Jay, my lawyer, again, and spill the whole thing to him over the phone, or just find some ordinary scrappy litigator right now to take me through the first hearing at least and deny everything. My word against theirs. And I wondered whether I should stick around and make the trial and mount a defense with the tapes or just assume it would all come out so badly for me, I'd better just clear out and go undercover. I hadn't gotten much done during the week in terms of preparing for a legal battle, but I'd managed to secure or hide a lot of my assets and get rid of any traces of my secret profession, right down to the shreds of Artificial Skin wedged into the floorboards.

I finally called Jay's office. He was still away, but the secretary set a meeting for Saturday, five days away, and I decided not to take anyone else into my confidence. I was kind of paralyzed anyway.

Karen's astrologer had been right. September was a very bad time for me.

As far as I knew, Minaz was still all right. Her movie was due for release in about a month.

I called Mark at the lab, for the tenth time in two days.

"I think it's causing some sort of reaction underneath, in the flesh itself," Mark said. "Karl's back, and he and I are trying to figure out what went wrong. We're working twenty-four hours a day."

I practically screamed into the telephone. "You *have* to figure it out, and not just that, you know, uh, you have to figure out how to make a presentation that's going to convince them that we can fix it completely. Completely! Okay?"

"I can't listen to this," Mark said. "I'm as scared as you are."

"Listen, this Iskowitz guy has absolutely no shame, and he really means business. And he's trying to intimidate me into signing over all rights to the tapes."

The call-waiting tone beeped. "Hang on a second," I said.

It was Minaz. She was in L.A. She'd heard. She was hysterical.

"How did you find out about Penny and Virginia?" I asked.

"Word gets around Tinseltown. You know. So am I going to turn into a Tale from the Crypt?"

"I don't think so, there are plenty of successful cases walking around, I think someone messed Penny and Virginia up afterward, after I worked on them. Maybe some rival doctors' organization or some secret directive from the FDA, I don't know."

"You don't know."

"No."

"I'm going to see a specialist this afternoon," Minaz said.

"Who?"

"None of your business."

"You'll just get messed up. They'll think there's something really wrong with you, and I'll get in incredible trouble when they screw up."

"You're already in incredible trouble."

She hung up. I didn't know what to do.

I felt a cold sore coming on. I've had them a lot through my life, and they've always been the most traumatic experiences you could ever imagine. Not only are they ugly but they carry the stigma of sexually transmitted disease, even though most people have them, even when they're little, or so I've been told. But it doesn't matter, you just feel like a leper. I got really mad at myself for not taking my acyclovir every day for the past six months. I dug the bottle out from behind the vitamins and minerals and herbal supplements and cod liver oil and stuff in the refrigerator and popped three, and wadded ten more up in tinfoil and put them in my pocket. I dug around in the bathroom cabinet (which was a strange shape and really hard to open, goddamned Postmodernism) and found some Blistex and the shade of concealer I use on my lips. I also found a Chanel lipstick that Katrina had been bugging me for months to find. I started rubbing Blistex on my as-yet-invisible cold sore. I wished it were so siccative, it would just dry the whole thing out and pull it up to the surface and purge me of infection. I felt impure and unclean.

I couldn't keep from visualizing a particular half-dried-out pimple that Katrina had had on her cheek once. I kept thinking about how much I had wanted to squeeze it, but she never let me because she said it would make a scar. Eventually it just ran its course and dropped off, but two years later I still couldn't keep from thinking about it. It had gotten all dried out, and just before it totally dried, when it was absolutely ripe, that would have been the perfect time to squeeze it. I imagined the semenlike pus welling up out of its hidden caves in the flesh, like a geyser.

There's some primal fascination with scabs and other skin irregularities and calluses and crud. Maybe it's analogous to the fascination with what Edmund Burke called the sublime—mountain crags seen from a safe distance. I always wanted to pick other people's scabs, and I always enjoyed it when I had scabs myself that I could pick. I'd generally make them worse when I was a kid, but eventually I learned to pick at them systematically, gently, kind of lovingly, without pulling them all the way off.

I also couldn't help thinking of an old dark-skinned homeless person I'd seen in India when I was a little kid. He'd had polyps growing out of his face. They were like little brown coral growths or twists of clay. I had wondered whether they were growing down inside his mouth and in his insides and all over his body, too. I shuddered then and I still shudder when I think about it. It's one of my earliest really strong memories.

That fascination is the flip side of my urge toward the smooth and the perfect, I guess. Anyway, I think almost everyone has it. But with me, it's at the point where I can't stop thinking about and imagining scabs and acne that I've happened to see over the course of my life.

It sounds really crazy, but I started to wonder whether maybe I'd really known all along that something like this was going to happen. Maybe I'd wanted it in some weird way. Was it some kind of crazy serial killer streak in me that I never knew I had? Was it a weird sexual obsession of some kind? I'm such a bookish sort of idiot, I wandered around the studio for a while, and then I found my notebook lying on top of the TV where I'd left it months before. There was definitely something in there from Bataille about destroying beauty. I flipped through the book, and there it was, enough to make you wonder:

> If beauty so far removed from the animal is passionately desired, it is because to possess is to sully, to reduce to the animal level. Beauty is desired in order that it may be befouled; not for its own sake, but for the joy brought from the certainty of profaning it.
>
> In sacrifice, the victim is chosen so that its perfection shall give point to the full brutality of death. . .
>
> Beauty has a cardinal importance, for ugliness cannot be spoiled, and to despoil is the essence of eroticism. Humanity implies the taboos, and in eroticism it and they are transgressed. Humanity is transgressed, profaned and besmirched. The greater the beauty the more it is befouled.

Bataille. Basically, You Always Hurt the One You Love. Maybe there was something I liked about the part *before* the PCS goes on, when I got to sand down their skin with little sanders and dissolve it with chemical-peel acids. You never know about yourself, my shrink says.

■

For the next two days, all I did was run around the Greater Metropolitan Area trying to liquidate my assets and get my thoughts together. I didn't sell the statue of God L, though. I needed to know I still owned it, that it was slumbering in its safe-deposit box. It was much harder to get rid of stuff than I had thought it would be, and I had to take some really bad deals. I knew that pretty soon the IRS was going to get wind of all the selling I was doing and investigate, but that was the least of my problems at the moment. Finally I started selling illegally. The low point was the night of Friday, September 30, the day before my meeting with Jay and four days before the hearing, when I stayed out all night haggling over my Lalique lamps and paperweights with some crook from São Paulo. I got in the cab back to my house at five in the morning. I felt empty, and poorer than I had thought.

43

It was six A.M. when I staggered upstairs to my door. It wasn't locked, but I knew I'd locked it. I pushed in, carefully, staying back in the hall. It was a disaster area. Papers and books and broken glass and open doors and clothes all over and everything. It had been broken into and searched without any regard for leaving traces of the search. It made me shudder to look at it, it was so messy. It was like a half-taken-down set for a film about Bohemian Artist Life. The banal trappings of creativity were piled up in cairns and ziggurats. There were iridescent oil pastels ground into the floorboards. Head shots and magazines and model books had collected into vast drifts around the bases of the bookshelves. Luckily, there hadn't been anything to find: the fireplace was filled with the ashes of whatever incriminating photographs and documents and flammable implements and supplies hadn't been valuable enough to put in a safe-deposit box and were too bulky to tear up and flush. Although flushing is definitely the best way to get rid of things, by the way. And the keys to the safe-deposit boxes were in the zippered compartment of my deceptively slim wallet.

The lit-up transparency table was badly cracked and covered with hundreds of expensive four-by-fives that cast disturbing shadows on the ceiling. Luckily, they were photos of all of my paintings, not of my surgery. I noticed an element from a sculpture I owned, a mirror ball, lying in the corner. When artworks get busted up, they look so forlorn. Especially trendy clean modern artworks. There was dirt on the floor from my knocked-over jade plant. I'd raised that jade plant forever, since college, and just as it was getting impressive, somebody'd knocked it on the floor and probably killed it and certainly ruined its symmetry. But the dirt and glass on the floor bothered me most. It looked all nubbly and jizzy, and I shivered. You know when you get those spinal shivers for no apparent reason?

I would have thrown some of the garbage out the window into the vacant lot in the back, but I'd been doing too much of that lately, and the other people in the building were mad.

The locks hadn't been broken, they'd been picked. That, at least, was classy. Had Iskowitz set this up, or had Penny or Virginia arranged it on their own? Was it safe to stay, or should I just get out of town immediately? I checked everywhere in the loft, and there was no one there. I even looked under the sink. I was so tired. I bolted and chained the surviving locks on the door. If I could only lie down for a minute, I thought. I pushed all the clothes and broken stuff to the side of my bed and kind of curled up on it. I'd deal with this in a couple of hours, I thought. I'd just have to get my head together.

When I woke up, it was sunset outside already. I'd slept the whole day. I guessed I'd missed my appointment with Jay. I'd had some dream, about cancer, but I don't remember what else. The lumps of cancer are a really primal fear. I remember passing an old tree with my mother one time when I was little, and it was all covered with huge lumps and twisted and misshapen, and she said, "That tree has cancer," and I got this ghastly shiver of horror and repulsion, and I was just shaking for at least an hour. I kept wondering what those big nodes of cancer would look like if you sliced into them. Would they just be beautiful and irregular, like burled walnut, or would they be filled with rotting abscesses and convolutions of worm-eaten crud? And one time our Labrador dog Rover (I'd picked the name) got some tumors on her stomach, and I found them when I was petting her, and I got the same shiver. They had to be taken out, and I wondered what they looked like sitting in a tray. I sat up, feeling crummy physically and mentally, remembering all this, and wondered what to do. Then the phone rang. The answering machine was broken. I didn't know what to do, but I thought it might be safer to pick up than not, so I answered it, and there wasn't anyone on the line. I put it down, and it rang again. There was nothing. It rang again, and I answered it again, and there was nothing. I hit the flash button and tried to dial David, but I hadn't gotten a dial tone, and the call didn't go through. I flashed again and dialed the operator, but didn't get anything. I put it down, and it rang again, and nobody was on. I hadn't heard of any phone problem like that before And somebody was really mad at me, to put it mildly. It looked as if they had gotten a whole lot of people to call me at once, like the "phone zaps" ACT UP does against drug companies. But maybe it wasn't even people, I thought, as I put the phone down off the hook. These days it was more likely to be some kind of computerized dialing system. Something like a "demon dial," like they use to keep dialing a busy number until the call goes through. And they'd turned it on me just to hassle me.

Or maybe, I realized, to keep me from dialing out.

44

The intercom buzzed like the trumpet of death. I'd never realized it was so loud. I ran over to it, and no one was on the little TV screen. I went over to the windows on the street side, in my bedroom area, and peeked through the Venetian blind down at the street. There was one blue car idling in front of the building. A big man was standing next to the car, and a smaller person, probably a woman, with a hood over her head was standing three floors directly below me. She said something to him, and he got back in the car. She rang the buzzer again.

I grabbed my jacket with the wallet in it and found my key on the desk next to it, and ran over to the door and picked up the intercom.

"It's Jaishree. I've got the key." Her voice sounded a little strange. Should I barricade the door? I wondered. Should I just run out onto the stairs and climb up to the roof and jump down to the roof of the next building?

Maybe I'd start off playing it cool. It wasn't a good sign that she'd called herself Jaishree. Was she coming to beat me up with some kind of goon squad? If she just wanted to kill me, I'd be dead already, I supposed.

Like an idiot, I just stood there for a minute. Her steps on the stairs sounded a little heavy, for her. I couldn't help thinking of *The Fall of the House of Usher*.

I didn't turn on any lights, but the light table was still on, covered with transparencies. I heard her key turn in the lock. I wondered what I should do. Should I pick up a heavy object? I couldn't stop thinking that I felt like a character in an Elmore Leonard novel and wondering if I'd choke up. The police bolt turned and I stepped back a bit. She came in.

When I was very little, my dad took me to the Lon Chaney *Phantom of the Opera,* and the unmasking scene scared me and I thought about it for days. When I had rented it again a few months ago, even though I knew it was coming, that scene still gave me a real shiver. Maybe even more so because I knew it was coming. And the scene in the remake of *The Fly,* when half of Jeff Goldblum's face falls off and the horrible fly head comes out, and even the scene in *Batman* when the Joker takes the mask off Jerry Hall's face, and it's all scarred with acid, even those scenes kind of gave me a shiver. There's just something very primal about those scenes. So I half-expected something like that with Minaz, too, and I was already inwardly shivering in advance. She took off whatever sort of a hood thing she was wearing, kind of slowly, but she was still turned away from me. She was putting on a kind of unmasking act herself.

The table lit her from underneath, and she cast a strange round shadow against the colored light on the ceiling. It was because her hair was partially gone, and what there was of it was tied back, so she looked bald. The light from the transparency table was multicolored and patchy, so I couldn't see her clearly at first, but as she moved out of the shadow into a patch of purple light, I could see her face was covered with dime-sized discolorations in a kind of measles pattern. Something must have reacted with some of the dye.

"You should be really proud of yourself. You're such a great artist," she said. She had the same beautiful low voice. "A regular Michelangelo. Maybe more of an Expressionist lately, don't you think? I do confess I feel a bit like a Francis Bacon. Don't you think?"

She walked around the table toward me. I edged back a bit, bumping into the purple vinyl couch. Suddenly, I realized the discolorations were holes.

"Or maybe not so much a Francis Bacon more of an Oscar Mayer bacon, don't you think?"

There were tiny networks of cracks running around the holes in her face, like ridges in a rotting pumpkin. And it seemed to be a weird mottled gray color. Her face definitely seemed smaller. I guessed that all my work had been stripped off. And there wasn't any skin underneath. Just flesh that dried and wrinkled.

Something immediately flashed into my mind, something I hadn't remembered for many years: my grandmother's face from one visit home when I was a little kid, at Christmas, I think. She had been operated on for skin cancer, and there were huge black-red scabs on her face, from where the doctor had abraded and stripped the skin, and even the front of her nose seemed to have been cut off, and its tip was flattened. I had been horrified but didn't want to show it. I remembered going into her bedroom and noticing she had a towel on top of her pillow so that the blood wouldn't stain it.

"Listen," I said, "you can't tell me this happened, uh, because of, uh, what I did on you, you know, it's happened too fast, someone did this to you, somebody didn't know what he was—"

"I've just been operated on for *cancer*!"

"I, uh—"

"It wasn't just skin cancer, either, you know, it's some kind of sarcoma, it may seed itself and kill me. I want you to know the whole story. Take a good look, okay? You're one of two people to see me, including my doctor."

She sat down on the couch. I just stood there. I could feel myself getting detached, saying this can't be happening, it's only real life, it's just like a movie, I'll just act the way you're supposed to act in movies and get out of the apartment before whoever she had in the car came up the stairs.

"I have a few security people downstairs in the car," she said, reading my mind. "I hope you don't mind. I'm still something of a star, you know, at least until someone wants to take a picture of me. I need protection. You know, I had a whole speech planned out for this occasion, but I just don't think I'll use it, I don't think you deserve to hear it."

"Listen, we'll fix it," I said.

"How?"

"I'll do an emergency treatment, we'll do everything absolutely right this time, I've got patients around who are perfectly fine right now—"

"Do you think I'd let *you* turn a knife on *me*? You, the Jack the Ripper of SoHo? Don't make me hurt when I laugh.'

"Well, I'm going to jail soon, so you can gloat over me while I get raped in prison."

"No, you've protected yourself too well, with those tapes and everything," she said. "We're not calling the police in on this."

"Well, Penny will."

"I don't care what Penny does. I want you all to myself."

It was strange hearing her beautiful soft voice come out of a gargoyle.

"I don't think you could really understand what it's like," she said. "To be a woman, to get older, to worry about being ugly, then to get a second chance, and to be beautiful, and then to have it all taken away in one day. I know it sounds like I'm asking for sympathy, but I just don't think you could ever—nothing that happens to you will ever, ever, ever—"

There was a tear running down the lunar landscape of her cheek.

"I love you," I said. "I, I—"

That's not true, I thought as soon as I said it. I'm just trying to squirm out of this, if I love her it's because I've destroyed her . . .

No, that's not true. I did love her.

"Jaishree," I choked out, "I love you for you. Faces don't matter. Faces are masks, masks don't matter—"

The Minaz Monster had crossed the room to the intercom. "You can come up now,' she said into it.

I moved fast and pushed her back toward the kitchen, hard, so that she fell over and knocked over one of the high bar chairs. I slammed the door and started bolting the two remaining locks, keeping an eye on her. She didn't seem to be about to attack me herself. She was holding back, listening for the footsteps on the stairs.

Get a weapon and try to hold her hostage? Jump onto the roof next door, out the studio window? Both too dangerous. I ran around the light table to the window that opened onto the fire escape and started messing with the catch. It took forever, but I got it open. I felt in my pocket for my wallet. It was there. I could get away. It had almost everything I needed in it to be on the run—five thousand dollars, my phony papers as well as my real ones, my safe-deposit keys. I was officially on the run.

She screamed really, really loud, *"Get in here now!"* There were a whole bunch of really loud bangs on the door. It's a really good thing that police bolt lock was so strong. Otherwise they would have gotten in immediately.

I wriggled out the window onto the fire escape. The light outside was a deep red. The ancient, rusty narrow bars seemed really flimsy and hurt my hands. I looked down once at the car she'd come in. Two more big people were trying to pull the lever-staircase of the fire escape down, one giving the other a boost.

Meanwhile, Jaishree had gotten the door open. I should have started climbing immediately, but I took a nanosecond to watch these big guys push in through my door. I'd seen really high-quality goons before, when I'd worked at the Davidian Gallery. Actually, just one, his driver, Marco. He was a big, stocky guy, very well groomed, soft-spoken, and well mannered, with dead-looking eyes, killer's eyes. And of course, I used to see John Gotti and his guards around the neighborhood. These two people reminded me of them. I only got a quick look.

I started climbing.

45

I swung up over the ladder and onto the asphalt roof. I looked over at the roof door that led to the interior stairs. There were dark yellow storm clouds building up all over the city. The sun was falling into the tiny gap between the two blocks of the World Trade Center, and it made magenta smudges all over the bottoms of the clouds. The sky was blue-gray behind the clouds. I couldn't help thinking of Poussin, even though I was scared out of my mind. Sometimes when you're really terrified, you focus on some trivial thing, something that seems safe and eternal, and I just kept thinking of the clouds in Poussin's *Flood*. But I couldn't bolt the roof door from this side, and they were probably on their way up the stairs, and the fire escape was already covered, so I ran to the far end of the roof and managed to get up on the wall that runs around our roof, and climbed over the metal railing. On this side there was a building attached to ours. I looked down. It was only one story down, but suddenly it looked like a long distance.

"*Hey!*" some tough-guy-sounding voice shouted behind me. I didn't even look around, I just jumped. When I was a little kid, I used to jump from heights like this all the time, and I was always great at it, because I didn't weigh as much, I guess. But even though I remembered to collapse and roll when I hit the asphalt, I still really hurt my feet and knees. It was tremendously painful. Then I sort of scrambled up and ran over to the fire escape. It went down in the back of this lower building, out of view of anyone on my roof, but as I grabbed on to the rusty metal and lowered myself onto the stairs, I looked up and saw a couple of dark figures above me, silhouetted against the brown sky. I hustled down the fire escape and wondered whether they were going to follow me down this way or go back down to their car and try to head me off on the street. I got down into this horrible little alley and ran out onto Rivington Street. From here it seemed like it was already night. I ran around the corner onto Norfolk and headed toward Delancey. I looked over my shoulder a couple of times, but there wasn't anything there. There weren't any cabs on Delancey when I got there. I ran out into the street and looked all around, kind of frantically, I guess, because I got stares. It's incredible, the way there are never any cabs around when you really need them. I'd never been so frustrated. And terrified. A couple of cabs went by with passengers in them. Then a cab went by with its off-duty light on. I ran up to it anyway and tried to grab the door handle, and he zoomed right by me, the bastard. Those fuckers just turn on their off-duty signs in this neighborhood because they don't want to pick up the lowlifes around here, the schmucks. Don't they know it's a newly yuppied-out neighborhood? I kept looking around for the goon squad while I ran west, past Ratner's Dairy Restaurant, past the Styles R Us, and out into Essex Street. Way east, by the FDR Drive, there was a free cab. I turned back and ran toward it, and just before it got to my block some artsy bitch lady hailed it in front of me. I was so disappointed, I nearly had a stroke.

There were some shapes way down the street that could have been Minaz's goons. I wasn't sure, but they were coming in this direction pretty fast. A big car turned the corner down there, too. It looked very bad. I was gasping out "Shit, shit, shit shit," over and over. I was really panting a lot. I had pains in my chest. I hadn't really exercised at all since I had swum a little in Key Biscayne. So I was way, way out of shape. There was an F train stop on Essex, and I started running toward the subway entrance, and then I realized its light was red, and I ran across the street to the green-lit subway entrance, and nearly got killed by a truck.

For once in my entire life, there was a train coming in as soon as I got down the stairs. A sign from heaven. I hopped the turnstile. What if I got arrested just for that? It's never a great idea to break the law.

I got out of the subway and
walked up the passage to Grand
Central Station. I passed the
Caruso Pizza, and the closed Hoffritz store, with its huge circular
radiating arrays of scissors and knives and evil-looking surgical tools
and whatever on black velvet, and past the newsstand—I practically
expected to see COPS SEEK MAD "ARTIST" on the front page of the *Post*—
and then the huge void of the main terminal opened up in front of
me, sending a shiver through me, as it always does, and I remembered the roof with the Zodiac signs and the information kiosk and
the message board with NEW HAVEN DEPARTS 8:52 at the top of the list from
all the times I had come through here on my way up to Yale, and I
thought for a minute maybe I was still just a student there, I'd just had
a longer-than-usual-bad-dream, and I was on my way back up to a
tiny comfy room on the Old Campus, and I didn't have anything more
to worry about than whether Harold Bloom was going to let me in his
Lyric class.

She'd said she wasn't going to the police. But she really wanted
me to suffer, and she didn't have much to lose. And since she might
decide there was a good chance her hired help wouldn't find me—
they might not be real Mafia people anyway, just a few corruptible
private detectives—it was possible she'd report me to the cops even if
Penny and Virginia hadn't already. On which charge? Reckless endangerment? Well, Iskowitz would probably have cooked up something

good enough to get me arrested. I suppose a ruined movie career would let you argue for a whole lot of damages. And he probably wasn't even that worried about the videotapes, because good lawyers don't believe in contracts. No matter what I had her saying on tape, he'd just yell that I'd led her on, and the idiot jury would take one look at her and crucify me. I could just see him dramatically unveiling her at the trial, and the scene in my mind immediately cut to jail bars clanking shut.

Still, I supposed I was safer with the police than with hired killers. I could probably still mount a defense of some kind, and maybe escape prison. The real danger would be getting killed on the street somewhere, without warning. And that was a chance I couldn't take without protection. I couldn't just walk around town like a target. I'd have to get away for a while and sort everything out from a distance.

The other problem was Mark. If they picked him up, and she knew where he was so they probably would, he'd crack pretty fast. He'd really always just been a science nerd, not really up for playing with the big boys. And his testimony would make me seem like the ringleader, which I guess I was. And if Penny and Virginia had gotten together, too, and somebody got them to give their stories out, well, it just seemed like the story was right up the *Post*'s alley, and Minaz was going to be the next Jennifer Levin, and I was going to be the next Robert Chambers. I could see the whole thing getting really out of hand. MAD DOCTOR "ARTIST" FAKES MOVIE STAR. MINAZ DISFIGURED BY "ART" SURGERY. Was I being an alarmist?

The board said the last train to New Haven would leave in a half-hour and get in at 11:32 P.M., late enough so that I wouldn't have to find a place to stay overnight before I went out to Torrington. For a minute I thought, maybe I'll just check into the Royalton or something and see whether I had a real problem in the morning. They'd never pick me out of all the hotels in the throbbing heart of Western Civilization this late at night.

But better safe than sorry. I bought a ticket—track 26—and started wandering toward the lower level of the station.

I had to call Mark.

First, I couldn't find a quarter and had to change a fifty, then two of the phones didn't work, then I had to get his number from information, but finally I got him at home.

"It's okay, I'm awake," he said.

"Listen, it was worse than I thought. Minaz had a goon squad with her, and I had to sneak out. And I'm afraid the cops are going to get on this any minute."

"Yeah, they already visited me."

"Are you serious?"

"Yeah, but they left. They didn't have a warrant or anything, they just asked a few questions about you and left."

Shit, shit shit. "What did you tell them?"

"I didn't tell them where you hang out or anything, if that's what you're afraid of. But I guess they've been over to your studio by now."

"What are you going to do?"

"Well, nothing, I mean, I'm not going to hop a plane to Tahiti. Why, is that what you're doing?"

Sometimes Mark was a real bore.

"Listen," he said, "There's something else going on. I called up some of the burn victims—you know, Paul and Rachel and Rebecca Casper—and *none* of them have had any problems. It's just those three."

"The famous ones."

"Yeah, I've been thinking, I shouldn't have told Karl who we were working on at all. I mean, he'd always ask, and I'd just tell him."

Oh, fuck. It was suddenly very clear.

"Karl put something reactive in the PCS," I said.

"I don't know."

"You stupid fuck," I said. "Could Karl have a *patent* out on PCS? Does he know everything about it?"

"Well, I know he's filed patent papers on some things," Mark said. "But I don't—"

I was practically shaking too hard to talk.

"So Karl set us up to screw up," I said.

"I guess so."

"He cut us out."

"I guess so."

"He's going to have a hundred percent of the business. He got free testing without having to go through channels, he'll get a ton of free publicity on our messing up with 'his' invention, and then even though it didn't work in a couple of the main cases, people are going to start to experiment with the PCS 10 out of curiosity, and it'll work, and there'd be articles in medical journals, and it will gradually get accepted by the medical community and approved for worldwide use."

"I guess that's about the size of it."

"And we won't be able to take the credit for it." My voice was shaking, but I was explaining things pretty clearly. Overcome by sudden comprehension. "You and I just stole his chemistry and screwed up with it because we used the wrong dyes, or something, supposedly, and Karl's salted all his share of the money away without ever spending any of it—and no wonder he never even set foot in my studio—and nobody'll believe us, and we'll get crucified while Karl will be explaining away on *Live at Five*."

"I guess that's it."

"So. Where is Karl?" I asked.

"He left again yesterday. He's on vacation, in the South, he said."

"How did he leave the lab?"

"He always takes most of his own records out of the lab and locks up his work."

"What about our records?"

"I haven't checked yet."

"I can't believe you were so stupid, Mark. You just signed your death warrant. You're a dead man."

"Is that a threat?"

"Not from me. Minaz is going to get you."

I had to put another couple of quarters into the phone.

"But why did he make us mess up?" Mark asked. "I still don't really get his motivations for that—"

"Well, maybe he was a little jealous. He wanted to be another Jamie Angelo."

And more important, he *knew* that with my personality, I'd overdo it and take risks. I mean, I'd known all along that this was a problem. But I just couldn't fathom so much betrayal, I'd just thought I was so great at what I was doing, anybody would be glad to be on board. I just couldn't imagine him or anyone doing something so horrible. Why, why, why, why? I mean, to mess up Jaishree. And Penny and Virginia and maybe others. . . .

Of course, if he hadn't made us screw up, he wouldn't be able to take the credit even if he turned us in for practicing without a license. Mark and I would still be famous even if we did get exposed and have to pay a fine or go to jail; Karl would just look like he was trying to cash in on our success. This way, he'd get a big publicity bash and come out smelling like a rose.

And even the spectacle of Penny's and Virginia's and Minaz's faces getting eaten away wouldn't scare people off, because people will do absolutely *anything* for youth. If they can put belladonna in their eyes to make them seem larger, and if Argentinian women can take arsenic to make their skin paler, and if they can chance horrible infections with face-lifts, and worse things from liposuction, and cancer from silicone breast implants, then they can certainly accept the risk of a little plastic. I had to hand it to Karl, he really had worked it out pretty well.

I was more than a little annoyed. To say the least. There's nothing like getting played like a fish to make you furious, and I was on the verge of going back into the subway and trying to track down Karl and strangle him, but somehow sanity prevailed, and I realized I didn't have time. I probably didn't even have time to try for one of the airports, I should just get on a train, get a bus sometime tomorrow or the next day, pick up my reserve supply of cash—it was in a safe-deposit box in Torrington under a name from one of my phony IDs, and *nobody* knew about it—and then just get out away from the East Coast for a while, before the shit really hit the fan. I went over the flight plan again in my mind, and it sounded to me like I was thinking rationally. In a way, I was proud of myself. My first real major crisis situation.

"What are you going to do?"

"What?" I asked. Mark was still talking on the other end.

"Where are you going to go?" Mark asked.

"I'm going—"

I thought better of it.

"I've got a flight to Paris," I said. "I've got to run."

I hung up I walked into the drugstore next to the Hoffritz and bought some light sunglasses and a cheap knit hat. Luckily it was cold enough so that I wouldn't look unusual wearing a hat, I'd just look like a jerk. But I supposed I was going to have to put my fashion sense on hold if I was going to stay a free agent. I walked over into the main room of the station, the one where, if you're a fugitive, you really feel like there are a hundred plainclothes cops watching you, and went to the Chemical Bank machine kiosk. I punched in my code—B-E-A-U-T-Y—and took out the maximum five hundred dollars. I love the feeling of new crisp warm twenties hot from the machine. I got out my other account card, from Dollar Dry Dock, and started punching it in when I suddenly wondered something. Did the cops have some way of getting into bank files and tracing people to the cash machines they use through their account numbers? I hesitated for a minute, but there was a line of antsy people starting up behind me, and so I just punched in my other account number and took out another five hundred dollars. If they could trace that way, it was too late anyway. I'd better just get on a train and not wait around to see whether I was in the evening edition of the newspapers.

I walked downstairs, and I thought about all the times I'd walked this way to take the train to New Haven, and I wished I were doing that again and going back to school instead of clearing out with the law on my tail, so to speak. I managed to stagger out onto the plat-form—my left foot was messed up somehow—and into one of the first cars of the train. I started looking for an "optimum defense seat," the way I had always done, even when I wasn't feeling particularly paranoid: a two-person seat, toward the back so I could see the whole car, but not near the bathroom with its disgusting smells, fac-ing forward, on the left side of the train, so my right arm would be free. I finally found one two cars back, put my jacket on the seat next to me to try to keep people from sitting there, and scrunched down in the corner of the seat. Only a few other people came into the car, and none of them looked like detectives or hit men. The train started up pretty soon. I was awake all night. It was hell. I sat on a bench in the station and dozed off just as it got blue outside.

I dreamed I was in my old high school and they were all after me, all three horrible, mutilated furies with scabby faces and hateful eyes. They were all coming to get me. When I woke up, I wondered whether maybe I *had* wanted to destroy the girls, like Bataille says, whether maybe I had known that my process wouldn't work, and that I wanted to wreck whatever beauty they had in order to possess it, the way a serial killer wants to possess his victims.

■

New Haven Station is pretty dreary in the middle of the night, and I felt pretty stiff and crummy, but I ate stuff in the coffee shop from 5:45, when it opened, until 8:30, and then I walked around outside for a while, in the cold, hoping I wouldn't run into any old schoolmates and looking up at Harkness Tower and remembering how impressed I had been by it when I arrived there for college back in the pre-Cambrian era, and finally I walked back into the station and found a newsstand that had just gotten the morning edition of the *New York Post*. Some murder in Queens was on the front page, and that reassured me a bit. But I hadn't been too much of an alarmist. There was a nice little piece on page four called "Artist Sought in Bizarre Surgery Case." It jumped out at me and sent a real chill down my spine and into my feet, which wriggled a bit. It sounded like the police and the press were pretty set against me. I got all self-con-scious, like everyone was staring at me. It was a worse feeling than it's possible to describe: a hollow glob of terror inside, and badly concealed involuntary shudders. The article didn't say much, but it mentioned my name. I was officially on the run.

There was a Greyhound station a few blocks away, on the way to School. You had to walk past the police station. But I made it and got a bus to Torrington, Connecticut. It's a very sleepy place with a couple of closed factories and big old white houses falling into ruins. I felt pretty bad about myself at this point, but I was kind of proud that I'd taken the trouble to set up an anonymous safe-deposit box out here. It was still only about one o'clock and the bank wouldn't close for a while, so I sat in a diner and got some doughnuts and coffee and cocoa and felt better. I wondered whether I looked strange to the people there, whether they were all looking at me and gossiping about me and would remember me the instant they saw my picture in the *National Enquirer*. It didn't really matter, though. I hadn't been to this bank in about a year and a half, but I didn't think I'd have any trouble. I'd pick up my bag of emergency cash and gold coins, which included $45,000 in twenties, fifties, and hundreds. Now I wished I'd put away more, but at the time I just couldn't bear losing all the interest. I also had keys to all the anonymous deposit boxes and art storage depositories that I hadn't been able to liquidate, and so maybe I'd only lose the stuff that was in the loft itself.

■

I bought some hair tint in a drugstore up there. There was another big wooden box I could pick up, at my parents' farm in the Berkshires, which was empty at this time of year. I wondered whether it was safe. I'd need a car to get there, but renting one shouldn't be too much trouble, with cash and my good fake ID. Also, I could sleep in a car, and I'd need sleep to plan my next move. I wished there were someone I could call to discuss my troubles with. My next move.

Renting the car under my assumed name—Alex Melmouth—was tension city for me, but I used my false-name Visa card, and they were busy, and I got the car. Later on I'd turn the car in at some other Hertz office and buy an old Volvo or something off the side of the road, for cash.

I called Jay from a pay phone and told him I was sorry I'd missed the appointment and that I'd called to just collect information about the case, find out what Karl and the girls were up to, and whether Jaishree was going the legal route or whether she was just planning on offing me privately. "Think about a defense," I said, "I'll call in a couple of weeks." I said he could say that I was currently afraid for my life and had to go into hiding. He seemed kind of eager for his firm to argue the case, even though he's not a criminal lawyer, because it meant big press. But I told him he'd have to wait.

Going by the old farmhouse was tense, too, and nostalgic. It wasn't being watched yet. I came in the back way, on foot. It made it easier that it was at night. But the smells still reminded me very powerfully of relatively happy times in childhood. I was glad to just grab some stuff and go. It was three A.M. when I left.

At least the tapes were in the vault, I thought. And Karl couldn't really use the procedure the way I knew how to. Maybe I'd just send the safe-deposit key to some rival of his, some ambitious young plastic surgeon, and see what happened.

I headed west on Route 80, thinking about my next move. But there wasn't any next move.

■

By dawn I got to the Delaware Water Gap, a pass over a rushing rapids with high gray raggedy cliffs rising on either side, and after I was through that, I was in Pennsylvania, and I felt I was really away from it all and safe, because you feel hidden there, with all the fog and mountains and little farms. I was almost tempted just to stay in some motel there, in some little town, but I knew the sense of security I felt was totally illusory. And it wasn't really a good place to hide out. I had a better spot in mind, one that I knew pretty well but that was still a place that people wouldn't connect me with because I had never talked about it. It was in this country, so I wouldn't have to cross a border, but it was near enough to Canada that if things ever really heated up in the United States, I could cross over, on foot if necessary, then even maybe arrange for a flight overseas. Maybe to Costa Rica. I had some friends there. But then I thought I should stay away from friends. I should gear up for a period of pretty intense solitude.

I got to Youngstown, on the state line between Pennsylvania and Ohio, around noon. It was still an overcast day. There were storms with lightning in them visible far ahead. I was tired and I was tempted to stop, but I knew I was also too keyed up to sleep. And too tired. One thing that worried me was my accuracy level on the driving. It wouldn't do to have an accident or even get pulled over. I wasn't sure my fake identification was good enough to pass inspection by a cop. Certainly not if they ran it through the computer. But I couldn't deal with a motel, so I pulled over at a rest area and climbed into the backseat and stretched out. I didn't actually sleep. Maybe I dozed in and out a bit. It was four o'clock in the afternoon when I started driving again. I drove through a drive-through McDonald's and got a couple of fillet-of-fishes and a few milkshakes and salads and coffee. Burger King and Wendy's are actually better than McDonald's, but McDonald's is packaged better for driving. It's easy to eat with one hand. The sky became rainy and stormy and scary, with really loud thunder crashes. Nothing was coming in clearly on the radio. For a few minutes I couldn't see a thing because of the rain. But it made me feel secure, in a way, the storm was a kind of cover.

Ohio starts out as a nice state, rolling pillowy hills with lots of big white barns faceted like crystals, but it goes on forever. It takes six hours. About midway through it, I emerged out from under the edge of the sheet of boiling storm clouds into a strange, lavender, silent evening. I passed places with poetic names, Eleiria, Erewhon, the Vermilion River. At Toledo I headed north on Route 23. It was getting dark again with more flashes of lightning, and I felt like I was getting close to the edge of the world.

49

I didn't fall off the edge of the earth and get eaten by dragons. After staying at a lot of Holiday Inns, I finally rented a room in a somewhat isolated house in a town in the Upper Peninsula of Michigan. It was a Dutch-American town and everybody seemed to be named after painters: Mrs. Van Eyck, who ran the house, Mr. Bosch the carpenter, and Bob Brueghel, who did construction and drove around in a tractor called, of all things, a Vermeer. The house was on the lake and had a sign on it that said ROOMS FOR RENT. It was like a forties movie, just the way you'd imagine a "rooms for rent" place—for escaped convicts and Uncle Charlies. Mrs. Van Eyck was very into arts and crafts. So I gave up the old geology-and-antiques cover I'd been using and told her I was a photographer working on a book about American beveled-glass windows. She loved it. She was my new best friend. The only problem was, her face was kind of dried-out and crunchy-looking, and I recoiled a bit whenever I saw it, especially when I saw it unexpectedly. I liked the room because it had a great view, just a strip of pure light salmon-colored sand and the big smooth void of Lake Superior. Once in a while a jogger would run past and leave a horrible scar of footprints on the sand, but it was getting on toward November and that kind of thing was tapering off, and the winds were getting strong enough to eradicate most traces of humanity pretty quickly. The room was pretty small but very spare and nice, except for the spotted old walls. The first thing I did when I moved in was get three gallons of Benjamin Moore Decorator White. It made me feel a lot better about things. The next morning, though, I noticed there were some irregularities and cracks and holes in the plaster, and I had to run out and get spackle and a big putty knife and I spent the whole day working with that. Finally I got it pretty good. I'd gotten some paint spots on the old tongue-in-groove floor, so the next day I went out and bought a small power sander and a lot of polyurethane and worked on that for a while. At about six o'clock I had to get out of the fumes from the polyurethane, so I went walking along the beach— not in front of my own window, of course, because I didn't want to mess up the sand.

Sometimes, at night, when the wind was screeching over the lake and there was the sound of sand being blown against the glass, I'd have to close the blinds because I would see faces outside the window. They were hardly visible except when they pressed up against the glass to look at me. They were of all ages, some nearly old men with beards, a lot of young men who had been rough-and-tough sailors, a few children, and fewer women. They had desiccated, wrinkled milk-white skin stretched over their skulls and bulging, imploring eyes. They were, of course, the shades of the crews and occasional passengers of barges and freighters, who had drowned shrieking in the wind in the awesome fall and spring storms out on the great lake. Somewhere three hundred feet below the surface, preserved in the airless fresh water, their bodies were swept along the sandy bottom like dried-out cactus flowers blowing across the desert, tumbling in and out of the half-buried hulks of boats and airplanes in the green twilight. The Ghosts' High Noon lasted twenty-four hours a day. I began to recognize some of them, on several successive nights, especially a motherly-looking woman with long hair matted with some kind of seaweed. She smiled at me and tried to say something to me, to get me to go out there, I think. After a while I kept the blinds shut all the time at night, and I didn't know whether the little scratching sounds were their dry fingers or just the blowing sand.

So apart from the nightmares and a general feeling of total despair—which came and went—I got along really well. I got hold of some Maya books and sent away for books and papers and did some more work on my pre-Columbian studies. I thought maybe someday

I'd go down there again and start learning Yucatec and really getting into it. It was a peaceful period. I celebrated my thirtieth birthday by myself. It was the only time all the time in Michigan when I cried.

The only other big problem out here was the flies. I couldn't stand having any of them around. Sometimes I got so mad at them, I started going outside to swat them.

I'd sit in bed and stare out at the lake for hours. Once in a while it would get ruffled up by the wrong kind of wind, but usually, even though it was wavy, they were nice smooth waves. I loved the surface of it. It just went on and on.

Then one morning I woke up, at eight, and there was something wrong with the lake. There had been a howling in the trees all night, and it was a gray day, and there were strange irregular geometric patterns building up on the shore. It took a minute before I realized they were ice. Toward the middle of the day more ice started drifting in on the waves, building up against the beach. Some of it had white clumps of snow on it, sticking up like pustules. By evening, the lake was covered with a network of white and gray lines, in an irregular crunchy-looking formation. It really disturbed me, it was so sharp and crunchy. So I kept the blinds closed after that and relied on the television more. Once in a while I got a glimpse of the lake as I went out to buy groceries. It wasn't just flat ice anymore; the chunks had piled up into big icebergy formations with sand all over them, and it sent shudders running down to my toes whenever I looked at it. Sometimes it would get covered by a heavy snowfall, and it would look fairly nice and there'd be blessed relief, but it didn't last long because the snow would blow off in the high winds. I should have moved, maybe, but inertia was becoming the biggest force in my life. At least the ghosts had stopped coming to my window. They were frozen solid in the ice.

I even toyed with the idea of getting fat. I tried eating a lot of fattening stuff, but it just made me feel sick. No matter what I ate, I stayed the same weight I'd been since high school. Finally I gave up. I went back to my very restricted diet of fish sticks, fish, and peas with olive oil and Parmesan cheese. It was kind of exciting to eat the same thing every day and not wonder about what to eat. After a while the breading on the outside of the fish sticks began to bother me and I just got plain frozen fish. I got a whole bunch of Conran's-looking white dishes from something called Safeway. I mainly ate and drank out of mugs, but I began to be bothered by the way no matter how carefully I drank, I'd always leave a little drop of liquid on the outside of the mug, where it shouldn't be. I started drinking only clear things so it wouldn't bother me so much, but that was only a partial solution. I washed my towels and clothes every other day in Mrs. Van Eyck's washing machine. Around Christmastime I revarnished the floor, just for the hell of it. You only live once.

There's a magazine store in Sault Sainte Marie that gets the *New York Post* and the *Times* and the *Daily News* and *Newsday,* and they agreed to hang on to a week's run for me. I picked them up on Thursdays and spent the rest of the week sorting through them. The whole incident ultimately got more press than I would have liked, but not enough to make me a household word. I got quite a scrapbook of tabloid headlines together, though. The *Post*'s MAD SCIENTIST'S "ART" MAY KILL 3 STARS was one of my particular favorites. It's a little hard to tell from the widely varying articles exactly what the charges against me are. And I'm not sure I want to call Jay to find out. Karl's been doing great, of course. He was on *Regis and Kathie Lee* in late November. I had my TV on an hour before the show started. Things prey on your mind when you're alone.

"Today we're talking with a plastic surgeon who's taken the phrase 'plastic surgery' to a new level of meaning and made headlines around the world," Regis said.

Kathie Lee went, "The process invented by Dr. Karl Vanders of Columbia University College of Physicians and Surgeons promises a new era in anti-aging, cosmetic, and reconstructive surgery. But his process made tabloid history when it was stolen and used incorrectly by two unlicensed colleagues. Dr. Vanders, do you feel the press's reaction to the incident has been blown out of proportion?"

"By 'the incident,' I suppose you mean the cases involving Minaz and Penny Penn," Karl answered.

"Yes."

"Well, I certainly feel those cases did some damage to the public's image of the process, yes. But you have to remember, I didn't develop these compounds for cosmetic surgery in the first place. I was researching burn victims, and I'd still like to make the process available primarily to people who really need it, not movie stars particularly."

Smart, I thought. Karl looked much less nerdy, almost stylish in a Ralph Lauren suit and contact lenses.

"Doctor," Regis said, "there's been some speculation that Penny Penn or Minaz may come to you for a reconstruction of their previous 'looks.' Can you confirm or deny anything about that?"

What bullshit. "Doctor." "Doctor" indeed. I've always hated doctors because they're hung up on their stupid title. They make you call them "Doctor." It's ridiculous. The whole point of the American Republic was not to issue titles, because the stupid public gets too impressed by them.

"I'm not at liberty to discuss that potentiality," Karl said. "It's true that what happened to them is tragic, but for the time being I can only pursue what I feel is the most medically responsible course of action."

50

There's no question, it's a little frustrating to sit in a rented room in Bar Harbor, Michigan—or, to be honest, a town with a name rather like "Bar Harbor"—and watch some talentless geek you barely gave a thought to in your former glamorous life flay you to death with your own ideas on prime time. I'm frustrated, I have to admit it. But I suppose I was living a little high, maybe I deserve it. I'm going to make sure Karl gets what he deserves, too, though.

Mark, on the other hand, didn't come out too well in the popular press. I have a feeling he's a very unhappy person. He hasn't been sentenced yet. He's been ranting and raving about me whenever there are reporters around the courtroom. Even more than Karl, he's responsible for the negative image I've gotten in the magazines. David hasn't been mentioned anywhere, and I like to think he got off with just minor injuries. Oddly enough, the best coverage of the incident hasn't been in the *Post* but in the art press. I got a very good mention in *Flash Art* in an article called "New Frontiers in Art About Science" by James Meyer and there's a long feature article in *Artscribe* this month on my series of beautiful faces—both the paintings, the last series I did from my beauty research, and the ones in flesh—by Robert Pincus-Witten himself. He says he's a little disturbed by the amorality of it all—well, he actually even called me a "sociopath," which I think is a little strong—but he'd be willing to bet, he says, that in another fifty years Jamie Angelo would be thought of as a major pioneer. Of something.

Unfortunately, the piece was illustrated with news and publicity shots of Penny and Minaz and not my own loving four-by-fives, or even Timothy's great session. Maybe I'd better get somebody to go to the bank and get out the good transparencies. All I've got here is a few snaps. But I'm starting to sound nostalgic. At least Karl didn't try to take the credit for my designs. And that's what I'm most proud of, the poetry, not the techy stuff. And to some extent, although it sounds corny, Virginia and Penny and Minaz will live forever on celluloid, and they've already had more of an effect on the world than most people ever had, so maybe, however they feel personally, their lives haven't been a total loss. Maybe they're better as fair shades. Maybe I should be proud. And maybe someday I'd be a major artist again.

■

On the other hand, I picked up another copy of that Bataille book *Erotism,* and it's made me question my motives a bit. Particularly this passage:

> I can link my revulsion at decay (my imagination suggests it, not my memory, so profoundly is it a forbidden object for me) with the feelings that obscenity arouse in me. I can tell myself that repugnance and horror are the mainsprings of my desire, that such desire is only aroused as long as its object causes a chasm no less deep than death to yawn within me, and that this desire originates in its opposite, horror.

■

I've got an old 9mm Browning-model automatic, an issue weapon from the Panamanian army that a friend of my dad's got at a gun show in Dallas in the fifties, and it's about as cold as they come, completely untraceable, and I've been taking it out and blowing away tin cans (always careful to pick up the spent shells) at a deserted rocky beach on the north side of town. I've been using new ammunition, but I still have a couple of boxes of the old hard-to-trace rounds that came with the gun, and they still work fine. It's an inaccurate weapon, but still reliable and hard-hitting at close range. So when I think of Minaz's scarred face, and what she must be up to right now, and how she's feeling, I figure I'll just take a bus into New York, wearing a wig and glasses and two completely different sets of clothes, one under the other, and stake out Karl's clinic, wait for him to come out late some night, fire all seven rounds into his head— well, I'd put the first couple into his knees and then his stomach just to wake him up a bit—and then leave him lying in a bloody spattery quivering heap, wipe off the gun with a Wash'n Dri, drop it in a trash can, walk down into the Seventy-second Street subway, strip off my outer clothes behind a pillar or something down there, put the old clothes into a suitcase—maybe I should even go in drag underneath, come to think of it—walk out the other exit, get in a cab, get on the next train leaving Grand Central, and get a bus back here, and I'd probably feel much better about everything. And they'll probably think Mark did it, for that matter, since he's not in jail yet. I'll have to pick a time when Mark is at home, unaccounted for. If he were more enterprising, he'd do it himself anyway. It's not a ridiculous notion. Stranger things have happened.

However, I also sometimes wonder whether, maybe, Karl had a point. After all, Mark and I were going to keep the whole process restricted to rich society ladies and movie stars. But I suppose it could really benefit the general population of the world, you know, people who are unhappy forever just because of some facial flaw. In the long run, expanded cosmetic surgery could make everyone much happier, even if it did level out differences in a kind of Huxleyan way. Or it might eventually even promote difference and originality in faces, but a kind of difference people had control over, not just something they were unalterably stuck with from birth. So what I'm wondering is, maybe in the grand scheme of things bringing the process out into the open is worth losing three girls' faces over. Maybe Karl was right. Mark and I aren't the most responsible people, anyway.

However, Karl can't do what I could do. Nobody could put the talent and learning and effort into it the way I did, I just know they can't. Certainly not without all my photographs and recipes and videotapes, all the stuff down in the Chase Manhattan vault on Fifty-seventh. Karl doesn't even do full-face reconstruction yet, as far as I know. He can't bring Minaz's face back, or even Jaishree's face. But I started wondering whether maybe I could. Of course, Minaz wouldn't let me. But I thought someone could probably do pretty well if he had all my tapes. . . .

The house in Massachusetts has an answering machine, so I could leave a message there and then call and give the retrieval code and people could pick up messages from it. But I could only do that a couple of times, because I could be pretty sure that they'd get over there and hook up a tracer after the first couple of times I tried it. I could also leave messages on other people's machines when I knew they'd be out, if I was pretty sure they weren't the type of people who'd have tracers. So I made some phone calls from the pay phone outside the drugstore. I called up this ambitious plastic surgeon, Paul Zinser, one of the ones who sent Mark a couple of "impossible" cases when I was just getting started. Now he's a surgeon to the stars. I couldn't talk long, because I was afraid he'd get someone to put a tracer on the call—they're pretty prevalent now—but I told him who I was, and of course he knew all about the whole case.

"How would you like to be in charge of my records?" I asked.

"I'd be very interested to see them," he said. No kidding. "Of course, the legal questions would all have to be worked out beforehand."

"I'm prepared to turn the records over to you if you'll agree to do three procedures, to my specifications, on three of my former clients."

"Well, of course, if we could work out the legal ramifications—"

"Otherwise, I'll turn my records over to the Vanders Clinic. We'll have to work out some guarantee system so I ll know you'll do the procedures."

"Could I ask you where you are? Have you decided to come back to the United States?"

Good, they thought I was abroad. I felt like saying "Yeah, I'm going to turn myself in so guys like you can take me apart, throw me in jail, and make an industry out of my ideas," but instead I just said, "Expect a letter from me," and hung up.

I put in one more pay-phone call, to my shrink, Dr. Brook.

"I think you'd be better off if you turned yourself in," he said.

"I don't think so."

"Do you want to tell me what really happened?"

"Sorry, no time," I said. "I'm uptight about telephones lately. You do prison calls, though, right?"

"Yes."

"So maybe we'll chat later," I said. "Thanks." I hung up. He was okay. He really did want to help.

51

So I got an envelope all ready to drop into the mailbox, addressed to Calvin, with another envelope addressed to Paul Zinser inside it, with a letter with all the information on it and the keys to three of the seven safe-deposit boxes, the relevant ones—the first two, which have all the explanations of the surgical procedures, and the last, with the tapes of the Minaz Project. I moved out of Michigan all the way to a motel in Louisiana, and I still drove two hundred miles off-route to send it, but I didn't think Calvin would show the cops the postmark on the outer letter. He's on my side. He'll just send the inner envelope on to Paul. I figure Paul will still be eager enough to get his hands on the other four boxes to do a reconstruction on Minaz for free. I said in the letter that I won't believe he's done it until I read about her in *Interview,* though. And she'd better look as beautiful as ever.

If she was still alive. The press had really clammed up about her lately. It's weird. I'd risked a call or two and asked Jay about her a couple of times, but he didn't know where she was and didn't seem to trust me anymore. The last few newspaper items just said she couldn't be reached for comment. I suppose I could call a few people in L.A. and try to track her down, but I'm just afraid to make too many calls. And frankly, I'm weary of the whole thing.

Actually, I'm trying not to think of this as a permanent stage. Instead, I'm just telling myself that it could be a weight-gain or a weight-loss experience, depending on how I look at it. It's a little strange living off pure cash, carrying around a shoulder wallet with hundreds of hundred-dollar bills in it wherever I go. Writing this has been good to make the time fly down here, but it's frustrating to write when you don't even have a printer. I suppose I could take my disk into a store, and they'd just do it. I mean, it's paranoid to think anyone in the computer store would have heard of the case. Besides, I may want to surface in a while anyway and take the credit for what I've done and try to get some of my paintings back. One just sold at auction for thirty, which isn't bad. I'm proof there's no such thing as bad publicity. Of course, I couldn't get the money, but I might get some of the art. On the other hand, I don't know if I have the energy left to go through all the legal stuff. And in a way, being on the run kind of rounds out my dramatic sense of my whole story. I thought at first it would be really difficult, having to deal with the locals and not being able to indulge any sense of fashion. And I wish I could call Zinser again and find out how it's going, but now I'm convinced he'd trace it. However, there seem to be some pretty girls down here, the scenery's great, I'm very unstressed—off the Konzak, off the Valium —and I'm kind of getting into the anonymity of it. As we all know, life imitates art, usually badly, but I've structured my life around the artistic properties I really like and imitated them very well. I've played Dorian Gray, Dr. Moreau, Frankenstein, Pygmalion, and Svengali, and now I'm getting a nearly equal kick out of playing the fugitive. Why screw it all up? Maybe I won't release this little memoir, or even just put it in a safe-deposit box the way I usually do. All fifty-one chapters—that's a good number to end on, by the way, all the cards in the deck except one—all the chapters are on one floppy on my laptop computer and I haven't made a single hard copy of any of it yet. A three-and-a-half-inch disk is a very ephemeral thing. Maybe I'll just hit F5—CONTROL ALT F6 once and delete this whole tangled skein out of the universe forever. I suppose the psychiatric profession would have a real field day with this manuscript if they got hold of it. I know my shrink got a big kick out of me until circumstances made further communication impossible. But I'm happy with the way things are for now. There's really no reason to be down here, even; at this point I could live in any major city without worrying about getting spotted. And anyway, if I did go back, even if I could make people realize

who I was, even if I could mount enough of a defense to stay out of
prison, and even if some people said I was an okay person, I'd still be
lonely, because, really, your face is your identity, and my friends just
wouldn't relate to me in the same way. I look so different now.

XXXXXXXXXXXXXXXXXXXXXXXXXXXXXXXXXXXXXXXXXXXXXXXXXXX
XXXXXXXXXXXXXXXXXXXXXXXXXXXXXXXXXXXXXXXXXXXXXXXXXXX
XXXXXXXXXXXXXXXXXXXXXXXXXXXXXXXXXXXXXXXXXXXXXXXXXXX

CONTROL ALT F6

It's funny. Just as I was sitting around wondering whether I should press the ENTER key that would erase this whole disk and launch my final testament into the infinite void of nonbeing, I heard on the television that Minaz was going to be on the next week's installment of *Entertainment Tonight*. I was pretty breathless to find out what had happened. I practically called Alan, but sanity prevailed. It's better to maintain telephone silence. So I hung around down here for a week, even though I was thinking of heading west. I ran out and bought a whole bunch of magazines and newspapers, but all I could find on her was that there were "rumors" she was going to have her face reconstructed. There was a lot of speculation on whether people would still want to see her on screen, or be able to identify with her, or anything, now that they knew that "some of her face was reconstructed out of plasticized compounds." I figured the public would probably get over it if Zinser did a good job. I was really glad I'd gotten all the materials to him and that Karl hadn't gotten to them first.

After all, the public identifies with *cartoon characters,* for God's sake, practically as much as they do with real people. More so, in fact. Take Bart Simpson. And I read an interview with Miss Piggy in *Woman's World* the other day, and I didn't get the feeling they were playing it as a joke. Let's face it, the public lost the distinction between fantasy and reality a long time ago. And it's a good thing, too.

So they're not going to mind knowing that one cf their favorite stars has a tad of polyethylene around the edges. It'll just increase her allure. The public will all wish they could afford to have the process done on them, and they'll rush to see her films to see how it looks. It'll be a whole industry, and I'll be the Freud of it. Think of the untapped market just in sex-change cases alone. And I'll have won, in a way, anyway. Minaz is my design. She'll be the first in a race of cyborgs, half-human, half-technology *Über*-beings. The new order of man. The dawn of a new age. *Next century's meta-level hyperreal aestheticized android today! Minaz ushers in the twenty-first. Forget all your old preconceived notions about the difference between man and machine. Throw that nature/culture dichotomy out the window where it belongs! It's over, it doesn't apply! There's a new day coming! A day when everyone, regardless of "actual" age (so-called) can look like a million billion bucks! Do you, sir, want to look like Montgomery Clift (pre–auto accident, of course)? You got it! Yes, madam, the face of Penelope Tree? Certainly. Yes, child, I can even dye your eyes to match your gown. Yes, sir, I can make you indistinguishable from Kim Basinger. But which age level would you prefer? Of course, we already have molds for her* Batman *period and her* 9 1/2 Weeks *period, but if for some reason you'd like to look a little "older" or "younger" we can custom-design a Kim Basinger face to your specifications. And will you be needing breasts or hair implants as well? Yes, good decision, it's very tiresome having to grow your own. Two long-lost siblings who'd like to look exactly like each other? What a story! Neither of you would mind if we wrote this up for the company brochure, would you? We've done two similar procedures already. We made a gay couple look exactly like each other a couple of months ago, at the Los Angeles branch. We actually blended characteristic features of each person together. Sit down and play with the imaging computer awhile, it's easy to concoct your own "celebrity mix": blend your own features with Celebrity Formats or our Standardized Ethnic Beauty Pattern Menu, or, if you prefer, allow one of our consultants to help you select and design the visage of your dreams. Honestly, L.A. has gotten so far ahead of the rest of the country in Facial Engineering, it's just not funny. I was only there for two days, and I talked to a Humphrey Bogart, a Dorothy Lamour, a Sarah Bernhardt, a Snow White—it's amazing how much she looked like the cartoon—and a*

Rudolph Valentino, and a Jean Harlow. That's not even the half of it. Do you know they're making a rock-opera movie version of the Bible with an all-engineered cast starring Lillian Gish, Marilyn Monroe, John Belushi, Yul Brynner, Errol Flynn, Olivia de Havilland, Joan Fontaine, Vivien Leigh, Laurence Olivier, Orson Welles, Edie Sedgwick, Nico, Rita Hayworth, the Marx Brothers, and the Beatles? Sure, some of the Beatles aren't dead yet, Tri-Star just bought the rights. Some of the other name-and-face combinations are still private property, too, but it doesn't matter. Just more work for entertainment lawyers, that's all. But personally, I can't imagine some of the faces folks are licensing these days. Imagine getting yourself turned into Peter Lorre! Or into a Milton Berle, even, can you imagine it? But people are doing it. And now there's this whole Fantasy Face thing going on in Holland and Denmark, it's absolutely out of control. People are getting themselves made over into the most grotesque things you can imagine! There's some singer over there called The Fox, because he's got a fox's head. And he's getting to be a big hit. And there's this S&M group that has these ugly, monstrous faces designed for them, they look absolutely cruel and horrible and mean and animalistic, and they have horns and strange bumps on them, and they come in all kinds of really garish colors. Can you imagine thinking that kind of thing is sexy? It's given Punk a whole new lease on life. And I was reading in Bomb *about the Smooth-heads, it's another Dutch/American group, they've had their heads redone into these really abstract, really smooth, pale-pastel designs, usually without hair and no ears and barely any nose, and they're tremendously alien-looking but actually in a way they're done so beautifully, you don't notice after a while, they even are kind of sexy, it's weird, there's something really great about the designs. Some of them are very rounded and soft-looking, and then the male ones—although it's kind of an androgyny thing—the male-looking ones are sort of faceted, and some of those are really shiny and robot-looking. There's some artist over there who designs most of them, he's becoming a really big deal. And then I was looking through the VandersGraft Corporation's fall brochure, and they're getting into all kinds of fantasy-inspired prosthetic limbs, they have things that can let you move your hair implants around in waves, and they think Spock Ears are going to be even more popular once you can curl and uncurl the tips, and they're offering extra arms and unfolding tentacle-fingers for "delicate work," although of course they're really making all that kind of stuff for sexual applications. I bet they're going to offer a whole range of new sexual organs, only they won't put them in the brochure. The Tongue Extension's just the tip of the iceberg. Double, triple, and quadruple penetration is going to be a matter of course. And they have all sorts of vibrator and massage and pleasure-center sensor implants all ready to go. It's certainly going to take the monotony out of sex, everybody's going to have different gadgets. I can't wait to start sleeping around again now that some of these things are coming out, it's going to be great. And I think I picked a sexy face design, too, don't you think? It's a combination of the young Diane Keaton, Carré Otis, and a Dutch Rabbit. What's your name again? Are you a boy or a girl? I know I knew you before your change, but I'm just so disoriented lately with all my friends getting made over. . . .*

53

Now that I'm one of my own works of art, it's kind of fitting. But I wish I'd been able to make myself a bit more imaginative. It was strange eradicating my previous face. It's hard to describe the blend of emotions. It was purgative and exciting but also immensely sad. Of course, I did it under very difficult conditions, and unassisted. I had to take tranquilizers and painkillers for two weeks afterward.

But maybe I'd even redesign my own face again, I've thought, and launch a new identity as a movie star. I probably wouldn't even have to do it again, actually, I'd done a good job even if it was kind of hurried. I'd based myself largely on Alex Pickman, that really good-looking young painter friend of mine whom we all used to envy because everyone thought he was so sexy, and partly on the young Basil Rathbone, with a hint of Raphael. I think I may have made my face excessively smooth-skinned, a little too angelic and perfect to be convincing. But it's what I want. The PCS feels pretty much the way I expected, numb but not unpleasant. One of the strangest things is not having to shave.

I'm pretty sure I used a batch of PCS on myself that hadn't been adulterated. It was a small amount from an old batch that I'd kept in my own "art freezer" on the farm in Massachusetts—where I also kept some film and brushes—just in case of emergencies during a procedure. There wasn't much of it to work with, but I did okay.

■

It was six-thirty on the last day. I was getting impatient for *Entertainment Tonight* to come on, for the first time in my life. The papers that day had mentioned that Minaz was going to have a press conference at five o'clock. That was why it was going to make it on to *Entertainment Tonight* before it got on the news. It was frustrating to have to sit back and watch everything from a distance and not be a participant.

I paced back and forth in my motel room. It had two double beds, and they made me feel lonely. It was very clean and that made me feel out of place, too, even though I'd become quite at home in motels. I was on the second floor, and the door/window looked down into a little valley with a six-lane highway at the bottom, with gigantic trucks carrying submarine-size logs going by every couple of minutes. The sun was going down behind a coniferous hill, and it was difficult for me to think of any blessings to count. I was free, relatively. I had lived a short but full and fairly hedonistic life up to the point before the "incidents." But it's funny how uncomforting memories are. On the other hand, I had no immediate money worries. I had some reputation or notoriety in the art world, and my paintings might survive time's wan wave. Best of all, I was about to see my greatest piece brought back to life—by someone else, of course, but she was still my piece. I settled down in front of the TV with a couple of cans of Cherry 7-Up and a McDonald's Chicken Salad Oriental, which was about all I ever ate anymore. I'd never gotten such a kick out of watching TV. The horrible host-persons of *Entertainment Tonight*—I forget their names—came on and said what they were going to be talking about. She was first on the list. But they only showed a glimpse of her talking to reporters on this screen behind their heads, and I couldn't tell what she looked like. I had to wait for the first block of commercials to run out.

I'd never been so impatient with commercials. The Nestlé's Sweet Dreams White Chocolate commercial seemed interminable, and then there was a "Night belongs to Michelob" spot, which I normally liked, but now it drove me nuts. And then they put on some local ad for some godforsaken furniture store called Klingman's with scabby rough-looking couches, and I nearly blew a fuse. And then there was another local ad for this place that customizes vans. It was mercifully short, and then they got back to the show. Another couple of seconds, and I would have had a hemorrhage. After a little banter What's-Her-Face led into the Minaz segment.

"The top story in Hollywood today was the reemergence of the actress-model Minaz from a cloud of rumor and speculation that has surrounded her since her disappearance eight months ago. Minaz electrified the world as a top model and in her one movie role to date, as Sita in Brian de Palma's film version of *The Ramayana*. But in the wake of plastic-surgery scandals involving two other actresses, Virginia Feiden of *Demon Spawn IV* and Penny Penn, the star of *Trucker* and many other films, there were allegations that Minaz had had her face completely rebuilt by a bizarre process that eventually destroyed it. The case, involving unlicensed associates of the Columbia researcher Dr. Karl Vanders, is still in litigation. But today, Minaz came forward to set the record straight."

There was a shot of her outside, at some sort of podium surrounded by reporters. It was kind of far away, so I couldn't get a good view. But from what I could tell, Zinser had done all right. She had her hair up, the way I didn't like it.

"I've had an illness," she said, "as the result of a new surgical practice. It's been difficult, but I've come through it well, and I look forward to working on another film."

The face seemed mobile. She smiled, and it lit up the TV. It was my masterpiece face at work.

Someone asked her whether the film had been set.

"Yes, it was announced today that I'll be appearing with Sigourney Weaver in a new film by Rob Reiner."

There was scattered applause. The shot cut to a closer angle. I think they edited out a bit, too. There was a voice asking, "Is it true that your face was disfigured by uh, surgery and is—has been rebuilt?"

"Yes," Minaz said, "some sections of my skin have been replaced by grafts."

She's smart, I thought, she didn't seem to be denying anything, but she minimized the extent of what really happened. She was doing great.

They said they'd talked to Minaz in person after the conference and we'd get to see that after some messages.

I didn't see the messages. I was practically jumping up and down, I was so excited. I ran into the bathroom and splashed water into my eyes.

She looked as good as ever, every loving detail was in place. I didn't mind being left out. I'd started a great thing. I'd get recognized someday, I was sure of it, and in the meantime I just wanted to watch her career grow. I was so glad I hadn't ruined her life. It meant I was a good person. I'd been starting to think of myself as a monster. Even though I hadn't meant to do damage, I'd done a lot. And now it was all right. Everything was just so all right, it was amazing.

The show came back on, and some reporter was talking to her up close. I could see a lot more detail. But her face looked the same —even the coloring, from what I could tell. It was going to be a long interview. I wished I had gotten a VCR. It was something I'd really want to save.

"Now, where are you from in India?" they asked her.

"Bombay."

"Is Bombay a very difficult city to grow up in?"

"We lived in a good section, Juhu Beach."

I began to feel uneasy about something. She seemed a little flip, different from the way she had acted before. Probably her experience had left her really traumatized, and her new flip manner was her way of dealing with it.

"And how many languages do you speak?"

"English, Hindi, Urdu, Marahti, uh, Spanish, French, and Italian."

She'd left out Sindhi. Her own family language. And it seemed like there was something wrong with her voice. It was higher, it didn't have her old range and expressiveness. And then she used some expressions I knew she just wouldn't have used. And she'd pronounced *Juhu* wrong, the way a Westerner might pronounce it. And suddenly I just *knew*. I started smashing things all over the room. I got my automatic out from under the mattress and shot her image on the television. The picture tube imploded with a satisfying shower of sparks and tiny iridescent spicules of glass, like a blooming chrysanthemum in ultra-fast motion.

Zinser had reused the mold. On somebody else, not Jaishree. It wasn't the same person.

54

And that was when I decided to turn my skills to the creation of monstrosities.

55

New York never really changes and hadn't changed much in nineteen months. I had, though. I'd altered my new face with spirit gum and putty and soluble dyes to simulate a very bad case of advanced psoriasis and piebald scarring. It was all completely removable and would wipe right off the PCS with solvent in a few seconds. But it was convincing enough to have fooled the assistant surgeons working in Karl's clinic. I had a dark wig and glasses, and they were enough to make me completely un-recognizable. I'd rehearsed stripping it all off in less than a minute, down to the beautiful angelic face I was so proud of.

I was face-to-face with Karl. I'd rehearsed my new voice quite thoroughly, and I was sure he didn't suspect a thing.

The clinic was beautiful and successful, so successful I'd had trouble getting an appointment with Karl at all. He was one of the richest doctors in the city. But now I was finally alone with Karl himself, in his tasteful Federalist-decor office, for a final pre-operation consultation. He'd filled out a bit and looked prosperous and self-assured. I'd watched the habits of the clinic very closely for three and a half days, and I'd specified an unusual time very late in the day—I was in arbitrage, I told him, and couldn't get out of work—when there would only be one secretary left in the rest of the clinic. I could handle her if she bothered us. But there didn't seem to be any buttons that could be alarm systems around where he was standing. I didn't want him to get back to his huge desk. I reached into my attaché case.

"There's really no reason for a personal appointment," he said. "This procedure is totally routine once you've approved the designs."

"You know," I said, "this may seem kind of melodramatic, but do you know what this is?"

It was a taser, or electric tranquilizer gun, a big twin-barreled single-shot air-powered thing that fired two electrode-darts wired together. Police use them to subdue crazies. It had cost a fortune on the black market. It was so mean-looking, every time I picked it up I heard the James Bond Theme playing in my head.

"It's not a fatal weapon," I said, "so I wouldn't be afraid to use it. It *will* knock you out and silence you until I can tranquilize you properly, so don't yell or anything. I just want to ask you some questions."

"Jamie?" he asked. I'd dropped the voice. "You'll be the first one they'll suspect if anything happens to me." He was sleazing over toward the desk.

"Stay where you are, please," I said. "Keep your hands visible." I aimed the gun more carefully. He stopped. I had to hand it to him, he was pretty smooth under pressure.

I sat down on a swivel chair. I took my left hand off my weapon and pulled a framed watercolor painting out of my bag.

"I had a whole speech planned," I said, "but instead I think I'll just show you a design I've prepared for you." I held it up to him. "I think it's about time for you to sample *your* procedure yourself, don't you think?"

The face was a masterpiece. To say it was hideous was an understatement. It was evil-looking, skull-like, with the convoluted protuberances of a vampire bat. I'd drawn in the projected scars and scabs with Ivan Albright–like obsessiveness. It was a face I'd seen in nightmares as a child. The face of God L, the Lord of the Dead.

It took him aback for a second. Then: "This is completely ridiculous," he said, in very measured tones. "I'll be getting calls and having some visitors in a minute. You'd better just leave, and you might get out of town safely."

"Maybe I want to get caught. It might be kind of fun to bring this to trial. I wonder how Mark will behave when he's subpoenaed out of jail." That seemed to affect Karl a bit. Mark would jump to damage Karl if he had a chance. "I dropped by Zinser's clinic on my way here and kind of persuaded him to give me back my box of videotapes." He looked at my bag. "They're in a locker," I said. "It'd be great to play them to a jury. I'm sure *some* of the truth would come out. And my lawyer says I'd get a suspended sentence or something and I could skip."

He was quiet, finally. He was just waiting and watchful.

"I'm going to do this operation on you with more conventional surgery," I said, "so it can be as permanent as possible. I think I've worked out something that will make my result very difficult for you to alter. I'm going to go very close to the bone. It's nice that all the equipment's right here."

"I know it's difficult to get through to crazy people—" he began.

"Is Jaishree alive?" I asked.

"Of course she is, I can get her on the telephone if you like. We designed a new face for her together."

Shock. I couldn't think for a minute. I sat there pretty impassively, but inside I was just confusion.

"Dial 914-3313," he said. "Just ask for Jaishree."

"You talk to her," I said. "Ask her to come over, alone."

56

"All right," he said. He started reaching for the phone.

"I'll dial it," I said, bringing up the taser and sighting on his right eye. He froze.

"Fine," he said.

"What's her last name now?"

"Still Manglani. On Franklin Street."

I punched the speakerphone button and dialed 411. I asked for Jaishree Manglani on Franklin, and they gave me the same number. I couldn't imagine that Karl would have set up her number as a trap for me. So I punched it in. She answered on the third ring.

"Hello?"

"Jaishree?" Karl asked.

"Yes?"

"It's Karl Vanders. Could you cab over to my office immediately? It's extremely urgent. Nothing health-threatening, but urgent."

She said she could be at the office in twenty minutes and hung up. Her voice echoed on the speakerphone, but it was her voice, all right.

■

The twenty minutes took a long time. I had a sneaking feeling she wasn't really coming alone. Karl made a few abortive attempts to reason with me, but this time I stuck to my guns, so to speak. I switched off most of the lights in the office.

I sat there silently. We were on the ground floor, and I could see some of the street through the windows behind Karl.

There was a terrible creature standing outside, a horrible grotesque wrinkled-faced dwarf in a strange bright-green outfit with a high hat. It was like some Pulcinello character out of a Tiepolo painting. Then I realized it was a little girl with a snow suit and a mask and witch hat. It wasn't Halloween, though. Why should she dress that way if it wasn't Halloween?

There were a lot of things I wanted to ask and tell Jaishree. I wanted to tell her how Karl had set her up and how I thought about her all the time. A couple of calls came through the intercom, but Karl said he'd call them back. It didn't sound like he was using any distress code. We just sat there, stalemated. Suddenly he spoke:

"Jaishree has an engagement at Lincoln Center starting next month," he said. "As Jaishree, not Minaz."

"What does she look like?" I asked.

"You'll see for yourself. She's very happy right now. She has a steady boyfriend, too. Some actor."

The secretary rang and said Jaishree was here to see Dr. Vanders. The door opened, and she walked in.

57

There was a shrieking, mechanical whoop. Karl must have set off the alarm somehow.

He was pulling out his desk drawer. I sighted and pulled the trigger on his mid torso. There was a satisfying thud as the twin darts hit him, and he yelped and shuddered spastically and collapsed, sliding off the chair, pulling a lamp down on top of him. It smashed and sprayed glass.

Jaishree had run out. I ran after her and barged past the secretary and out into the lobby. The alarm was even louder out there. Jaishree was pushing through the revolving door to the street. I blocked it with my foot and trapped her inside the triangular compartment.

The desk guard came up at me, but I waved the empty dart pistol at him. He wasn't armed. He backed off and started yelling into his hand radio. I realized I'd left my conventional gun in my bag in the office. I should have used it on Karl and killed him.

I looked at Jaishree through the glass. She was frightened. Her new face was kind of pretty, but human-looking, not flashy. A bit of her old Jaishree face. But not much. She was kind of recoiling from my new ugly face. But she knew it was me. My foot was giving out. "I'm not going to hurt you," I yelled through the glass. "Karl set you up. Think about it. He sabotaged your operation."

"Karl saved me after you nearly killed me," she said. It was definitely her voice.

"That's bullshit—it was Karl all along. None of the other—"

"If you run now you may get away," she screamed at me. She stopped pushing so hard on the glass. I pushed the door around in the other direction, so that I ended up on the outside and she was inside. She didn't run. There were already sirens coming closer on Park Avenue. Maybe she'd called them herself when she came over. It didn't look like I had much of a shot.

"Why didn't you keep our face?" I asked.

"It was *your* face! I didn't want *your* face. I didn't want to be your creation. I didn't want to be some weird goddess freak. I didn't even want it in the first place! You just made me feel so bad about how I looked, you tricked me into it! I wanted to be me."

"But that isn't Jaishree's face," I said.

"I guess you can never go all the way back."

I looked in at her face again. It wasn't really so ordinary as I'd thought. It was something like Jaishree's original face, but it had an echo, a very subdued echo, of Minaz. It made me proud to see it.

"It's a good face," I said to her. I got ready to run out into the dark. "I really like it, it's really pretty. It's a really good face."

I felt a sudden pain in the back of my head.

58

I woke up in a hotel room. It was evidently somewhere in New York. I could just *tell* it was New York, from the rumble of traffic. It was late at night. There was one light on, maybe in the bathroom. I couldn't move. I was in some leaden, drugged state. I felt like I was wearing a water-drenched gorilla suit. I looked around, as much as I could. My neck hurt when I moved it. There was something familiar about the decor. It looked like the first-class cabins on the *Queen Elizabeth II* or something. Then I realized it was the Royalton. My favorite hotel.

I had a few memories of the time since the revolving door incident. The phrase "He's a patient of ours, he's deeply disturbed" kept returning to my mind. I remembered being strapped down, looking into bright light, feeling the telltale floating effect of intravenous Valium. I remembered Karl's face, very close, moving a light around over me.

For some reason, I also kept hearing the phrase "only fifty-two cards in the deck." And two jokers, I thought. What did that mean?

I just lay there. My throat was sore and cottony. My face throbbed.

After what seemed like a couple of hours, I managed to roll out of bed onto the floor. It was painful to move any part of my body. I'd fallen asleep on codeine before, in college, and it was always hell getting up after not moving for fourteen hours, but I'd never felt anything like this.

I was facedown on the carpet for a while. I knew I had to get out of here immediately, though. I was having a silent, motionless panic attack. My enemies would come back any second.

I noticed I was wearing somebody else's dark jeans and dark, thrift-shop jacket and a sweater. And green Reeboks, an odd touch, I thought.

After great effort, I stood up. I walked toward the gloom where I assumed the door would be. It was unlocked and I went out into the dark hallway. The halls are very dark at the Royalton, which is nice. There wasn't any goon squad around to stop me. I found the bank of elevators and punched in, but then I drew back into the dark hall in case there were any guards coming up in the same elevator.

The elevator door opened. It was empty. I stepped into the dark mahogany box and pushed LOBBY. I was very dizzy on the way down. I felt I was about to throw up, but there wasn't any food in me.

The door opened onto the overdesigned lobby and bar. It must have been about midnight. The slip-covered couches and round drinking tables and bar stools, all set against the long wall about thirty feet away across the Italian rugs, were filled with the usual fashionable crowd, drinking and talking and laughing. There were striking Japanese women and young men in dark emerald green jackets. It made me nostalgic for the art world.

I started out, wondering if any guards would try to stop me. If I could just make it to the street, I thought, I'd be all right. I could get out of town somehow.

The room seemed to have gotten quieter. I noticed that some people were looking at me. But there was something funny about their expressions, as though they were trying not to look at me. A couple of people seemed to be shivering spastically. Then a young girl came in through the outer doorway, looked up at me suddenly, and screamed, loud. There was an expression of complete, utter terror on her face.

I brought my hands up to my face. It was craggy and rough-feeling. But there wasn't PCS there, there was feeling and pain in my face. Whatever had been done to me was structural.

There was a glass-topped table with a black tablecloth under the glass a few feet away. I walked toward it, trying not to look at any-one. There were another couple of screams. I looked down at my reflection in the table.

It was the face I'd designed for Karl, the horrible face.

59

I screamed, shrilly. I'd never screamed like that before. There were a lot more screams from other people. My legs practically gave out. But I panicked and ran through the big wood doors to the street, pushing past the terrified handsome young doormen. They have such handsome doormen at the Royalton.

It was clever, really. Everyone would think I'd done it to myself.

It was a cold night. Forty-fourth Street was empty except for a few idling limousines. There was a drugstore across the street with a huge plate-glass window, with a gigantic rear-illuminated lightbox Revlon Cosmetics ad behind it. And Minaz's face was on the ad, full front view, against a black background, staring out at me, the new, false Minaz, with a cold expression, inhuman, seven feet high, staring at me, mocking, cold-looking, photographed in blue light, a giant luminous lavender-magenta oval of pure beauty.

The only things that would do anything for me at this point, I decided, were pain and blindness. I started running across the street. I built up quite a bit of speed, the old lungs and leg muscles still working pretty well despite all the abuse, and as the big sheet of plate glass loomed up at me, I took a flying, headfirst, face-forward leap into the center of the window, right at the Face. Oddly enough, I heard the crash a long time before I felt it closing around me. It felt cold and liberating, like diving from a great height into the surface of a frozen lake.

60

But, of course, I didn't die. And I don't think I'll be in here much longer.

I'm dealing with Karl in my own time, in my own fashion. Mark knows what kind of soap Karl uses, and how it gets delivered to his house. And Mark's been doing some experiments with heavy carcinogens. Each day this thought consoles me more and more.

Jaishree may never understand what really happened, and I've about given up on trying to get her to listen.

I'm not Jamie anymore. But I have a core of me inside. I wonder when I get back into the world whether I will get into some other genre of art. Maybe not portraiture. Maybe something to do with landscape.

ACKNOWLEDGMENTS

Jackie Cantor; Brian DeFiore; Susan Schulman; Barbara D'Amato; Jamie Meyer; Amy Adler; Manisha Mirchandani; Maria-Teresa Concepcion Lucia Gabrillo Ignacio

Serafina Clark; Suzanne Telsey; Terri Gotti; Jeanette Lundgren; Robin Arzt; Evan Boorstyn; Phil Rose

Jonathan Adler; Janine Cirincione; Professor Anthony D'Amato; Karin Greenfield-Sanders; Timothy Greenfield-Sanders; Peter Halley; Professor Robert Pincus-Witten; Leslie Roberts; Barnet Schecter; Andrew Solomon; Justin Spring

William Bailey; Andre Balazs; Rob Boynton; Daryl Bright; Leo Castelli and gallery staff; Chantal Coombes; Dana Cowin; Paul D'Amato; Mort David; Rona Pondick and Robert Feintuch; Larry Gagosian and gallery staff; Erwin Hauer; Sylvia Heisel; Diane LaVerde; Stef McDonald; Kathleen Cullen and Robert Mahoney; Professor Mary Ellen Miller; Isaac Mizrahi; Jay Oles; Angela Orlow; Helena Kontova and Giancarlo Politi; Mariza Scotch and Dièry Prudent; Alexis Rockman; Dr. M. S. Trupp; Jaime Wolf